Richard Calder was born in London. He spent many years in Thailand, where he lived in Nongkhai, a border town overlooking Laos. He currently lives in the Philippines. His short stories and reviews have been published in *Interzone, Science Fiction Eye* and *Omni*, and his novels include *The Twist, Malignos* and *Impakto*.

Also by Richard Calder

Lord Soho

'A Time Opera'

RICHARD CALDER

EARTHLIGHT

LONDON · SYDNEY · NEW YORK · TOKYO · SINGAPORE · TORONTO

www.earthlight.co.uk

First published in Great Britain by Earthlight, 2002
An imprint of Simon & Schuster UK Ltd
A Viacom Company

Simon & Schuster UK Ltd
Africa House
64-78 Kingsway
London WC2B 6AH

Simon & Schuster Australia
Sydney

www.simonsays.co.uk

A CIP catalogue for this book is available
from the British Library.

ISBN 0-7434-0896-9

1 3 5 7 9 10 8 6 4 2

Typeset in Melior by SX Composing DTP, Rayleigh, Essex

Printed and bound in Great Britain by
Bookmarque Ltd, Croydon, Surrey

'I announce myself, "Madame, a gentleman from the birth, and a gentleman to the death; but *not* more than ordinarily honourable. I despise such a weak fantasy." Thereupon she is pleased to compliment. "The difference between you and the rest is," she answers, "that you say so." For she knows Society.'

Charles Dickens, *Little Dorrit*

Lord Soho

On my twenty-first birthday I killed a man. It was during my maiden speech in the Lords. In those days member privilege not only extended to sexual peccadillos and the kind of malfeasance ruthlessly prosecuted in men of less exalted rank, but to capital crimes whether committed inside the chamber or out. Given the moral climate that prevailed amongst the Darkling Isle's ruling class, few of us would have escaped the gallows if it had been otherwise.

'*Bastard*!' I cried, as I pulled the blade free of my swordstick and leaped over the benches towards my foe. The assembly parted, ermine-cloaked fools scurrying for the shadows. '*Vermin*! *Unlettered savage*! *Dog slobber*! *Obscurantist*! *Quack*!' The Lord Chancellor's eyes grew wide with astonishment as I vaulted the woolsack and closed upon the man who had traduced me.

Bayswater was five decades my senior and had only recently recovered from a near-mortal illness. But neither grey hairs nor convalescence could dissuade him from keeping his ground. Disdain informed every inch of his bearing. He had not even deigned to draw.

Mindful that his long military career had included victorious campaigns in Northumberland, Mercia and Kent, and that, in his day, he had enjoyed a reputation of being a cunning swordsman – a reputation that extended, unfortunately for me, far beyond the confines of a lady's bed – I checked my momentum.

My blood was hot, but I had always been conscientious about who I called out, and the thought that this old warhorse had, perhaps, more mettle than might be supposed effected a cooling whose rapidity was such that I soon felt a chill extend to my marrow.

'This chamber,' said Bayswater, 'does not take kindly to being lectured to, especially by a pup who has only, this day, come into his inheritance.' He raised a hoary eyebrow and cast a mocking glance about the benches. 'Such as it is. For we cannot help but recall that in his veins runs the polluted blood of our enemies.'

'You go too far,' I muttered. 'You will apologize for that remark.'

'Too far?' he said. 'You have today told us that we must embrace the *new science*—'

'We have on our hands a peasants' rebellion. Nothing more. An insurrection of thralls. The giants of the ancient world would have long ago settled these continual, petty wars, and so would we, if we only had the courage to study their example. Instead, we fight with swords and musketry. No wonder we cannot consolidate our successes and bring matters to conclusion.'

'The *new science*,' he continued, ignoring my interpolation, 'which all dispassionate men know is merely a euphemism for diablerie.' I looked around. The red mist that had fallen on first hearing his calumnies had now completely lifted, and I was left with a vision of terrible clarity, the conviction that I would soon be fighting for my life. 'Not that we can expect a man such as this,' he added, playing to the crowd, 'to be able to distinguish the two. After all, his family line is one contaminated by the *diabolical*.'

It would, I knew, be necessary to commit myself before sound judgement called the retreat. Retreat – an option I would have gladly embraced in other circumstances – would earn me, on this my first day in the chamber, the eternal derision of my peers.

I pressed matters home.

'Apologize,' I said, 'or die.' There was a rumble of hostility from the benches to my immediate left, where my opponent's lickspittles had congregated. Farringdon, Kilburn and Aldgate stood with their hands fingering their sword pommels, and Battersea and Kensington, in whom old enmities against my own all but extinguished line still burned bright, fixed me with baleful stares.

'I call a spade a spade, sir,' said Bayswater, committing himself now, 'a jack a jack, a knave a knave. And, as my duty urges, indeed, demands, I call you a *witch,* sir, a man of *dubious allegiances*. Remove yourself from this chamber. You have no business with true men.'

There were cries of 'Hear, hear!' From the tiered benches on either side of me a mass of raised fists underlined what was already obvious: I had won no new friends.

I readied myself.

I fought Eastern style, as my father had taught me to do, and as his father had taught him. I turned and presented my left side to my opponent, an outstretched hand gripping the ebony cane so that I might use it to ward off a blow. I leaned backwards, displacing my weight so that my full one hundred and seventy pounds was supported by my right leg. My right hand – my sword-hand – was tucked just beneath the hip, the slim, sixteen-inch blade pointed towards the groin of my prospective attacker. Parry, left kick, right foot forward, thrust. That was the order of things, the ancestral style that had put many a man in the ground.

Bayswater had still not drawn. I studied his face for signs of weakness. But the man was like adamant; there seemed nothing I could exploit. I could only hope, it seemed, that his antique veins were sufficiently adamantine for him to be seized by an apoplexy and that he drop dead upon the spot. I grimaced; bared my sharp little teeth; flared my nostrils and, with an angry flick of my head, let my locks fall over a gunmetal face so heavily lined as to seem a counterpart to my scrotum. My appearance had often benumbed the sword-arm of those I closed upon. But Bayswater had seen the enemy at close quarters. And the countenance of an octoroon whose orc-blood came courtesy of a grandmother whom he had neither met, nor knew much about, did not, it seem, have the power to disconcert him.

'I am as proud of my lineage as any man,' I said. 'My grandfather was known to some of you here, perhaps even to you, Bayswater. Acknowledge, then: he saved London from being overrun by the armies of the Netherworld!'

'*But not his bed*!' shouted one wag. I glanced about, trying to pick him out from the welter of faces. I could not find him. A pity. For I would have enjoyed making him the day's second kill, if I should be so fortuitous as to make a first.

6

Lord Soho

Bayswater looked at me with restrained condescension. 'You, boy, have more cause than most, I think,
to appreciate the manner in which the legions of the
perverse have impinged themselves upon the world. It
is barely a hundred years since we drove their armies
into their underground lairs where, licking their
wounds, they still lurk but, happily, no longer give us
trouble. Except, of course, by way of their proxies left
on the Earth's surface. I speak, of course, of *your* kind,
Master Pike. Hell's miscegens.'

I felt my skin prickle as my blood recalled its
patrimony.

'Master no longer,' I said. 'Today you address me as
Lord Soho, or you do not address me at all.' I edged
forward, my right leg bent, my left leg and arm ready to
kick and block, respectively. I swung the blade's tip
through a clockwise circle, then repeated the exercise,
anti-clockwise. And while I did so, I focused on
Bayswater's vitals.

My opponent slipped the ermine casually from his
shoulders. The air between us blurred. My wrist went
numb, and I sucked in an exorbitant amount of air,
hoarding it in my lungs for long seconds, in the
unconscious hope, perhaps, that it might provide an
anodyne to the terrific pain that had begun to course
along my arm. My blade clattered to the floor. Its ebony
sheath followed as I relinquished hold of it to grasp my
offended wrist. As I struggled to suck more air into
lungs already stretched to capacity, I felt tears sting my
eyes like hot beads of alcohol and heard a squall of
laughter from the benches.

It was as if I had been struck with a steel bar.

Which, of course, I had. Bayswater, with a skill and speed that were beyond my powers to reciprocate, had brought the flat of his rapier down across my sword-hand.

As I at last realized what had exactly happened, I expelled the musty air I had been accumulating in a long, yodelling moan that was punctuated with the foulest of imprecations.

I had always been a poor swordsman. A shame, my father had said, and what was more, an imponderable shame, given the fact that the family boasted so many ancestors either famous or infamous for their martial expertise.

My gaze darted around the chamber. I was encircled by Bayswater's grinning henchmen and toadies. I knew I could expect no mercy from them; first, they would play with me, like cats with a mouse, then despatch me on a journey into that void that, these last hundred years, we have been pressed into supposing a heaven; and I wondered, as my injured hand sought refuge in my pocket and fingered the artefact that lay sequestered there, why I had until now been so merciful myself. The ruling classes of the Darkling Isle: they were all crooks, some more nakedly so than others, but crooks, thieves, murderers, whores nonetheless. I was no different, except that straitened circumstances had, since my late teens, compelled me to act with less hypocrisy. My civil list income was supplemented not by usurious loans, embezzlement, simony and graft but by a life of crime so artless it was almost plebeian. But whatever I and my surrounding peers had in common, and whatever our differences, mercy – or so my present situation made obvious – was not a fitting companion for those, like myself, who wished to live long and accrue their share of intellectual accomplishment, women and loot.

'You should not dismiss the new science so glibly, Bayswater,' I said, taking the artefact from my pocket and proffering it towards him. 'It may yet prove this nation's salvation, as I averred in my speech before I was so oafishly interrupted. You should have attended more closely.'

For a moment, the thought that my speech had been deliberately sabotaged irked me more than the growing suspicion that I had been set up, that, unlikely as it might seem, my drawing out was part of a conspiracy. But for a moment only. Damn the speech. The question of why Bayswater was so intent on my assassination was, of course, paramount. I was hated and feared by many, but I could not think of any one who would greatly profit by my death. Being at mortal loggerheads in this chamber, though not without precedent, was unusual enough to be perplexing in itself. Though member privilege might be seen to encourage it, it was remarkable that the proportion of nobles who fell victim to each other's resentments was not higher than it was. The knowledge that a bloody fit of offended pride brought swift revenge had, I daresay, much to do with it; as did the fact that one often satisfied one's pique upon thralls, something that, for a peer of the realm, did not even rank as a peccadillo. Bayswater would not risk killing me unless he had backing and the rewards were substantial. Since the nobility were for the most part impoverished, it would seem someone from London's powerful, emergent merchant class would be the most likely instigator of a plot. And as soon as that consideration struck home, my true enemy stood revealed.

My father-in-law.

I tried to filibuster. 'I spent many hours crafting today's statement,' I murmured, speaking largely to myself, a single name – *Peachum* – percolating into my consciousness and filling it till my skull seemed fit to crack from internal pressure.

The assembled lords and ladies looked at the artefact with bemusement. It was no more than a black, oblong box, its mother-of-pearl inlay giving it the appearance of chinoiserie. I had found it amongst the possessions of a squire's daughter whose coach I had ambushed on the Brighton to London road. At once, I had known it to be an artefact of the Ancients. It had been non-functional, of course – indeed, it had taken me some weeks to establish just what its original function was – but I had at last revived it from its millennia-long sleep.

'A snuff box, Soho?' said the assassin. 'Or do you mean to present us with a lady's paints and powders?'

'A jewellery box, but also a contrivance for a lady's self-defence,' I said. 'Over four thousand years old. La! I don't need to tell you those times were almost as dangerous as our own.'

I lifted the box's lid. Opened correctly, the mirror set in the lid's back would have been the first thing to greet a lady's vanity; but unfastening its clasp, as I had done, without taking the necessary precautions, the mirror, which I knew to be a portal that opened upon intelligences that lay, half awake, half asleep, in the great cities buried hundreds of miles beneath us, would do more than reflect a prospective thief's likeness.

Bayswater was the first to have an intimation of the device's nature, and the concomitant danger it presented. 'Diabolism,' he whispered. 'You truly are the Devil's spawn.' And then his eyes exploded in their sockets, like the eggs that I have experimented with in my chamber *mirabilis* – using a revivified artefact bought from a pedlar during one of my excursions into the wastes, I found that I was able to heat them to many hundreds of degrees Celsius from within.

His screams were overlaid with a hideous *pop*! *pop*! *pop*! as his cronies were similarly afflicted. Their own screams drowned out his own.

Soon, a dozen, perhaps two dozen lords and ladies were a-leaping, their hands clenched over their eyes, blood and vitreous humour oozing between their splayed fingers. Blind, they thrashed and flailed, toppled over benches and rolled upon the floor like a pack of slathering hounds. One old dame, in her confusion, strove to attain the throne, where, tripping and stumbling in a grotesque parody of a curtsey to a queen who had yet to visit us that year, she fell and, hitting her head against the exposed marble edge of the steps, added the red of her blood to the deep-red pile of the carpet.

I slammed the box shut before those still unaffected should fall victim to a fatal curiosity and themselves stare into the mirror's cruel depths.

It had been my intention to defend myself, not bring down the state.

Slipping the box back into my pocket, I scooped the blade and its ebony sheath from the floor, reintroduced them to each other, turned on my heels and then, taking advantage of the general panic, fled the chamber.

My maiden speech had not gone well. It would be some time before I could dare return to the House of Peers and again present my arguments. But return I must, I thought. The nation must embrace the new science. Surely, that was obvious to any rational man. My country's still-born renascence was being squandered in its haste to return to an age of superstition and darkness. The shameful status quo had to be redressed.

I raced through the corridors of the Palace of Westminster, past the disused Commons, and on until I reached the vestibule that stood adjacent to old Westminster Hall. Exiting through an archway that had not much changed since Pugin and Barry laid the foundations of the pile that, some three score centuries on, was an eclectic ruin compromised of countless forgotten architectural styles, I exchanged the fusty shadows of governance for a bright, summer's day. Outside, my coach was waiting.

I would have to pay my father-in-law a visit.

But not today. Today was my birthday.

My confederates lifted their glasses: Jemmy Twitcher, Crook-fingered Jack, Wat Dreary, Robin of Bagshot, Nimming Ned, Henry Paddington, Mat of the Mint and Ben Budge. We sat at a table in the Beggar's Banquet, a noted chocolate house in Wardour Street.

'A health to your lord's majority,' said Wat Dreary, in that monotonic manner of his that had earned him his moniker.

'Long life,' said Crook-fingered Jack. The rest, sheep

that they were, fell into line, and offered me their own toasts, each felicitation distinguished by an unimaginativeness that vied with its predecessor. My confederates were, in truth, unimaginative and despicable company. Thralls, like witches, were not true men, and were not usually suffered to live within the city walls. But I needed them. They were familiar with the wastes.

'Long life,' repeated Jack, then added, 'and prosperity.' He gave me an unpleasant and meaningful look.

'Jack,' I said. I paused, wondering how to deal with this idiot. Like his accomplices, he was descended from human detritus that a previous age had called the 'information poor'. His congenital slowness was the result of drug-based pacification measures practised upon his ancestors. Those humans outside the walls were no longer 'simplified', as the euphemism went. The anti-toxin that had found its way to the Darkling Isle from the East had restored old man Crook-finger to something approaching full mental competence. But the millennia-long wounds of simplification could not be so easily taken out of the equation of inheritance. Jack was a dull boy. 'Listen,' I continued, 'I come today into a thousand a year. After I have paid off certain debts, I'll probably have just enough left over to pay for your drinks. For now, at least. Genuine prosperity will come the way it has always come: through ingenuity, valour and hard work.' I looked searchingly into his face, and then into each of their faces, to try to ascertain whether I could detect any flickers of comprehension. None. Resignedly, I returned my attention to Jack. 'If it weren't for me, if it weren't for my influence and my propensity to threaten and bribe, you would still be working in the chain gang by which you first entered this city.' I gave him my most threatening stare. If this ploy did not work, I thought, then I would have to resort to violence. 'A little gratitude might be in order, sometimes, I think, don't you?'

'Very pleased and proud,' said Jack, backing down from whatever criticisms he might have been about to make about my leadership, 'proud as punch, you might say I am, sir, to serve as your guide.'

'And your bodyguard,' added Nimming Ned, who, a tad more intelligent than Jack, knew that I could send him and his friends back to the chain gang, or even the gallows, whenever I might feel so inclined.

'Money,' I said, in a spirit of conciliation, 'will come to those who help themselves to it.' I lifted my bumper of *aqua vita* to my lips, quaffed, and slammed the glass down on the table. 'Gentlemen, let's get down to business.' I could not bear to enter into what, amongst their kind, passed for celebration. I wished to impart instructions while still sober, and then leave. I would have my own little party, later, in the privacy of my own chambers. 'I have had intelligence—'

'Good goblin intelligence,' interrupted Ben Budge, eager, it seemed, to ingratiate himself into my good books after witnessing my earlier impatience. 'From our best contact, too.'

'—that a merchant,' I continued, unabated, and flashing Budge a scowl to show him that I disdained dogs as much as I did sheep, 'by the name of Underwood is on his way to London from Reading. This man has been known to trade in the things I seek—'

14

'Artefacts,' Budge interrupted again, undaunted and fairly panting, so desirous was he to be tossed a scrap of my favour. 'Stuff from the Netherworld.'

'Quite so,' I said, acknowledging the dog only to stop him yapping. 'Relics from the ancient days.'

'No gold?' said Mat of the Mint.

'Oh yes, gold and guineas a-plenty, as well as linen, lace, plate and all the other things you so covet. It's only artefacts that interest me, as I'm sure you know.'

'Glad to hear it, my lord,' said Mat, rubbing his hands. 'Peachum will give us a good percentage, I should guess?'

'I feel we shall be having to drop Mr Peachum,' I said. 'For I believe he has it in mind to drop us.'

'Give us over to the law?' 'Strike us out?' 'Do the filthy on us?' 'Make us do the Jack Ketch rigadoon?' said one and all, in tones of village-idiot outrage.

'Yes. Drop us. And stretch our necks to boot. I'm afraid it's all down to this business between me and his daughter.'

Jemmy Twitcher, who, like most of us that afternoon, had drunk more *aqua vita* than chocolate, thumped his fist down upon the table and broke into song.

> *'Through all the employments of life,*
> *Each neighbour abuses his brother;*
> *Whore and rogue, they call husband and wife:*
> *All professions be-rogue one another.*
> *The priest calls the lawyer a cheat:*
> *The lawyer be-knaves the divine:*
> *And the statesman, because he's so great,*
> *Thinks his trade as honest as mine.'*

'Be quiet, Jemmy,' I said, with all the restraint I could muster. I had had a trying day, and had no desire to have a subordinate cant me with his tuppenny ha'penny summation of life's little ironies.

I gazed over Jemmy's shoulder, my attention captured by the sight of a young woman, framed in the open door. An aureole of golden, summer light surrounded her, as if she were a plaster saint seated upon the candlelit altar of my own private chapel. Or at least, upon the equally hypocritical altar of my expedient love. Polly Peachum, my most recent wife, who, until this morning's business in the House, I had thought worth the sacrifice of my proud name in return for the supplement she brought to my income, walked into the Beggar's Banquet.

I retrieved my swordstick from where it leaned against a table leg, got up, muttered my excuses to my men, and sauntered over to her. Taking her by the arm, I ushered her into a corner, where we might confer with a degree of privacy.

No sooner had she sat down than the tears started flowing.

'Oh Mackie, Mackie, he knows. Somehow my mother found out, and she told him.'

'I know he knows,' I said, a little irritated. 'He tried to have me killed.'

She looked at me with wide, enamel-blue eyes, less comely than usual due to a certain blotchiness precipitated by her unseemly and wholly unhelpful jag of weeping. '*Killed*?' There was a rustle of hoop-petticoat as she leaned back in her chair and put a hand to her brow, as if she were more acquainted with the boards at Drury Lane than the sexual theatrics that went on in the surrounding streets. I was normally amused by her country-girl affectations; today they served only to provoke my exasperation. I had married the loopy slut at a time of acute financial embarrassment. But I had, it seemed, merely exchanged one embarrassment for another.

'Yeah, *killed*, my little chitterling. Our marriage was supposed to be a secret, remember? But now the secret's out, your dad wants me dead. I came into my inheritance today. God knows, it's not much, but old Peachum doubtless thinks you're worth more to him as a widow than as baggage.'

'We'll run away,' she said.

'Oh sure, we'll run off into the wastes. If we're real lucky, we'll get to work under the whip, on some farm, perhaps, or quarry, along with a ragbag of thralls and converted witches. No thank you, madam. I'll have to straighten things out with your old man, that's all.'

'You won't hurt him, Mackie?'

'We'll have a little heart to heart,' I said, thinking, With his heart on the end of my swordstick. 'I'll be paying him a visit tomorrow, with my men. Tell him it's business.' Should I let him fence for me one last time? I wondered. Good fences were hard to find. And my gang would need a good fence after tonight's escapade. Perhaps I could profit by him, before I slit his throat. To take his money, then his life, would be sweet. And then again, perhaps I would merely use the excuse of business to gain entry to his house, and then have him summarily bludgeoned to death by the vacuous wretches who followed at my heels. 'Now run along like a good little slut and find yourself some pimply soldier boy on leave, or better still, a man of my own rank, if not one so detestably impoverished. I'll be seeing you tomorrow.'

'Not tonight? Oh promise it'll be tonight, Mackie. Please, oh pretty please.' She was putting on her little-girl-lost act. There had been a time I had been captivated by it. Contrariwise, there had been a time when such a strategy had seemed like the most calculated, most hideous form of whining, a time, when, for the sake of my sanity, I had had to resort to slapping her face. That time was coming round again.

'Tonight I have business to attend to,' I said, gripping the arms of my chair with both hands in an effort to resist the temptation to strike out. Sublimation, I found, was, in the end, the key to resolving my dilemma. As she rose I gave her a *thwack* on her behind, ostensibly to show that she could count on me. It was a vicious goosing, and went some way to exorcize the disgust with which I had come to regard her. But she took it, as I had meant her to, as a bestowal of my troth. Glancing over her shoulder, she grinned her saucy, milkmaid's grin, knowing that, by so doing, a dimple would indent her left, candy-apple cheek, and remind me of the time it had been chief amongst the wiles by which she had ensnared me.

'I'll be waiting, Mackie. I'm always waiting.'

'So you are,' I said. And I gave her a tired little salute as she swept out the door. I looked round. At the other end of the chocolate house the amused faces of my confederates were turned in my direction. Once again, Jemmy Twitcher began to sing.

'Man may escape from rope and gun,
Nay, some have outlived the doctor's pill:
Who takes a woman, must be undone,
That basilisk is sure to kill.
The fly that sips treacle is lost in the sweets,
So he that tastes woman, woman, woman,
He that tastes woman, ruin meets.'

I had left the city walls far behind. Here, in the wastes, the road was little more than a earthen trail furrowed by wagon wheels. The horses that carried me and my band of brain-damaged followers through the wooded darkness were strong and fleet. We had covered much ground. But though my heart quickened to know that we drew near our rendezvous, it would freeze, in momentary terror, whenever the thought crossed my mind that without my guides I would be lost.

Though no more than a few miles outside London, the forest that grew on either side of the trail was almost impenetrable. The air was still; the canopy dead. There was no sign of life, or habitation. And yet, negotiating my way through the overarching thicket, I could sometimes believe that I had not left the city at all, for I seemed hemmed in by masonry. The trees: they did not belong to Earth-Above. They were indigenous to the Netherworld, transplanted by the enemy during long centuries of war in an attempt to choke humanity out of its cities. Cultured in the Earth's depths, they were made of living stone. They were trees of granite, basalt and hypabyssal. Trees with brittle, carbonaceous leaves that rattled like the desiccated bones of men in gibbets swaying in a midnight storm. Florescent structures, resembling morbid growths, protruded from their slate-like bark, maroon, puce and mulberry – the sickly heirs of the flowers I had read once covered the English countryside, before the grafts from the Netherworld had taken hold.

As I rode, I would glance to left and right, half expecting the glint of subterranean eyes to light up the shadowy recesses that lay between the Gothic tangle of branches and boughs; eyes that belonged to a people who would be almost forgotten but for the progeny they had left behind. I shook my head; but my fears could not be so easily dispelled, even though I knew the Netherworlders had long chosen to exile themselves in their underground fastnesses. I was one of those creatures they had sired upon humanity, and at such times as I passed through the darkness of these forests my blood was haunted by atavistic memories of great underground caverns and the joy of dark, sunless seas. And by eyes: the dark, reptilian eyes of my cousins. Sometimes, on these rides, I half wished the shadows *were* filled with goblins; half wished that my cousins watched, waiting for their chance to snatch me from this world and take me back to the cavernous mother-land I was in terror of, but for which my blood yearned. I passed a hand across my face; blinked. It was not good to indulge in such morbid irrationality. Never, in all my journeys through the wastes, had I witnessed so much as the flit of a bat or the swoop of an owl; neither had I seen gnats, midges or fireflies. Only the stone trees could claim life, and they jealously admitted no other. Nothing but darkness and stone everywhere, except in those little settlements blasted out of the ubiquitous forest and worked by slaves of the state, and in regions held by rebels.

For if a man were not a Londoner, what was he but a slave, a barbarian, a witch or thrall? And what had such dispossessed people to lose from taking up arms? Could we ever really expect to prevail in such circumstances, unless we enjoyed some significant military advantage? The kind I had offered, only to find myself spurned?

At a crossroads I held up a hand, and my little troupe came to a halt. A cloaked rider with a cowl pulled full over his face stood in our path, waiting.

'Good evening, Melchezidek,' I said.

'Hello, Master Pike,' replied a thin voice emanating from the bundle of rags, a voice so like the wind that whistled through the stone branches, that anyone but myself might have supposed the bundle filled with rocks, and that the speaker were alive only in the inexplicable manner of the trees.

I nodded to my men to indicate that they should remain where they were. Then, lightly bringing my spurs against my steed's flanks, I went on alone to where the witch blocked our passage.

Without revealing his face, he spoke again. 'The coach will pass this way in about one hour.' Though the missionaries had done a good job of teaching him English, they had failed to eradicate his accent, an exotic oddity in a world where not only most languages were extinct, but most dialects, too. Beneath the familiar words and grammar, I seemed to hear the sounds of the Netherworld, just as I had previously sensed its presence amongst the trees.

He pulled back his cowl. Melchezidek was always

reluctant to reveal himself fully, even to me, who had known him since childhood when I had accompanied my father on archeological digs under the shadows of the city walls. He was a half-breed. And if I had looked as he did I might have been equally reluctant about showing my face. My father had been a half-breed, too, of course, but the familial tie had, for me, softened his terrible demeanour, as the trappings of civilization had perhaps softened it for others. Melchezidek had had no such advantages. His face was as stony as the surrounding trees, so lined and pitted that it seemed almost squamous. His hair was white, and hung to his shoulders, reflecting the moonlight with an albedo that was comparable to that of mother-of-pearl, or vitreous silica. And two small, curved horns protruded from his forehead. I had never seen a true Netherworlder, those creatures we commonly called goblins, orcs or teratoids. But if Melchezidek represented a *dilution* of their blood, I had often thought that I would not care to see one, no matter how curious I sometimes grew about my own damned ancestry, and no matter how much I recalled my father's admonishments when I had been a boy. He had told me that though my mother was human, I was not to disparage those other beings, one of whom belonged to his own distaff side. His mother, he said, had been as beautiful as his wife.

I had not realized that the witch had been studying my face as intently as I had his. 'You're not looking well, Master Pike. Has coming into your inheritance had so little effect on you? I had hoped it might reverse the decline I have witnessed of late. Your father would not have liked to see you like this, the last of the line so dejected, and dealing out the family's patronage' – he tweaked an eyebrow towards my men – 'so ignominiously.'

'You've become quite the prating evangelist, Melchezidek.'

'You know my opinion of Christians,' he said. 'I am a freed thrall, but the wars have made me a refugee for over thirty years. And the only place I have found peace is beneath London's walls. It is wise, in such circumstances, to come to some accommodation with the powers that be. You too, Master Pike, have made your accommodations, I suspect.'

I cast a glance over my shoulder to see that we were not in danger of being overheard. When I faced him again I let the disgust that had seized and distorted my face on having gazed upon those I 'accommodated' remain. For a moment, I thought I gazed into a mirror.

'I suppose we all do,' I said, with a shrug. 'I have this new name they've given me. Mackie. Or Macheath. Seems it's to do with some kind of Soho fairytale. I've been adopted, in other words.'

The old witch leaned forward in his saddle.

'Fairytales, legends, myths. They are abroad in the land. Dark tales from the darker depths of the heart. The world is caught in cycles, Master Pike. Mythic cycles. Formerly, it was that which we called the *perverse* that captivated our imaginations and lives. But the perverse lies buried underground, and will not emerge again in our lifetimes nor those of our children and grand-children. We are caught up in a new cycle now, the myth of this new, resurrected church that so plagues us, and which resists all our efforts to revive the learning of the Ancients, something that has been so long your dream, Master Pike, just as it was your father's.'

'And your dream too, old man. Are you disappointed?'

'Yes, but not yet in despair, Master Pike. Or else I would not be out here in the middle of the night, risking my life. The struggle must go on, and without artefacts to experiment with, that struggle is still-born. I only worry that *you* despair. These people you mix with. And these bigamous marriages I have heard of—'

'Expediency,' I said. 'It's hard for a witch to live in the wastes. I know that. But inside the city, life is difficult for our kind, too.'

'Witch? You do not qualify. Only one-eighth of your blood is that of an orc. You have rights. You are a citizen.'

'Rights? I have the right, like all our kind, to be insulted and passed over. That is why I am here, with a pistol in my belt, resorting to the tricks of a common highwayman. I do not pretend to understand the full extent of your hardships, Melchezidek, please do not presume to offer me advice.'

'*Mackie!*' came a sharp whisper, cutting through the night's stillness. '*Mackie, I can hear a coach approaching.*' Again, I glanced behind. Ned was on his hands and knees, backside in the air and right ear flush to the ground.

'They're early,' said the witch.

'It doesn't matter,' I said, a hand pulling the flintlock free from my belt. I had often considered bringing one of my militarily adapted artefacts along on one of these nocturnal capers. But the contents of my chamber

24

mirabilis were too unpredictable, too ungovernable. I wanted to hold up a coach, not initiate a cataclysm. 'I'm ready.'

'I will leave you to go about your business, Master Pike,' he said. 'Or should I say Macheath?' He grinned, the moonlight reflecting off his serrated teeth, and playing in his silvery-white hair. 'But think on this: if the world is caught in mythic cycles, then so are some families, too. In such circumstances, a man may lose his soul. Make your own story, Master Pike. This business with artefacts, it has been necessary, I suppose, but I have begun to suspect that our experimenting is taking us along a path that may ultimately prove sterile. The world, perhaps, should make its own story, just as we should. We should not look so to the past.'

He turned his horse round and disappeared into the darkness, as quietly as if his steed had been shod with cotton wool, a ghost, a figure cut loose from the narrative that had given the world my teratoid forebears, that old, calamitous narrative imposed upon us by strange gods, a narrative that had drowned out the song of who we were, where we had come from and where we might yet go, in its strident fanfare of dark lusts, derangement and hysterical amnesia.

Our enterprise went successfully. I let my men do the dirtiest of the work. And I let them take their share of the dirtiest of the pickings: snuff boxes, fine linen, a few swords, timepieces, silver candlesticks and a lady's mantle. I took, I must admit, a little dirty lucre myself: a purse of crowns. But, as usual, I reserved the main thrust of my cupidity for things antiquarian: a handful of curios, and, most interestingly, the decapitated head of a mannequin used to display wigs which, I suspected, had originally belonged to one of those mechanical men that the ancient world had used as thralls.

I would get back to London, I calculated, before midnight. First thing tomorrow, I would see Peachum. But I set my sights now on the little birthday celebration that I had been promising myself all day.

That purse of crowns was going to be put to good use.

'The ladies are here, sir,' said Filch, my valet.

In they came, some as far as from Hockley-in-the-Hole, Vinegar Yard and Lewkner's Lane, but most from the environs over which I was the titular head, good Soho lasses all, many of whom had entertained me on previous occasions: Mistress Coaxer, Dolly Trull, Mistress Vixen, Betty Doxy, Jenny Diver, Mistress Slammekin, Sukey Tawdry and Molly Brazen.

Discreet as ever, Filch withdrew, if with the hint of a prurient leer on his tightly compressed lips.

'Dear Mistress Coaxer,' I said, helping the slut off with her light wrap, 'how charming you look so bedizened with your paste and painted with your most vicious rouges.' I felt a forefinger and thumb squeeze my left buttock, as if I had sat down upon the muddy banks of the Thames and had had a crab disabuse me of the notion that I could do so with impunity. 'And Dolly Trull! As amorous as ever, eh?' Speaking of crabs, I thought to leave Dolly to last. The last time I had sampled her I had done so without the degree of impunity a man might wish. 'You're always so taken with stealing hearts that you don't allow yourself time to steal anything else. Shame on you!' I glanced from one face to another, going through my selection like a greedy child eager to sample his comfits without further delay, but spoilt for choice. 'Mistress Vixen, I'm yours! And Betty Doxy – come here, girl! Do you drink as hard as ever? And Jenny Diver, too. Never did a whore have such a sanctified look and such a mischievous heart. Mistress Slammekin, Sukey Tawdry and Molly Brazen – free-hearted floozies all, each with the ogle of a rattlesnake. Before you seat yourselves, ladies, please – a dance I insist!'

I turned to the musicians I had hired and cued them. They set to with enthusiasm, too much enthusiasm, in fact, sawing at their strings as if determined to use up the city's supply of catgut in that one evening. I had promised to pay them in flesh, as well as in guineas, and the sight of the itinerant ladies had undoubtedly stoked their lust so that they were eager to be remunerated as soon as possible. I stamped my foot on the boards and the quintet, looking a little abashed, fell back from a *prestissimo* to an *andante*.

I had drawn up the programme some weeks ago. I owned, amongst my collection of ancient manuscripts, a book of antique airs, ballads and chamber music. The scores were all damaged, and it had amused me to add my own interpretations where notes and sometimes, whole staves, were missing. The piece I had selected to introduce the proceedings had been entitled 'Surabaya Johnny'. In the programme notes – I had written them purely for my own pleasure, the tavern musicians I employed caring as little for such refinements as my illiterate whores – I had dedicated it to the memory of my grandfather, the only real hero of my family, who had spent much of his life in the Far East, and may, for all I knew, have visited that mysterious Javanese city with his beloved goblin woman, Gala.

'Sukey,' I said, 'may I have the honour?'

'No, but you may *take* it, my lord, as befits your station.' She smiled and displayed two imperfect rows of tobacco-stained teeth. 'Though I fear,' she concluded, with a hoarse giggle, 'that a girl like me's got little enough honour left in 'er for you to avail yourself of.'

Her blood, like mine, had been infused with the alien, though hers was a cocktail that was one hundred percent *Homo sapiens*. (Not that the nomenclature of the Ancients had much meaning any more, at least, not when applied to the genus we stubbornly called 'human'.) Her mother, I would have guessed, had at some time slept with a sailor from Cathay. It seemed appropriate that the issue of that cynical union accompany me to that sad, languid 'Surabaya' conjured up by the music that filled the room.

I pulled her into the middle of the floor. Filch, with the assistance of a few street boys he had pressed into service, had removed the furniture earlier and, save for the podium that accommodated the string quintet, the long, panelled dining room was bare. Sukey pressed her head against my chest. I put an arm round her and we shuffled across the boards, her skirts sending up a frou-frou that was so wonderfully venereal that I almost convinced myself that it might signify that she desired my person as much as my purse. I looked good tonight, in black velvet breeches and white silk hose, my silver-buckled shoes shining in the lamplight. My waistcoat was embroidered so finely that it had doubtless cost the eyesight of a few, poor, little thrall seamstresses, and my cravat was starched and magnificently frothy. But it would take more than an attack of the hots to make Sukey Tawdry forget the imperatives of her trade. In her the venereal and the venal were perfectly counter-poised.

I looked over Sukey's head. Her sisters-in-whoredom leaned against the walls, bored, but brave, as if ranged before a firing squad personifying 'unspeakable tedium' that their profession required them to outface. They gazed at me coyly from behind the spread lunettes of their fans, their eyes evincing an appropriately intense, if staged, longing. They would get their turn, I told myself, even if there were no male guests to leaven the task that I had set myself (the musicians would have to wait until I was through); they would get their turn even if it killed me.

As my father used to say: 'I love the sex; and a man who loves money might as well be contented with one guinea, as with one woman. I must have women. If it were not for unprincipled bucks like me Drury Lane would be uninhabited.' I had, if not my father's skill with a blade – as I think today's business in the chamber proved – then at least his propensity for unwearied swordplay with the women, and most particularly, women such as these. Perhaps such swordsmanship might have allayed his disappointment in my lack of martial skills. If so, I hoped his ghost looked on.

'I usually prefer the *old* 'uns,' she said, as I studied her impressive cleavage, breasts forced into their uncompromising attitude by the long, tightly laced corset that she wore over her crimson, silk mantua. "Cos I always makes 'em pay for what they can't do. But young bucks like you, my lord, are just too much of a temptation. Tell me: can I call you Mackie?'

'Yes.' I sighed, the sudden mention of that name more exhausting, more disturbing, than the sum of the day's events. 'Everybody else does. So why not?' I pulled back my lips and showed off my rows of spiked enamel; she giggled, the trilling notes as little girlish and as manipulative as my pretty Poll. 'I thought once I might have amounted to something,' I continued. 'Become a player in the "new age" I convinced myself was waiting around the corner. But I'm not a Pike. I'm a criminal, no different from others of my class, except that my crimes are somewhat less obfuscated by hypocrisy. So why shouldn't you call me Macheath?'

'Oh, you *do* know how to talk.'

Perhaps I did. But sensing that the pleasures of intelligent conversation were, tonight, not to be had, I kept my peace, and danced her through the doors. Outside, in the hallway, I loosened my grip of her waist and offered her my hand. She took it, in ironic imitation of a lady of quality. I took it, the irony no less rich, in imitation of a lord. I often think there's such a similitude of manners in high and low life, that it is difficult to determine whether (in the fashionable vices) the fine gentlemen imitate the highwaymen, or the highwaymen the fine gentlemen. I certainly was no longer clear about where the role ended and reality began.

'To the roof garden, I think,' I said. I led her past the

iron-braced doors behind which lay my chamber *mirabilis*, its stock of artefacts now including a lady's device for self-defence that had been strenuously combat proven. We proceeded through the arch that lay at the end of the corridor and up the staircase that wound towards the top of the house's bell tower. 'A warm summer night awaits our fornication.'

As we ascended, we passed various family portraits, glowering down at us through the yellow light cast by the great crystal chandelier that hung like a plummet from the stairwell's uppermost shadows. Under the gaze of so many other accursed Pikes, my legs grew heavy, my breathing laboured, my youthful vitality sapped by the grim weight of my ancestral past.

'Ohhh, Mackie, that one looks scary,' she said. I believed very little was capable of frightening Sukey Tawdry, but the little attack of the shudders that she affected gave her an excuse to throw her arms about me. The avaricious gesture had me suspect that she believed that the anxieties I suffered whenever I passed beneath these family likenesses – and which, I supposed, had manifested themselves in my face – threatened to spike my appetite, and that she might stand to be cheated of her fee. Her supposition was wrong, but not by much. There was something about those portraits which I had always found intensely disturbing. Something that threatened to unman me.

'That's my father,' I said, trying to ignore the dread that swirled in the pit of my stomach. I put a hand into my breech's pocket and jingled some loose change so that my squeeze might be as reassured by the sound of ready money, as by the calm, cool timbre of my voice. If

I was somewhat enervated by all that I had crowded into the last twenty-four hours, and bowed by the recollections of my history that these portraits summoned up, then I was still determined to make good on my investment and make a night of it, even if the night would soon be subsumed by the dawn. 'My father, the antecedent Lord Soho. Painted, here, in the uniform of the Order of Black Knights, of which I too am a member, if something of a nominal one. The portrait was executed shortly after he was ennobled, when he moved from Greenwich to this, his sinecure. A parvenu, his enemies said. Bought the title after making a fortune importing goods from the East, a fortune which, in his last years, he lost, largely due to the envy and chicanery of the Darkling Isle's real aristocrats, the Batterseas, Kensingtons and their ilk. Died when I was still a boy and left me his name, title and debts. Very good of him, I'm sure.'

I pointed to the portrait that hung next to my father's. 'And that there's my paternal grandfather, Richard Pike the First. Perhaps you've heard of him? A famous soldier, if somewhat indiscreet in his amours. Entered into a liaison with a goblin girl. Died in exile.'

'You don't look much like him, Mackie.'

'Of course not,' I snapped. 'He was fully human. Not—' Involuntarily, I put a hand to my face; ran it over the pocks and rills that had been transmitted to me through my family's polluted bloodline, flesh that, though not as squamous as a goblin's, was non-human enough to mark me out as one of the enemy. No matter that my father had not only acquired citizenship, but had bought his way into the establishment, I would always be an outsider. 'He had three sons and two daughters,' I continued, taking my hand away from my face as soon as I became conscious of it there. 'Only one son returned to the Darkling Isle. I am ignorant of what became of the others.'

'They *let* him return? said Sukey, somewhat incredulously.

'It was before the blood laws were enacted,' I explained. 'They certainly wouldn't accept him now. You shouldn't have more than an eighth. Preferably—'

'Less than an eighth,' said Sukey, like a schoolgirl reciting from a primer on civic responsibility, 'preferably less than an eighth of teratoid blood in you if you're to qualify for citizenship.'

'Quite so.' I averted my face so that she might not see my sneer.

As we ascended past the portraits of my immediate forebears, my little, gaily wrapped, ninety-six-pound parcel of bought flesh stopped and drew me to a halt. She looked up at me and put a hand to my cheek, exploring its trammelled skin with a long, red fingernail. 'You look nice, Mackie,' she said with a tenderness I had not suspected her capable of, and which I found unaccountably moving. She began to walk ahead. I followed. 'I mean, with your grey complexion and all. It's nice. It's nothing to be ashamed of. Don't let anybody tell you different.' I skipped up the handful of steps that separated us and took her arm.

We reached the summit. I led her forward into the little roof garden. Still somewhat distracted by my encounter with my ancestors, and touched by Sukey's curious display of empathy, I disengaged my arm from hers and walked to the parapets. I wanted to be alone. Glancing round, I saw that my companion idled, going down on one knee to smell various horticultural marvels that had been plucked from the countryside before the stone forests of the Netherworld had overrun the land. A series of trellises formed an arbour at the garden's centre, above which the cross of St George flapped atop a long, steel flagpole, listless as a dying bird. Beneath the flag, on bended knee as she was, she seemed to be making obeisance to the nation's forgotten gods, or, perhaps, more in keeping with her character, was mocking that symbol of our heritage, just as she mocked me, perhaps, by pretending to love the goblin within the man, and by deeming it appropriate to await my pleasure in that florescent bower, with its hackneyed associations of romance and lovers' bliss.

Fortified by this surge of cynicism, I placed my hands on the parapet and looked down upon Soho Square.

My own house was the largest of the several imposing edifices that formed the square's perimeter. The dimensions of the big, gloomy pile were a burden, and I would have readily exchanged them for the unknown, mysterious, but infinitely more wonderful dimensions of wealth. But these old buildings were impossible to sell. And I had only its draughts and shadows to comfort me. I had my valet, it's true, but I had retained his service only by the strictest of economies, a financial regimen that had involved relinquishing much of the house to bed sheets, cobwebs, woodworm and the ruin of general neglect. A few private rooms, my chamber *mirabilis*, and the chapel dedicated to the old gods that I had had reconsecrated to the new in order to appease the city's burghers and demonstrate that I was not of the devil's party, but a man of God – these apartments alone remained for my use. The rest of the house was like a sealed tomb.

I looked up, squinted, and focused on a section of skyline beyond the square: the fashionable new buildings along Oxford Street whose gigantic proportions relegated my own Soho quarters to the status of a foothill. Like all buildings thrown up by the massive rebuilding projects that had followed the peace between Earth-Below and Earth-Above, their parabolic arches, absurdly extended finials, ornate stonework, and mosaics made from shards of porcelain and glazed earthenware brought to mind the ancient Catalonian structures attributed to Gaudí. Carved from the imported, living stone of the wastes, their façades were angry, eruptive, where the husbanded rock had been slaughtered after it had met the requirements of the city's engineers and masons. Each assemblage of steeple, tower, pinnacle and spire stared back at me like some troll who had awoken from a distant age, only to be frozen in stony horror at the spectacle of the modern world.

The buildings were terrible, more terrible than the trees that they had been hewn from, with a terror that flowed from their deadness where it had once flowed from life. It was our death they housed, our mortality they celebrated. Our final despair.

'We are in danger of entering another dark age,' I muttered. 'Who could have believed it?' I was suffering from my own personal dark age, of course. On the low horizon of my flattened life, the possibility of what those damned Christians called 'redemption' would sometimes present itself. I might still, I would think, be able to slough off who I am or, rather, who I have come to be. I may yet become a different person. But I was trapped. Trapped by my own weakness. How might I find the strength to free myself when the world was trapped within its own similarly false identity, the bars and walls of its manifold pseudodoxies and lies? 'A hundred years ago,' I said, 'it seemed that we would enjoy a new renascence of learning, but the energy of these damnable *Christians* has undone so much. We are falling back into ignorance.' On a clear summer's night such as this I could see, if not the city walls themselves – the snaking, circumambient mass of stone, mortar, *chevaux-de-frise* and cannon that protected us – then the lights, the thin, lantern-dotted line that indicated the city limits. 'Atlantis is *in extremis*,' I said, continuing my self-scarifying monologue. 'Coptic armies have ravaged Afric like swarms of locusts.' I put a hand between the loosened folds of my cambric shirt, found the lanyard, and then, fingers slipping down its length, settled my hand around the key which unlocked my chamber *mirabilis*. It was reassuring to know that it was there; like the city walls, it was a bulwark against barbarism, even if it could do little to protect me from my civilization's inner demons. 'It's this accursed True Word that these Christians claim to have discovered in the East. The one intact copy of their wretched Holy Bible. Ha. It's an artefact, of course, that Bible, just like those I've set such store by over the years. How can something from the ancient world contribute to our destruction rather than our enlightenment? Does history have as cruel a sense of humour as this damned *Christian* God?'

I felt Sukey's sweat-streaked breasts against my back, wet and warm as big, soapy sponges. She pressed herself closer, and the heat intensified. I shifted, restless.

'Hold me, Mackie. Don't let the barbarians get me. A girl needs someone to look out for her these days. So many bad things are loose in the wastes. Save me from them, Mackie. Save poor little Sukey.'

Swinging around, I took her by the arms and bent her over a merlon. Her head pointed towards the cobbles some two hundred feet below, her hindquarters, offered up by the bevelled stone that supported her waist, providing sufficient inducement to snap me out of my miserable reverie and attend to the *raison d'être* of our little rooftop one-on-one.

She gave a squeal. I think it was genuine; the capstone that dug into her belly must have been quite sharp. Then her innate and admirable professionalism took over, and the sound effects that followed – while conceding that there was to be little foreplay – were stage-managed with the expertise of one used to satisfying the demands of rapscallions, rakehells and the occasional mad aristocrat.

I kicked at her ankles, first one, and then the other, sweeping her legs to either side of the merlon, so that her thighs hugged its respective embrasures. For a while, I studied the tendered rump. Then I fell to pulling up her petticoats, eager to bring the affair to conclusion and rejoin my other guests, each one of whom, I had promised myself, would serve or be serviced in a different part of my rambling mansion.

For a while, I was frustrated by her underskirts' sheer voluminousness, until, tearing at them like a wild dog, I fell to, sending a cry out over London's rooftops which was a celebration of my goblinry and a release of twenty-one years of pent-up sorrows and hatreds.

There is a traditional way in which a lord and commoner achieve congress. It involves what is known as the 'minimalist embrace', what contact there is being confined to the genital area. And so we continued, I with hands locked behind my head, eyes raised to the moon, baying like a feral animal, while she wiggled and waggled in that exemplary way of hers, making little moans, gasps and other appropriate noises, and occasionally offering a comment on my virility, skill, omnipotence and general savoir faire by way of elegant variation. Our rhythm gathered pace. Became almost absurdly frenetic. We raced each other towards the finishing post. I, because I had much other fleshly business to attend to that night and, she, because she undoubtedly despised the ground I walked upon. At last, to both parties' considerable, if qualitatively different, relief, the goal of our carnality was achieved in that complementary voidance of desire and pretence that has always characterized my relationships with womankind.

It was only then that I became aware that I was being watched.

I turned, hands automatically occupying themselves in the discreet adjustment of my breeches. Peachum, flanked by a posse of constabulary, was pointing an accusing finger at me and indulging in a stupid, lopsided, but horribly triumphant grin.

Wobbling a little, Sukey got to her feet, crossed the roof garden and stood by his side, patting down her skirts and glancing backwards with eyes that were lit with the same malicious glee that animated the face of my father-in-law.

'You are an adulterer, sir, as well as being a notorious bigamist,' he said.

'I'm a lord of the realm, sir,' I countered, surprise giving way to indignation, 'and I am not to be held accountable for such trifles.'

'And what you did in the chamber today, sir, was that such a trifle?'

'Indeed no, sir, but member privilege does not make me accountable to you.'

'You are free with your member privilege, sir.'

Sukey essayed a laugh, but sensing that a whore might not indulge her humour, here, without incurring some painful recompense, she hurriedly accepted the purse which Peachum extended to her and scurried down the stairs.

'I told you I liked the *old* 'uns,' she said, by way of a parting shot, 'Mr Mackie Messer, *sir*.'

Peachum drew himself up. 'Yes, you are free, sir. Too free. We shall have to rectify *that*. You have injured my daughter.'

'Her reputation will survive its association with my name, Peachum. It has, after all, survived its association with yours. Her position as one of Soho's most prominent strumpets will not, I think, be compromised by a few street urchins calling out "*Lady* Poll"! after her. It is not *I* who am accountable to you, but *you* to me, sir.

Yesterday morning you made an attempt on my life. Do you deny it?'

'Arrest him,' said Peachum, quietly, to the constables.

I smirked. But on seeing the constables advance, the smirk withered on my lips.

'There is some mistake,' I said. 'I am Lord Soho. I may only be judged by my peers.'

'And they *have* judged you,' said Peachum. 'But you have perhaps been so busy as not to be aware that the House was in special sitting tonight. A bill has been passed revoking all previous legislation that made it possible for you and others of your filthy kind to reside behind the city walls. It is not only half-breeds who are now to be denied citizenship, Macheath. It is quadroons, and, yes, octoroons too. Your citizenship is revoked. You are no longer a lord. And as such—'

One of the constables interrupted him, eager to secure the last lot of doom-laden words for himself, and to squander them in my suddenly dispossessed presence. 'As such you are accused of murder, kidnapping, wounding, grievous bodily harm, actual bodily harm, petty larceny, grand larceny, compound larceny, fraud, bigamy, living off immoral earnings and procurement. And, oh yes,' he added, his laughter bright where mine had dulled, 'you are also accused of being an illegal alien.'

It was thus I came to Newgate.

> *What gudgeons are we men!*
> *Every woman's easy prey.*
> *Though we have felt the hook, again*
> *We bite, and they betray.*

Lord Soho

The bird that has been trapped,
When he hears his calling mate,
To her he flies, again he's clipped
Within his wiry grate.

If there were ever to be written a comprehensive anatomy of bleakness, or a world encyclopaedia of misery, I would, I believe, make an excellent contributor. A mere paragraph or two focusing on the twelve all-too-bleak, all-too-miserable hours spent in the dark, labyrinthine depths of Her Majesty's prison would elevate any account of my life's travails to a level that would necessarily resound down the years and have me lauded and commiserated by posterity.

The unbearableness of my ordeal was due largely to my visitors: Polly Peachum and, as misfortune would have it, Lucy Lockit, the gaoler's daughter. Indeed, the conjunction, which until now had been unheralded was worse than that of certain, unlucky stars. A year or two ago, I had not only flirted with Lucy in order to stock up credit in the event of future arrest, but had upped the ante of this 'get out of gaol free' *affaire de coeur* by marrying the silly girl.

My two wives stood outside my cell regarding each other evilly. Each held a small lamp close to her face, and their heavily painted eyes glinted, yellow and phantasmal.

It was necessary, of course, to disown Polly. Only by so doing might Lucy come to my aid. I must admit I would have gladly disowned Polly even if my life hadn't depended upon it. She was, I told myself, with an attention to reason somewhat skewed by the

41

previous evening's misadventures, the one who had brought me to this pass, indeed, the source of all my recent troubles. Lord Soho, by virtue of his vast resources of self-pity, was absolved of blame.

'Be pacified, Lucy,' I said. 'Polly's not my wife. She's just desperate to be thought my widow.'

'You have the heart,' said my pretty Poll, 'to persist in this?'

'And have you the heart to persist in persuading me that I'm married to you? You're a very aggravating child, Polly.'

'You expose yourself, Mistress Peachum,' said Lucy. 'Besides, it's barbarous in you to worry a gentleman in his circumstances. Decency might teach you to behave with some reserve with the husband while his wife is present.'

'Seriously, Polly,' I said, 'this is carrying a joke too far.'

'My father's the turnkey here, Mistress Peachum. If you are determined to raise a disturbance I shall be obliged to ask him to show you the door.' And after he's done that, I thought, you can persuade him, with a daughter's sweet, wheedling words, or, if it be more persuasive, the promise of incest, to show *me* the door. 'I'm sorry, madam, you force me to be ill-bred,' concluded my little fail-safe.

I would, I believe, have successfully prosecuted matters and earned, by my brave gainsaying, an eventual salvation, if, at that moment, the fruits of several years of fervent philandering had not caught up with me.

One of the prison guards materialized from the

shadows that curtained off the rest of a corridor so long it had taken fifteen minutes to walk to my cell, but so obscured by darkness that I knew it to be populated only by the sighs and screams that would sometimes drift through the damp, fetid air. 'Four women more, Pike,' he said, laughing, 'with a child apiece. See, here they come!'

I looked away and spat on the floor. 'Tell the hangman I am ready,' I said.

And there it should have ended. But a tale is vulgarly served by poetic justice; especially, I would like to add, when that tale is my own. That I survived my life as a serial bigamist and all-round cad was due, quite astonishingly, to the fact that I chose to survive it; that I chose to go against the poetic grain. A person is shaped, they say, by environment. But that's nonsense, deterministic nonsense. Studying the Ancients, I had known that a man's character owed as much, perhaps more, to heredity. That is, to those mysterious entities called *genes*. I have since decided that this too is a gross simplification. Perhaps even an error. A man, I believe, is shaped by his ability to choose, to exercise his will and imagination. It is only thus that he truly defines himself.

What occurred to me on the road to Tyburn prefigured a later revelation that would bring an end to Macheath as effectively as the gallows: the revelation that I was free to remake myself in my own image.

Yet as well as choosing, I felt that day that I was chosen, too – chosen by a deus ex machina that entered this world somewhat like the fabulous 'grace'

Christians like to cant about. A deus from another universe . . .

The cart rolled up Holborn, past Lincoln's Inn Fields, through St Giles and into Oxford Street. It was there, as I passed the outlying streets of my own stalking ground of Soho, that the pavements became filled with pretty maids, each one of whom made an ostentatious display of dabbing at her eyes. Women are partial to the brave, they say, and think every man handsome who is going to the gallows.

> *The youth in his cart hath the air of a lord,*
> *And we cry, There dies an Adonis!*

My jaw was set, it's true, but the emotional adhesive that bonded it emanated from a disposition to get the thing done and escape this life rather than from courage.

There were, amongst the fair sex, of course, those who were not so impressed by my comportment. Polly, Lucy and a dozen or so other women, some of whom I had married and some of whom had received my matrimonial overtures, took considerable delight in bombarding me with eggs and rotten fruit, and this brave Adonis soon looked like a fairground Aunt Sally. My ears were also subject to filth – the hurled imprecations of a mob raised on tales of goblins, 'Devil', 'Archfiend' and 'Mephistopheles' being the least objectionable, if enjoying a pertinence that, thanks to my countrymen's new-found sanctity, made them all the more vindictive.

We rattled along towards Edgware Road, on whose

corner the Tyburn gallows cast its shadow over the cobblestones, as it presently would my life.

I looked up into the clear, blue sky. It seemed ready to receive me. I had never believed in much, but I *had* believed that the world might not have a lid, and that the azure empyrean might be limitless. That possibility seemed lost now, the sky blanked out by the dark, overarching buildings, murdered remains of the accursed present cramping all existence just as the halter would soon cramp the tiny portion that had been allotted to Richard Pike the Third, second lord of Soho.

Then to whom should I address my prayers? I was, I suppose, of the old religion. My chapel still contained, suitably hidden away, the little clay images that celebrated the trinity that was the Null, the Zero and the Void. Gods of progress? Gods of nought. My own negation of authority – whether it be family, church or state – and my commitment to rationalism and scientific truth, negated, now that my end was near, life itself. The old gods would not hear me.

A coach and four swung out of a sidestreet and pulled up to the cart. Throughout my progress, other vehicles had held back, allowing us swift passage. But the coach seemed intent on defying the commonly accepted etiquette awarded a condemned man. The din of the raucous crowd subsided a little as heads turned to see what its arrival portended. I had achieved such a state of detachment that it took me a while to notice that my coat of arms – a sphinx, couchant, above crossed rapiers – was displayed on the coach's side. Dazed by this apparition, I hazarded that my old, faithful conveyance had been leased out as a funeral hearse to defray the expenses of my inhumation. I turned my attention to the figure on the driving-box. He was shrouded in a cloak that was as black as the coach's panelling. A cowl was pulled down over his head. This was no hearse, it dawned on me, it was a getaway vehicle. For I knew that bag of bones – would have known it anywhere – whether it were perched on a driving-box or astride a black mare in the drear, stony forests of the wastes.

'Melchezidek,' I said, my voice breaking, 'Melchezidek, is that you?'

'Prepare yourself, Master Pike,' he replied.

A flap of his cloak fell open; through it, a bony, long-fingered hand appeared, clutching that dear implement of perambulatory refinement and cruelty, my sword-stick. The old witch flexed his arm and threw. The swordstick described cartwheels, its silver knob flashing as it caught the rays of the noonday sun. How beautiful it looked, that dandyish length of ebony and steel that had captivated the eyes of the ladies and whose concealed blade had despatched more than a few impudent thralls. I half stood and, though manacled, endeavoured to raise my hands to snatch it from the air before the guards seated to either side of me could intervene.

Everything suddenly seemed so right, so fated, that when I plucked the swordstick from the air, I knew, with a surge of gladness in my heart, that *possibility* still existed. Above me, the sky seemed to open up. Sunlight streamed through the matted vault of the overhanging buildings and was everywhere. I placed the black shaft between my knees and then, with both hands clasping the stick's hilt, twisted and pulled, releasing the blade from its oiled confines.

What I did next was largely due to the insight that, on grasping the short, thin sword, suddenly irradiated my brain like an exploding cannonball filled with magnesium.

I'm not Macheath, I said to myself. I've never been Macheath. That was a name given me by my Soho confederates. I'm Richard Pike. I'm Richard Pike the Third. And I'm also something marvellously other . . .

A searing consciousness of my patrimony burned through my veins. From the depths of those hot, salty streams and rivulets, I heard the voices of my father and grandfather, and deeper down, the voices of orcs. But from the deepest abyss of my being came a terrible, alien voice that pre-dated not only my family, but the Earth itself, and the universe that it was a part of. And it was that unspeakable presence that guided my hand.

I screamed, then jabbed the blade under the ribs of the guard to my right, who was in the process of rising to disarm me too casually, too confidently by far, it transpired, to save his wife the expense of widow's weeds. I hobbled forward, the ankle chains clanking on the straw-covered boards. The cart's driver glancing round failed to appreciate the peril of his situation. Within the time it took me to make three swift hops, I skewered him through the left eye.

I spun about, killing the remaining guard with a slash that carved a neat, conic section out of his oesophagus. I screamed again, as I was spattered with his blood.

The coach was now almost flush against the cart's big, right wheel. If I had not been shackled I believe I might have leaned out, opened its door, mounted the cart's side, and leaped into its velvety interior. But constrained as I was, I knew that simple act of athleticism to be impossible; I stood transfixed, staring at the coat of arms that decorated the varnished, black wood, its propinquity eliciting a low, rising growl of frustration. The cart's horse had bolted, and both vehicles thundered along Oxford Street. Cane stuck between my thighs, knees bent, and hands held before me, grasping my blood-slicked blade, I began to sway and stumble. Soon, it was all that I could do to prevent myself from being pitched on to my face.

The voices within me became louder, drowning out the shouts of the mob, some of whom had flung themselves at the cart, obtained purchase, and hung suspended from the sides and chassis. I feared they would at any minute induce it to topple, or else clamber aboard, tearing me to pieces in their desire not to be cheated out of a hanging. As I watched mouths open and close in silence, the coarse plebeian utterances of these zealots swamped by the clamour inside my skull, I at last began to attend to what my voices said. They didn't communicate in English, or, it seemed, in any human tongue, and the sub-verbal transaction was almost instantaneous. But in that second of communion with forces personal, yet supremely alien, I knew for the first time in my life who and what I was and what I was to do.

I focused on my wrists, jerking at the chain that restrained them. The links snapped. Tucking the blade under one arm, I bent down, grasped the restraint that fettered my ankles and, with one fluid motion that brought me back to a standing position, freed myself. I waited for the surprise that should, by any reasonable expectation, have been forthcoming. But there was none. Surprise would come later, reserved, not so much for the discovery that the highwayman, Macheath, had never really existed, but for a deeper truth: that the scientist I had thought was my better, nobler self, was equally unreal. The Ancients, with their claims to possess objective knowledge of the world, and, indeed, foolish as it seemed to me now, all worlds, were as much victims of superstition as our latter-day Christians. They both belonged to a distant past that remained best forgotten. From that moment, I knew I would hunger for a different reality.

One of the mob had managed to pull himself up over the side of the cart and fell, in a sprawl of outsized limbs, amongst the straw. Tottering, I assumed my fighting stance: weight supported by my right leg, blade held snug against my hip. In my other hand I held the ebony sheath before me, to turn or block a blow.

Swiftly, the intruder got to his feet, bunched his meaty fingers and, finding his balance, came forward. I used the cane to knock one of his arms aside, and then kicked, the toe of my left boot connecting with the soft, fleshy underside of his chin. He stepped backwards, choking. I followed – he was a big brute, and wasn't going to go down easily – right foot stepping over my left as I put all my weight behind the blade and thrust its needle-like tip into his sternum.

I pulled the blade free. He fell, dead, I think, before he hit the boards.

Quickly, I scanned the street, the coach, the sky, the cart. Those that still clung to the cart had grown tentative enough, I decided, for me to reach out and open the coach's door. I did so, and, after putting a foot on the cart's side to gain leverage, flung myself across the intervening space. The blurred cobbles rose to meet me and dash out my brains, or else consign my bones to iron-rimmed wheels, or the hooves of the team of four. But I impacted on wood. Feeling the embrace of velvet, and smelling old leather and fresh varnish, I knew that I had attained my goal. I scrambled to lock the door. An afterthought, in which the ugly faces of my persecutors largely figured, also stirred me to pull down the blind. I heard the snap of reins against horseflesh, and we began to accelerate, swerving through the crowds, sometimes successfully, sometimes, to go by the odd holler of outraged flesh that stung my ears, not so successfully. The gallow's party soon reduced to a diminuendo of disappointed bloodlust.

I rejoiced in their pain.

'You've learned much today, Master Pike,' said Melchezidek. He drew his cloak more tightly around him and shivered. His ancient bones alerted him to every change in direction of the cooling breeze. 'I am glad that you put that narrative behind you. Like a mirror, the past has been shattered but its shards still fly through space and time and sometimes find a place in our hearts. It falls to us to become our own surgeons, remove those splinters of perverted history, and in so doing, set ourselves free. For if we do not, we will see reflected back at us, not our true faces, but the faces of those others who no longer have a place in this world. You must choose, now, Master Pike. Choose to be your own man. Choose to be *free.*'

'My own man? But what man is that?' I said. The forest was behind us, and I looked down upon the city I knew I would never see again. For though Melchezidek had rescued me, I had only the life of an outcast to look forward to. 'And am I really a man at all? The things that I felt today, the *power*. I know I'm part orc – a witch, like you. But today there was something else I discovered within myself. Something more alien than I ever suspected.'

'There is an alienness that came before the orcs, came even before the people whom legend calls the lost tribes of the perverse. It is the fount of all the strangeness in the world, and it emanates not in the universe in which we exist but in another. It is that which truly makes you an exile, Master Pike. It is that which is the demarcating line, not only between you and the human race, but between the human race as it is now constituted, and humanity as it was in the confused, forgotten past. Your contaminated blood owes its origins not to the liaison that your grandfather entered into with an orc, but to something vastly older and more otherworldly. A liaison our world entered into with a parallel dimension, four thousand years ago.'

'How do I find out who or what I really am?' Today, I thought, today I had been a superlative swordsman. How had that metamorphosis come about? 'How?' I said aloud, with an earnestness that could not be compromised by a weariness of limbs and spirit.

'Time enough for that, Master Pike. You must think now upon surviving. You're not a lord out here in the wastes. It is now, perhaps, that your true education begins.'

I sighed. 'Begins? It only begins?'

'You've learned what you are not. I suppose that's a good enough start for any story. Now you must learn what you are. What you can be. Now you must create your own narrative. It is not enough to revive artefacts. Not enough to look to the Ancients for your example. You must not be a slave to the past. You must subvert it, re-invent it, and in so doing re-invent yourself, and, perhaps, all mankind.' I felt his long-fingered hand on my shoulder. 'You are a member of the Order of Black Knights, Master Pike. And you have reached your majority. Do not fear. You can do anything.' I put my own hand over his. I owed the old witch my life. It had been foolhardy of him to enter London. A proscribed half-man, he could have easily ended up on the gallows, alongside me. More than friend, I realized he was the only family I had, now the human family had turned their collective back on me.

I had heard voices: my father's, my grandfather's, all the bloody line of the Pikes, and I had heard the voice of my orc-grandmother, her dark song of the Netherworld. And under all this had been the ground bass which prefigured the strangeness and perversity that had proved a dividing line between the Earth of my own age and the Earth of the Ancients; perversity that had emanated from another universe and had confounded our attempts to win objective knowledge. But beneath even this I had heard, for the first time, the inspiration of that chorale: the ground of Being to which the multitudinous spheres owed their harmony, the Love that moved the stars. I knew, once heard, that that music would change my life for ever and give it meaning.

I had been trapped in a narrative in which I was the Soho highwayman, Macheath; but I had also been trapped in my mechano-materialistic view of life. Only in a philosophy that attended to Being as well as Becoming could mankind rediscover itself and set itself free.

Like the Christians, I had placed my faith in a pseudodoxy. Truth was not all of one order, and neither was the self.

Could that lost article of faith, Man, be truly revived? Yes, I thought. But not by grubbing amongst the flotsam of the past. Artefacts, holy books – they only offered us an escape from what, in the end, was an ineluctable responsibility. I would redefine what it meant to be human, I decided; I would make it my life's work. I would accept that I enjoyed an atrocious, if heady, freedom, and that I could choose who to be and what to do.

The breeze whistled through the stony branches, like a child playing with a tin whistle. London was lit, its lights cold and distant. And in its maze of stony streets I tried to descry Soho, where a boy once came to be known as Macheath, and a man lost that name only to find himself without a new one.

The clouds were lucent with moonglow. I gazed down until London's black outlines stood out in relief from the greater blackness of its heart. From that heart, streets extended like capillaries, the red street lamps of Soho the corpuscles in a dead man's inert bloodstream. Towers and tenements tangled with the moon-bright sky, like the branches of the gnarled and blasted trees under which I sat. London was a petrified forest. A place of decease. I looked away, into the depths of that other, strangely familiar forest that was to be my place of exile. Unlike the city, the stone about me was vital, full of a strange sap that promised new life, a rebirth from the ashes of the alien. Perhaps my exile would not be so hard as I had supposed.

I became aware that I was about to set off on a long and hazardous voyage. But however far I might journey, and whether or not I might find myself eventually stranded, lost in some distant night of the soul, I was buoyed by the intimation that there would be others who would come after me.

The thin fluting of the wind in the boughs conjured up the catch of an old song. I fastened my gaze upon the Pole star, and made my wish.

Now I stand like a Turk, with his doxies around,
From all sides their glances his passions confound;
For black, brown, and fair, his inconstancy burns,
And the different beauties subdue him by turns:
Each calls forth her charms to provoke his desires,
Though willing to all, with but one love he retires:
But think of this maxim, and put off your sorrow,
The wretch of today, may be happy tomorrow.

Incunabula

'Each Pike contains within himself the spirit of a sword, and the name of that sword is *Espiritu Santo*.' My father gave his razor a disdainful glance, and then proceeded to sharpen it on the strop. 'But the sword is lost, both in actuality and in spirit, and all our family is left with are the incunabula, such as we have in you, my boy. Though it sometimes seems a curse, as much as a blessing.' Dad was a great one for genealogy. He had a family tree pinned up on the shop wall. He liked to point out to customers that his own father had had noble blood, and that, if our family's enemies had not been so devious, I, his son – instead of being the valet of a local sheriff – would be destined to occupy a seat in the House of Peers, Richard Pike, the fourth Lord Soho. The regulars would twit him. Call him a dreamer. A fraud. But neither mockery nor the knowledge that our dispensation was surely irrevocable could inhibit my father from concluding his boasts with the assertion that we would one day regain our title. He had spent his whole life duelling with phantoms. And if he had no rapier, he had determined – and determined, I should think, at an early age – to lunge, jab, pink and stab at fate with words. Indeed, so determined was he to overcome the enemy, even if the foe was as far beyond reach as *Espiritu Santo* – our family's lost, mystical heirloom – that my poor mother had died, I think, of eight and a half years of sheer unrelieved aural proximity to such a fanatic. Pride, in him, was relentless, as I too had discovered, shortly after my mother's death, when he had despaired of bringing up an only child alone.

But today his volubility had been chastened by the lack of a suitable audience. Apart from the old man – a regular customer, I had learned – whom he was about to relieve of three day's worth of stubble, and who was either deaf or affected deafness in commensurate degree to the promise of being once more subjected to one of my father's harangues, the shop was empty. There was no one to fence with but myself. 'Ah yes,' he continued, pinching the tip of the old one's nose and delicately applying the blade to an inchoate moustache, 'to be an uncorrupted text, a living book which represents a re-interpretation, or subversion, of the past, is a burden. We Pikes have all felt it. The way history is repeating itself. Not in fact, but in fiction. Or rather, in fiction that yearns to become, and indeed so often succeeds in becoming, fact. Fiction as embodied in those new examples of humanity called incunabula. Men and women, boys and girls, who suggest a rediscovery of Man.' The cut-throat razor skimmed across a richly lathered cheek. The old man grimaced, less, I knew, at the application of steel to flesh than in apprehension that my father was about to launch into a too familiar round of interminable speechifying. But Dad checked himself. 'I feared little good would come of you entering the count's employ,' he said at last, somewhat anticlimactically.

He was being disingenuous. And I almost told him so. Mother had not been the only one to be wounded – if not so mortally – by his quixotic idée fixe. Eighteen years ago I had, in effect, been sold, my journey into bondage dressed up as 'the chance of a lifetime' and 'an avenue by which the family might bring the injustices it has suffered to the attention of a sympathetic noble', such as, I suppose, Count Almaviva was thought to be. I had forgiven Dad his cant, if only because I too, over the years, had come to share and thus understand the constant, neurotic ache that was his sense of dispossession; but it had been hard. The conviction that the family's estates and fortunes would be one day restored was a slippery one. Nevertheless, he lost no opportunity of grasping it whenever he could, whatever the consequences. And, just as there is a point where toleration of injustice becomes complicity, there was a similar point when desperation such as his became callous self-aggrandizement.

But I chose not to go over old ground. I was still comparatively young, and, in the young, a flirtation with bitterness yields the kind of unhealthy glamour that has always elicited my disgust. I am, I like to think, a man of good sense, cheerful in adversity, someone who refuses to bow to life's rankness. And if I acknowledge that the world is a dark, dark place, I see no reason why such darkness cannot be filled with laughter. No, I would have nothing to do with bitterness. I would, I had decided, concentrate instead upon the future. And Suzanne.

'You still haven't offered a shred of advice as to what I should do,' I said. Even as I said it, I wondered why I had come here. It was my first visit in over six months. My familial past was as obscure and unloved as that ancient world .that humanity found itself hopelessly separated from. The future, I thought. Think only upon the future. Depart.

But my legs might as well have been clamped in irons. Outside, the branches of the trees tapped against the mullioned windows. The black, dew-lacquered boughs summoned up an image of glistening seams of coal, and, for a moment, I felt the shop might have been some goblin redoubt deep beneath the Earth's surface. I remained seated, as petrified as the alien woodlands that crowded in from all sides, and as isolated as the handful of rude, mercantile domiciles that dotted this lonely stretch of highway.

'You are thirty years old,' said my father. 'And in this world, this rough, feral world we Pikes have been thrust into, you occupy a position that represents a modest step up the social ladder. You are old enough – and indeed, experienced and independent enough, I hazard – to do without my advice. At least, you have thought so until now. But if you want it, have it: I've told you for some time that, until you attain some reversal of our fortunes, marriage will only serve as a distraction. And yet you persist. Why not satisfy yourself with one of the local trollops? Why yearn for one such as this maidservant, this Suzanne?'

'You can only understand if you are an incunabulum,' I said. 'There is this need to realize one's self, to make one's narrative complete. And that can be only achieved through having knowledge of another of your kind, one who has a stake in the same storyline, one who shares your destiny.' I sighed. For thirty years my subjective life had struggled to realize itself, but, in ignorance of the totality of its own nature, had failed to achieve holistic integrity. Only union with another incunabulum would complement and bring the mystery of my being to fruition. 'But of course, I may not be married at all. That's the problem.' I still stared out of the window. No matter how much I tried to make good the decision to get up, bid my adieus and walk through the door, I remained paralysed by a vestigial sense of filial duty: something I had clung to ever since I had been compelled to leave home as a twelve-year-old: the notion that, in return for honouring him, my father would award me his protection and love. 'As I've told you: the count has a determination to revive his droit de seigneur.'

'For which, I understand, he will give Suzanne a handsome dowry.'

'And take the knowledge that was meant for *me*.'

'But can you blame him? He's a collector. How many incunabula does he have these days?'

'His library extends to some nineteen,' I said. 'But most are misbirths. They are frozen in suspension amongst his grimoires, floating in a cocktail of exotic antioxidants. Suzanne and I are the only incunabula actually in his service.'

'There you are then. Why should he go to all the trouble of keeping you, bringing you up, giving you a good education, if he stands to gain nothing by it? Forgive me, son. I don't want to sound unsympathetic. But we Pikes go through life with our eyes open, I hope. People like Count Almaviva are doing us quite enough of a service when they're not actually doing us any real harm. So leave well alone. Let the count enjoy your popsy for one night, and then take her to your bed regardless. Forget that anything untoward ever happened, eh?'

'But the *knowledge*, father. Only I should have the right to share her knowledge and make it my own. The count is not like me. He can't hope to enter into a perfect, psychic communion with her. But I believe he's studied incunabula long enough to know how to wrest elements of Suzanne's fictiveness and incorporate them into himself. The man's a bandit, no better than the rest of England's aristocrats. Not content with robbing us of our freedom, they want to take our very *souls* for themselves. It's rape, Father. Nothing less. *Rape.*'

'You seem filled with that spirit of sedition that appears to have taken root in the school. *You'd* have been a pupil there, perhaps, if it hadn't been for my foresightedness.' He wiped his razor clean of lather and whiskers and then reapplied himself to his work. 'You always seemed a boy destined to abuse his freedom, someone the magistrates wouldn't have thought twice about stripping of what measly rights he possessed. Better to be valet to the count and a free man outside the city limits than be inside London's walls only to find yourself the plaything of a rich master or mistress or the factotum of some government drone.' He clicked his tongue against the roof of his mouth. 'I knew the count would be interested in an incunabulum. Knew he'd want you in his household, so that he could verify what I had said about you – that you were as powerful and healthy as I'd claimed. And I knew that, as a collector, he would not think of informing on you to central government. Now listen to me: you should turn your energies to using the count as he uses you. We Pikes have much to redress. It's a long climb back up to the great eminence we formerly occupied, as your grandfather never tired of reminding me. But it is only by using the foot and handholds that the count offers that we may even begin the ascent.'

I turned from the window and stared Dad in the face. I did not remember much of my grandfather. But he had seemed a man who, like me, had little respect for social niceties or station, except, that is, when he might stand to profit by them. It gave me hope that, if the inveterate snobbishness of the latter Pikes was a matter of blood, then my portion was that of Richard Pike the Third, second Lord of Soho, and not that of his much fallen, if overweening, barber-surgeon son.

'Perhaps, one day,' he continued, 'we may even recover the sword of our ancestors – *Espiritu Santo* – lost to the savages and panjandrums of the Far East by the man who polluted our bloodline, your great-great-grandfather.'

And is that where it had all begun? I wondered. With a distant forebear who had a goblin girl for his doxy? With the first Richard Pike? Was that the man to whom I owed my curious status as a living book, or incarnate fiction? Was the curse that he brought down upon my blood the same agent that conferred knowledge and made me an incunabulum?

Perhaps. It was the fifty-fifth century. Mankind was extricating itself from the smother and obscurity of the last four thousand years by discarding its grimoires in favour of those creatures whose existence provided a link with the all but forgotten past. Creatures like myself. Living books that had survived the corruptions – both psychic and material – of the interregnum. Books treasured, but feared almost as much as the mutant clans of rat, cat, shark, bear and insect people that had overrun the Earth in the days of the perverse and which, just beyond the bounds of living memory, had been confined to the Netherworld, where they had passed from manifest danger into legend. In London, my great-great-grandfather's heirs had been feared because, though nominally human, they represented what was left of the Netherworld on Earth-Above. All that was alien, perverse and – to concede that vanity, in me, has compensated for any lack of inherent Pike-ish *snobbism* – what might still be thought brilliant and beautiful. But despite what my father had earlier averred, the narrative – the twisted, half-formed, preternatural narrative of my soul – *was* a blessing. And more, infinitely more so, than a curse. If my status as an incunabulum really had arisen out of the habitual viciousness of my line, then I thanked the new God. And thanked my ancestors, too, for their wantonness and taste for miscegenation.

At last, I stood. There had been more that I had wanted to confide. For instance, the problem I had, not just with the count's droit de seigneur, but with Marceline. My father avoided my eyes, making a point of studying his customer's blue, newly mown jaw line, almost as long and betraying the same contaminated blood as my father's. Grandfather had evinced more noticeable witch-like features, but Dad still had the gunmetal complexion, yellowish eyes and pointed ears that would have identified him as having, sometime in the distant past – even if the genealogical chart on the wall conspicuously omitted to mention it – an orc for an ancestor. And the cracked, fly-specked mirror behind him that threw my own image back at me recalled the fact that, if my outward appearance had been mercifully diluted by three generations of intermarriage with human women, then the inner man had become more, and not less, alien, with time.

It had been pointless to come here seeking advice. I had fallen victim to a sentimental need for reassurance. For approval. The past was a dark pit. For years, I had stood upon its friable edge, giddy with a desire to pitch myself forward, to leap, to fall, to drown, so much had I wished for its bleak emptiness to be filled. It had taken many years to summon up the courage to walk away. And now that I did walk, I would make sure I did not play the victim again. That wasn't my role. Every fibre of my narrative told me so. No; I was born to prevail. And the time had come to prove it, to embrace the narrative line that, if dim and incomplete, made me more than myself.

I determined I would outfox the count, take my beloved's hymen and appropriate her vast, psychic energies; determined upon hatching stratagems and plans that would risk all. I was Richard Pike, a lord of the imagination, if not of the Darkling Isle. And damn all humans for a crop of thieving, palsy-minded yesterday's men if they got in my way.

I turned towards the door; opened it. 'Goodbye, son,' murmured my father. 'I'll be at the castle tonight, of course. If I disagree with you, it's only because you're dear to me and I don't want to see you get hurt. I wouldn't miss my boy's wedding, now, would I? No; not for anything. Even if its consummation should have to be necessarily delayed. Take care, boy. And remember: you're a Pike.'

I swept out of the shop in silence and hurriedly crossed the highway so that I might be enveloped by the sombre, black woodland. I had gone a hundred yards or so when, in a weakening of resolve, I stopped and looked backwards, filled with the temptation to retrace my steps. Why, I wanted to demand, should I be put in a position of opposing my father? Why should I care so much that he would or could not accept the conditions of my love? The candy-striped barber's pole that I espied through the tangled, ebony branches whirled lazily in the gathering, early morning breeze. Above it, creaking on its hinges, was a sign that displayed three bleeding cups, a hand with an eye in the middle, and the motto 'Consilio Manuque'.

It seemed to me that that sign had always been there. But I was no longer sure of anything. The psycho-dynamic aura that radiates from an incunabulum had been at work ever since I had been born. Wherever I had gone, it had warped local space-time. And over the years 'reality', if never responding with an infinite, or sometimes even partial, plasticity, had, I knew, gradually changed, as people, places and things accommodated themselves to the imperatives of my fictive core. The world about me was not the world of my childhood. Because of me, and, perhaps, Suzanne, life in this small part of England was different and suggested unbounded possibilities. How could I guess, then, just how much that sign owed its origins to the greater world? Maybe it really had always been there. And then again, maybe it had been pressured into being at the metaphysical urging of the parallel universe that I carried about within me.

As I continued to stare through the dead, matted vegetation at the swinging, creaking sign, my mind grasped one abiding fact, and clung to it, hungry as it was for a little certainty in the flux between outer and inner existence: I was my father's son. For like him I was the 'nimble brain' and, like him, I possessed the 'swiftness of the hand' so blatantly advertised by the traditional barber's hoarding. And my name was Richard Pike, too, despite the fact that the people of these parts dismissively called me 'Figaro'.

These parts. These people . . .

I walked through a tract of desolate land north-east of London's high, interdictory walls. It was called the Sink. A dark, barely cultivated waste of petrified trees and coarse, stagnant vegetation. That its denizens were either thralls, slavers or, like my father, men whose delicate state of freedom was predicated upon slave mercantilism, had always seemed to me entirely appropriate, for the dead landscape was thus admirably mirrored by the lifeless, abject curs for whom it was home. They had lived once, truly lived, those slaves and slavemongers, just as the trees in these parts had once been constituted of living, as opposed to dead, matter, even if that matter should, paradoxically, have been stone. For the forest here, as in much of the Darkling Isle, had been transplanted from caverns and galleries far beneath the Earth's surface, where, it is said, all inanimate things have life, and baleful, stone plants, flowers and the demons and demonesses who might conceivably pluck them for nosegays, flourish under a black sun, much as life does under our own sun, though in stranger, more perverted, ways. The once unchecked growth of granite and limestone forest cover was intended, they say, to drive men from their cities and into the hands of the armies of the night. But as the wars with the Netherworld and its orcs had been eclipsed by treaties and the retreat of all goblinry into the deepest parts of the Earth, so had what remained of the subterranean *élan vital* that had taken root on the surface begun to wither and become no more than a vast, country-wide necropolis of deceased, atrophied boughs and blooms, an obsequy to the dark past, as forgotten, almost, as the time of the Ancients.

The path I had taken provided a short cut to the castle, but was not without its dangers. Robber bands of men and half-men – those witches whose number I sometimes found myself uncomfortably accounted among – often lurked amidst the gloom of the dense woodland, waiting for unwary travellers. But the sun had been up a good hour, and my familiarity with the terrain had long bred a contempt that vied with that which I felt for the Sink's population.

I pushed onwards. Oblique rays of early sunlight flickered through the fossilized, overhanging branches, and patches of refulgence swam across the crisp mulch that carpeted the ground like argent petals cast before the feet of, whom? A returning hero, I thought, doggedly apportioning myself a little cheer. Yes. A hero. For I had no wish to think of myself in starker terms of a back-returning, truant drudge.

Lord Soho

I passed into a large clearing.

The low buildings of the slave school lay to my right, surrounded by a chicken-wire perimeter. The school served the capital as an indoctrination and processing facility for factotums and pets and was one of the few outposts awarded anything more than cursory notice by central government. Its staff, pupils and garrison supported those few dozen shops and businesses that, like my father's, parasitized the lifeblood of hard currency that flowed in from London. I dawdled awhile, screwing up my eyes to focus on the phantasmagoria of forms silhouetted by the jaundiced light of the windows: boys engaged in horseplay, or else dragging their feet to class, girls performing little gymnastic routines, massive velvet curtains framing a cartwheel, a handstand, a somersault, each big, oblong casement like the black-bordered frame of a strip cartoon whose figures have yellowed with age. The school was no workhouse such as might be found in the forests of the midlands and the north; its graduates had little to fear of long years of back-breaking travail or a shorter, if equally grim, career as cannon fodder; its intelligent, amusing, wholly submissive boys and girls – so fantastical, this morning, in their multitudinous arbours of sallow light – were destined to become alumni whose grace and charm would be the talk of his lordship's smoking room and the scandal of every other lady's boudoir.

Of course, their submissiveness was not something that had to be taught or otherwise inculcated into them. The denizens of the Sink, and its correlatives strung out across the Darkling Isle's wastes, had, at some indeterminate point in their history, chosen to glory in their thraldom; a choice that was, over centuries, and then millennia, to become ingrained to the point of being instinctual. In embracing submission of their own free will, and happily, too, they had evolved their own culture, and, to a certain extent, their own idiosyncratic philosophy, a *Weltanschauung* that extolled the virtues of abjection. In other times of acute urban and social apartheid when the world had been populated by species of swinish commonality now extinct, there might have been found a corresponding type of voluntary thraldom, a survival mechanism, perhaps, some process of natural selection favouring those who most avidly sought and accepted the life of a craven submissive. All that was certain was that those who had been born in the Sink – and who, unlike my own family, were here not for reasons of political exile, but who traced their origins to a time before the interregnum – were only content when under the thumb of that authoritarian spirit that ruled the land and which I had myself been born to personify but for misfortune and the implacability of my family's enemies.

In the wastes, there were, it was said, only slaves and free men such as roamed alone, brigands and malcontents who might band together in small raiding parties, or sometimes congregate in vast, locust-like hordes. But of late, another variety of human life had come to colonize the heaths, moors and forests of the Isle's wild, defunct counties and shires – the agitator, the dissident, the mutineer were abroad, inspiring the freeborn, and sometimes, it seemed, even the slaves, to dream of revolt. Rumours of sedition circulated within the school's gates. Impossible tales of pupils assaulting their teachers. '*Once we were witches,*' I would some-times hear a gaggle of sullen schoolgirls sing, defiantly, as they passed beneath the castle's walls, '*but now we're just bitches.*' And the boys that followed would answer, '*Once we were punks, but now we're just hunks.*' I remembered a passage from one of the grimoires I had seen in the count's library, a passage that seemed prescient of the delinquent spirit infecting the Sink or, which was, perhaps, only one of many indicia of the eternal state of an England whose people were meta-morphosing back into their mad, surly originals after thousands of years:

What, then, is Darkest England? I claim it for the Lost, for the Outcast, for the Disinherited of the World. These, it may be said, are but phrases. Who are the Lost? Reply, not in a religious, but in a social sense, the lost are those who have gone under, who have lost their foothold in society, those to whom the prayer to our Heavenly Father, 'Give us day by day our daily bread', is either unfulfilled, or only fulfilled by the Devil's agency: by the earnings of vice, the proceeds of crime, or the contribution enforced by the threat of the law.

I had first read that passage when I had been a child. It had been on the occasion when the count had intro-duced me to his library therein to explain my worth to him: how and in what degree, that is, I differed from the collections of fragmented texts that were all that was left of ancient science and art. But was the memory of

71

that reading sound? As ever, childhood returned to me smacking of unreality . . .

I pulled back my shoulders, tipped my chin to the sky. I was a servant, not a slave, I reminded myself. Salaried, with a degree of initiative and petty privilege that, to the class of humanity that were the thralls, made me seem like a scaled-down model of my master. Rebellion, for me, would be subtle. More potent. More lasting.

I left the clearing and turned into the path that led to Aguas Frescas, the castle of Count Almaviva, Lord High Sheriff of the Sink, my guardian, patron, mentor and suzerain. The forest canopy, which resembled the dome of a blasted cathedral, was here surmounted by the castle's battlements, themselves so like the rooftop of a forest of the night. Those battlements suggested the nature of this woodland as it had once been; for Aguas Frescas had been hewn from the living stone of the trees during the time of their dark florescence, its arched galleries and fan-vaulted chambers a baroque homage to the netherlife long vanished from Earth-Above.

The path narrowed, and the branches – the pyre-blackened bones of what might have been long-dead, gibbet-hung orcs – formed a colonnade, so that I would sometimes have to bend my head to avoid bruising my uncovered poll. The path – the remains of a thorough-fare that excavations had proved was the last remnant of a sacked village or town – was rarely used these days by horse, carriage or even man. Yet when I turned about a sharp bend and found myself confronted by three figures, I had no excuse for astonishment.

The man who stood in the middle of the group was, if

a menacing apparition, also a familiar one, instantly recognizable by his stooped shoulders and ominous, little black bag. Here, about to make his tiresome introductions once again, was Dr Bartholo, the local quack, much feared by the thralls on whom he practised the black arts of beautification and reshaping. Bartholo. As the doctor's small eyes arrested and then commanded the attention of my own, I knew that his name might as well have been Vendetta. For he had surely appeared, as he had done regularly over the past ten years, to appease himself of the grudge he felt for me and the count, but which he could only safely satisfy on Figaro, the despised servant, and not on the one who, alone of all sapient life in this region, was allowed to call himself a true man.

The two thralls who stood to either side of him were, to go by their livery, members of his retinue. And if both were a head taller than the good doctor, then they shared his slovenly appearance and shambling ways. They were not graduates of the school, but pinheads: burly, small-brained retainers favoured less for their social accomplishments than for their junkyard-dog aggressiveness and slathering desire to please. Along the coastland fortifications of the West Country, they manned the martello towers that were the Isle's first line of defence against Hibernian reavers. And sometimes the Sink's gentry, such as it was, employed them to collect rents and other debts. Like the debt, I suspected, the doctor felt I owed his *amour-propre*.

'Who goes there, then, eh?' said Bartholo, knowing full well. Though the shadows were deep, he had obviously seen me leave the castle and had lain in wait for my return.

'Anonymous is my patron saint,' I replied, praying that the shadows were thicker than I had reason to hope. 'May he bless you in commensurate degree to whatever disposition you have for allowing me to pass in a state as innominate as I have enjoyed hitherto.'

'So you might wish it,' he said. 'But no: it's little Pike,' he continued, 'Dick Pike, the barber's boy. The Figaro of the Sink. Good morning, thrall. Good morning, *Figaro*.'

'Figaro qua! Figaro la!' said one of the retainers, thickly, as if his tongue were too big for his mouth.

'Figaro su! Figaro gui!' said the other pin, as well-rehearsed, it would seem, as his sidekick, if as equally in need of some form of oral surgery, as well as lessons in elocution.

'This feud has gone on long enough,' I said, in my best, no-nonsense manner, all the while feeling for the cut-throat razor I kept in my belt, suitably obscured by my coat's gold-trimmed flap. '*Espiritu Santo*' – but I spoke to myself, now, whisperingly, as I always did at awkward moments such as this – 'wherever you are, translate yourself into my arm and let me fight as my forefathers did.' As I recited this heretical little prayer, something rose up within me. I heard voices: those of my father and grandfather, and of his father and his father before him. And then I heard, or rather felt, the low vibration that was the ground bass of the perverse radiate through my body and into my right hand. I was possessed by the Holy Spirit. Not the one that the newfangled Christians talk about, but the spirit of the old gods of the perverse, a wholly alien spirit that offered me power – dark, reality-forging power – if only I should acknowledge it. I did acknowledge it. And knew myself an incunabulum. In the hot crucible at my being's core I felt myself remade, and, as at other such critical times in my life, felt also the world about me shiver and then resettle itself in accommodation to my desire.

I forgot, for the moment, that Bartholo was gentry. I gazed upon him as I might a pig, hen or bullock about to be whisked off to market.

'This feud has gone on long enough?' he repeated, mockingly. 'Not so long as to have me forget what you once did to me, lapdog.' The two retainers who flanked him took a step forwards.

'Why, no,' I said. 'How could I forget, old lecher? I helped Count Almaviva cheat you of your ward, Rosine. Though I sometimes rue it. Not for the hurt it did your overbearing pride, you wretched bundle of bones, but because her ladyship seems not the happy woman she was when the count first took her for his own, and so saved her from your stinking bed.'

If my father had chosen to acquit himself of injustice through the desperate medium of language, then it was in this respect, and this respect more than any other, I think, that I knew myself to be his son. To lunge, jab, pink and stab at fate with words, and words alone, had often been my only option in a life that had denied me more appropriately steely means to satisfy the requirements of offended honour. But language is a terror. A razor-sharp barb can wound, not merely the object of a man's ridicule and disgust, but, by way of a misapplication of vocabulary, grammar or syntax, come to injure the subject, too. For if a sally of wit, a greasily enunciated slur or a medley of clever, stinging insults have always represented the thin pie crust of civilization across which I customarily tiptoe, safe from the rancid stew of my birthplace, then so did mispronunciation, a stutter, a single, inelegant aside threaten to open up the ground beneath my feet and commit me to perdition. How much better, then, to have another, altogether more palpable, kind of razor-sharp instrument to defend myself with.

With circumspection, I drew my little blade, choosing, for the moment, to keep it concealed within the voluminous lace cuff of my sleeve.

'I care not for your pathetic tirades, boy,' said the doctor. 'Only for an atonement that I would have you achieve through contusions and bloody wounds. Perhaps then the sight of your scarified, slavish hide when I go to visit the count on my rounds will, if only by virtue of its ruined beauty, vex me the less.'

And it was true: I was beautiful. A hundred or more conquests, of chambermaids, parlourmaids, housemaids and scullery-maids, and the applause of not a few gleefully serviced ladies visiting the castle on their way from London to the north, testified to the snake-like charm of my eyes and my handsome, if somewhat reptilian, profile. I had no wish to have the singular, and – to the fairer sex – wonderfully dangerous charms of my countenance and bearing compromised by one such as Bartholo and his pinheaded proxies.

I pulled out the razor with flamboyant dash and grinned, showing my glittering rows of sharp, orc-like teeth. The blade caught the rays of the rising sun. Its mother-of-pearl handle was cool in my grip. I chortled, my laughter as dry as the barren splinters of leaf and bole beneath my feet. 'You might have a word with Marceline, if you're visiting the castle,' I said.

'Marceline?' The two pins closed in, their gait ungainly but certain. 'The housekeeper?'

'Someone the count is using to defer my marriage so that he might have the chance of enjoying my bride, whether he has droit de seigneur or not. Marceline, you see, loaned me money some time ago, and now she says I either return it or marry *her*. A pretty pickle. But I have heard Marceline is a former lover of yours, doctor. And if the old sow's so hot out of season as it were, I'd have thought a man like you, someone with hair as grey, and even a carbuncle or two to match her own, as well as sharing so many other degenerate characteristics, might be better suited to fit her, so to speak. In short, doctor, why not give the hag a roll in the hay and get her off my case?'

'Impudence in the face of catastrophe has always been your style, barber boy, has it not? Look at you, you jumped-up little pleb. You have no respect for even the sumptuary laws!'

I made a pirouette, letting the tails of my magnificently embroidered coat fan out, and then, as I came to a halt, slapped a thigh to emphasize the sleek, satin-blue luxuriousness of my silver-buttoned breeches. Not content with such a modest display of exhibitionism, I circled a foot in the air to bring attention to my immaculate white stockings and bright-buckled shoes. Then I made another pirouette. At the conclusion of this second twirl I stood with feet set wide apart, tugged at my splendid, frothy lace neckerchief, and, by way of a finale, made a sarcastic bow.

'My life has necessitated a certain foppishness,' I said, 'in apparel, I suppose, as much as in language. I have walked a tightrope, you see. Beneath me, the steaming midden of the Sink and its prospect of enslavement, to either side the machinations, greed, prurience and viciousness of those I serve, buffeting me like a wind. I have had only the long, straight, pliable line of my own wits to keep me safe all these years.'

The first retainer pulled a bludgeon from his belt, ready to do me some horrible injury. I executed another impromptu bow. Maintaining that mock-humble attitude, I raced in, got under the blow even as it was falling, and, hugging my assailant about the waist with one arm, hamstrung the brute, slicing neatly through the tendons that ran down either side of his knee even as I heard the bludgeon swish past my shoulder.

I sprang back. An inarticulate query seemed to form on the slave's lips. It rapidly converted itself into a half-apologetic howl, as high-pitched and senseless as that of a skewered marmoset. The pin – his tiny head rocking back and forth on the disproportionately large body – tried to advance, button-like eyes wide with an alarm that was all that he had to substitute for intelligence. He fell to one side as he made the attempt, crashing into the brittle undergrowth that bordered the path.

The other retainer hesitated. But, servile dog that he was, he had to be reminded of his duty by no more than a nod from the doctor before he hoisted his own bludgeon and entered into the fray with a joyful cry that celebrated not just his own slavery but that of all slaves in the Sink.

I jinked; slashed across the outstretched arm that swept through space and whose payload had been meant to crack my skull; felt the razor meet resistance as it cut through a black velvet sleeve and connected with flesh and sinew. The big, meaty hand opened and the bludgeon dropped on to the ground.

I feinted, the razor carving at the air this way and that a bare half inch from the big loon's face, as if I were demonstrating just how fast and close I could shave him, if I should choose; indeed, shave the wretch to an early grave, if it should have been my intention. He stumbled backwards, looking left and right for his master, his puny head cocked pathetically for some word of command or discipline by which he might orientate himself.

But Bartholo had already taken to his heels.

I ignored the two bleeding pinheads and continued my walk down the path. I did not choose to pursue the doctor. It would go ill with me if I should hurt him. But I knew he could be relied upon to continue in his persecution, and would meet with me on some other lonely, abandoned piece of ground. Even as I wiped my razor clean of gore on the parchment-like leaves of an overhanging creeper, and tucked it back in my waistband, I knew I would have to keep it sharp. And would have to do so, probably, for many, many years. Bartholo and his kind would always be around. And I – like all men near the very bottom of the social order – would always have my back to the wall.

If I had known, then, how much things were to

change before the end of the day, I might, I think, have run after the fleeing poltroon and cut his throat from ear to ear, with as little compunction and as little fear of retribution as if I had exercised my congenitally morbid barber-surgeon's imagination on dissecting a bug.

The countess's boudoir was heavy with the perfume of her own patrician status and the rougher, somewhat cat-like scent of the thrall-born soubrette who, like me, was a living fiction: Suzanne. The tangy, invigorating notes of the older woman's bergamot mixed with my betrothed's darker, plebeian musk and ambergris, offering an effect that was akin to some piquant amalgam of virtue and vice – that is, of privilege and subjection – that had been sprayed promiscuously about the room. As I had entered Suzanne had looked up at me through her long, sooty lashes, and then addressed herself again to the task of arranging her mistress's coiffure.

What a beauty was my betrothed. She was dressed in a full-bodied white satin gown, the bodice decorated in the Basque fashion, her own high-coiffed hair set off by a cute little toque. And what a tale was hers – a pert, coquettish, lively narrative for those who had ears to hear it – and how much more wonderful that tale for one such as myself who could make it his own. I have always had a penchant for vulgar women. A decided weakness. And in Suzanne, the gestalt of the Sink was salvaged and transformed into an eminently vulgar loveliness; for if she had been born a thrall, she was also an incunabulum, and would not bow her knee readily to any man, except, I hoped, the one she loved.

'I have been giving our mutual problem some thought, my lady,' I said, as I took up position by the mantelpiece, my elbow resting on its chipped, marble edge a few inches from the ormolu clock. 'And, in the course of the last hour, I have translated thought into action.'

'Without my authority?' said the countess, looking into her vanity mirror with a cool, judicious appraisal of the cruel effects of time. I looked up at the ceiling. The hand that I had a moment before held insouciantly akimbo was working its way up the mouldering wall-paper, a long fingernail picking at the peeling flock. 'But then what does it matter?' she concluded. 'I am ignored by my husband, and so I must expect, I suppose, to be overruled by his servants. Do you know why I especially asked Suzanne to attend me this morning, Figaro, on this, her wedding day?' I shrugged. 'Because there's an old rustic saying that it brings luck to neglected wives.'

'Overruled? Nothing like that, my lady,' I said. 'And if I've been a little precipitate, I hope you will consider the state of mind I am in. I am worried. Anxious. Confounded by matters that a man of my background – cursed by fate, as it has been – can have little control over, even if he feels the sting of insult none the less.'

'Tell her what you've done, Figaro,' said my soubrette, patting the countess's hair into place and picking at a few stray locks. 'Tell her your plan.'

'A plan, eh?' said the countess, 'With you, Figaro, that means intrigue. Bizarre intrigue. That is your element, yes?'

I looked at Suzanne and smiled. I sometimes

81

wondered at her faithfulness. I must admit, I think I
sometimes enjoyed wondering; for it was the common-
ness of her origins, the slave glint in her eye that vied
with the lively independence of an incunabulum,
which generated, in me, such a frisson of interest. But
her ready accord to go along with my plan – a plan that
would allow her to gain the dowry the count had
offered while at the same time preserving her chastity –
convinced me that with all men, perhaps but myself,
the incunabulum was ascendant. She wanted to be the
count's slave as little as I. But there was always that
delicious doubt. And it was a doubt that, I think, she
herself deliberately cultivated, knowing, as she did,
that the suspicions I entertained regarding her sexual
probity excited my amorous propensities to a white-hot
pitch.

'An anonymous note has been passed to the count
saying that a stranger – a man – has been seen with the
countess while he has been out hunting.' The count, I
had calculated, might be discouraged from appro-
priating what was mine by giving him concern over
what was his.

The countess leaned forward in her chair and looked
away from the mirror. Her eyes, when they found my
own, were red with sleeplessness. 'Are you mad?' she
said, steadily, but in a timbre designed to leave no
doubt about where the authority in this house rested,
despite her former rhetorical concession to being ruled
by underlings.

'Not mad, madame,' said Suzanne. 'Inspired.'

'But a man as hotheaded as the count—'

'Exactly. As a woman you must surely understand

that this is the best way of getting him annoyed,' I said. 'The note states that your lover intends to make a secret assignation with you at tonight's festivities. The count will spend the day cursing and gnashing his teeth, looking here, looking there, and suspecting all. He'll have no time for Suzanne, of that I can assure you. And no time to prevent the wedding!'

'I *must* be reassured by that, I suppose,' said the countess.

'Oh, but there's more,' I said, proudly. I turned to Suzanne. 'You've sent word to his lordship that you'll meet him tonight in the roof garden?'

'I'm not sure I've ever been happy with *that* idea, Figaro.'

'Neither am I!' said the countess.

I clucked, impatient with the two of them, but especially with Suzanne. Did my soubrette wish to ensure that the count was true to his bargain and bestowed upon her a dowry, or not? I focused on my betrothed, my eyes narrowing. I was tempted to blurt out just how much we needed the money. But I resisted the impulse, and redirected my attention to the countess. 'Nothing illicit will occur, your ladyship. I'll simply dress someone else up in Suzanne's clothes,' I said.

'And who would that be?' said Suzanne, blowing out her cheeks.

'Why the count's page, Cherubin,' I said. 'He's such a pretty slip of a boy that it will take no more than a little application of the powder-box, a dress and a new arrangement of the hair, perhaps, to make him quite convincing. And the ruse will not only serve to distract the count and secure Suzanne and I the payment that is rightfully ours, it will, when all is later revealed, surely chasten him. Do you not think so, madame?' The countess studied her image in the mirror, mystified, it seemed, by the smile that she saw crossing her reflection's face. I clapped my hands. Cherubin, who I had left waiting outside, with his ear pressed to the keyhole, acknowledged his cue. He knocked on the door. 'And I do believe . . . '

The door opened. The boy – a recent graduate of the slave school – stood before us, a miniature libertine with sly, downcast eyes, the peril of many of the little scullery wenches and, most particularly, of the gardener's halfwit daughter, Fanchette. He was no wordsmith, it was true – which is why he was here rather than in London; his virtue lay in his exceeding beauty. Indeed, he was so delicately made, so fair and smooth of skin, that he looked like an adolescent girl who had been caught trying on her older brother's clothes. To transform the little brat into the appearance of my betrothed would be simplicity itself.

Leaving the two women to effect the wretched epicene's transformation I had retreated outside, where the autumnal sun had risen sufficiently for me to enjoy a little warmth from its rays. I was sitting in the garden, my back against a tree, contemplating my plans and thinking of ways in which I could make them more complicated still (until the count found himself enmeshed in a web as devious and inescapable as any courtier's), when my attention was arrested by the sight of a topsy-turvy mass of petticoats and satin tumbling from a first-floor window. Recognizing Suzanne's habiliments even before the falling body had turned rump over crown, righted itself and hit the flower beds, I was on my feet and dashing across the short stretch of lawn that separated us, reaching my sprawled, groggy but otherwise intact betrothed before she could raise herself from the dirt.

I bent over, held her under the arms and pulled her to her feet. I was just about to communicate an anxious enquiry as to the state of her no doubt much bruised constitution, when, peering deeper into her half-covered face – she held up an arm as if to shield herself – I realized just how easy gulling the count might indeed prove if only I could overcome this propensity of my confederates to launch themselves from windows. I smiled, waited for her, or rather him, to lower his arm, then gave the annoying boy a sharp slap across the cheek, whereupon it flushed, as if with outraged, maidenly modesty.

'It's not my fault,' blubbered the page. 'The count came in just as they were putting the final touches to my toilette. I had to hide in a closet, and then, oh—' I put a finger to his lips and glowered, silencing him. I pushed him along the stretch of wall we stood adjacent to until we had passed into a scrub of bushes and away from any danger of immediate discovery. 'Then,' said the boy, more quietly now he understood that I wished him to continue, 'then the count says he's found this letter, and, like, what is it with her ladyship, and who's this bastard she's supposed to be meeting tonight. Then as ill-luck has it I knock something over – it's so dark in that closet, it really is – and the count gets all accusatory like, saying to her ladyship that she'd better let him see who she's got tucked away in there, or else. The countess pretends it's Suzanne. Suzanne chose to hide too, you see, just before I got shoved in the closet. And the countess she's going, "Ooh, ooh, ooh, how could you, my lord, you philandering dog and whatever, how could you suspect me of unfaithfulness when it's you who's been running round with every mobcap and petticoat between here and London." Anyway, the count goes out to get a jemmy so he can break the closet open, and I'm like shitting myself, but then next thing I see is Suzanne. She had the key, understand, and she's opened the door and – one in a million that that girl of yours is – she's telling me that she's going to get everything sorted like by substituting herself for me. But just as we shut her in and turn the key the count comes back and her ladyship urges me to do a bit of self-defenestration. I don't mind telling you, Fig, she didn't have to ask twice. The state the count was in he'd have eviscerated me, for sure.'

What a mess, I thought. 'I'll get up there and try to calm things down,' I said. 'Get yourself out of here, you preposterous boy, before someone sees you.'

I hurried back into the house, up the stairs and into my lady's bedchamber.

The count was standing in the middle of the room. He was dressed in 'cruel seducer' attire – all riding boots and tight pantaloons – a 'look' that it had been my duty, as his valet, to help him cultivate. He had come directly from the stables, it seemed, interrupted before he could join the hunt by the green-eyed monster that, in his vast, aristocratic conceit, he was so unfamiliar with that its sudden appearance that morning would have proved less disconcerting than traumatic. However, though his face was red, he seemed otherwise in control of himself. Over the years I had learnt that the depravity of the count's morals in no way detracted from the elegance and coolness of his manners.

'I heard her ladyship was unwell,' I said, my tongue as limp as a wet lettuce. The countess sat in her chair, pale, shaken, but with a set to her lips that indicated she had triumphed, at the same time knowing her victory to be small and of a temporary nature, and that men, beasts that they are, must eventually prevail in their heartlessness and cruelty. 'I'm delighted to see that she is recovered,' I added, my gaze darting from master to mistress like a man trying to determine which one of the wild animals he has recently had under his control will rebel, leap and devour him. Suzanne winked at me, her hands on the back of the countess's chair. It wasn't a saucy wink, I knew that; indeed, it seemed fearful. But I was otherwise at a loss to understand its import. I found myself wondering what effect she had had on the count when, in his jealous fit, he had broken open the closet only to discover that his wife had, ostensibly, been telling the truth. Little, I hazarded. The count was without shame. 'Since she is so recovered, perhaps I might ask your lordship's permission to allow me to conduct my bride to—'

'And who will look after her ladyship, then?' said Almaviva.

'She *is* ill?'

'No. But there is this question of a man coming to visit her, it seems. Tonight.'

'A man?'

'The man in the letter you had arranged to have given to me, Figaro. You two-faced cur.'

'Figaro,' said the countess, 'the joke's over. I couldn't dissemble any more . . .' The countess, it seemed, was as shameless as her lord. Suzanne and I were mere toys who, if failing to alleviate the gloom of their day, would nevertheless provide a catharsis for their respective sulks.

'I'm very disappointed in you, Figaro,' said the count. 'I had hoped you understood me, and what I have been trying to achieve.'

I decided I would outface them both.

'Oh come, my lord, enough. Let's go to the roof garden where everything's being prepared. Let poor Figaro and Suzanne have their wedding.'

'Figaro,' said the count, in an undertone of disgust. 'Ah yes, how everyone calls you *Figaro*.' He turned to the countess. 'It will be our downfall, that name. Even *I* have started to call him Figaro, damn it, despite the fact that—' He swallowed his conclusion, grimacing as if it had been as unpleasant as a clot of bile. And then he again brought himself to bear upon me, his face like proverbial thunder. 'And do you know why, Dick Pike? Do you have any understanding of the influence you are having on us all? The malign influence I've spent years trying to unravel?'

'I've given your lordship nothing but faithful service!' I said, genuinely put out.

'It's true,' said the countess. 'The man sometimes has trouble telling the truth, but—'

'My wedding, count,' I said, trying to suppress the tremor in my voice. 'You'll not forget my wedding.'

'Your wedding, ah yes,' said the count, rather nastily. He nodded to someone over my head. I spun about. In the doorway stood Marceline.

'Wedding indeed,' muttered the old housekeeper. 'And soon, it's to be hoped. But you'll not wed any but me.' She turned to the count. 'He has obligations. And I'd implore your lordship to make sure they are fulfilled.' Big, viscous tears began to course down her yellow, snuff-stained cheeks. Her face, which always reminded me of a rotten cheese, did so doubly now that the jag of weeping underlined its resemblance to a runny piece of Cheddar. 'He promised to make me his bride! *Whaaaaa!*'

'A condition –' I said, resisting the impulse to flinch, but nevertheless thinking it politic to edge away from the bawling harridan before her frustrated passion culminated in an act of violence '– a condition relating to the loan of some cash.' I looked at Suzanne, seeking understanding. Sympathy. 'Nothing more.'

'Marceline,' said the count, in a tone of infinite self-congratulation, 'how right you are. Everything must be held up – both ceremony and celebrations – pending a careful examination of your claims in the courts.'

'But that could take weeks,' I said. 'Months!' The count's eyes burned with lascivious suggestiveness. I fixed him with an angry look, daring him to bring matters to a head. For several seconds our staring contest went on unabated. At last, I turned away. It was not that I conceded defeat, but, rather, had thought to wait until I could find a more favourable battleground. One upon which a cat might not only stare at a king, but take his head. 'Pike,' said the count, 'I would have a word with you. In the library, if you please. It is time you and me came to acknowledge each other's place in the world. Our *rightful* place.'

I tried to issue some measure of mute reassurance to Suzanne. But she had her back to me, miffed, it seemed, but, I hoped, not bitter. She knew the way things went in the castle. And she would know, too, it followed, that my relationship with Marceline was purely mercenary. Indeed, how could it be anything else?

I followed the count out of the door, taking care to step on one of Marceline's oversized feet as I did so, humming a refractory little ditty to myself. 'Sue – Sue – Suzie,' I think it went, 'she's my suzerainty, not this master of inanity, Sue – Sue – Suzie, my story, my cherry pie!' Pathetic, no? But the only way, at present, I could defy him. Until, that is, Figaro of the nimble, if by now somewhat confounded brain, had cooked up another stratagem.

Few were allowed within the precincts of the library. Maids, scullions and the like had no place here, for this was a sanctuary dedicated to true men and the redis-covery and, perhaps, re-invention, of that nebulous species, the human race. My duties were those of an amanuensis. I had normally not the time, and certainly not the inclination, to exchange my quill for a pan and brush. In consequence, a thick patina of dust covered those few tables and chairs that I had not taken the trouble to shroud in bedsheets. And each time I entered the library I felt as if I had wandered into one of the castle's more neglected areas, an abandoned wing, perhaps, walled off for long years.

We walked beneath towering rows of books, stepping fastidiously over rat droppings, and sometimes the carcass of a rat itself. Shafts of sunlight poured through the high, ogival windows, scattering golden lozenges across the floor. The stained-glass vignettes of Christ and his harrying of the Netherworld evinced that the library had once been a chapel, and that we strode down a nave constructed during the first flush of revived monotheism which had emanated from the Far East. Ladders set in brass rails ran the length of the long, deconsecrated room. They allowed me to dolly the count back and forth as he inspected those volumes ranged some eighty feet from the ground immediately below the rows of stained glass. Our footsteps echoed off the tiles, hollow as the promises of salvation that radiated from the stone mullions above us, promises that so many of my poor, deluded countrymen had chosen to place their faith in little more than two hundred years ago.

We came to a halt at the library's median point, about us the rotting parchment of the incomprehensible centuries, the gobbledegook of a civilization's ruins. The count stood before the writing desk he habitually used for his studies. It formed the hub of a little group of furniture that included a chaise longue, an ottoman and a prie-dieu. Upon the desk was a small oil lamp and, spread so that its vast leaves took up most of the table's surface, a grimoire, opened at a series of passages that he first glanced over, and then ran a long, elegant index finger across while mumbling distractedly to himself.

'It is like all the other volumes, of course. An anthology of fractured texts out of which scholars like myself have tried to reconstruct the arts and sciences of the ancient world. But these more often than not senseless fragments, which sometimes seem to promise so much, are obstinate, are they not, Dick?'

My gaze, however, as it always was when I entered this place to assist the count, was fixed upon the rows of vivaria that divided the upper bookshelves from those within unassisted reach. They lay to either side of me a little above head height, a line of tanks whose pickled occupants were strange, misshapen human foetuses and infants, or else adolescents who had succumbed to some of the debilitating afflictions common to incunabula, and had been placed in suspension until such time as they could be cured. But I knew there were others, almost as fully adult as myself, whom the count had had put in the tanks for other, more sinister reasons, not least of which was, perhaps, that he had learnt to fear them.

'Whereas *these* books,' said the count, as if prompted by my thoughts, and flinging out his arm to encompass the rows of those who either slept or were dead, 'how different *these* are from my dusty, confused old grimoires! How much these children and their like promise to reveal of our glorious past!'

And that was how he thought of me, of course. As something to be used. I cleared my throat. 'Only that the past is in danger of repeating itself, surely, your lordship,' I ventured. 'Is that what humanity has come through so much for, just to relive the past?'

'Spoken like an insurrectionary, Dick Pike. Spoken like a *subversive*.'

'And you, my lord? How do you speak?'

'Like a man of my class *should* speak. Of maintaining England's patrimony and the social order. Outside London, there is only anarchy, leavened, in parts, by sad outposts such as it is my dubious honour to command. There has been too much turmoil. Too much madness. We need stability.'

'Suzanne and me. Is that want you hope to gain from us? Or from thwarting us, rather. Stability?'

'It is what *you* hope to gain in life that we have to talk about, Dick Pike.' He turned his attention back to the grimoire, his brow creasing with a pedant's sedulity. 'We may never know how the Ancients really lived. Most scholars accept that now. The only complete, uncorrupted book of theirs we have is their damned *Bible*, rediscovered, to our nation's spiritual cost, by those knavish monks in Cathay. But, quite miraculously, we have found that through human mutations such as yourself, we may come to know ancient *fictions*. That is, we may rediscover the past's imaginative life, its stories and its narratives.' Once, twice, three times, he stabbed a finger into the parchment, a small cloud of dust circulating about his hand. 'Yes, the past is repeating itself. Reasserting itself. Race memory, it seems, extends to individual imaginative artefacts, and not merely collective myths.' He laughed. 'It is ironic, is it not, that the very earliest books, so to speak, those that possess the greatest integrity, should resurface, not as physical texts, but as dream texts, embodied in the psychic life of a new race? The sub-species we call incunabula?' His laughter died on his spittle-flecked lips, but its harsh, ghostly music continued to reverberate about the library's vault, like a comment on the ancient past whose echoes filled my soul. 'Or maybe it is not so ironic. For those old stories seem, by virtue of their very age, to have resisted the corruptions of the interregnum. They have merely lain in wait, *in posse,* as it were, until, four thousand years later, the human, or perhaps superhuman vessels necessary for their rebirth, were themselves born. Or reborn.' He looked me in the eye, and his brow creased the more with irascibility, and maybe, a little terror. 'And that's the real question, eh, Dick Pike? Are you really a mutant, or are you a throwback? A true human, such as we had thought long vanished from the world?'

I had heard this rhetoric before. It did not impress me, much less flatter me. I was concerned only with his initial remarks, which had made a direct appeal to my inherent opportunism. 'You said I have something to gain. How do I stand to gain anything if I'm to be denied Suzanne?'

Almaviva sighed. 'I know much about you, Dick. Much that you yourself are unaware of. I have, after all, not merely conducted research into grimoires in this library of mine; it is incunabula that have been my primary study. Your great-great-grandfather, for instance. Also called Richard Pike.'

'A hero, some have said.' I straightened myself, and became at least two inches taller, as if I were literally standing upon my dignity.

'He distinguished himself during the wars with the Netherworld, but rather let himself down, it is thought, by taking a goblin woman to his bed, and making her his paramour. The opprobrium he met with was considerable. He chose exile.'

'And he chose to take *Espiritu Santo* with him,' I

whispered.

'His fabled sword. To which some have attributed alien powers. Powers, it is thought, he took into himself while living in *Las Islas Pilipinas*. You, perhaps, have inherited that alienness, just as you have his mistress's goblin blood. It has made you twice as powerful an incunabulum as those you see around you.' And perhaps, I thought, more of a human than you, count, for is it not said that the true human heart is a mix of rationality and the bestial, and that beauty, true beauty, is inseparable from strangeness? 'It has given you the ability to survive,' he concluded.

'And Suzanne?'

'Suzanne's heritage is something of a mystery to me. Though the fact that she shares your extraordinary powers seems incontestable. Which is why, Master Pike, I cannot allow the two of you to enjoy a union.'

I bit my lip, clenched my hands and bored holes in the outspread grimoire with the hot, poisonous lead that dripped from my lowered, if far from humbled, eyes.

'My researches have revealed this much,' the count continued. 'Marriage between you and Suzanne could spell disaster for the social order. It could even provoke revolution.' He looked away, scanning the bookshelves. 'What we have to maintain is the current precarious balance between innovation, or what was until recently called the "new science", and the retrograde tendencies of the *ancien régime* represented by an absolute monarchy and the Church. Men such as myself have achieved much: magnetism, inoculation, quinine and now, if we are to believe it, the mechanical harnessing of steam. But freethinking can only go so far if it is not to endanger society's delicate fabric. The anarchy of the wastes would breach London's walls, and all would be a wilderness of slaves, witches and mad scientists, if respect for the social order were lost.'

I smiled. 'You overestimate the effects,' I said, speaking determinedly to the back of his head, 'the probable effects from the union of two incunabula. Suzanne and I are—'

'Are already distorting local space-time in the manner we scholars call a time opera. And have been for some years. Look –' he turned smartly about and again ran a finger down the page of the grimoire that lay on the table '– you have never been master of your own destiny, Dick. The narrative that is the kernel of your soul has distorted your own identity as much as it has that of those around you. Figaro, we call you. And we may learn from certain passages here that you are the psychic reincarnation of a fictional character who did much to foment revolution in the ancient world.'

'But that, as you say, was fiction. An imaginative event, not an event in the real world.'

'No. This was a case where a fiction directly affected reality. It was a fiction that crystallized long-standing discontent, acted as a catalyst for revolution, if you will. Have you any idea what effect you have on the slave school, Master Pike?' He shook his head, with mordant regret. 'You have been my amanuensis, my assistant. But there has been so much I have necessarily kept from you. Now listen to me. The thralls know little about you, it's true. But it's the name. The psychic reverberation of the name. Figaro, Figaro, Figaro, Fig-a-ro. Ah, that damned, *damned* name. Four thousand years ago there were men called Danton and Robespierre.' He pointed to the relevant passage. 'They interpreted that cry of "Figaro!" as a clarion call to arms. To social war. To lopping the head off the established order.' He removed his finger from the page and tapped it against his forehead. 'The same psychic aura permeates the Sink, and has done so for years. It is only recently that I have recognized it for what it is, and realized the danger. Your mediumistic powers, Dick. Think of them. Combined with those of Suzanne, the psychodynamic force of this *Figaro* narrative would become overwhelming. What has been until now but a half-realized story would become something that may have disastrous consequences. For us all.'

'All this, my lordship,' I said, careless of just how much my voice might express my rising contempt, 'to inveigle me into surrendering my betrothed? What should a man like me care for the social order?'

'Look at the passage before you, Dick,' said the count, unperturbed. 'However the story is consummated, you stand to lose something dear to you, by virtue of the very nature of the narrative imbedded in your being. Here, see? In this section called Act III, you discover that your mother is not the woman you have thought her to be, but—'

'Marceline?' I said. 'That's impossible.' I spat out a nervous laugh.

'And more to the point, your father is—'

'Bartholo? Ridiculous!'

'Farcical, I admit. But it is the way things are, or will

be, if you do not cut a measure to *my* tune. As I have said: like the rest of us in Aguas Frescas, you are not master of your own fate.'

'But,' I said, thinking quickly, and almost conceding to a hysterical whoop, 'if it transpires that Bartholo is my father and Marceline my mother, then Marceline, at least, cannot exert a claim on me. How can I marry my own mother?' I felt emboldened. 'Count, you have merely opened the way for me to marry Suzanne. All hindrances swept aside! But for your desire to enjoy her by way of your antiquated, detestable droit de seigneur, that is.'

'But think, Dick: if the narrative really is fulfilled, and Bartholo becomes, or is revealed to be, your father, then that would mean that the father you have now would cease to acknowledge you. You would no longer be a Pike. And that means you would no longer stand to regain your title. If the narrative runs true you remain Figaro for ever, and never a lord, whether it be of Soho or anywhere else. As I say, Dick, you stand to lose however the story ends. If it ends my way, you lose Suzanne. But if it ends your way, you stand to lose your precious *name*.'

The words cut deep, as he must have known they would. My innate snobbishness, which I often tried to pooh-pooh, was, I knew then, as strong as any in my line, including my father's. I had hankered after the title so long that I had despaired of ever regaining it; but that did not mean my appetite for a reinstatement of my family's fortunes was any less keen. Indeed, its keenness, made all the more sharp by the prospect of losing my past for ever, was suddenly quite savage. I shared the vices of my master, I knew that now. I was like him, if dispossessed. Cynical, world-weary, ambitious, and yes, fearful. Fearful of change.

'Let us come back to the original point,' I said. I listened to the calculation in my voice as if to a stranger. The chance that I might somehow become Lord Soho quenched all desire for other things in this life, however much the fiction at the core of my being urged their realization. 'His lordship said earlier that I might stand to gain?'

'If you do as I say, Master Pike.'

'And it is within your lordship's power to . . .?'

'Though I'm a mere sheriff, I have friends at court. Friends who are the enemies of your family's enemies. A word here, a word there, and a little purse of gold thrown in the right direction – you really have no idea what such things may accomplish.'

'A time opera,' I mused, my own finger, now, on a line of text. 'I begin to see what his lordship means. Yes, most dangerous. We cannot have the thralls forget degree and station. Not when men such as ourselves –' and I rested a hand familiarly on his shoulder; something that, until that moment, I would not have dared to do, and would surely have never been allowed to, in any case '– not when this country's hereditary ruling class has so much to lose. And then, as you say –' and I choked back my inclination to laugh at my own hypocritical audacity '– we must maintain the balance between progress and the conservation of order. Where would this country be without its lords and ladies, after all?'

'Where indeed. I'm glad you've seen things my way,

Master Pike,' he said, shrugging free of my lowly hand. 'I really am.'

I bet he was, the lecherous old bastard.

The thing was, what was he going to do with the knowledge and power he would acquire in the act of sexual union with Suzanne? For any normal human male, of course, the encounter would likely prove sterile. But, as I had told my father that morning, the count had studied my kind for many years. And he had for an almost equal number of years played a part in the narrative pattern Suzanne and I had imposed on Aguas Frescas and the Sink. He was distinctly *abnormal*. No doubt he hoped that, in communing with, and perhaps taking part control of, the narrative in which his own fate was embedded, he might consolidate the authority he exercised over this despised, if economically important, petty sheriffdom. And perhaps his ambitions were not as misguided as they might have at first appeared.

The day had been crazy enough. I tried not to think about how it might further proceed.

I locked myself in the library, dusted books, and then, tiring, but unwilling to commit myself to any line of thought, sat and stared at the rows of tanks wherein the suspended incunabula floated, blind, cramped – their bodies curled in foetal attitudes – or else swimming about with nervous, rudimentary and, I had always supposed, entirely unconscious movements of their arms and legs. What tales were there? I wondered. Amongst those whose brains were still preserved, if not intact, what operatic flights of fancy that, if those spastic, jiggly creatures were to be released, would make of the Earth a vast stage for the re-enactment of forgotten narratives?

Odysseus, Almaviva had called one. A Greek name. Over the last fifty years, scholars had come to discover quite a lot about the Greeks. Grendal, another was called. And there were incunabula whose names were Faust, Butterfly and Orphée. I could feel their dull but persistent energy field all about me.

But how many of those incunabula were in fact 'suspended'? Most, perhaps nearly all, of the vivaria were in truth sepulchres, within whose glass walls corpses floated in an inert amniotic fluid which could do little more than mummify its occupants, like the preserved oddities of a freakshow, each exhibit serving only to warn my kind not to overreach itself.

When night began to fall, I could restrain myself no longer. Suzanne, of course, had arranged to meet the count in the roof garden. It had been my ploy to dress Cherubin in her clothes to give old Almaviva a shock, and part him from his money. But now Suzanne would be there alone, waiting for me, I suppose, in the hope that I would arrive with yet another nimble plan by which to snare the count. And a morbid inclination somewhat out of sync with my cynical acceptance of my situation urged me to go and spy on the couple, and thus either hopelessly mortify myself or put the seal on my predilection to laugh in the black of these times.

Night poured through the stained-glass windows. Darkness was everywhere. I turned down the oil lamp, got up and walked down the nave. And then, with a salute to my fellow incunabula who, I felt, I might well join should my expedition go amiss, I unlocked the doors and left.

Go amiss? Something within me wanted to do more than play the voyeur. Something within me wanted to smash and rend.

Perhaps all incunabula were overreachers.

Moonlight played over the chaotic arbours, the orangery, gazebos and tubs of exotic dead plants that stood to either side of the lanes serpentining through the garden's black, petrified undergrowth. The brittle vegetation, frozen in the act of crawling over the castle's flat roof, erupted in irregular clumps of scrub, thicket and boscage. This wax museum of botanical out-rageousness was, like the very stones of the castle itself, a homage to the weird, twisted anti-Nature that the goblin people had brought with them when they had sought to colonize Earth-Above. What a fitting backdrop, I mused, bitterly, for a romantic assignation so *contra natura*.

On tiptoe, I walked through the shadowy pathways, my passage lit only by an occasional paper lantern. Bunting and other examples of the half-hearted attempt to decorate the garden in preparation for what was to have been my wedding would sometimes brush my cheek, eliciting the kind of disgust I normally reserved for walking unsuspectingly into a spider's web. Angrily, I tore the gaily painted streamers aside. Then, hearing voices ahead, I forbore and held my breath. Creeping forward, I came to a clump of stunted trees. I sidled into their depths and went into a crouch. Hiding thus I was able to spy on the count and Suzanne, who stood nearby. He had his mouth close to her ear, doubtless murmuring noxious sweet-nothings into lobes that I, and only I, should have been allowed to nibble and pollute. Yes, I was like him: I had all his vices, and more. And I had the supreme vice to boot: treachery. Was this what, in the end, made me, and would sustain me, as a Pike and lord of the realm?

I heard an exhalation of breath to my right. Smelling a perfume that I at first hesitated to place, and, at suddenly placing – my nostrils stung with the sharpness of bergamot – wished only an ignorance of as sure and fit as the surrounding shadows, I spun about to discover the countess on her haunches by my side.

'So my errant husband has achieved his goal at last,' she said, ignoring me, her eyes fixed upon the philandering count. 'What will become of us, Figaro?'

I darted a look at the wanton twosome. It was as I had always suspected. My betrothed was a slut. The sight should theoretically have had me panting with excitement. But, despite my predilections for a feminine vulgarity whose apotheosis – at least, for a sick mind such as my own – always seemed the suggestion of easy virtue; despite the fact that I had engineered my betrothed's unfaithfulness and had, indeed, rejected her for the paltry suggestion of a name and a piece of ragged ermine; despite all this, I seethed with anger. That Suzanne did not scream, claw, bite and scratch his lordship's eyes out, now that the count had clipped her within his arms and rained passionate kisses down upon her brow, her cheek, lips and neck, was an affront that I took as badly as I might an assault upon my own person.

'Let us avenge ourselves, my lady,' I said, the devil-may-care timbre of my voice so extreme that it almost seemed the voice of another. 'Let us get down upon the ground and act like the animals we and, it seems, all human beings secretly are. Let us snort, bellow, and have at each other. Let us indulge in mad, bestial coition!'

The sting I felt as the countess struck me a resounding blow across the face should not have come as a surprise; but it was so concomitant with the recognition that I faced not the countess but my own sweet Suzie – she had moved a little out of the shadows in order to strike – that I almost jumped out of my skin. And then, before my syncopated heart could fully regain its accustomed rhythm, I fell backwards, choking back a flurry of laughter and tears, even as I collapsed beneath her blows, my ears boxed until I could feel them glow like the painted lanterns that hung all about us. Not that anything compared with the luminousness of her face. My soubrette, my beloved incunabulum and opposite number in the story that was unravelling before me with a speed that made me almost retch, gazed down, as furiously pale as the moonlight that bathed the garden.

'It's the countess that Almaviva makes love to,' she said, in a hissing, angry undertone. 'We women have some stratagems of our own, I'd have you know. Yes, the countess wears my clothes, and I am dressed as she, but you, Figaro, stand revealed for what you are. Do not think of squirming out of this one, you mealy-mouthed dog. Your nimble brain is good, it seems, only for mendacity. I'll have no more of it!'

She lifted up her skirts and straddled me. 'First, I learn that you've promised marriage to Marceline, all for a purse of coins. And then I discover that you've sold me out to the count. This farce has gone on long enough. It's time it was brought to conclusion. But not the way you wish, Figaro. Nor the way the count may wish. But the way *I* wish.' I felt the warm, dark mystery of her crotch settle upon my manhood. 'I suppose the count has been telling you that you are helpless, a victim of your own narrative. He's tried that on me, too. But it's a lie. We can subvert this psychodrama. We can choose to make it what we will, just as we can choose to be whoever we want to be. And to punish you, sweet husband, I'm going to show you exactly what I mean!' She snorted back a laugh. 'How stupid clever men can be!'

It was a swift and rather brutal coupling. My breeches pulled down with angry despatch, and my nether parts harassed until they did as they were ordered, she introduced me to the vestibule of Hymen's temple in the manner of a tour guide who shows Master Priapus the sights with her eye continually on her timepiece, her gestures and words mechanical, performed by rote, all the most interesting sights passed by in a flash until, the exit looming just a little way ahead, the hapless traveller is ejected with only a few bruised memories of the marvellous encounter left to him, and not one lousy souvenir. It was what some, I suppose, who affect aristocratic lineage, call the 'minimalist embrace'. Whatever it was, it was certainly no Grand Tour. But what went on in my mind during that episode was, if less fleeting, more brutal. Inside my skull, time distended and another kind of tour took place. I stood, it seemed, at a crossroads, an infinity of forking paths.

As I hesitated, unsure which way to take, I found myself bundled by unseen hands along a rough highway alongside which I glimpsed the faces of all those I had ever known: my father; the count and countess; the scullions and thralls of Aguas Frescas; Bartholo, Marceline and a score of supporting roles; and finally Suzanne. She was leading the way. Dragging me along her storyline. But rather than participating in that narrative, I found myself overwhelmed by it, parasitized by it, raped by it. I gave her all that I had; she took it, made it her own, and then allocated me a part in her own psychic household.

I was Figaro still; but her Figaro, it seemed, not the count's. I was not even a Figaro of my own imagining. I took heart. Whatever Suzanne's heritage, it was older than my own, and certainly more noble.

'Listen, husband,' she whispered, inside my head. 'I'm going to tell you what you are. What we both are . . .'

I screamed as I was granted a brief vision of beginnings and ends, plots and sub-plots, acts, scenes and grand finales, then felt that vision radiate outwards, wave after wave of raw energy pouring from us and invading the outside world.

'Louis XVI told the author – that is, the author of our being – that he would have to demolish the Bastille before the play could be performed. The opening night at the Comédie Française in April 1784 was remarkable, a milestone on the road to revolution. Something was born that night, or rather, found its way into our universe, that changed it for ever. For all fictions are as much pre-existent as invented, alive in what used to be called Platonic space, and yearning for incarnation. It is

Time that they desire, the sensuous dimension of Time, where, at last freed from eternity, they may replicate themselves down the centuries by parasitizing the body of civilization, mankind's collective host. Such was the destiny of our own story, until the perverse came and civilization died. But if human culture became fragmented, its Platonic Forms endured. They turned from their natural host, human society, and transmigrated to individuals, propagating along a genetic line in the manner of a "time opera"—'

'Time opera,' I echoed, grunting. At that moment, my backside was being ground into the mulch. And I no longer doubted that those machines called jackhammers really existed. My love's pelvis fitted their description to a tee.

'All culture is fragmented,' she had replied, though without moving her lips, 'but music cannot be paraphrased. Especially not our music. Not our grand, millennia-spanning opera. It has retained its integrity for thousands of years. It has resisted the depredations of the interregnum. It is not humans like us who have mutated, Figaro, but the Forms, the Platonic Forms. They have achieved a kind of independence. They live through us, but are independent of us, too. And independent, finally, of reality. But it is I who will have the last say. I who, even now, choose to be a slave no longer, but an artist. I who choose to be like the humans of old, to create, invent, assert my own independence, and use this moment to at last fully realize myself . . .'

I had screamed again, and louder, too, for I knew that I coupled with a true human, a reincarnation of those beings who had walked the ancient Earth. And as my scream ebbed, I heard the count exclaim in response.

Suzanne fell off me and lay in the dirt, her mouth gulping at the air and her breasts heaving with such violence that they threatened to burst from the constraint of her tightly laced bodice. I raised myself to my elbows just in time to see the countess – for all the world, at this remove and beshadowed, the double of Suzanne – run down the pathway and into a little pavilion. The count – who had been distracted by the triumphant, orgasmic cry of two incunabula who have enjoyed perfect communion – was unable to make out where she had gone. 'Who is that?' he said, more boldly. By now recovered, Suzanne rose to her feet and, smoothing down her skirts and struggling momentarily with the tangle of the obscuring branches, left our hiding place and walked towards him.

'Count Almaviva,' she said, coming to a halt at a spot where she remained still half-cloaked in shadows. 'All has been concluded. Your days are numbered. My husband and I are one.' She had spoken, I noticed, in the manner of the countess.

'What are you talking about? And where did you vanish to?' cried the count, believing Suzanne to be his wife. 'And why is your dress so torn and muddy? And who is that figure with you, skulking in the trees?' he added, pointing in my direction. 'You! Yes, you over there! Come out this instant!'

I got to my feet, adjusted my breeches, and walked out into the clearing, a little behind where Suzanne stood.

'You!' said the count, astonished. My flamboyant clothes made me instantly recognizable, it seemed, despite the shadows. 'You – and my *wife*!'

'No, of course not,' I said, 'this is a simple case of mistaken identity. A popular dramatic device. Look. Let me explain—' But Suzanne had calculated what would happen next. Or rather, she radiated an energy field which, now it had harmonized itself with my own, was so intense that all within its bounds lost independent will and became an extension of her storyline. She would have her revenge on the count. And, it seemed, on me.

'Explain?' The count drew his rapier. 'I am expected to listen to my valet's explanations when he has been caught in flagrante delicto with my *wife*?'

He moved towards me. I felt for my razor, knowing that there was no alternative, now, but to fight and play my part in whatever dénouement Suzanne had chosen for the two of us.

'Lights!' cried the count. 'Servants! Guards!' It was evident that he had no wish to engage with a lowly creature like myself on such a compromised field of honour. A gentleman confronted in his own backyard by a lout with a cut-throat razor will let his retainers sort matters out. I had, however, no intention of waiting for my fellow flunkeys to appear and give me a mortal thrashing such as befitted not only my supposed crime, but station. With a will that he seemed to find as astonishing as discovering his wife post-coitum in the presence of his valet, I ran forward, low, and, it transpired, with sufficient fleetness to avoid the arrogantly lazy sweep of his blade. I slashed at his thighs, but the count, not so soused by wine, rich food and general dissipation as to forget his weekly fencing practise, managed to avoid my own blade's parabola, and I succeeded only in effecting a tear in the silk of his breeches.

Then I jabbed, but he had recovered enough to skip back a step, the rapier's cruelly honed extremity suddenly hovering an inch in front of my Adam's apple before I, who had not his advantage in a *salle d'armes*, could reposition myself, either for attack or defence.

'So here it ends, barber's boy,' he said. 'And to think that you have such airs and graces as to have believed that I might have chosen to have ennobled you and made you into an image of myself. You – a half-man, half-orc, a travesty of humanity, a witch whose ancestors were thrown out of London for having the *perverse* in their veins. Whose family's title was, in any case, only held for two generations. Lord Soho indeed!'

'Count Almaviva!'

The count looked over his shoulder and then, recognizing the countess, who stood but a few feet from him, turned about full to confront the ghastly doppelgänger.

'It is as Suzanne has said. Your days, and the days of oppression, are over. This is the end of our story, I fear. If the beginning of another.'

He was, I think, in the process of spinning about to double-check that it was his wife that spoke, and that the one he had mistaken for her was, in fact, her maidservant, when I pulled back my right arm and, with a cry of '*Espiritu Santo*!', sent the razor flying through the air. It caught him just below the left shoulder blade and, I believe, must have immediately penetrated his heart, for his spin was checked. He turned to again face the true countess, dropping the rapier as he did so.

He staggered a little, and though his heart could no longer have been capable of performing quite all the errands necessary to sustain life, it still beat with sufficient celerity to keep him going for a few seconds more; enough time, at least, to enable him to cross the part of the garden we occupied and, with a melo-dramatic concession to approaching mortality, tip himself lordly over the battlements and into space.

I rushed to the embrasure which had been Count Almaviva's last acquaintance with the material things of this Earth. Peering down into the darkness I found that I was in time to witness his corpse arcing away from the wall and towards the moat, tumbling, over and over, a scarecrow incongruously apparelled in rich silks and brocades. But the other spectacle that confronted me was so grand, and so contrary to the small thrill communicated by the sight of his lordship's demise, that I paid no more attention to him, not even when I heard the far-off splash that confirmed he been committed to the cold, murky waters far below.

The courtyard was filled with children, each of whom carried a fiery brand. Others – thousands in number, and likewise carrying flaming torches – approached from the dark margin of the woodland. Amongst that mass of humanity I spied soldiers – soldiers who, until now, would have regarded those they stood shoulder to shoulder with as no more than contemptible play-things: boys and girls to be spat upon as soon as applauded for some clever trick or turn of phrase. Then I looked out, far out, over their heads and over the forest canopy. Standing some three hundred feet in the air as I was, I could see, in the distance, a greater conflagration – the slave school itself was ablaze. Tiny, dancing figures ringed its flickering shadows, or else broke away to converge on the castle to join their rebellious comrades. Shaken from the trance-like hold of this spectacle by a growing murmur from immediately below, I looked down to see multitudinous eyes staring up at me, as the thralls who had followed the arc of Almaviva's descent found its point of origin. And then with one great voice the mob called out '*Figaro, Figaro, Figaro, Fig-a-ro!*'

I retraced my steps, holding my pounding head with one hand, seeking my way forward with the other, like one who is about to swoon. As I beheld Suzanne, I recovered, breathed deeply and held out my hand to her. She took it.

'It's all changed now,' she said. 'Do you think you can accept that you'll never be a lord?'

'I believe I can,' I said, smiling. For that impossibly far-off prospect of ennoblement had only been a symbol, I think, of the remaking of myself. 'This is better,' I concluded. 'This person who I've always been, if I'd only known it. Better, yes, better by far.'

Those amongst the castle's retainers who had responded to Almaviva's summons encircled us. Scullions and gardeners, chambermaids, parlourmaids, housemaids and scullerymaids, snot-nosed little boys and girls of all work and even the drunken gardener, Antonio, and his little daughter, Fanchette. Cherubin – that ridiculous milksop the late count's true apprentice in matters of libertinage – goosed the little girl while the general attention was upon Suzanne and me. Cherubin. Ah yes. Let him say goodbye to pastime and banter. I would send him off to glory. I would send the little clod-tongued nincompoop off to war.

I looked from one face to another, seeking signs of resistance. There were none. Neither were there signs of that happily embraced submissiveness that usually informed their bearing. Even Bartholo was there, and Marceline too. They held each other's hand, mirroring the pose Suzanne and I had adopted, acknowledging that they loved each other, too, but no longer felt any enmity for me. If the retainers had abandoned their slavishness, so had Bartholo, and perhaps all gentry in these parts, abjured their rank. All was transformed. All was made amiable, strong and new.

And then my gaze fell upon my father.

'So this is how you celebrate your wedding?' he said. 'What will become of the family now? No one to help us regain our title, and, if this sort of thing catches on, no titles left in all the Darkling Isle, I should imagine. No, none at all! Still, to be an uncorrupted text, a living book which represents a re-interpretation, or subversion, of the past, is a burden. I've always known it. All the Pikes have known it. What a business! What a night!'

'I'm still your son,' I said. 'I always will be. Richard Pike, that's me.'

'There will never be another Lord Soho. And the sword is lost, now, forever.'

'It lives,' I asserted. '*Espiritu Santo* lives. In spirit. My spirit.'

And just as I believed that, contrary to what I had

asserted, Suzanne's rewriting of all our lives had served to confer on me the name Figaro, too, as well as my real name, and confer it upon me for all time, so that, in effect, my identity was interchangeable, I heard the cheers outside the walls demur, then rise again, reconsolidating as they adopted a slow, chanted rhythm.

'*Lord So-ho,*' came the cry, '*Lord So-ho, Lord So-ho.*' And hearing it, I knew that my power and influence as an incunabulum was in direct proportion to Suzanne's own, that I was choosing my destiny, as she had chosen hers.

We would be married forthwith. I set the retainers to organize the proceedings, and called for music and wine and dancing to follow.

If I was Figaro, I would be a Pike, too. A Lord Soho. If a Lord Soho of the mind. A lord of the imagination and spirit. For I was a human. A true human. Not like those blue-blooded pretenders in old London town, whose human lineaments were soiled, and who, fools that they were, proudly called that sterility their 'pedigree'. I was one of the ancient men reborn. I knew that now. Had known it ever since entering into communion with Suzanne. Our heritage was no enigma. Glorious mongrels, amalgams of animality and the life of reason, we heralded a new age. That the rebirth had been enacted in a confluence of strangeness and perversity was right. For the heart of mankind was an erotic union of the angelic and demonic. And wherever we should go, the aura of that truth would infect and reshape reality. Let the Earth make way for our kind. Men and women who would choose who they were to be, but were at the same time embodiments of older selves, of humanity's ancient, collective soul. Men and women who would not blindly relive the past, but re-invent it.

I tilted my chin to the stars. I no longer cared for the fine line that sometimes divides fiction from fact. My will was set to roam through the world of the imagination and the real world knowing no limit or restraint. And later, as I slipped my arm about Suzanne's waist and kissed her powdered cheek, and as celebratory fireworks burst in the skies above Aguas Frescas and the music rose and song and stars conspired to make a celestial harmony that was like laughter in the dark, I knew a man can hope for nothing more of destiny.

The Lady of the Carnelias

I stood by her graveside amongst a dozen or so other mourners. The glass coffin – showered with that horrid bloom, the carnelia – was lowered slowly into the earth. Though distempered by a riot of reds, pinks and magentas, enough glass remained uncontaminated to reveal that, shortly before death, she had become like the flower herself, her flesh a tangled bouquet of thorny vines, exploded calyxes and dank, suppurating petals. Death is the great promise of life, she had said, it is a reconciliation with otherness. The febrile air of an unusually hot Parisian summer filled my lungs, choking me with its dissonant correlative to grief. How could I believe in that promise after all that had occurred? We are born alone. We die alone. And between 'you' and 'me' there is always the insurmountable gulf. Like those that, looking up at the night sky, Violetta would say, lay between, not just the planets and stars, but the spheres of pre-existence and afterlife, the past, present and future. 'Life is a discontinuous phenomenon,' she would conclude. 'As bleak as those voids that I have traversed merely so that, it now seems to me, I could be with you. And as full of strangeness and terror.' But she could be with me no longer, nor I with her. The gulf had opened up for all eternity. About me, all was void, and strangeness, and terror such as I had never known. The terror of infinite loneliness. Of separation, irrevocable, complete.

I remembered when we had first met, a few months ago. And if the encounter had, as she often suggested, been no more than a dream, as uncertain as memory itself, then I clove to it still. For dream or no, it was the only substantiality that my life was ever likely to possess . . .

I had been invited to the Théâtre Nationale de l'Opéra to see a staging of an opera buffa inspired by the life of my paternal grandfather, Richard Pike the Fifth, the infamous revolutionary. I had not been informed that the almost equally infamous courtesan, Violetta Valery, would also be attending.

'Ah, so you are called Richard as well, then?' she had said, looking up from her programme, after we had been introduced. She spoke my mother tongue prettily, with only a trace of an accent. Nothing unusual in a world where languages other than English were virtually extinct. But in Paris – citadel of some of the world's last verbal chauvinists – surprising, nevertheless. 'Everything is repeating itself,' she added. 'Or so our *philosophes* say. Ideas, fictions, even history. But I had not thought' – and her generous lips parted in a smile that was too arch to be kind, but too coy to be completely unfeeling – 'that God's grand design for *l'éternel retour* might include a man's Christian name within its purview.'

Our host, the director, retired discreetly to speak to his other guests. I wondered if she was his mistress, or belonged, for the time being, to one of the other men who circulated about the box: industrialists, landowners, civil servants, prelates and the usual sprinkling of idle rich. I seemed to detect, amongst their number, a few meaningful exchanges; and it occurred to me that I might be the subject of some elaborate joke. A joke made at the expense of my dispossession: the fact that I could never afford such a woman as Violetta Valery myself.

'A name?' I said, darting vicious glances at those who potentially mocked me. 'Like God I believe I do not care for very much at all. Certainly nothing for a *name*.' I strove to ignore the haughty looks that the preening scrum of men about town returned, and concentrated solely upon my interlocutor's face.

'Oh,' she said, still smiling. 'But I had heard different.' I affected coolness, boredom, even. It was difficult. For if, along with the other guests, she secretly laughed at me, she was still the most beautiful woman I had ever seen.

'But it is true,' I said, with a shrug of conciliation. 'The first-born males are always named Richard. Not because our line is so alike. But because we labour under the same curse. And have done for seven generations.'

'The rumours, then, are equally true?' she said. 'That your family has orc blood in its veins?'

I bridled. 'How disarmingly candid,' I began. But then bit my tongue. Stung as I was by the blatancy of her allusion, I knew I had, by citing the family curse, raised the issue of my polluted heritage myself. I could hardly rebuke her for taking the proffered bait.

'There are some,' she continued, 'who believe that a woman like me is as defiled. Like you, monsieur, I am sometimes called a witch.'

'A witch,' I murmured, raising a questioning eyebrow. 'Indeed, madame's powers of bewitchment are legendary. But I cannot believe any man would be so low as to suggest that you were of compromised stock.' Hardly conscious of where the words came from, and unmindful of how absurd they might seem, I concluded: 'I would kill such a man.'

Before I could even think to stop her, or marvel at how she flouted propriety, she touched my cheek. The long, feline nails caressed my squamous flesh, and then I felt the softness of the hand itself; and its contact would have been warm, sisterly, almost maternal, if it had not carried a sexual charge flagrant in the extreme. I knew then that, though she evinced no obvious signs of hereditary pollution, she was, like me, a creature of the perverse, if unlike any such one as I had seen before, or even suspected to exist. The fact that she was a woman of the *demi-monde* had nothing to do with it. Her whole being was informed by the dark energy of the Netherworld.

She took her hand away, and I felt my cheek flush invisibly under its scale-like epithelium. 'I have been looking forward to meeting you, Monsieur Pike. Or should I say, Lord Soho?'

'That title is no more,' I said, gripping the brass handrail and steadying myself. During the few minutes of our encounter I had gone from a man overly suspicious to one about to cast all doubt aside. And I was afraid. Afraid that – despite my recent avowal – I was confronted by something that I *did* care about; cared for more than my lineage, and feared far, far more than those dangerous abstracts such as justice and freedom that, during my long years of exile, I had vigorously campaigned to have remitted to the trashcan of history. The emotion I felt, if not wholly novel, was so rare that the accumulated disappointments of my life seemed to fall away, like the scales that, less proverbially, made a grim, ashen latticework of my skin. 'There will never be another Lord Soho.'

'Is that your sincere belief?' she said. 'Is it really?' The earnestness of her tone suggested the miracle that perhaps she cared, too. And my distraction was such that I did not, for the moment, question the wherefore. 'But come,' she continued, 'the curtain is about to go up. And I want you to tell me all about your family so that I may enjoy a greater understanding of tonight's performance. Your grandfather' – she swept aside the great bell of her long, opalescent skirts and sat down – 'was an incunabulum?' I pulled back a chair and joined her.

'An incunabulum, yes,' I said, 'an embodiment of the intellectual life of our distant forebears. A living artefact.'

We sat at the front of the box, below us the bejewelled ranks of the City of Light, the orchestra and proscenium arching away in a rapture of glass and iron, recalling me to the St Pancras of my boyhood and youth, and the recently built, and even more magnificent, St Lazare.

'Yes, of course,' she said, 'I have read of the incunabula. When civilization died, books were burned, artefacts destroyed, but their ghostly, intelligible structures lived on.'

'They transmigrated,' I said, 'and now, through the

medium of the incunabula, the Forms use us for their own ends.'

'But you do not fear the incunabula, surely? The Forms they embody reflect an ideal. It is through them, and through them alone, that we have begun to rediscover the glories of the Ancients.'

'I do not fear them,' I said. 'I oppose them. Not because I am superstitious, but because I hope I am rational. A Form, imprisoned in matter, is always but a dim reflection of the Ideal. And these are mutant Forms. They are not beautiful. They are not true. Neither do they any longer require an artist, or man of science, to body them forth. In parasitizing the deepest levels of the human mind, these entities have become autonomous.' I paused, my lip curling with rancour. 'Fear incunabula? Incunabula are no more than vectors, familiars, human beings who are possessed. But, nevertheless, they are *dangerous*. Wherever they go, their radiant intellectual will distorts space-time until it harmonizes with the ancient pattern that lies at their core.'

'But,' she said, with a simplicity that might have been interpreted as a reproach, if it had not been for the girlish ingenuousness that shone from her eyes, 'are you not too an incunabulum?'

The gaslight dimmed. She lifted her lorgnette. For a moment, her profile reminded me of some legendary beauty from a masked ball – and not of Venice or Rome, Prague or Muscovy, but from beyond, a place more distant, perhaps, than even fabled Cathay.

'Just because my grandfather—' I floundered. My father was normal. But I had always feared that I had

inherited much, perhaps over much, from Richard Pike
the Fifth, the family iconoclast. And I felt a rush of
something akin to shame. 'No, no, I don't know what I
am. I do have goblin blood, of course. The first Richard
Pike took a goblin woman for a paramour. But I know
nothing else about myself.' She rested the lorgnette in
her lap's pearly mousseline-de-soie. The darkness
deepened still more. I felt my usual self-restraint, along
with my shame, vanish, as if I were ensconced in the
gloom of my own apartment in the early hours of
morning, alone, oblivious to the burdens of past,
present and future, and slipping into the blissful
vacancy of sleep. 'Yes, I know nothing, except that I
have wished, and wished for as long as I can recall, to
slough off the responsibilities my family has imposed
on me. You realize—' I took a deep breath; began again,
more quietly, for in the passion of mounting my
hobbyhorse I was becoming overly excited, and somewhat loud. 'You realize that my father has taken the
whole of Essex? That, after he takes London, all Europa
will be swamped by a tidal wave of manumission that
will destroy the work of the last few hundred years?
Slavery is the bedrock on which human culture has
been rebuilt. Without it . . .' I swept my hand through
the air to indicate the reversal in mankind's fortunes
that would follow.

'*Liberté, egalité, fraternité*?' she enquired, coolly.

'Barbarism comparable to that of the days of the
interregnum,' I asserted, with a happy nod of agree-
ment. I leaned back in my chair, swallowed and looked
away into the auditorium's shadows. I had begun to
sound like one of my pamphlets. To ape the gestures of

a demagogue. It was perhaps not the most fitting way to win the respect and admiration of a beautiful woman. 'I can no longer have anything to do with my family,' I continued. 'Nor with my country. Not as it presently is, not if I am to retain a conscience.' Family and country, of course, no longer wished to have anything to do with me, either. The rants that bore my assumed name were execrated. Even Londoners, whose vested interests lay in the maintenance of a slave state, thought my ideas beyond the pale. 'My name is Germont,' I said, with finality. 'I wish for no other.'

'Germont it is. But I tell you, Germont, do not believe that there are not others who may grasp the elements of your selfhood better than *you* do.' She leaned towards me, staring up from beneath long, velvet lashes. And if her eyes – the lids inclined sharply upwards towards the brows on the temple side – were typically those of a femme fatale, and spoke of a nature wanton and cruel, then I understood that this was only due to my lingering inability to grasp their essential, and overpoweringly marvellous, non-humanness. A quality less wicked than amoral, or, at least, as beyond my own poor, stricken morality as I prided myself in being above the general fray. The eyes narrowed, reinforcing the oriental character that, until then, had been only suggested by the deviant lids. '*I* know who you are.' And, in a moment of revelation, I knew she knew. Knew more about me than anyone had ever done. And I felt that, at any moment, I was due to partake of similar insight, and know her as thoroughly.

The orchestra struck up with the overture. 'We must talk more, Germont.'

'Yes,' I said, benumbed by what had seemed her transfiguration. 'I must learn about you. I must learn *everything* about you.'

For the first time since we had been introduced, her smile vanished. 'Be assured: you will.' One side of her powdered face caught the illumination of a remaining lamp, and she seemed to glow, pale as some night bloom drenched with phosphorescent dew, a bloom such as might be found amongst the dead forests of my own lost Darkling Isle.

I was so entranced that I had not even once taken more than a cursory note of her corsage: the red and pink bloom that so resembled an obscene wound: the night bloom that paralleled her own ineffable beauty, and whose wet, flesh-like petals I had seen reflected in her eyes: my first carnelia.

The performance concluded. As we were leaving the box, I saw, to my pleasure, that I had provoked the surprise and wonder of the other men. If a joke had been intended that evening, I began to feel that it had rebounded. I had been chosen. And though cynical enough to know that I was possibly being used – though just how, I could not fathom, for my straitened circumstances were well known – I retained enough youthful spirits, vanity and arrogance to believe that the beautiful woman on my arm might simply be my due.

My barouche passed down the Boulevard St Germain. To either side of that bleak, depopulated canyon rose the colossal ruins of the Latin Quarter, one of Paris's oldest *quartiers*, and one through which few chose to pass, except by necessity. Its crumbling edifices might have been twin mountain ranges composed of glistening, black soap for whom a slow percolation of water had effected a deterioration that had stopped just short of complete deliquescence. Might have been, that is, if its decay had not precipitated effusions that one most readily associates with a graveyard rather than a bathhouse. Like many of Paris's less salubrious environs, the masonry here had been hewn from those forests of living stone that the Netherworld had loosed upon Earth-Above during its long war with humanity. Those forests had died, leaving only petrified remains. And in the Latin Quarter it had seemed, at first, that the stone had died in like manner. But an unknown factor had initiated a process akin to putrefaction. The stone rotted – not like wood, or some analogous compound – the stone rotted like *meat*. Eaten from within like gigantic carcasses, riddled with strange, wormy growths, a brief rigor mortis had given way to general corruption, until each building's skin had burst and the dark, corrosive sap that it had long harboured could be seen coursing down St Germain's façades. The mephitic odour that would sometimes waft through the neighbourhood, if tonight palliated by summer weather that had gone some way to drying out the sweaty, cadaverous stone, was unbelievable; almost as unbelievable as the fact that people lived in these ruins, people as rank and unsympathetic as the scuttling, verminous life harboured within the architecture's viscid walls: the dreaded apaches.

I am not a brave man, but the fear I had of discovering that Madame Valery might be toying with me abrogated the greater, and surely more sensible, fear that the apaches familiarly generated. When I had earlier put it to her that we might share the late supper that would have been prepared by my maid, implying – by way of those submissive, feathery little inflections of the voice that I had picked up from childhood associations with thralls – that I did not expect, indeed could not hope for, anything more, she had accepted, even though she must have known that I did indeed hope for something more. But before I could further reflect upon my absurd good fortune, the carriage slewed to a shrieking halt, and an inarticulate cry from the coachman alerted me that we had, perhaps, either run over some unfortunate drunk, or fallen victim to the Latin Quarter's rapacious denizens.

'Germont?'

I raised a hand to still her. I reckoned I knew the unreconstructed parts of the city better than most, and did not want our safety compromised by a kept woman's hysterics; a woman who, no matter how much she had bewitched me, could, in the final analysis, I knew, be trusted as little as the next human female.

I girded myself, trying to ignore the hooting and hollering that emanated from the gelatinous warrens of dens and lairs, and peered out of the window.

The street was like pitch. Ahead, almost directly in front of the horses, stood a cloaked figure, its outline picked out by the glare of the gig lamps. The figure was impassive. But it seemed to exude a mysterious vitality. Shadows, as black but no obscurer than its own shrouded form, swirled across the otherwise deserted cobbles, as if the figure imposed some kind of hyper-kineticism upon the very darkness. A hand reached out, frozen in that imperious and universal gesture to stop that, if it had not been for the quick wits of my coachman, would have proved an improvident, indeed fatal, gamble. The figure's head – cowled in the sable cloth that covered the body – turned, and invisible eyes seemed to lock upon my own. The figure advanced. So smoothly did it move over the cobbles that whatever legs were concealed beneath the cloak might have been attached to wheels. Wheels muffled so effectively as to make them utterly silent.

I slipped a hand under the moleskin lapel of my frock coat and found the pearl-handled paperknife I habitually carried in the inside breast pocket, less for cutting the leaves of books, or opening letters on the wing, as it were, than for self-defence. On several occasions it had proved an effective pseudo-weapon, warding off the attentions of drunks, hooligans and political opponents. Reassured, I left it in place, to be called upon if the extremity of the situation demanded it.

'It's all right,' I said, calling up to my man. 'Let me talk to him.' My driver kept a firearm beneath the coach box; I didn't want him discharging it in a blind panic. Especially since I was almost certain of who it was that approached.

Madame Valery had already taken off her necklace and rings in preparation for appeasing the robbers with as much expeditiousness as circumstances might allow. I leaned forward, almost thinking to touch her, or in some other way assuage her fear. But she was still the great courtesan, and I was still the impecunious émigré. 'He's not apache,' I said in a whisper. 'I'm sure of it.

Stay here while I go and find out what he wants.'

I opened the door and jumped out. The man – his identity, as much as his gender, becoming quite unmistakable, now – had reached the carriage, and stood but a few feet away, mercifully out of Madame Valery's line of sight.

'Melchezidek?'

The cowl was thrown back to reveal the face of my father's aide-de-camp.

He was old, they said. Very old. And, in truth, his face was like that of the old gentleman himself. His skin was like pewter. And horns – those clichés of the diabolical – rose from his scaly head. His argent hair was like spun glass. And his saurian complexion made my own seem almost human. It was rumoured that, beneath that cloak, he sported the vestiges of a pointed tail. And, perhaps, for all I knew, cloven feet, too, and a multitude of other attributes that revealed him to be, if not a scion of the Netherworld, then a cousin-german.

'Good evening, Master Pike,' said the old devil.

'You again? And what news have you brought from father this time, lickspittle?'

'Come home, Master Pike. The life you lead here – '

'The life I *choose.*' I began to wring my hands as involuntarily as if I had been a fly. And then I grinned, relaxing just enough to relish the taste of bile in my mouth, such an epicure had I become, during my years of exile, of acrimoniousness. 'And what awaits me at home? Vilification? Sanctimony? The rights of man, eternal, inalienable, trumpeted in my ear from dawn to dusk? Tell my father, tell him—'

'I am not here,' the half-human interrupted, 'to argue natural law, or whether such doctrine does or does not recognize the legitimacy of slavery, but to tell you that you are in danger.'

'From Father?' I choked back a laugh. 'You astonish me, Melchezidek.'

'What I say now has nothing to do with your father. I have been on this Earth a long time, Master Pike. Above it, and below it. I have seen many things. And in you I see disaster. I have had dreams, Master Pike. Dreams of you. You fear the past. In particular, its concepts of individual freedom. The release that it implies of certain psychic energies, so repressed these last four thousand or so years. You fear your childhood, your country, your responsibilities, your fate. But I say to you it is not the past you must fear. No. Fear instead the *future*.'

'I'm to fear the future, eh? Oh Melchezidek, can't you do better than that?'

But with that, the witch turned upon his heels. I watched his measured progress as he proceeded down the middle of the road, away from us, as if retracing his steps along the arrow of time that, tonight, had briefly bisected my own, leaving futurity to me in a manner that implied I was welcome to it. Very soon he became again, not a man, and less a demon, but rather an uncertain figure about whom the shadows danced, then coalesced, shrouding him, until he and the darkness were as one.

I heaved myself up into the carriage and sat down. Madame Valery looked away, frowning, engaged in a detached, somewhat schoolgirlish contemplation of the monstrous architecture that surrounded us.

'Did we really have to come this way, Germont?'

'My family has accrued wealth, madame, much wealth, but I share little of it. That is why I live where I do. St Germain, I am afraid, is the only route to and from the Île de la Cité.' My bewildered companion's gaze remained fixed on the putrefying ranges that rose on either side of our defile. I gave the driver his order. Soon, we were continuing on our way. 'The man stopped us,' I continued, 'due to a misunderstanding. There is no need for further concern.' But until we reached the Île de la Cité she remained silent, like a child lost in the perusal of the illustrations contained in a book of cruel fairytales, or one, rather – as I was soon to find out – lost to herself.

Madame Valery and I sat outside, enjoying the cool breeze. It blew in from the west, made its way over the Seine and the ruins of Notre-Dame, and briefly decamped on my balcony before bidding an adieu, to continue on its journey towards Germania, the seat of Holy Empire, and the wildernesses of the savage, unconverted East.

'My father is misguided,' I said, in answer to her queries. She pulled her mantle more tightly about herself and, with a shiver which ran from her shoulders to the trim ankles that showed below her skirt's voluminous hem, leaned back in her wickerwork chair and cast her gaze upward, deep into the night. It was one o'clock and the breeze had come to be invested with a certain keenness. But she still listened. I was sure of it. Sure that she hung upon my every word. 'For thousands of years, those denied access to civilized life, and confined beyond the boundaries of the world's great walled cities, had been pacified by a chemical programme of psychic castration in order to prevent organized rebellion or unrest. It was only when the Netherworld, wishing to sow discord on Earth-Above, discovered and disseminated a universal antidote to what had become known as "simplification" that the programme was gradually abandoned. But long before it *was* abandoned the Darkling Isle's disenfranchised masses had willingly accepted their status as slaves. Whether this was due to their cultural imperatives, the "slave culture" that they had evolved, or whether factors associated with the long-term effect of the drugs that had permeated their food and water for generations had had the prevalent influence, it is difficult to determine. But the general manumission, both legal and psychological, which my grandfather, and now my father, are imposing upon the country is leading to that very unrest that "simplification" had, for so long, precluded. In time, I predict, it will lead to the destruction of our culture. To internecine warfare. Yes, that end of days will parallel the coming of the perverse, when, towards the end of the twenty-first century, mankind chose to forget how to interpret the objective world and instead embraced the dark forces of the cosmic libido!'

I paused, conscious that I sounded like some callow student who hopes to impress his new girl with an ill-conceived and somewhat naïve rant on how *unfair* life is. I had long known that I could not escape my past. But sometimes, when I stood revealed to myself as less the seasoned politico than a malcontent whose resentments were rooted in adolescent pique, I was abashed, if only for so long as it took to explain away the epiphany as weakness, a surrender to my shadow-self.

'The coming of the perverse,' she said, her words echoing my passion with all the breathlessness of a communicant's response. 'Yes. Are we really emerging from four thousand years of chaos to find ourselves merely at the mercy of another dark age? One that resurrects the dead language of *natural law* and the fallaciously subtle arguments of *conscience* to wreak changes in our society that, however it may flatter our newly revived powers of reason to assimilate them, will, in the end, have us repenting at leisure?'

I tried to mask my surprise. She had done more than excuse my inclination to demagoguery; she had understood me in a way few others had the courage to do. I got up and walked to the balcony's edge. There, my arms outstretched and grasping the filigree balustrade so firmly that my knuckles grew as white as the moon, I decided to test her further, hardly daring to conceive that this beautiful, notorious woman might have chosen to associate with me because of the sympathetic vibrations I set up in her soul.

'You have read my work?' Far off, I heard the whistle of a train, a sound that always summoned up images I associated with childhood, when the great steam locomotives which ploughed through the knotted wastes of England had still been a novelty, and I had been happily unaware of just how much the Darkling Isle was to change.

'Of course. Where I come from, *everyone* has read your work.'

I turned. 'Where you come from?' I gazed down at her, quizzically.

'There are some who disagree with your arguments, of course. Just as there are here. People like your grandfather, and now your father, it seems, who say that slavery has no foundation, either in societal terms, or as a matter of evolved human psychobiology. It is a construct, they argue, which is as much an article of bad faith as the paradigms adopted by the tribes of the perverse.' Flushed with ardour, she took a deep breath. Her bosom heaved. 'But *I* have never believed in such arguments. I, like you, Germont, have always known the truth.' I was unable to prevent myself from breaking out in a boyish grin. 'Your critics question what to me has always been obvious: that, at this point in time, civilization may be rediscovered only at the expense of a small body of human beings holding the rest of mankind in thrall.' It was her turn to smile. And how girlish was the transformation she effected upon herself, the left cheek dimpling prettily as her lips parted to reveal perfect little rows of teeth.

I shuddered, turned away and looked down at my knuckles afresh; saw them whiten the more, until they became like the perfect enamel that lined Madame Valery's mouth. 'Four thousand years of darkness against the four hundred years that represent the human renascence,' I said, as if in a dream. 'Yes, slavery seems a small price to pay.' I filled my lungs to capacity and scanned the horizon. Despite the unreconstructed slums of the Latin Quarter and Montparnasse, Paris was a glory of soaring towers. Everywhere, boulevards glittered with dance halls, hotels, cafés and emporia.

Screwing up my eyes, I focused on the city walls, and beyond, where the reminders of barbarism, in the form of dead, twisted trees and vegetation, covered the Earth's still unreclaimed wastes. And I thought upon the filled-in adits that dotted those wastes and which led below the Earth's surface; of the vast, subterranean caverns of the Netherworld, last redoubt of the perverse, whose buried spirit I often felt rise up within me, and which I had been at such pains to expunge all my life.

I emptied my lungs in a great sigh. 'It is only by maintaining the purely human status quo of the last four hundred years,' I continued, 'that we can hope to remain human. It is the only way we can keep the perverse in check. We have been given this wonderful opportunity, don't you see?' I raised my hands, as if I were addressing the entire population of Paris. 'Because of various random factors, such as "simplification" and the evolution of a slave culture, which, but for outside interference, has had thralls gladly accepting their abject fate, we keep the perverse itself in thrall. For it is the slaves, *our* slaves, who, living outside the world's cities, have, over millennia, interbred with all manner of perverse creatures: rat people, snake people, cat people, insect people. Bred with the creatures those tribes became when they sought refuge under the Earth from a resurgent humanity: the orcs whose blood contaminates even my own veins! The thralls are in truth the last vestiges of the perverse on Earth-Above. It is *imperative* we control them.'

'Ah,' she exclaimed, 'you really *would* be Lord Soho, I see!'

'I told you, that title is—'

'Lost. Yes, I know. Your ancestors were dispossessed and sent to live outside London's walls. And all because of their polluted blood. But control is your darling, is it not? Of the world, and perhaps, yourself? Oh, Germont. Be Lord Soho. Be the proud lord you were born to be!'

I heard the clipping of high heels over tiles and spun about. My maidservant, Musyne, brought out two brandy balloons, cognac, chocolates and a selection of my best, handmade cigarillos. Madame Valery's eyes never left her. When Musyne had deposited the silver tray on our little folding table and had disappeared back into the apartment, she spoke again. 'That girl. She was the cause of your exile, wasn't she?' She half turned in her chair, her eyes trained upon the darkness of the interior, as if she descried things there she did not wish to see, but was compelled to. 'A slave.'

'Yes,' I said, walking a little sheepishly back to my chair and slumping down. 'A slave.' Musyne had been the flashpoint of my life, and, if not the cause, had certainly provided the excuse I had needed to impose upon myself the conditions of self-exile. 'But between her and me there is no longer—' No longer, I had meant to conclude, if I had not felt suddenly so utterly exhausted with life, no longer a connection.

'But she is very pretty.'

'Yes,' I said, annoyed. The telling way in which she had enunciated that 'pretty' rankled. I had had Musyne's age, both mental and physical, arrested, in order that she for ever resemble the young woman who I had once thought I had been in love with. But love dies, dies sometimes even before obsession, and the years, if leaving my maid untouched, had worked their evil upon my soul. Love, like so many things that belonged to my past, had disintegrated, like a pressed flower exposed to the raw air of a harder, more bitter clime. 'But that was many years ago. When I believed that it was possible that love and passion might not be doomed to be always distinct and irreconcilable.'

I poured her a measure of cognac.

'And so,' she said, as she accepted her balloon and peered into it while swirling its dark-red contents about, first clockwise, then widdershins. 'Not knowing who you were, and perhaps not caring to find out, you ran away to France.' I inclined my head in sad acknowledgement. She had learnt much, it seemed, from those who still remembered the wild-eyed young man who had entered their drawing rooms only to summarily demand that France should declare war on his native land. 'You ran to Paris, where a man may still own a slave, or even breed them, with impunity. You ran away for *love*.' And her expression modulated into one I had first seen at the opera, its frank worldliness diluted by simple, common feeling. It seemed to suggest that life might not always be so contradictory as it had been hitherto; that – though I could not help but balk a little at the sheer ridiculousness of the hypothesis – love might exist outside the exigencies of power. 'I am impertinent, perhaps,' she continued, 'but I hope you will believe me if I say I empathize. I too have run away.' She looked up at the night sky. 'Where I come from, there is also revolution. At the end of time, where the spheres of pre-existence meld with those of the afterlife, and past, present and future are one, we have our own cursed abolitionists.'

It was at this point, I think, that the first dim alarum reverberated through my consciousness. 'I'm sorry – what do you mean?'

'I speak of those who seek to undermine a happiness that it has taken the multiverse an eternity to achieve.' Before I could make another appeal for clarification she coughed, violently.

'Madame Valery, are you all right?'

Except for two livid dots, which punctuated her cheeks like dabs of paint on a porcelain doll, all colour had left her face. She pulled a small handkerchief from her purse and held it to her mouth. She coughed again, this time with even greater violence, then leaned back in her chair, as if the blood had been drained, not only from her cheeks, but her entire cardio-vascular system. She took the handkerchief away from her mouth and quickly replaced it in her purse; but not quickly or surreptitiously enough to disguise its dark, arterial stain.

'Yes, where I come from,' she said, 'men and women consider you their messiah and take your word as that of God's own. I suppose –' her smile returned, and a little of her colour; but both seemed equally unhealthy; her cheeks became hectic, and the mouth broadened into a lively, red crescent of manic delight '– I suppose I should tell you the truth. I am from the future.'

I looked away, up, up, into the starlit firmament. Alarm, dim no longer, seemed to fill the entire night. I gripped the balustrade. Again, my knuckles whitened. Like her teeth. Like her face. Like the moon that, quite unexpectedly, seemed to have left its trammelled course and revealed its dark side.

Was this why the other men in the box had exchanged those secret little smiles? Because they had known I was subject to the attentions of a woman whose sanity had become questionable? I remembered Melchezidek's veiled threat: 'It is not the past you must fear. No; fear instead the *future*.' Had he, mocking devil, known too?

'It is late, Madame Valery,' I said, not daring to look at her. 'Perhaps—'

She began to giggle. 'Oh yes, where I come from, that is, the Omega Point, we have all read your pamphlets. You are our hero. Our god.'

'My carriage, Madame Valery, is at your disposal. It might be better if—' I heard a rustle of skirts. There was a catch in her voice, as the infantile fit of laughter threatened to metamorphose into an equally grotesque unleashing of tears. And then, after a long diminuendo, silence.

When I at last turned about, she had gone.

I found that she had left her corsage on the table. A little card embossed with her name and address lay on top of it. Picking it up, I saw that, before leaving, she had hastily scrawled out an invitation to her Thursday evening salon, and underneath it the words:

YOU ARE MY SLAVE AND I AM YOURS.

After breakfast, I stood before my cheval glass, naked, wincing at a fresh contemplation of my ugliness. As we Pikes grow older, it is said, so do we grow more corrupt. I was of middling years. And corruption, I liked to think, was in equipoise with my finer qualities. But my outward aspect belied this moral homoeostasis. The gnarled, embittered old man I would soon become stared back, accusingly.

Few of my ancestors, I hazarded, had cut so grim a figure. If we Pikes grew corrupt with age, then so, it seemed, did we degenerate with each new siring of the line, despite the care that my father, grandfather, and, as far as I knew, his father's father's father, had taken to invest their seed in fully human women, in the hope, I suppose, that some kind of hereditary compound interest would at last purify and release our family from its curse. I had no horns. No tail. No claws. No bat-like wings. But, sad to say, I otherwise approximated the appearance of those creatures who presumably still populated the Earth's depths, and whose demoniacal aspects could be witnessed amongst the reliefs and statuary of Notre-Dame and Sacré-Coeur.

Yet Musyne had always found me personable. Musyne had always adored me.

'Over there,' I said, as she entered the bedchamber pushing a trolley burdened with coffeepot, hot croissants and a small glass of cantharides, my midday and evening aperitif. She too was naked, except for the little chiffon gloves, choker, stiletto mules and white candy-striped stockings, gartered at mid-thigh, that was her customary dishabille when we were alone.

Parking the trolley by my escritoire, she walked to where I stood. As she approached, and her own image filled the mirror – the reflection of a small, buxom girl whose silken appurtenances glistened like scalded milk in the mote-filled light that fell through the jalousie –

the pleasurable anticipation that had animated her face was overtaken by puzzlement. Just as a dog cannot recognize its own likeness, due to its inadequately developed sense of selfhood, so too do some slaves fail to know themselves when confronted by a looking-glass. Long ago, when she had still been a child, Musyne had embraced a state of consciousness wherein her will had become inseparable from that of the Darkling Isle's ruling class. Not for her the fear and trembling of self-consciousness. Her life was one with the universe of things, a mirror herself, really, a passionate but dull vessel which had reflected my needs and wants for over twenty years.

Something like a growl formed inside her throat, a rumble that grew until it visibly rattled her delicate trachea, like a far-off thunderstorm might a window or door.

'It's all right,' I said, stroking her long, platinum hair. 'It's all right.'

'Make her go away,' she said, peering deep into the glass. 'That girl is a nasty girl. Musyne has seen her before. She doesn't belong here. Musyne hates her.'

I grasped the mirror by its frame and tipped it, so that it rotated on its swivel and presented us with its impotent, silvered back. 'Is that better?' The jealous growl subsided. 'I said is that—' She nodded, compliantly; but her peevishness refused to be so easily mollified; may indeed, I ruefully considered, have been only exacerbated by my show of concern. Of late, her once rare, coquettish bouts of refractoriness I used to find such a charming antidote to a subservience that, being so total, threatened to make her attentions insipid, had begun to surface with alarming frequency, as if twenty years of being owned by an almost universally despised Englishman had begun to sow in her an unthinkable contempt.

'Did you bring the books I asked for?' I said, addressing the skittish girl with a sharpness that I hoped would bring about a reversal of her mood. The ploy worked; immediately, her face lit up. Skipping to where the trolley stood, she pulled back the white linen that covered its surface and hung down its gleaming, metallic sides. There, on the racks designed to accommodate hotplates and tureens, lay several new tomes I had recently added to my library. 'Good,' I said. 'That's all for now, Musyne. I have work to do. But remember, today's the day of your injection.' Her face fell a little. 'To keep you young and beautiful, my bonbon, yes?' Gradually, a smile enlivened her impassive features, in slow recollection of the delight she took in her own body. 'We must be grateful, I suppose, to the incunabula for one thing: mankind's technological prowess is less cumulative than a matter of uncertain leaps and bounds. According to what we know of the chronology of the Ancients, the chemicals which, in you, have arrested the ageing process, are so out of sync with our own attainments that, without benefit of intervention by such an agency as represented by my grandfather, you might have had to wait another two hundred years or more before enjoying the advantages you presently have over other women.'

She simpered, uncomprehending. And I paid her back with a sick, ironic grin.

Those advantages I had spoken of had, of course,

apart from making her somewhat sillier than the average slave, shortened her natural lifespan. In a few more years, when she had attained Christ's age on the cross, she would die, having entered her own, final passion. Such was the cost of arresting Time. Such the reason why the chemicals I regularly introduced into her bloodstream were available only on the black market, and why human beings still grew old and died.

I watched her leave. Then I threw on a dressing gown and put on my tasselled cap. Affectation that it was, that facetious little headpiece seemed nevertheless to act like a talisman. On more than a few occasions it had tickled my brain into some sterling excogitative feats.

I walked to the escritoire and sat down. Last night I had acted like a fool, I decided. The worst kind of prig. And what is more, a man wholly ignorant of himself. If much that Madame Valery had said could be reasonably ascribed to some dysfunction of the mind or soul, I had still fallen under her spell. I could not forget her.

Nibbling abstractedly at a croissant, I opened the little compartment in which I had placed Madame Valery's corsage. As I retrieved the flower, a sheaf of yellow, dog-eared pamphlets, dislodged by my too eager hand, fell out and spilled on to the desktop. I looked down at them – my nom de plume staring back, accusingly – and pride conceded to disgust as I briefly reflected upon the wasted years. My soubriquet's original purpose – to allow me to pass unremarked amongst Paris's salons and cafés – had become redundant sometime ago. My father's emissaries had seen to that. But my life, and its purpose, had become, it seemed to me, redundant long before.

I swept the pamphlets aside and deposited the flower upon the blotter. From another compartment I took out a magnifying glass. I placed it next to the bright-red bloom. Then I swung my chair about, bent over, and hefted up one of the heavy tomes. Placing it adjacent to the object of my enquiry, I opened it and set to work, my fingers trembling a little with what, if I should have taken the leisure to think about it, was an almost sexual anticipation.

The corsage, I discovered, had seven overlapping petals that surrounded a tight mass of yellow stamens. I picked it up, my fingers exploring its silky corolla. My fingers delved deeper; the sepals dropped on to the leaves of the outspread book. They ranged in colour from pink to red, and, at their outer fringes, exhibited a darker, almost purplish erubescence, such as that which one associates with a bruise. The smell too was bruise-like, overripe, like a decayed fruit, sweet, but at the same time morbid, not unlike rotting flesh. Indeed, the most astonishing quality about the flower was its flesh-like texture. Its luxuriantly silken, but rather creepy tactile quality, and the unaccountable manner in which it seemed to squirm, wriggle and even pulse whenever I would palpate it, reinforced the impression communicated by its scent: that this was a flower of death.

I could find nothing like it represented in the book – a catalogue of French flora, compiled before the Netherworld seeded Earth-Above with its own vegetation – but I did discover a few parallels. Most notably, an extinct shrub of the genus *Camellia*, whose lurid, rose-like blooms owed something, perhaps, to convergent evolution. It was listed as an oriental evergreen named after a certain Kamel, Latinized as Camellus, a Moravian Jesuit who collected plants in *Las Islas Pilipinas*, coincidentally the same archipelago that my distant ancestor, the first Richard Pike, had chosen for his own self-exile. Species, I read, had been introduced into Europa and Atlantis since before the time of the interregnum.

I pulled another tome from the trolley and set it upon the book I had already opened.

This book listed Netherworld flora, the plutonic, granite, basalt and hypabyssal trees and plants that would have choked and extinguished Europan civilization if they had not died out shortly after the orcs had been driven permanently underground. Again, I was unable to discover, amongst the lists of strange flowers, any exact resemblance to Madame Valery's corsage. But, as with the previous catalogue, I came across something to which that bloom seemed unaccountably related. A stone flower called the *cornelian*.

The plate showed a translucent, semi-precious mineral whose reddish-brown petaliferous angles and planes were − or so ran the text − due to colloidally dispersed hematite. It might have been sard, or some equally familiar, if somewhat exotic, stone, differing only in its brighter shade, if its superficial inertness had not been informed with such dark, subterranean vitality.

With a flash of insight, I realized that the corsage was an unheard-of hybrid, an artificial, or more likely, completely natural cross-fertilization between a flower of the Netherworld and one of Earth-Above. A syngamy resulting in an unprecedented life form.

I studied it with mounting wonder, and then self-pity. It was perhaps not so miraculous, or even unheard of. Like other 'witches', I was myself a hybrid, a life form that, if composed of human flesh, was at the same time related to the perverse. I too was the result of a strange, somewhat obscene cross-fertilization of species.

Rescued from what threatened to become an increasingly despairing reverie by the creak of an opening door, I glanced over my shoulder. The door had only opened a fraction, but it was enough to allow Musyne to spy on me, her face half occluded by the jamb. I got up, walked to where she stood and, opening the door fully, lifted her up into my arms, proceeded to the big, four-poster bed, and deposited her upon its crumpled, unmade sheets.

I let my dressing gown slip to the floor. Then I lay down by her side and examined her. First, with a cursoriness befitting her station and my own, and then with the same unhurried, if less reverent, attentiveness that I had recently bestowed upon the flower. Like the flower, she would, I knew, require a lifetime's study. And even then I felt I was unlikely to apprehend anything more than her most superficial elements. She was hidden from me. Like life itself.

I took her in my arms. Outside, the air was still, as if before a storm. The closeness had extended into the bedchamber. It pressed upon my inner ear, and converted itself into a sharp, ferrous-oxide taste whenever it came into contact with my tongue. I caressed her milky thigh, idly toying with a lace garter. I felt no inclination to carnality. I felt only the need to forget the meaninglessness of my life, the pointlessness of a struggle to control something I had no real comprehension of. In the twenty-odd years of my association with Musyne, who had been slave, if not I? 'What is it like, Musyne?' I said, softly. 'What is it like, and what does it mean, to be a slave?' She stared back, blankly, as ignorant of my interior life as I had always been of hers. 'I must know. Is it good? Is it the *answer*? Tell me.' I grasped her by the shoulder; shook her. 'Tell me, please.' I don't think I had ever said please before. Not to her. Not to one who could not love, but only beg. A slave. '*Tell me*,' I said, angrily now.

She nuzzled my hand. And her impenitent vacancy filled the bedchamber, oppressive as the close, summer's day.

I had been ushered by the butler into the drawing room. But even before stepping over the threshold of her front door, a reminiscent scent – a sharp *altitudo* ballasted with gamy base notes – had heralded my re-acquaintance with Madame Valery's unique flower. That scent: I wondered how her guests could stand it. Perhaps custom had defanged its lacerating properties; or perhaps – and my intimation was, in part, at least, to prove accurate – Madame Valery's salon tolerated that killing fragrance much as the aficionados of the coca leaf exchange the occasional bleeding nostril for the enhancement that the drug lends their senses.

Tentatively, I edged through the press of bodies and towards the centre of the room. There, amid laughing, and, it seemed, more than a little drunk, company,

Madame Valery lay upon a chaise longue, attired, as when I had first met her, in a glistening, opal-white gown. Her favourite, scarlet-mouthed blooms were arrayed about her, sprigs, bouquets and wreaths rising like gross, inflamed organs of generation from what must have been over a hundred faience vases, urns and celadon flutes.

Her languid gestures, her wan complexion, the inanition that each flutter of her eyelashes, every twitch of her nose, seemed to confirm, all spoke of her worsening condition. But like the flock of callow men who flitted about her orbit, or who had gone down on their knees, adopting poses befitting fatuous, all-adoring youth, she laughed, and gaily held up a glass in a salute to Bohemia.

Before her stood a great samovar. The steam that swirled about its bulbous, silver lid compounded the malodorousness that permeated the room. My head began to reel. I stopped dead in my tracks, and, if observance of the proprieties had not been quite so deeply instilled in me, would have pulled out my handkerchief and employed it as an improvised pomander, so powerful, so disorientating had that scent of heaven and hell become.

'Theaceae,' said a voice to my right. I turned. A short, fat man wearing a purple biretta looked up at me from over the tops of metal-rimmed spectacles. 'Of the tea family,' he continued. 'One of the new plants to take root in the wastes. Hope, yet, that the world may become fecund again!'

'Theaceae,' I mused. 'Is that then what is creating this fug?'

He smiled, indulgently. 'It is what we are drinking.'

And he held up a cut-glass bumper. It was filled with a dark, red liquid that resembled port or brandy. The same beverage, I saw now I cast a more alert eye about the salon, that was being sampled by all Madame Valery's guests. 'But let me introduce myself. Monsignor Teste, at your disposal.'

'Germont,' I said. I pointed to one of the macabre bouquets that filled the room. 'The tea, I take it, is a tincture of the flower? The one you call theaceae?'

'Of course.'

For a moment, I seemed unable to wrest my gaze from the bloodshot, almost sentient *knowingness* of the engorged, thrusting blooms. 'It seems an ugly name,' I said. 'And it is hard to believe that such a plant yields anything that is not noxious. It is a remarkable flower, nonetheless. Where does it come from?'

The Monsignor frowned; shook his head. 'I do not think—'

'And what is its genesis?' I went on, attempting to override whatever fuelled his discretion. 'It is my own belief that this theaceae is a cross-fertilization of the camellia and the cornelian.'

He beamed once more. Quite fortuitously, I had stroked this amateur botanist's ego. 'My own thoughts exactly,' he said, as discretion succumbed to conceit.

'And so I have christened it the carnelia.'

He let forth a brief, expectorant laugh and clapped his hands, a little of the red tea spilling over the lip of his glass and spattering the prelatial shirt. 'Did you hear that?' he said, as he turned to gain the attention of our hostess. 'You have a new name for your flower, madame. The carnelia!'

'Germont!' she said, seeing me for the first time. Her eyes were glazed. She seemed to be comprehending me as if through a mist. 'I am so pleased you could come.'

'Carnelia,' pressed the Monsignor, somewhat piqued at being ignored. 'If it is somewhat demotic, is it not delicious, too?'

Madame Valery did not afford him the benefit of her gaze. That gaze belonged to me alone, a correlative to the illusive but unsettling vegetable scrutiny of the hypnotic, circumambient blooms. 'So much better than your own taxonomic suggestion, Teste,' she said. '*Theaceae*! So inelegant.' And then – even as I sensed the little Monsignor wilt a little – she lifted her glass above her head, and, shrugging off her languourousness with what seemed a pure effort of the will, announced: 'The carnelia!'

A young blade sitting near her raised his own bumper and seconded the toast.

'To the Lady of the Carnelias!' he cried, to the general laughter of all.

'And why not?' said our hostess. 'I gave you this flower. I gave you all that it offers. Why should it not be dedicated to me!' There was more laughter.

The Monsignor spun about, presenting Madame Valery with his back, a sulk that would have brought forth more laughter if only the little man had been at all conspicuous. '*I* gave you the flower, madame,' he muttered, in an undertone that I am sure no one heard but me.

Madame Valery coughed. One of her admirers offered her a napkin, another, a fresh bumper of the tea.

'Consumption?' I enquired, in an aside to the

Monsignor, my voice as low as his had been.

He took off his spectacles and furiously polished them on his lapel. 'I have been attending her for several weeks,' he said. 'I am' – he cleared his throat somewhat theatrically – 'a doctor of medicine, as well as a divine. And I can tell you her health has steadily declined. But no, it is not consumption. There is pulmonary damage, of course. And I thought at first that a bacillus might well be responsible. But the damage to the lungs, like the vesicles, pustules and lesions of the skin, which, initially, at least, so resembled lupus, had, I discovered, nothing to do with *Mycobacterium tuberculosis*. No. Nothing at all.' Meditatively, he gazed down at his spectacles and then replaced them on the bridge of his nose. 'God help me, but I have seen nothing like it.'

'The prognosis?'

He looked up at me with rheumy-eyed circumspection. 'I have no idea. But I fear it is an ailment, a progressive degeneracy, that everyone in this room may one day share. She was the first, you see. The first of these people to experiment with the preparation we extract from theaceae.' He plucked one of the long-stemmed, bright-red flowers from a nearby vase. 'Have you tried the tea, Germont? The tea made from the quintessence of the flower's sap? Is that why you are here? If you have not, no doubt the fascination Madame Valery exerts over all she meets may convince you to try it, no matter what I might say, or predict.'

He proffered the flower. I took it, and held it to my nostrils. The incipient nausea I had felt on entering the salon was abating, and the carnelia's scent, though powerful, also possessed a certain allure, like the smell of sweat, cooking oil and cheap perfume that one associates with the cocottes who loiter in the Bois de Boulogne.

'It is, of course,' he ventured, detecting, I think, a blasphemous sea change in my face, 'merely a flower, however curious its anomalies.'

'It represents a marriage between the Netherworld and Earth-Above. Between hell and heaven,' I said, dreamily.

'Be assured, monsieur, it has the power to transport you to both.'

I looked round at those who constituted Violetta Valery's salon. Of two score faces at least a handful mirrored the pallid countenance of their hostess. Those remaining displayed subtler but no less sure signs of creeping atrophy; enough to convince me that the gathering was indeed doomed. 'This narcotic,' I said. 'Have they *all* tried it?'

'They are addicted to it, monsieur. That is why they are here.'

'And you?'

He hesitated. A shadow, like that cast by self-loathing, fell over his plump, otherwise innocuous visage, giving him a new, somewhat frightening demeanour, like that of a priest who has performed one too many exorcisms, or has taken to exploring, with a dedication as inappropriate as it is perfervid, the cult of the flagellum. 'Of course. It was I who introduced the drug, first to Madame Valery, and then to her circle.' His face glistened, its patina of perspiration like diluted lard. 'And it is testimony to the drug's potency that I still take it, no matter how well acquainted I have become with the inevitable consequences of its continued use. But you must not think that I, like the others in this room, monsieur, am in any way *dissipated*. No, I am a scholar.'

'A scholar,' I said, with sardonic flatness.

The little priest flushed. 'The drug allows us to experience the past! It allows us to walk amongst the Ancients!'

Calm down, little man, I almost said, but contented myself with merely raising a doubtful eyebrow. 'In the manner of incunabula?' I enquired, coolly.

'No, no. I am not talking about the re-experiencing, or embodiment, of lost fictions, but of *truths*. The immediate apprehension, not of civilization's fripperies, but of its elemental bedrock: the objective knowledge that is eternal, and not hostage to the vagaries of culture or time! It is those *eternal* Forms that we have access to now. And with them, we may no longer have need of the incunabula.'

Despite my inveterate cynicism, I found myself instinctively rooting for anything said to undermine the influence people like my grandfather had had upon the world.

'They are an unstable element in our civilization,' I agreed. 'Puppets, the marionettes of old concepts better left dead. With them at the tiller, our human renascence is out of control.'

'But the tea,' said the Monsignor, 'the tea of the theaceae – or carnelia, as you fancifully call it – allows *any* man to peer through the dark, obscuring mists of the interregnum! Like opium, it opens up the gates of memory; and like that drug, allows the user to relive past events. But the tea does not work upon personal memory; no, it allows the exploration of *collective* memory. Deep, racial memories of ultimate truth!'

'And the user retains independence?'

'More importantly, the user looks upon the face of God. Those Forms that the incunabula embody are created things. But the vision conferred by the tea is of primary knowledge, the ideas – mathematical, musical and morphological – that make up the universe's underlying structure, its ground of Being.'

I looked away, again scanning the faces that filled the salon. 'But these side-effects . . .'

He sighed. 'Call it parasitaemia. The damage to the internal organs is followed, after a while, by a deterioration of the cognitive faculties. Time travel does not come cheaply, monsieur.'

'And these people here,' I said, unable to prevent a trace of mockery entering my voice, 'are they too then *scholars* engaged in disinterested research?'

'They are as you see them,' he said, careless that he made his contempt plain.

'And why then did you introduce them to the drug?' Of course, I already knew the answer. 'Is humanity expected to place its faith in such people? Is it by their agency, and theirs alone, that we may hope to discover the *truth*?'

Whatever disdain he might have felt for Madame Valery's hangers-on, my own, I think, served only to remind him of his degradation.

His eyes flashed with anger. And then almost as quickly saddened.

He shook his head, walked away and disappeared into the crowd. He had bought himself into this company with the promise of cheap pharmaceutical delights. Because, like me – like perhaps everybody here – he loved the Lady of the Carnelias.

'Can you truly re-experience the past?' I asked her later, after her guests had left. For much of the evening, I had roamed, disconsolate, amongst the gigolos, popinjays and twittering pretty boys of her salon. I was offered the tea many times, but I deferred. And not solely out of fear. It was Violetta Valery I had come for, not her egregious narcotic. Then, just as I had begun to wonder whether I should not retreat into the prospect my old life held, of manic bouts of scribble, scribble, scribble followed by equally manic bouts of coition with Musyne, all about me began to depart, and Madame Valery appeared, at last, by my side, urging me to accompany her into the garden.

On plunging into its balmy shadows, I had entertained the conceit that I was, perhaps, entering upon a garden of delights, a gorgeous labyrinth in which I might be lost for ever. Moonlight bathed the shaded walks of dead, Netherworld foliage that had been sculpted into arbours and little pavilions wherein older, living plants grew. After strolling a while, we seated ourselves beneath a trellis polka-dotted with white chrysanthemums and heavy, black tulips. The atmosphere was so ripe that, in a fit of daring, I had requested, and then prevailed upon her, to call me by my adopted first name.

'Is is possible to walk with the Ancients?' she replied. 'I used to think so, Freddie. But I learned that it was an illusion.'

'But the Monsignor—'

'We must all be grateful to the Monsignor for what he has given us, and indeed, the world. But I know more of this, this –' and her stuttering mouth puckered into a mischievous grin '– this *carnelia*, than he does. The visions of the past are what we tea drinkers experience first. But after that comes knowledge of the truth.'

'The truth?' I thought of what the Monsignor had said. 'A vision of universals? Of Forms unadulterated by the works of man?'

'The truth that nothing is true, that *all* is illusion. A dream. There is only one true Form, you see, Freddie. The Form of Forms. And the Form of Forms is *Love*.' An almost imperceptible breeze insinuated itself through the trellis's slats. The shadows of leaf and petal trembled, dancing across the bench and the ground about my feet. 'Don't you wish to try the tea?'

'I don't know,' I said, remembering all that I had been told of its deleterious effects, evidence of which, in the shape of the patently sick Madame Valery, sat only a few inches from me. 'I . . .' There was a failure of nerve; and then, as in the opera box, when I had first felt the stirrings of passion, words tripped off my lips as if of their own accord: 'I don't know if I need to imbibe a hallucinogenic, or, if you will, *visionary* narcotic, to realize that I am in love.' I could not face her. But I knew she was staring at me, and that her eyes blazed, dark and flecked with red. 'I am not a rich man. And my best years are gone. Besides which, I have never been accounted regular of feature. Why then bestow upon me this intimacy? If intimacy it is.'

'I told you I was from the future, Freddie. Do you remember?'

'Yes, I remember,' I replied, warily. 'And I should apologize, I feel, for my behaviour that night. I did not mean to be so—'

She put a finger to my lips, stilling their propensity to assume a life of their own. 'In the future, there is no separation,' she said. 'The unborn and the dead live in harmony. As do the free man and the slave.'

'Your calling card,' I said. 'You wrote that—'

'That I am your slave, just as you are mine. That is what love is, is it not? Surrender of the self. Extinction. Death. A death that leads to life.' I turned then, and braved her eyes. They shone with the same fire I felt in my loins. I peered more deeply, wondering how I might distinguish passion from madness. 'Freddie, when I first read your pamphlets—'

'They are political tracts,' I said, eager to keep the conversation on an even keel. 'They are in no conceivable sense mystical.'

'Oh, but they *are*, Freddie. Must I believe I have been the only one to notice it? The only one to read between the lines of your shoddy, political harangues? To realize that you are a man who has spent all his life seeking love? And not a domestic, bourgeois love, no, but the blowing out of individuality, a dying into an ecstatic union with otherness.'

'This is slave talk,' I said, shifting on my seat. 'This is the philosophy of *eroticism*.' But if her longing was fit only for a slave, and not to be countenanced by proud, free humans, it was, I knew, a longing I shared, if one I could seldom give expression to other than via the repressed, stultified medium of political agitation.

'The Omega Point,' she said. 'That is where I have come from. To seek you, and you alone, because of what you are famous for, Freddie. For the legend you will become. For your belief in enslavement to the Ultimate.'

I stooped and put my head between my hands. Like the passion she had engendered, her madness was, perhaps, communicable. But it was too late to seek an antidote. Closing my eyes, I began to perceive my life's mission as having a secret goal, one that, until now, I had only glimpsed in moments of extreme fear, want or carnal surrender: fusion. With a world outside of Becoming. The world that she called the *future*.

'Why are you doing this to me?' I said. 'I love you. I have loved you ever since I first saw you.'

'You want to escape? I know, I know.' I felt her hand on the back of my head, playing with my thick but greying hair. 'You believe your life is meaningless. You have begun to doubt your crusade. But I tell you, you *can* escape.' She pulled at a few stray locks in a manner that, on another occasion, would have seemed playful, but which now seemed to taunt. 'Don't you wish to escape, Freddie? I know you do. All your life you've wanted to escape. Look at me, Freddie. Tell me you don't want to be mine. Tell me you don't want to follow me back to the Omega Point. Tell me you don't wish to *die*.'

'I can't, I can't. Please, please,' I said, 'don't make me.' To my consternation and anger, the tears had begun to flow. The silence crowded round, relieved only by the sound of my breast's convulsive heaving.

After some minutes, when I had managed to restore a moiety of my manhood, Madame Valery spoke again: 'You need only take the tea. And then you and I will be one. You *will* take the tea, won't you, Freddie?'

'Is escape so easy?'

I sat up. One of her maidservants stood before us with a tray. She set it down on the bench, and then swiftly retired back to the house. On the tray stood two glasses of the dark, red tincture of the carnelia.

'And have *you* escaped, Madame Valery?' I said.

She got up and walked to a swing that stood nearby. Sitting down, and arranging the capacious folds of her skirts, she began idly to push herself to and fro, her face as serious as a child's. 'I escaped a long time ago.' She swung a little higher. 'Human beings go through life entirely alone, Freddie. And when they die they remain alone, as alone as they were before they were born. As separated from each other as are the categories of time. No escape – or so I long thought. But this loneliness: I'll have no more of it. All space, all time, everything that keeps us apart. I'll put an end to it all. That's *my* crusade, Freddie. That's why I'm here.'

'And so,' I said, a little sanity returning, and seeking to humour her, 'why have you come from the future? Because of me? Because I justify slavery? Are you here to change the past, and so save your time from these abolitionists you talk so freely about?'

'But you don't understand. *This* is the future.' I waited in the moon-fringed shadows, waiting for her to go on. She kicked at the ground each time the swing crossed the equinox of her slowly magnifying arc, sending herself progressively higher, until, at the apogee of each passage, she seemed to meld with the night and its flashing stars. 'This *is* the future, Freddie, here, now and always. It is the future dreaming of the past. This moment exists only because we in the future dream it. All is a dream. The virtual manifestation of future desires.'

With a great scraping of her calf-skin ankle boots across the hard soil, she narrowed the swing's arc until she achieved stasis. She closed her eyes and flung back her head. 'We are both of us unreal. But that is the nature of the universe. *Everything* is unreal, a dream. With the tea, we come to understand. And come to understand, too, that, in dreaming, we may know reality. The reality of love, and death.'

Slowly, she rose and, with her head now lolling forward, so that she stared at the dark undergrowth to either side of her feet, walked towards me. And as she did so, she unbuttoned her right sleeve and turned it back.

'Yes, I'm dying, Freddie. But now you're here, I no longer care. In death, you see, I will finally understand love's absoluteness. I will no longer be alone. I will be one with the Form of Forms.' The denuded arm revealed a series of lesions which, as she drew close, I saw to be growths – angry, red, petaloid malignancies that were fleshly approximations of the carnelia. And as she grew closer still, I saw that those eruptive lesions writhed, squirmed and wriggled, that she was alive, with a seething life not her own.

I jumped up, knocking the tea tray on to the floor. The glasses smashed against the cobbled path. I backed away, unable to wrest my gaze from the horribly enflowered limb. And then, as I at last summoned up the requisite strength, I spun about and – mind empty of all thought – ran deep, deep into the night.

I never returned.

It was not, I think, the memory of her ravaged body that dissuaded me. Whatever I may be, I am not so bereft of compassion as to be ruled principally by disgust. No. It was the fact that I found her illness, both mental, and it must be said, physical, inexplicably seductive. And I was afraid. Afraid of the stirrings of my shadow-self. The dark, potent desires that had been with me since childhood, old, vengeful and as appallingly numinous as the perverse itself.

Several weeks passed, and then one night, quite unexpectedly, the little Monsignor knocked at my door. I asked Musyne to show him in. And, after she had taken his hat and coat, he joined me on the balcony, where, in pensive anticipation of enjoying my slave, I was taking my customary glass of cantharides.

'Madame Valery is missing,' he said.

I shook my head. 'I am not, you must understand, privy to her movements. But of one thing you may be certain: she is not *here*.'

'She has sickened greatly, monsieur.' He took the proffered seat. 'And, of late, has talked unceasingly of you. Yesterday, she received a visit from a man who, though I was not present at the time, would seem to have been a half-human.'

'A witch? Like myself?'

'You, monsieur, are hardly—'

'Spare me your delicacies, priest. What of this man?'

'He said he represented your father.'

Melchezidek, I thought at once.

'And?'

'And, according to Madeleine, the housemaid who provides me with intelligence, and who, on this occasion, as on many others, had her ear placed faithfully to the door, this man, this witch, told her that she must renounce you. That her hold upon you was evil. That your family would suffer greatly – your father, in particular – if she should further add to your woes.'

'Damn him,' I said. 'Damn them all!' I made a fist of my right hand and punched it into the open palm of my left. 'My family. Ha. They are nothing more than a nest of officious vipers.'

'She loves you, monsieur.' He sighed, like one whom defeat has liberated, and who is allowed, now that he has nothing more to lose, to embrace the possibility of grace. 'I fear for her. But I think I know where she may be found. If you could help, then . . .'

'Yes,' I said, eager that such grace should extend to me. I had been a poltroon. I had refused to engage with what, ever since that night in Madame Valery's garden, indeed, ever since first meeting her, I had known to be my destiny. Whatever terror, or revelation, awaited, I would meet it. Now. 'What can I do?'

'You once asked where the carnelia might be found. Monsieur, I have long kept that a secret. Those who frequent Madame Valery's salon have, I regret, been so unworthy of her as to sell the flower. And others, outside our little circle, have begun to clamour for a ready supply of the tea. It is to the carnelia's source, monsieur, that Madame Valery has flown. The flower's sanctum sanctorum. Yes; she has gone there to die amongst the blooms that are her heart's delight, and, in death, to receive from them one last, immortal vision. I am sure of it.'

'You cannot go by yourself?' I said, getting up. Musyne peeked interrogatively about the frame of the door, as, of late, had been her impudent want. I indicated to her that she should ready herself to dress me. 'What is this place?'

'We must go into the Latin Quarter,' he said. 'And deep, too. Deep into its byways and alleys.'

I clucked my tongue.

'I have come to learn that you are a Pike,' he said, gazing down at the floor. 'Your family's exploits are legendary.'

'Fame is fame, perhaps, ill or no,' I responded. 'But I'm no swordsman. No bloody adventurer. I'm a hack. I hope you do not think I will provide you with an adequate bodyguard?'

He pursed his lips. 'Whether or not you are a swordsman, monsieur, you are Madame Valery's love. You *will* come, won't you?'

'I have said I will.'

Musyne brought me my frock coat. I slipped it on, patting its breast pocket to make sure that she had put the paperknife – whose extra-literary offices might well be called upon tonight – in its customary place. I looked the diminutive priest in the eye. 'Sometimes, the pen is mightier than the sword. Or if not a pen . . .' The priest took off his spectacles and, with brisk, nervous flicks of the wrist, began to rub the lenses against his lapel. 'The

Latin Quarter is not so dangerous as is sometimes supposed,' I muttered, unhappy that he seemed to need my reassurance.

'I go there often,' he said, resettling the spectacles on his nose, and looking up at me, owlishly, 'for supplies of the flower. But as the fame of the carnelia has spread, so have there been people willing to kill to get their hands on it. So far, we remain undetected. Though some of my couriers have met, in the last few weeks, with some *extremely* unpleasant fates.' He stared, abstractedly, into the apartment, made an almost inaudible *tsk-tsk* as his gaze alighted on Musyne, and then shrugged, as if in nonchalant concession that such a fate might soon be his. 'Shall we go?' he added.

We took the Monsignor's coach and four – an equipage bereft of ecclesiastical, and indeed, all other signs of pomp – and proceeded towards the Latin Quarter.

There, the Place Maubert awaited, and its tangle of dark, riverside streets.

The re-sanctified pile that was Saint-Séverin had once belonged to a purely human world. But the sump created by the surrounding tenements had seeped into the church's foundations and been drawn into its walls and façade. Its ancient stones were now like those of the other, more recent buildings in the Latin Quarter. As black as gangrenous flesh, they glistened with perverse ruin, infected as they were with that weird petrophysical entropy that had transformed this portion of the City of Light into a single, putrefying abattoir.

Lord Soho

We debouched on to the wet, sticky pavement. Telling his coachman to wait for us, the Monsignor led the way to the west door. Before following, I glanced about apprehensively, conscious that obscure streets such as these – carpeted in mucilaginous rubbish, and lined with once proud, but now all but liquefied architecture – harboured, perhaps, as many hooligans and cut-throats as the Boulevard St Germain. Seeing nothing, but feeling as if I were in danger of being transfixed by a thousand pairs of eyes, I hunched my shoulders and scurried after the priest.

He knocked on the door. Almost immediately I heard a lock being shot. The door opened, if only fractionally, and we were greeted by a murmurous voice urging us to eel between post and jamb. Inside, our doorman stood revealed as a Benedictine.

'Is she here?' said the Monsignor.

The monk nodded. Enquiringly, his gaze met my own.

'A friend,' explained the Monsignor. 'Or rather, a friend of Madame Valery. It is my hope that he can help her. I fear no one else can.'

'Only God can help her now,' said the other. 'It is enough, I feel, that we concern ourselves with praying that she may emerge from her derangement in sufficient time for us to administer last rites.'

'Very noble of you, I'm sure,' I said, 'especially since you brought her to this pass.' I cocked my head towards the priest. 'Aren't you the ones who introduced her to the tea?'

'Our Order had nothing to do with that.'

'And I wish by Christ's bones it had had nothing to do

167

with me,' said the Monsignor. 'I have been weak. But I am a man, monsieur,' he said, looking up at me, and evoking the hoary old excuse, 'and I have but a man's heart and a man's flesh.' He began to walk down the nave. 'Come, let us go to her.'

The monk and I followed in his wake.

The nave was littered with fallen masonry: crescents of fan-vaulting and multitudinous shards of slate, all of which bled corruption. The mess oozed across the flagstones and under the pews, an impossibly cool pyroclastic flow that would be forever settling into a gelatinous variant of basalt or obsidian. But whereas the church's effluence was as livid as congealed blood, its walls were as fresh wounds, rampant with a burgeoning, deep crimson. The carnelia was everywhere. It seethed across maggot-eaten stucco, and hung, dripping its intemperate sap, in great, pendent clusters that suggested obscene haematomas, from a mucous membrane that had spread across the blasted vault. I walked through some kind of hothouse, it seemed, an incubator gravid with an unprecedented, aberrant vitality, a florescence of death.

'Where has it come from?' I murmured. 'What does it mean?'

'The flower is from the wastes,' said the monk. 'And it means that, outside the Earth's cities, there is a new parturition afoot. Life that represents both humanity and the perverse, but which is due to supersede both.'

'A mongrel life? Hardly new. I myself—' But I chose not to surrender so easily to the confessional.

'Mongrel? You may call it what you like. For centuries, now, the restored order of St Benedict has sought to preserve and recover such learning as flourished under the dispensation of the first Christians. But the grimoires we compiled were little more than collections of incantations and spells. It has not been until the coming of the incunabula that we have had a real chance of connection with the Ancients. But then my brothers discovered another route to the past. A better route. One over which our monastic order could exercise total control, and so dedicate knowledge to the greater glory of God, rather than heathen amusement. The new life that is transforming the wastes, and whose evidence you see all about you, is a sign of that greater life to come, the promise and hope of resurrection in Our Lord, Jesus Christ!'

We had come to a halt. Moonlight fell through the east window.

About the altar were a group of monks. They squatted, tailor-like, on their hams, coarse habits pulled over their knees. Eyes half-closed, with quills poised at the ready, they executed jerky, and, it seemed, quite involuntary movements, as one by one they emerged from trance to make a few, swift marks on the ledger-like tomes spread before them.

'The scriptorium,' said the monk at my side.

The assembled scribes, after making their entries, as quickly resumed their drugged, sentinel-like poses at the gates of the land of dreams.

The Monsignor ascended the altar steps. As he bent over the rectangular stone, in what I at first thought to be a ritual genuflection, I saw him tear at some of the vine-like tangles of the carnelia that had hitherto obscured my line of sight. The sleeping, or unconscious, form of a woman was revealed, who, after several more streamers of bloody vegetation had been pulled free from what seemed the woman's body itself, I knew to be Madame Valery.

'She is debauched,' said the monk. 'She has brought this disaster upon herself. The tea must be used sparingly, with respect.'

I ran up the steps and was presently at the Monsignor's side.

She lay supine in one of her opalescent gowns, all about her a gaudy confusion of blooms, thorn-encrusted stems – as savage as reels of barbed wire – and little pools that constituted the red crushed excrescence of the carnelia. The shock of seeing her smothered in that morbid foliage gave way almost at once to a graver concern, one predicated upon the sure knowledge that the flowers, rather than attacking her from without, had erupted from within. They had had their origins, here, in the fleshly stuff of stones and mortar, and had migrated to other flesh with a horrible ease. Humanity, for them, was but a stage on the highway that led to the new parturition. For as I raised my eyes to heaven – a hoarse shout ascending to the vault – I beheld the great pod that hung directly above: a gigantic blood sac which the uplifted tendrils of her body reached towards, as if to offer nurture.

'The sons of God,' said the monk, from behind, in a jubilant, antiphonal shout, 'have lain with the daughters of men and found them fair!'

To what unknown, perhaps even more horrible metamorphosis, was her blighted loveliness being this night transposed?

I gathered her up into my arms. Not only death was at work here, but birth, a monstrous birth.

'Stop!' screamed the Monsignor. 'You're killing her!'

'No,' said Madame Valery, stirring within my embrace, 'let us be. All of you meddlesome clerics, let us be. It is him I came here for. And now at last I have him. It is finished. I can at last return home.' The white gown was slowly turning crimson, as the crushed blooms radiated sap and her very body offered up its own converted essence. Something snapped within the bustier. The sodden fabric gave way, and a rosette of diseased flesh exploded from her breast with cathartic insistence. A necklace, to which was fastened a small phial of what looked, at first, like blood, but which I guessed was the tincture of the carnelia, hung within her cleavage. Even as I watched, it vanished beneath a corolla of overlapping flaps of tissue. She groaned, as one in labour. Then a series of stems – stems that had until then been rhizomes and tubers, but which now burst into the air, quivering with alien life – wrapped themselves about what was left of her bosom, and then they too rose, adding to the long, whip-like strands of febrile discharge that already reached blindly, pathetically, towards the pod.

'Violetta Valery died a long time ago, Freddie,' she said, her pupils dilating with approaching mortality. 'It is the flower. It is the flower which is from the future. The flower that has parasitized my body. It comes from a time when all will be put right. Oh, the travail it has endured so that it might come here, through voids of terror, through hearts of nothingness. Through the darknesses that demarcate the dimensions. But it is true what I told you. I am from the future, too, and I remember everything of the journey. Of the falling from eternity into time. And of the dreamtime, where I knew I would find you. Yes, Freddie, I remember everything. For I am the flower. I *am* the carnelia.'

Behind me was a thunderous rending of wood. And then a great roar of voices. I swung about, carrying Violetta off the altar, and, giving the invading mob only a cursory glance – my blood had frozen with recognition at hearing their massed cry – sought out shadows, a door, a hole in the ruined walls, anything, indeed, that might facilitate our escape.

'Apaches!' cried the Monsignor, crossing himself. A swell of raggedly apparelled men and women surged forward. The monk who had opened the door to us ran back down the nave, his hands extended in protestation, abjuring those who had profaned the house of God to leave.

He died as he reached the first apaches who had run to meet him, instantly succumbing to a battery of rocks, blows, cleavers and staves.

'Quickly now,' I said to the Monsignor. 'How do we get out of here?' He went a little way down the altar steps and then retreated. An idea – born of terror, or conceived in a spirit of rational, if somewhat un-Christian, self-preservation – seemed to occur to him. Continuing to back away, he reached the line of entranced scribes. There, he squatted down, half-closed his eyes and, affecting an expression as vapid as their own, took his place amongst them, as if hoping that he too might find refuge in the past.

To follow his example, with Madame Valery in my

arms, would have been impossible, even if I had thought that the apaches might be impressed by such a show of non-resistance. Grimly, I stumbled down the steps, leaving the Monsignor and the Benedictines to provide the apaches with whatever cruel, sordid entertainment their low-born minds might devise.

I knew, with a certain fatalism that revived a dormant spirit of intractability within me, that the western door provided the only exit. I lay Madame Valery down at the foot of the steps and withdrew the paperknife from my coat pocket. The vanguard of the apaches closed in.

'Give us the flower, priest!' said one.

'He's no priest,' said another. 'He's an aristo. A slave master.'

'No priest, that's certain,' I said. 'I'm—'

'He's Lord Soho,' said Madame Valery. I glanced behind. She had eased herself on to one elbow and surveyed the invading barbarians with all the contempt befitting a great Parisian courtesan. 'And yes, he is an aristocrat. Of the spirit. As am I. The flower belongs not to you, but to those who will inherit the *future*.'

'Lord Soho,' I muttered to myself, as if I were only now cognizant of that name. 'Lord Soho,' I repeated, relishing the title's bitter-sweet taste. And then, remembering our peril, I gave all my attention to the enemy. They were a pug-ugly bunch of reprobates. Fungous tumours covered their skin, and the reek of the Latin Quarter came off their breath and seeped from every pore.

'Freddie!' cried Madame Valery. Two of the vanguard broke off from the main body and loped towards us, skipping over the accumulated debris that cumbered the nave. They carried flaming brands and cudgels. I readied myself. 'Freddie!' she cried again. 'You told me that you do not know who you are. I tell you: you have many selves. I can sense it. The witch, the swordsman, the lord, the rake, the seditionary, and . . . and the traitor. But you will be reconciled with yourself. I know you will. Become what you are, Freddie. Here. Take it. Please. It's the only way. Know that you too are an *incunabulum*.'

Daring to take my eyes momentarily off the two on-rushing, mire-bred belligerents, I turned and saw Madame Valery hold up the small phial that had hung between her ravaged breasts. I knew then that I was condemned to follow her, to be with her wherever she should go. And if, in some measure, I had always known it, but had lacked the courage to embrace the fate that was concomitant with embracing her, both in mind and body, I now sought swift redress. Rapidly, I knelt, snatched the chain from her neck, pulled the cork with my teeth, and swallowed that cold, bitter tea. And the seal was set upon our spiritual union.

I awoke.

And it was as if I had awoken from a suffocating dream, wherein I had thought myself to be someone else, and now laughed with joyful relief: No, no, I was never that person, never that person at all!

The world about us had stilled, leaving Madame Valery and I isolated on a little promontory about which were ranged impotent, if misbegotten, horrors, a nightscape of frozen, vaguely human shapes.

'*Espiritu Santo!*' I screamed, remembering the old war cry of the Pikes. I darted forward and slashed the throat of the apache who stood nearest me.

For what seemed an age, he did not move. Only the thin, spurting pulse of a severed artery, and the pitter-patter of blood upon the floor, testified that, somewhere, time still existed. Then slowly, as if in concession to seconds, minutes and hours that, if displaced, were still exigent, he tipped sideways and collapsed upon the stones.

'Be careful,' said Madame Valery, 'the drug will at first speed up your reactions and distend your sense of time. But your body is unaccustomed to the tea. Soon, too soon, you will go into trance and fall back into the past!'

I despatched the apache who provided the next immediate threat with like celerity. But time was already gathering up its skirts and preparing to run. In his death spasm, the caitiff whose throat I had elegantly partitioned cast his flambeau high into the air. Looking round, I saw it come to ground, roll under the choir stalls and enkindle them. The wood – unaffected by the rot that permeated the church's superstructure – instantly began to blaze.

The surviving vanguard began to move somewhat more fleetly. Knowing I would not retain the advantage for long, I pocketed my blade, hurried to where Madame Valery lay, bent over, scooped her up in my arms, and proceeded down the nave. I wondered at how the drug not only speeded up my reactions, but released such a quantity of adrenaline that it seemed pertinent to fear for the structural integrity of my heart.

Elbowed aside, the tardy apaches groped at empty space, or else fell, the shimmering, convective air like a veil about to be rent, the fabric of reality giving way to the world of fabrication, the wilful narrative that lay at the centre of my being.

I burst through the western door. And, fuelled by what was now a truly unimaginable reserve of energy, I ignored the waiting carriage and continued to sprint, the carnelia burning in my veins like brimstone.

Only when I reached the river did I come to myself.

I fell to my knees, letting Madame Valery slip from my arms on to the embankment. Then, with an exhaustion descending upon me so profound that I might have been pole-axed, I sank down beside her. But I was conscious, still, as was she.

'I am your slave, Violetta,' I managed to say, before the delicious chill that was suffusing my body and the swoon that was overtaking my thoughts became complete. 'I have always been your slave.'

'And I yours,' she replied, a small dribble of blood issuing from the side of her mouth as she turned her head on the rough stones to look into my eyes.

The truth. Yes, this was the truth. The truth the Monsignor had promised. Great wards fell off the rusty locks of my soul, and I soared, free, like an unchained bird. Cities, great cities, came into view; I winged over their gilded rooftops. And I saw the glories of the ancient past. But it was another truth that was all-important, not this phantasmagoria, this mummery of lost time. Through the mist-like vision of another age I saw her face, and, with my last vestiges of strength, reached out to touch it, as she had once touched me, long ago, in the Théâtre Nationale de l'Opéra. She was what I had always desired, but not allowed myself to surrender to; that which all my life I had sought to control. I was like my father, and his father, and his father before him. I was perverse. Something alien in human shape. Something wrested from both Earth-Above and the Netherworld.

An incunabulum.

That is why I had run away from home. Because I could not bear to look at myself in a mirror. That is why I had abjured freedom and justice. Because of a craven need to keep my essential self in chains.

The tyrant in me released its hold; I fell into darkness, my exhaustion now as absolute as it was sweet. And I knew the bliss of liberation.

All was one. The witch, the swordsman, the lord, the rake, the seditionary, the traitor. All was in equilibrium.

She had triumphed. The perverse had overcome all human resistance, and mated itself with my soul, an acknowledged equal. I was, at last, myself entire.

Hearing a great drum-roll of falling masonry I crooked my head about, and, with what remained of my strength even then leaving my body, descried the church on fire, the tongues of flame like the blooms of great, shrieking flowers sending their last perfumed chorale to heaven. The festering walls ignited and fell in upon themselves, revealing a crimson interior. Out of the flames – from the exploding blood sac that had been the gigantic pod – I saw a shape emerging, a form that was like a man, but not a man, immense in proportions, and evilly fair. I saw wings unfold. Light shone from a beautiful, malefic face. There was another explosion; the vault began to collapse. And as the creature fell backwards into the fire, the fire in my own veins finally carbonized my overexcited senses, and I saw no more.

The coffin's burden of sickly wreaths glistened like watered silk in the few rays of sunlight that broke through the gathering clouds. The air was close. Thundery. I threw a scattering of earth into the open grave, and walked away.

In the end, did it matter what Violetta Valery had said about the future? I had spent my life living a lie. Mine had been the real madness. The truth, life's ultimate truth, for me, lay in her absence.

A little way off, Melchezidek and Musyne waited. We could all go home, now I no longer feared, now that I was free.

It had begun to rain. Paris would soon be as insufferable as a hothouse. If one robbed of the marvellous atrocity of its most valuable bloom.

I would put my affairs in order. There would be other flowers. Other examples of new life. The seed of their resurrection would spread, from here, and from wherever the carnelia, or its like, had taken root, to germinate the petrified countryside with a new and terrible bounty. And something, perhaps, the like of which I had glimpsed from the banks of the Seine before I had succumbed to trance, would be born. A race of giants, a race of angel-demons, as magnificent as they were evilly fair.

She was gone, but I was sustained by the knowledge that I travelled towards her, to that strange, absolute land of futurity. The place where Violetta dwelt. For I knew, in my heart of hearts, that she had been right. Life was dream. Insubstantial. As lonely as it was long. Only in surrendering to the absolute could separation be annihilated. Only then could the gulf between 'you' and 'me' be spanned. Death and love, the tea had shown me, were the paths by which we attain our future state, that is, our destiny; death and love, whose distinctions were as illusory as time itself.

I looked down at my hands. Saw the lesions, the first signs of lurid buds, that would, enflowered, take me to the long-hoped for communion, and rest.

I was a slave. A slave to the love, the new love, that I had become addicted to. The love that was final oblivion.

The Nephilim

At some point I must have succumbed to the soporific rhythms of our railway-carriage. When a blast of the whistle at last returned me to full consciousness, I discovered that we were travelling through the outskirts of Epping and would soon be at Castle Thorn, my brother Reginald's country seat.

My grandson sat opposite. Throughout much of our journey he had stared at me relentlessly. Now his eyes were again locked upon my own. Bruised, insomnious, they disconcerted me almost as much as the small but voluptuously modelled doll that he cradled and, sometimes, might be heard whispering to.

'Are you looking forward to meeting your Uncle Reginald?' I said. More than ever, I was desperate to establish some kind of rapport with the child. 'Perhaps you would like me to stow your little friend' – I glanced down at the doll with distaste – 'in my valise?' By way of reply he scowled and jealously hugged his porcelain inamorata the more tightly.

Unwilling to suffer his scrutiny any longer, I turned my head and gazed out of the window. The train had begun to slow, the trees to thicken. 'You will find these parts quite different from the Naze,' I said, drifting into a welcome state of abstraction. The reclaimed country-side had given way to older, less human vistas that, despite the fine, late summer weather, were shot through with shadows that might have emanated, not merely from another age, but from a climate of affect that had been all but banished from the world – the squall of pleasure and pain that had informed the interregnum, when the gods of the perverse still enjoyed dominion over men's hearts.

A public house came into view. Ranged outside it, in grubby shirtsleeves and vests, were loud, drunken examples of the newly enfranchised. I studied the crapulous multitude with all the civility that fear and disgust will allow. For how many generations had they been free? Two, three, four? And what had they learned in that time? Nothing. These slaves in all but name might have made of themselves something beautiful; they had, after all, money in their pockets and time on their hands; yet they had turned their backs upon art, music and poetry, and, like perfect case studies of the effects of the fifty-sixth century's industrial revolution, embraced the *ignis fatuus* of commonplace happiness. And it occurred to me – as it did whenever I was confronted by such demotic leavings – that mankind, if it were to rediscover that beauty led to ecstasy and ecstasy to transcendence, might do worse than resubmit to the perverse, that all but forgotten zeitgeist as mysterious to us, now, as the spirit of the ancient world had been to my distant forebears.

The Pikes, of course – at least those of comparatively recent vintage – had contributed so much to the Darkling Isle's present-day state of decay that my inclination to unambiguously damn the dull, swinish commonality, in word and deed, was always tempered with self-recrimination.

'Are you aware of our family's lineage?' I said, reluctantly turning to face the boy. Ties of blood – if powerless to override the antipathy I felt – could, at least, remind me that he was an orphan. 'Did my poor son instruct you in the genealogy of the Pikes?' I waited, determined to have an answer out of him.

The bulbous forehead – plastered with a lick of greasy black hair – glistened coldly with the same inverted feverishness that raged behind the eyes. The boy took a big gulp, then exploded into utterance. The verbal shock wave pressed me back into my seat. '*He said I must get the title back!*' Hurriedly composing myself, I nodded in encouragement. Anything, including a spasmodic barrage of distempered words, would be preferable to that quasi-autistic glower. 'He said we were robbed of our lands and estates' – his tongue was tripping hot and fast – 'because we have goblin blood in us. He said I must, must, must, *must* make sure I reclaim our rights, re-enter London and become Lord Soho!' As he had spoken, he had twined a length of the doll's horsehair ringlets about an index finger. The finger was bedizened with the ring and seal I had relinquished to my son and which my grandson had inherited by right of primogeniture. 'He said it didn't matter what the other children said,' he continued. 'I was human. Human through and through! And I would one day walk amongst the quality. Wear the ermine. Have a coronet, eight balls on tall points with strawberry leaves! Yes, he knew it. He *knew* it.' He switched his attention back to the doll, staring into her eyes with a sadness as much at odds with the repressed fury with which he customarily regarded me, as it was with the cooler, if no less chilling, aspect I had seen him turn upon the world. 'Isn't that right, Flagelleta?'

The boy was mad. His brain curdled by loss and grief. And by something else, too, of course. The curse of the Pikes. Ah thy people, thy children, thy chosen, marked cross from the womb and perverse . . . His soul, like my own – like that of all my ancestors – was besmirched with shadows. Shadows of the same genus as those that fell through the deepening woodland outside. Shadows that had veiled the past, distorted our perception of the present and pre-empted the future. Shadows that it had taken over four thousand years of turmoil for the Earth to dispel, but which still haunted those whom the perverse had secretly made its own.

I felt a sudden, if accustomed, metaphysical weight descend. My muscles crimped; I hunched over, borne down by a grief no single death could engender, not even that of my beloved son, Richard; no, I mourned my line, and its wretched apotheosis in this crazed, morbid boy.

I felt pity, too, of course. I am, if self-absorbed, no monster. But I was glad that pity, along with gentleness, understanding and all the rest of it, would not have to be put to the test. At least not by me. I looked up. My charge was still consumed with petting his doll. Soon, and soon enough, perhaps, I would turn the little horror over to my brother, who might assume patronage in whatever way he saw fit. And then I would return to Oxford and my studies.

'The first Richard Pike,' I said. I paused and peered once more through the window; the train was pulling into the sidings. I would, I had decided, acquit myself of my present responsibilities to the child by way of a swift recapitulation of our family's history. I continued, as expansively as time would allow: 'The first of our particular offshoot of the family, that is, sired a half-human upon a female orc. An orc whom, to the outrage of all, and his own eternal disgrace, he had made his paramour. For that crime of miscegenation, Richard Pike the First died in the Far East, in exile. His son, however, returned to London and, as those in our materialistic times might opine, "made good", for he was in time ennobled for services to Mammon and the state. *His* son, alas, soon came to know the exile of his grandfather. And if different in kind, it was an exile more lasting in its consequences. On the very day he succeeded to the title our family's enemies raised the issue of his goblin blood and had him cast into the wastes. Not such countryside as you see about you here. But the legacy of the wars between Earth-Above and the Netherworld. A wasteland of living stone, populated by rogues and thralls. Now *his* son was little more than a mendicant – an itinerant barber, I believe – but the next Pike, that is, Richard Pike the Fifth, was one of those humans we call incunabula. The spirit of the ancient past had been reborn in him, and its radiant, preternatural energy changed everybody and, perhaps, everything, he came into contact with. He was the one who made this part of the Darkling Isle his own, by freeing its slaves and leading them into battle against the forces of reaction. My grandfather consolidated his work, though his own son, Richard Pike the Seventh – that is, my father and your great-grandfather – was a black sheep. A retrograde. For many years he lived in

Paris, and filled the ears of any who cared to listen with his outlandish amateur politicking, justifications of the master-slave relationship and the like. But, coming to relent his ways, he eventually returned to the fold, and settled once more in England. Or so my mother told me. My father died young. I was barely weaned, Uncle Reginald a mere babe in arms. I too have tried to be faithful to our family's ideals – for God knows, man needs the Ideal – even if our once noble enterprise has been tarnished. The philosophy of Utilitarianism that permeates the Free Counties, and to which, you'll discover, your Uncle Reginald has dedicated his life's *apologia*, has everywhere left a stain of ugliness and philistinism. Still, there is much to rejoice in, I suppose. If we never have London, and never regain that fusty old title, it would seem a matter of small consequence. You are Richard Pike the Tenth, and you will inherit, in time, all that you see about you. Enough land for any man, I would hazard. A country within a country, you might say. Quarrelled over, indeed, fought over. But ours, and ours in perpetuity, by indissoluble right of conquest, and by the consent' – I could not help but grimace – 'of those we govern.'

'We are born to be great lords of the Darkling Isle,' murmured the boy, still looking down at the doll. 'Lords, not merely of Essex and its satellites, but of Northumberland, Mercia, Wessex and all the southern counties, too. We are born to be lords of *all*.'

But there would be little hope of that. For any man. Neither in space, nor in time. With each passing year, humanity became more unreal. More insubstantial. Such a state of affairs had been prefigured by the

188

incunabula and underwritten by the somnambulistic existence led by those of my contemporaries who resorted to the pharmacopoeia offered up by the new forests. We were a fiction, a dream that had had its day. All we could do was make a graceful exit, retire into the wings and let the Nephilim assume the stage.

Let us then prepare humanity's last refuge, I thought. A true Ideal. An artificial realm of Beauty.

The train lurched, and then came to a halt, a plume of smoke and steam billowing down the platform. I raised the sash window and made to call for a porter. But before the words were out of my mouth my gaze fell upon the family's old gamekeeper, Meyerbeer.

'Master Richard, sir, Master Richard!' he cried. He disappeared, momentarily, in the pale welter of the locomotive's emissions, then, re-emerging like a spindly wraith, he sped towards our carriage, arms raised in welcome. 'Oh, so many years it's been, sir, and you now a famous man an' all. So delighted, sir. Just hand me your bags. That's right, that's it. Got the cart waiting. We'll be home in a shake. And the boy, sir!' Meyerbeer had raised himself on tiptoe and peered over the window's lip. 'Oh, what an image of his father, sir! What a quintessence of Pikery!'

I turned about, wishing to award the boy, on the occasion of this, his adoptive homecoming, a tolerant, if not beneficent, pat on the head. But his aspect remained unchanged, and my arm hung limp at my side.

'There, there,' he said, quietly, rocking the bisque-headed girl, his eyes screwed into knots of unhealthy introspection, 'there, there, my snuff stuff, my pain slut, my death strumpet, my little exhibitionistic tart. Many names you've had, in many universes, Poison, Trash, Mascara, Treacle, Panic, Impurity, and yes, yes, Despair. Ah beautiful passionate body, that never has ached with a heart! But to me, my sweet, no matter what falls, to me you will always be my darling Flagelleta.'

'Gawd love us, Master Pike,' said Meyerbeer, 'but your grandson's a poet too!'

The dogcart trundled along the meandering bridle path.

'Is it safe? I said. I thumbed over my shoulder. 'I mean, the boy . . .'

The little psychopath rode in the back, where he was able to indulge his brooding uninterrupted by displays – sham or otherwise – of grandfatherly concern.

'Quite safe,' replied Meyerbeer. 'Your brother's had the whole woodland sterilized. Did it some years ago, too. No bugaboos here, sir. Just all the nice things we can rejoice in since this land of ours again burst into bloom.'

And he was right. The forest was beautiful. Beautiful in a way it had never been in my youth. But that florescence had come at a cost. The trees of living stone that the orcs had deployed to lay waste to Europa's arable lands had died a few generations after the war's conclusion. But unknown to humanity, a cross-fertilization had taken place between the still vital pollens of Earth-Above and the plutonic spore of the Netherworld. The plant life yielded by that union of vegetable and mineral gametes was appropriately eldritch: flora that communicated a beauty infused with terror and a vertiginous sense of loss. About me, twisted forms of red, pink and carmine that sometimes brought

190

to mind a particularly exotic karst formation, sometimes a mad labyrinth of fungoidal growths, rose with desperate, twitching fingers and snatched angrily at the still fallow sky. But these impressions were nothing compared to the creeping realization – one that would have been appalling if the forest had not indeed been so beautiful – that compounding each sticky leaf, every raw, incarnadined stalk or petal, was the morphological suggestiveness of *flesh*.

The forest was like a great, open wound quivering with exposed nerves, cartilage and tendons. Or if not a wound, an interior world, perhaps, like that most perfect of interiors, the maternal belly, the shafts of sunlight that fell through its rosy pink integument a dim foretelling of a life that, for the moment at least, we were able to keep at bay.

'Yes, sir,' the old servant went on while chewing on the long stem of his pipe, 'Master Reginald has seen to it that we have no Nephilim in these parts. He has a detachment of black knights at his disposal, bless him. They've cleaned things up, and no mistake.'

'The black knights,' I mused aloud, 'are they then still with us?'

Meyerbeer – sensing, I believe, the need for discretion – said no more, and I fell to pondering on what ulterior motives my younger brother might have for retaining such an unpredictable company of mercenaries in his employ. Our borders were secure; London had even opened an embassy in Colchester; and our satellites – including the one I had made my home – were loyal. We no longer needed the black knights.

A flash of light burst through the tangled branches. As

I blinked my eyes and strove to regain the fullness of my vision – the light had been intense – I heard a voice call to me, a human voice that emulated the twitter of birdsong. My vision cleared. Meyerbeer seemed unaffected. I glanced over my shoulder, half suspecting my grandson of some inscrutable mischief. But as usual, the boy was insensible to anything but the Grand Guignol of his inmost thoughts. 'The light,' I murmured. I focused on the boscage where the afterglow of that sudden refulgence seemed to linger, coruscating like fairy dust.

'A light, Master Richard?'

'Pull up here,' I said, trying to mask the unaccountable urgency I felt.

'Really, sir, I don't think—'

'Pull up. You said the wood was sterile, didn't you?'

'Yes, but it has its *presence*, sir. A most definite presence. It has . . .' He shook his head and reined in the horse, conceding to my seigniorial authority.

I jumped down from the dogcart and walked towards the locus still defined by the residual light, orientating myself before it could wink out and leave me unsatisfied as to its origins and meaning. Either because of my susceptibility to Meyerbeer's inarticulate evocation of some indefinable 'presence' in these woods, or because some invisible power really did lurk within the twists and folds of its lurid, bucolic gorgeousness, I began to feel absurdly isolated, cut off from retreat.

I pressed forward. The undergrowth closed about me. Viciously mutated forms of brier and bramble sliced at my calves and hands. When the afterglow did, at last, suddenly disappear, it was as if I had been jerked out of a swoon; I found myself stumbling through a shadow-infested brake, lost, directionless, without a quarry. I came to a halt and looked up through the canopy and its haze of pink leaves and late afternoon sunlight – a light too near, too credible, to be confused with the unearthly beacon that had momentarily blinded me on the bridle path. A pollen-rich scent filled my nostrils, sweet, yet musky, like the hot, perfumed skin of a thousand sylvan nymphs. I lowered my gaze and scanned the undergrowth afresh. The breeze had relinquished its hold upon bloom and bud. Time had slowed, as if yearning for its own cessation. Petals that had flapped like excoriated by-products of some exquisite and fathomless torture found their longed-for quietus. Beads of sweat hung cool and unmoving on my brow. I too then felt, I think, the same yearning that this new, transfigured Nature shared – a yearning for release such as I had always felt, but refined, in that breathless moment, to such a pitch of feeling that – if I had not at once resolved to push deeper into the thick, pulpy shrubs – I might have given way to the overwhelming temptation to sink to my knees, stretch out upon the soft ground, close my eyes, and give myself up to the mystery that called out to my soul.

The vegetation was like a sucking wound – a microcosm of the great wound of the forest itself. The playground of my boyhood, which had previously offered up glimpses of familiarity, was now displaced, and displaced utterly, by the alien landscape of the new parturition. Wading through its torpid confines, tearing at branch and leaf, the air seemed filled with an almost sentient tremulousness, as if it were attempting to confer upon me the mystery of its life. I held a hand before my face. It was stained with crimson sap. It too trembled, like the air and all else. But I knew I would have no answers until I had penetrated the forest's utmost depths.

Something, I knew, waited for me there.

I soon came to a little glade. The light here was mellow, a gloaming that would not have been out of place in a reawakened Arcadia. If Arcadia's twilit bowers, that is, had ever been so frankly visceral as to suggest that one had walked into the gullet of a fabulous beast. I stood, I knew instinctively, at the forest's centre, its very vitals. And the light, despite a disparateness in intensity, was the same as that which a few minutes earlier had so assaulted my senses.

A girl-child sat upon a stool milking a cow. I was not a believer, but the manifestation of a saint, angel or the Virgin herself, could not, at that moment, have more profoundly surprised me. The sight I was met with was so unexpected, so intimate, so sanctified by the most precious of memories, that I was smitten by a sense of revelation as effectively as if I had been brought suddenly face to face with the divine.

Stooped over her pail, and consumed with milking, the child had not seemed to notice me. But then softly, she began to sing.

> *'Long years ago – fourteen, maybe,*
> *When but a tiny babe of four,*
> *Another baby played with me,*
> *My elder by a year or more;*

A little child of beauty rare,
With marv'lous eyes and wondrous hair,
Who, in my child-eyes, seemed to me
All that a little child should be!

Ah, how we loved, that child and I!
How pure our baby joy!
How true our love – and, by the bye,
He was a little boy!'

I crept forward. 'Patience?' I ventured.

She looked up and held my gaze. There could be no mistake. Here was the girl I had grown up with, the russet-haired daughter of one of our tenant farmers, a child who, in my infancy, had been my constant play-mate, and later, my adolescent love. Here was the girl whom Reggie and I had quarrelled over. The girl an old widower could not forget. The girl he still adored.

I drew a hand across my face, as if to wipe away all possibility of having fallen victim to a cruel illusion. She remained, more real than ever, as immutable as the sepia photograph I kept in my rooms in Magdalen. The pathos of her ghostly form glowed with such numinousness that I felt my throat constrict. 'But Patience you . . . you are *dead.*'

The crepuscular glade deepened to maroon. The vermilion shadows grew longer. And the fire, the holy fire that was immanent in all things here, became correspondingly more profound. The shadows burst into flame. The light was infused with a dark resplendence. Approximations of furze, hawthorne, fern and thyme shone, delirious with that indwelling *presence* that, I now knew, was beyond the articulation of not only a Meyerbeer, but all men. My heart brimmed with love; the quiescent landscape shivered. Leaves rustled like dry, chapped skin, heralding, perhaps, the approach of afrits, fetches and flibbertigibbets. And then once more all became deathly quiet, the stillness punctuated only by the dull tom-tom of my pulse.

'I'm not dead, Ritchie,' she said, her voice so at one with the spirit of place that the silence seemed unbroken. 'I'm fate. Your fate. Don't be frightened. Come close. Please. There's something I must tell you.' An inchoate smile played upon her lips. She might have been one of Krishna's playmates, about to invite me to a game of celestial hide-and-seek or some other rumbustious sport of eternity. And when the smile burst forth it was indeed so transcendental that I did as I had been bidden, careless of whatever might lurk behind her enchantment. 'Here, in the forest, we are out of time. Time is your universe, Ritchie. The universe of men. A universe that I and my kind cannot yet inherit. It is of time I would speak.'

I stood by her side. Unconcerned, she continued her work, the rhythmical noise of milk impacting against the side of her pail echoing across the glade. 'I'm sixty-eight years old,' I said. 'But you . . .' Time? She was untouched by time. And free, mercifully free, of its scars. As Epping's petrified vegetation had given way to a strange, new life, it had thrown up a strain of cowpox that had been fatally related to the causative agent of its human equivalent. What had once conferred immunity upon England's milkmaids had, in our modern world, proved their undoing. Patience had died a few days before her eighteenth birthday.

I mustered my resolve. Tentatively, I placed an open hand upon the crown of her head, much as a grown man might bestow a respectful caress upon a little niece, or grandchild; then, abandoning myself to the moment, I slipped my fingers through the silky, tumultuous locks, and allowed myself to luxuriate in her corporeality. 'You're real,' I gasped. I smelt the sweat on her, musky and sweet as the forest itself; and her flushed complexion – almost vulgar in its stark, workaday matter-of-factness – provoked in me such a hyper-aesthesia that I became giddy and feared I might black out. In certain women, the prosaic world that I usually decried was transformed, made supersensual, and the ethereal affectations I cultivated to serve as a bulwark against 'the commonplace' would be fatally undermined. 'You're not a ghost,' I added, with the simplicity of a man whose poetic defences are all down, the literalness of her truth and beauty allowing no paraphrase or abstraction. 'Yet . . .' Without forethought, I looked to where I had entered the glade. Poking above the long, tendril-like grass that grew about the clearing's perimeter were the remains of old tombstones. Seeing them, I was seized by an immediacy of recognition as potent as that which I had felt when first confronted by the resurrected Patience. 'My God. This is the place where we buried you. Amongst family, friends and beloved servants. The old forest cemetery. But how it has all changed!'

'I haven't changed, Ritchie.'

She had stopped her milking and swung about on her stool so that she looked up into my face. Grasping my hand, she gently disengaged it from her massy locks. Then she pulled it towards her lap. I hunkered, obedient to her will. Our eyes levelled. I felt my old bones protest at the strain. And unable to gainsay the years as glibly as could my dead love, I teetered backwards, my fortuitously commodious rump cushioning my fall. I crossed my legs. Groaned, then sighed. Now it was she who looked down at me. I was a child again, an overgrown boy in cut-away coat, flannel trousers and spats, about to be told some fantastic story.

'Ritchie, I *am* alive. But I am not yet fully realized. The crucible of my becoming is the same as that of the new Nature. I am human and I am perverse. But I am something else, too. Something that yet struggles to find expression.' She pressed my fingers gently within her own. Then, with the hint of a frown creasing her brow, she gazed towards the tombstones. 'They buried me just as the forests began to change. They had thought this little acre of the Netherworld dead for ever. But the soil within which I had been interred was possessed of a dark vitality. I slept, and as I slept, I dreamed that I became as the flowers, the vines, the trees and the creepers that you see about you. And when I awoke, my body *was* the forest, my spirit its spirit. I had become the waking dream that will soon consume all mankind.'

'Yes,' I said, wonderingly, 'I know the dream you speak of. It is the Ideal, the refuge of art, music and poetry.'

'You are still such a little boy, Ritchie. The new world that will shortly come has no place in it for your kind. And yet . . .'

A stillness descended, greater than any before, a

silence like that possessed by the unmoving winds that fill the deserts of everlastingness. I followed her eyes. She looked out across a border of the glade where a handful of cropped treetops allowed a view of the sharply rising countryside immediately beyond. The turrets of Castle Thorn were plainly visible.

'And yet, if humans have had their day,' she continued, 'then we sometimes still need their services.' She seemed to tire of the forest vista; her big, black eyes once more looked into my own. The pupils were so radically dilated that they might have been infused with some novel variety of belladonna. I straightened my back. Breathed deep. Loosened my studs. 'Will you help us, Ritchie? Will you be one of the mortal harbingers of the new dawn?'

'For you, Patience—'

She put a finger to my lips.

'It's the boy,' she said. 'The one you have in your charge. It may not seem so now, but he will restore your line. And *his* grandson . . .' She removed the finger; I made to follow it, like a lapdog teased with a choice morsel, my lips pursed to steal a kiss. She tapped me on the nose, in playful reproach, and smiled. 'I cannot speak of that. But remember this: it will be a Pike who ushers in the new heaven and the new hell – the union of Earth-Above and the Netherworld. It will be a Pike who will bring an end to the human world and deliver the Nephilim into Time. That is why the boy must be protected.'

I shrugged, and, despite the sombre music of the glade's stillness, almost laughed. 'Is he in such danger?'

'Your brother means to kill him, Ritchie. You have

renounced all claims to the title. With the boy out of the way, the succession falls to Reginald.'

If I still had reason to feel amused, my certainty that she was sincere, if possibly misguided, killed the laugher at its root. I shook my head. 'Reginald? We've had our disagreements, but this—'

'I cannot say more,' she said, more excitedly. 'Just remember. Please. The Nephilim cannot achieve full incarnation until the present world passes away. Then, when time comes to an end, we who have been dreams and myths will take your place, becoming real even as you become insubstantial. Please, Ritchie. I need you. The Nephilim need you.' She touched my cheek. A tear glistened on one of her long, black eyelashes. 'Help me, Ritchie. Help all the Nephilim. Look over the boy and become one with your fate. Fulfil the time opera of the Pikes!'

'Yes, of course,' I said hurriedly, 'it's just all that you say is so . . .' The sensation of her hand against my cheek gave way to that of a breeze. A vagrant outline lingered; and then all trace of her disappeared. The stillness, which until then had been disturbed but once by an all but imperceptible soughing and rasping of the leaves, was now punctuated by the susurration of insects, birdsong, and, most stridently, a holler of 'Master Richard, Master Richard! Are you all right, sir? Are you all right?'

At the entry point to the glade stood Meyerbeer, and behind him, staring at me through a crook of inflamed undergrowth with his usual baleful intensity, the boy, the loathsome, burdensome boy a ghost had urged me to guard with my life.

Time had begun again, and the destiny that it had been suggested was inextricably linked to its progress – the metaphoric 'grand opera' in which, it seemed, I played a leading part – had forced me centre stage, careless of how little I knew of plot, libretto or score.

I leaned back in the red morocco armchair. I was a big man – as corpulent as I was unkempt, some had opined – my brother, though only thirteen months my junior, slight and dapper. But if Reginald's constitution remained sprightly, then time had found other, more malicious ways, of effecting its ruin. His eyes, for instance. Their capricious, almost epigrammatic, twinkle could not disguise the smoulderings of bitterness that only three score or more years can confer. He knew, as did I, the fallacies of friendship and love, and had learned to live without benefit of the everyday affections that provide our existences with a necessary palliative. Time, it seemed, had stopped for no one but Patience.

'You seem in parlous want of irrigation, Ritchie. Pink Villain?'

'You remembered, Reggie.'

'Pink Villain it is then. Still a man with the tastebuds of a viper, I see!' He signalled to the butler to mix, pour and serve me my accustomed tipple, then dismissed him. The smoking room was softly lit. I took a long drag on my cigarette and contentedly exhaled, a blue-grey whorl issuing from post-prandial lips that still carried the greasy aftertaste of an excellent goose. We were alone. 'So how's life amongst the dreaming spires? Still serving the lapidary muse?'

'I haven't had anything published for some time, Reggie. It is put about that I am one of yesterday's men.'

'You were always the futilitarian, Ritchie.'

I raised my eyes ostentatiously towards the bookshelves. 'Better futile than utile, Reggie.'

'Now don't get into a freak, Ritchie.' He took an equally long drag on his own cigarette and then gazed meditatively into the contents of his brandy glass. 'Sick-making, really,' he continued, after sending another cerulean plume circulating above the reading-lamp to sport about the cardboard spines of his meagre, eminently functional, library. 'The amount of mis-understanding, and – let's face it, Ritchie – bad blood that there's been between us over the years, does neither of us credit.' He gave a shy little grin. 'Bad blood, to the contrary, should prove our bond. We both have orc in us, do we not? The blood that provided our enemies with the excuse to deprive us of our rights? Now there's the question of the boy. Another point of common ground. Let's bury the hatchet, eh? Let's look to the future. *Little* Ritchie's future.'

'The boy has problems.' I sighed, inclined to wax upon the boy's loathsomeness, if only to prick the bubble of my brother's condescension. 'He's quite disturbed. *His* past will not be buried so easily, I feel.'

'You say he looks . . . different.'

'You and I have got off lightly, Reggie. We have this slaty, somewhat squamous skin –' I placed an illustrative forefinger to my jowl '– but there's little else to show that our lineage is contaminated.'

'But all that was so long ago in the family's history, Ritchie. No Pike has got a goblin woman with child since the black knight, old Richard Pike the First, entered into a *mésalliance* with his accursed Gala.'

'Bad blood will out,' I said. 'The boy is ugly. Supremely ugly. Not just in aspect, but in mind, I fear. Yes, he is disturbed. Very disturbed. But you must form your own opinions, of course, when you meet him.'

'When you said the lad was feverish and should be taken straight to bed, I readily concurred, Ritchie. But perhaps I have been too precipitate.' He sipped his brandy and frowned. 'Disturbed you say?'

'Horribly disturbed.'

'Perhaps – perhaps some kind of confinement might be in order?' I lowered my eyes. I could sense his thoughts racing towards some happily life-threatening prognosis. 'I will have to consult a doctor, of course. There is no doubt medication to be had. All kinds of medication.'

'No doubt,' I said.

'Perhaps exercise would be in order, too,' he continued. 'We have a boating lake. And then there's riding, of course. And shooting. All manner of expedients, in fact.'

'You have your philosophy, Reggie, and I have mine. But since you are assuming full responsibility for the boy's upbringing, I do not consider it appropriate to say more.' I smiled with all the complaisance of a man practised in the art of cut and run. But my guard was up. I was here, not merely to discharge myself of certain responsibilities, but to take up new ones. Responsibilities that Patience had allotted me. Responsibilities I knew I could not deny. 'Let me just conclude that boating, riding and shooting, wonderfully dangerous activities that they are, should not compromise the lad's education. Have you thought of sending him away to school?'

'Away? No, no,' he said, easing himself deeper into his chair's leather folds. 'Certainly not. He shall have his education here.' He took a thoughtful lungful of smoke, then exhaled with the peremptoriness of someone eager to get down to business. 'I shall begin it by having him recognize that humanity has only two real masters: pleasure and pain, and that the moral high ground is occupied by those who promote the former at the expense of the latter.'

'Hedonic calculus,' I muttered, unable to hold my peace.

'What was that, Ritchie?'

'I said life is more than a balance of pleasure over pain. You haven't changed, Reggie. You still place your faith in the Darkling Isle's old gods, the Null, the Zero and the Void.'

He tipped his head in suave concession. 'If you like, yes. I am a Positivist, a Materialist and a Utilitarian. I believe in scientific truth. Yes, yes, I am a *Nihilist*.'

'And aestheticism?'

'I *hate* aestheticism.' Though he smiled, his hand trembled, a little brandy spilling over the rim of his glass. 'Quantity of pleasure being equal, a game of whist, poker or baccarat is as good as poetry.'

I lifted my own glass to my lips, tipped back my head and downed in one go. The cocktail, pink, villainous and indeed – in the proportions in which it had been mixed – quite infernal, released me from the inhibitions wrought by long years of brotherly dissociation.

'The quest for ultimate knowledge of Nature is misguided, Reggie. In order truly to know something it is necessary in some sense to have made it. Humanity can only hope to understand its own created universe – its world of fictions: linguistic, plastic and mathematical.'

'Spoken like a true incunabulum, Ritchie.'

'I am not, nor do I wish to be, an incunabulum, Reggie, no matter how many other Pikes have been blessed, or perhaps doubly cursed, by providing a host to the past's spiritual, or artistic, forms. But fiction is to be *understood*. Yes, and emulated, too. For extra-textual realty is being annihilated. And man must go *somewhere*.'

'Ah, now there you go again! Ultra-poetical, super-aesthetical!'

'Listen, Reggie: this age's utilitarian philosophies must die, along with its philistinism. Only the text has value in itself. But in the end, the textual world merely points the way. The material universe is but a copy of the Ideal, and art, until now, has been but a copy of a copy. I wish to go beyond mimesis. I wish to discover, or invent, if you will, *new* truths and *new* worlds. Supersensible worlds not yet conceived! A new universe we can retreat into, after this one collapses under the weight of its own contradictions.'

My brother snorted. 'Except that it won't collapse. Mankind is here to stay. A new humanity based on sound principles.'

I gazed up at the electrolier. The Pink Villain had set me on fire. A current, an inspired, poetic current, passed through my body. 'Our time has passed. Mankind is doomed to leave this world, and leave it soon. It is the Nephilim who will inherit the planet.'

'They will inherit nothing,' said my brother. He put his brandy glass down on the little table by his side, then leaned forward and stubbed out his cigarette in the chromium bulb of the long, columnar ashtray that stood between us. 'Can't take your snifter any more, eh, Ritchie? Perhaps it's time we—'

'But what do *you* expect to inherit?' I said, indeed rather drunk by now. 'This evening, I've been treated to your usual cant about how we should all seek to increase the world's small stock of pleasure, how we should legislate against pain! But what is your purpose? Your real agenda?'

He rose from his chair, took a few steps forward, and stood over me, the sallow light casting his shadow across my armchair. He had changed. No longer the *viveur* bubbling with the latest, trite ideas, he seemed old, terribly old, imbued with an ancientness that was as primordial as the curse of the Pikes.

'You are the Ideal poet,' he said. 'But I have always been a dithyrambist of the *fleshly*. It is the world I care about. This world. And if you'd have ever ventured far beyond your anaemic little Oxford, and taken a look at the pit villages, slums, bestialism and sheer wretched-ness that surrounds you and serves to bolster your privileged life, you might care, too. I am a practical man. For me, power is the thing. The power to shape, change and yes, increase that "small stock of pleasure" you so airily deride. And the only real power in this divided land of ours is London. That is my rhyme, Ritchie. And if you can't see the reason in it, too bad.'

I compressed my big, meaty hands into fists and

brought them down upon the upholstery. 'You are a fleshly sham,' I burst out. I strove to moderate my tone. I was a little cowed by the force of his proximity. 'You want to be Lord Soho. That's the truth of it. The rhyme *and* the reason, eh, Reggie?'

His face darkened. He did not reply.

'I've heard things about Castle Thorn,' I continued. 'That you keep a detachment of black knights here, for instance.'

He pulled back his shoulders. Sighted me along his aquiline nose. 'You have chosen the path of escape, Ritchie,' he said. 'But I choose engagement. Mercia is making belligerent rumblings, our satellites are growing querulous and all the time these damnable Nephilim continue to spawn. Be assured, London will take advantage.' He pivoted on his heels, turned, stepped forward, picked up the brandy glass, swiftly drained it, and slammed it back on to the table's scarred marquetry. 'But I will unite this fell nation of ours. I will be the first Pike to return to his ancestral seat. I will make London open its gates to me, Ritchie, do you hear? Or I'll put the whole bloody city to the torch! And once I am installed I will reconcile the rebel counties with the Darkling Isle's autocracy.' Without turning to face me or bid me goodnight, he slicked back an errant, grey lock with his hand, then walked across the room towards the door. 'You renounced the title a long time ago, Ritchie. You have no right to interfere.' He opened the door, and, as he stepped through, he at last glanced backwards. 'Go back to your silly ivory tower. Your life: it has been . . . *unmasculine*. Leave politics to grown-ups. Men who are not afraid to *realize* their dreams.'

And then he left.

After a few minutes, I got up. The war between us was old. And it was old wounds that prompted me to action. I would not have the lapidary muse sacrificed to a shallow, self-serving trumpeting of the 'greatest happiness of the greatest number'.

Man was made for transcendence.

I went directly to my grandson's bedchamber.

I entered, stealthily. The drapes were pulled, and the room's panelling was lustrous with moonlight. A canopied four-poster, boasting the family's armorial shield, stood before a massive wardrobe, the doors of which stood threateningly open. The furniture was familiar to me from my own childhood. It had long seemed to have been designed for the sole purpose of seeding an infant brain with nightmares. As I crept forward, I noticed the small, fidgety body on the bed, its outlines illuminated by the silvery light as softly as the ancient, cherry-wood walls. My grandson was awake. I stepped over a shuffled-off eiderdown and sat down on the mattress's edge.

On arriving at Castle Thorn I had sent the child directly to his room. Meyerbeer had escorted him. I had wished, of course, to keep my grandson out of harm's way until I could properly ascertain the measure of my brother's intentions. But the 'fever' that I had cited as a pretext for his seclusion had seemed to have actualized itself, as if to task me for telling such a bald lie. The boy's glazed eyes made no acknowledgement of my presence and he was covered in a patina of sweat. I was uncertain what to do, or even say. Then I noticed the doll that sat propped up against the bedside lamp.

'They have electricity, here,' I said. 'My brother's very modern. Would you like the light on?' I reached out to pull the lamp's cord.

'Don't touch her,' said the boy, very quietly.

'I was just . . .' I let my arm drop to my side, content to sit in the moon-bathed shadows. To one side of the doll stood a jar. Peering closer, I saw that it contained a cockroach. 'Did you bring that with you, too?' I said, with resigned disgust. The boy turned his head on the pillow. The whites of his eyes shone luminously in the darkness.

'Do you know what I think of, when I lie awake on nights like this?'

'Please tell,' I said, expecting the worse.

'Of the East,' he said. 'It's in the East that all will be decided. The Far East, where our family line was accursed.'

'Ah yes, the *first* Richard Pike. I remember telling you, of course.'

'Father told me,' he said. 'And other things, too. About how our line will remain accursed until we expiate our crimes. That's why I have to go there. If I'm to be Lord Soho, that is. But I think of other things, too, when I lie like this, with the shadows all about. I think of the other world. The world that's my home.'

'And what world is that?'

'I don't know its name,' he said, his eyes widening with what might have been longing, or fear, 'but I'm most near it in the dark. Lying in bed. Or wandering through midnight alleys, deserted warehouses, the towpaths of disused canals, late-night underpasses and dockyards. Yes, that is when I sense the nearness of my home. The one I long to return to. A nameless place I only half recall, a place of violent ecstasy and beauty.'

I looked away. The perturbation I felt whenever he held me with his stare had returned. 'You speak like many a Pike before you,' I said. My voice was as quiet as his own. I was conscious that I could not disguise its tremor. 'We are invested with something alien that is only partly accounted for by our hereditary curse. Yes, there is something in us more alien by far . . .'

'Father would say it was the sword.'

'The sword?'

'Our family heirloom. *Espiritu Santo*.'

'Ah,' I sighed. '*That* sword.'

'Its spirit is in us. An alien spirit. At least, that's what father would tell me.'

'That is what *I* would tell *him*,' I said. 'But the sword is lost. As are we. There is another holy spirit abroad. It informs the forests and woods. And soon, very soon, I think it will displace us, spirit *and* body.'

I tensed, and cast a swift glance at the supine boy, unaccountably heedful that he might be about to sit up on the bed and spring at me like a feral animal. I need not have feared. His eyes shone, wolf-like, out of the shadows, but his insomnious form was otherwise expressive only of the prickly agitation felt by anyone who has to suffer the unremitting consciousness of a long, hot summer's night.

'But why' – I found myself studying the jar and its skittering occupant – 'the cockroach?'

I heard the boy's feet ruck the bottom sheet as he once

more surrendered to his fidgeting. 'Uncle believes that pleasure is all, does he not? That pain must be banished from this world?'

'Yes,' I said, surprised at the boy's intuitive grasp. 'But much of what he says is rhetorical. It is power that he wants.'

'Of course. He is a Pike. He knows, deep down, like you know, and I know, that pleasure and pain are one. And that happiness is a lie. A vulgar lie. Power is all. The blood and the life. Power is beauty.'

The cockroach's skittering became more intense. Repeatedly, it tried to scale the jar, only to collapse upon its back. Its feelers whirled like sabres. Then it charged at the walls of its glassy confinement, as if it would smash through, leap and tear at my throat in compensation for my grandson's impassivity. The noise it made filled the room. And then the noise found its way inside my head. An army of its confederates had crawled into my ears and infested my brain, all to the greater glory of the insect empire.

'The roach knows too,' said the boy. 'Isn't she superb? She loves power. The power that is death. Oh yes, my pretty, we hear you. We hear what you say. You want to die in the arms of your beloved!'

And then the insect noise disappeared, overwhelmed suddenly by the shrill, metallic ululation of the thing at the open window.

I shot up from the bed so fast that my foot snagged on a corner of the rug. I was sent sprawling. The titanic vibrations engendered by the infelicitous meeting of three-hundred pounds of flesh with the floor amounted to a minor earthquake. Several picture frames slid from the wall; the night table fell over. Clocks, chamber pot, crockery and other less collectable but more noisome items jumped into the air and then smashed. The barrage ceased. On rising – I was as swift about it as my bulk, years and panicked heart would allow – I came to a swift assessment of the situation. And I knew that if I did not act at once, both I and the boy would be killed.

Countless genotypes figured amongst the variegated life that had emerged from England's new forests. Some appeared human, like the form I had met with some hours previously. Such creatures were shapeshifters. Non-corporeal. But the creature into whose eyes I stared was wholly flesh and blood. Therein lay its danger. One that, if less grave than that presented by its ghostly brothers and sisters, was more immediate. In the brief interlude of my pratfall and recovery it had pulled itself up on to the window ledge, where it crouched, ready to spring.

It was a sphinx. I had, until now, seen such creatures only in copperplate engravings. Like so many of its kind, it was beautiful.

Its slim, graceful body was that of a great cat. Across the moon-kissed fur of its shoulders and haunches – limned with silver thread – were two folded, gently curving wings. And its face was that of a young woman. The delicate, Mediterranean features were crowned with a long-tiered coiffure of black curls, like that of an ancient Greek or Egyptian princess. The keening had stopped, and the creature's satiny gaze darted from the boy to me and back again, the uncertain flick of its tail underlining the obvious confusion it felt at my unscheduled presence.

I rushed the thing, yelling some hoarse warning to my grandson as I crashed past the bed.

I need not have been so solicitous. Bent, as I was, on frustrating the sphinx's patently murderous plans, I had not seen the boy take the twelve-gauge shotgun out from under the bedsheets; did not hear him cock its triggers; neither had I indeed recognized the thunderous discharge for what it was until I had had time to come to a sudden halt, hunker, and watch – with shoulders pulled up to my ears – the Nephilim splay its claws, forsake its hold of the sill, leap backwards, and, with a single, piercing shriek, vanish into the night.

I placed a hand upon my chest, unable to believe that my manically beating heart was still intact. Then I straightened myself and staggered to the window. Gingerly poking my head between the thin, ogival casement and out into the night, I surveyed the treetops. Their shadows revealed nothing. Neither did the ground two floors below show evidence of a body or blood. Not wishing to make further reconnaissance – I feared I might at any moment be rewarded by the sight of the thing bearing down on me, or meet with an abrupt decapitation – I retreated inside.

After I had locked the window I turned about. My grandson knelt on the bed, the shotgun still against his shoulder. He squinted down the sights, the smoking barrels following me as I moved across the room.

'I'm not going to hurt you,' I said. 'I'm here to help. Really I am. Now put it down.' As I neared, he reluctantly let the gun sag in his hands so that its muzzle pointed towards the mattress.

'I fired both shells anyway,' he murmured, talking as

if to himself, his gaze averted and taking in the broken glass and peppered drapes.

I leaned over the bed and grasped the gun by its barrels. One tug and it slipped out of his hands. I pulled it across the sheets, towards me. I broke it; saw that what he had said was true; then placed the gun upon the floor.

'Did I hit it?' he said. He rubbed at his head with his knuckles as if trying to shed the scarious folds that covered the bumpy flesh.

'I don't know.' My whole body shook with the effort of catching my breath, from the knowledge of what my grandson was capable of, and the apprehension of what he might do next.

'It's Uncle, isn't it?' He lay back and stared up at the ceiling. 'Uncle wants me dead. Fat chance. I'm no roachboy. I'm a lord. A master. I fight back. But what do we do now?' Before I could think of a suitable answer, the door was thrown open. Between the jambs stood Meyerbeer, a shotgun like the one the boy had used raised and pointing irresolutely into the bedchamber's shadows.

Behind him, emerging from the darkness of the hallway, to be illumined by the dusty electrolier outside, was my brother, the look of perplexity and outrage that he affected as sham, I knew, as his philosophy.

'I've dismissed Meyerbeer, of course,' he said at breakfast.

'I don't really see that it's his fault, Reggie. The boy is persuasive. Cunning. A subtle child. Besides which, it was certainly lucky – and lucky for us all – that he *did* prevail upon old Meyerbeer to loan him the gun.'

'It's unforgivable. Someone could have been killed. No, really Ritchie, Meyerbeer has to go.'

'The threat was real, Reggie. I saw it. Nephilim. In the form of a sphinx.'

He shook his head and shovelled a forkful of bacon and egg off the *rose Pompadour* Sèvres and into his mouth.

'I've told you, Ritchie, the forest has been sanitized. Look, I'll get you to meet the captain of the black knights. He'll vouch for what I've said. He's billeted a few miles down the road. Take the boy with you if you like. Drop of fresh air and all that. I'm sure the captain will—'

'And it's not the only thing I've seen, Reggie,' I interrupted, setting my silverware upon the mat and gazing across the long, highly polished table.

'What do you mean?' he said, his face frozen in a mid-masticatory grimace.

'Do you remember Patience, Reggie?'

He too put down his knife and fork. Then he put his hands together underneath his chin, steepled his fingers and let them take the weight of his jaw. He began to chew again, slowly, with infinite care, as if eager to conceal as yet unsuspected machinations.

'Ah yes. Of course. Patience. The cause of our estrangement, Ritchie. Never forgotten. No indeed. Not poor little Patience.'

'If there *are* Nephilim in these parts, like that sphinx I saw last night – chimeras you're either too abashed, or too circumspect, to talk about – then other Nephilim will undoubtedly be present here, too.'

'I really can't see what you might be alluding to, Ritchie.'

'Why did you sanitize the forest, Reggie?' I sucked the fat off the tip of my right index finger. 'Is it because you fear her? Is it because you fear Patience?' I drew the wet finger across the sheeny black table top. A snail-like trail glistened in its wake.

He looked at me very steadily. 'You're a child still. You really are. You and that boy make quite a pair. But some things are better put behind one. Patience, for instance. It seems you have not outgrown her, Ritchie. Just as you have not outgrown your other youthful follies, such as the idealism you affect, your *décadence*.'

'She's alive, Reggie,' I said. 'I don't believe she's one of those you *can* kill.'

For a time, and it seemed a long time, he said nothing. Then, as he took up his fork, reached out to the serving dish, stabbed a rasher of bacon and transferred it directly to his mouth, his coolness at last gave way to undisguised antipathy.

'Mankind has been too obsessed with the past. Our desire to rediscover the science and art of the Ancients has been like some absurd need to recover some mythical, lost innocence. But the thing about innocence, Ritchie, is that you only really know what it is after it's been lost. Truly lost. In engaging in hopeless attempts to resurrect it we become the past's slaves. We must resist such enchantments. There's no going back. We need to be our own men. Patience? Forget about her. She was nothing but trouble.'

My brother was always a poor liar when it came to matters of love. And in his eyes I saw that he still wanted her for his bride. Wanted her so much, in fact, that he might well try to kill her to prevent her loving anyone else.

The boy and I sat on the village green. The road we had taken had led through an area of cleared forest, where my brother planned to erect 'model homes' for those of his labourers employed in the mechanized dairy industry he was in the process of establishing. But there was no sign of mechanization here. Only pleasant reminders of childhood. Sights that summoned up the world that had existed before the new industrialization had spread its blight across the land.

Eager to get myself and the boy out of Castle Thorn for a few hours I had taken up my brother's suggestion to walk into the village and meet the captain of the black knights. But now I had arrived I felt disinclined to follow through. I might, after all, be leading the boy into a trap.

Still, follow through I must. I needed to appease Reginald. Humour him. As yet, I had nothing but the prophetic entreaties of a long-dead girl and my own suspicions to calibrate the extent of his guilt. That he was a cad I had no doubt. That he was engaged in dirty business I was certain. But despite all that had occurred, I marvelled to think of him as a murderer.

I watched the hands of the church clock – as notably regular, I hoped, as the captain's drinking habits – move towards opening time. The meeting would be in a public place – the village pub that stood opposite. My brother had wired ahead; the captain, it seemed, would be waiting for us in his customary snug. No assassination, I tried to reassure myself, could possibly be attempted before witnesses.

Ten minutes to go. I looked about, my stomach fluttering with misgiving. Village maidens strolled along the margins of the pond. The sight of them at first calmed me, so much did each one remind me of Patience; and in that calmness I was lifted out of time and filled with bitter-sweet delight; but their conversation, when it became audible, brought me smartly back to earth. It was unutterably distressing. A colloquy anti-idyllic in the extreme.

'Oh, That Reginald Pike, you mean, the master of the manor!'

'Such a darling! So practical!'

'I adore a practical man.'

'A man flash, pragmatic and utilitarian!'

'A man who puts the sex in sexagenarian!'

'But while he, the very cynosure of our eyes and hearts, remains icy insensible – what have we to strive for?'

Handsome, *comme il faut*, a dashing man of the world whose family curse only lent him a hint of dangerous glamour, my brother's erotic successes had been as legion and effortless as mine had been modest and hard won. Indeed, even my late wife once admitted that, if it had not been for the long years I had spent refining my wit, wardrobe and *boutonnière*, I would have likely been doomed to a life of fat, poetic celibacy.

The maidens passed by. Their mortifying chatter receded. And I was left alone with the boy.

During our sojourn on the green I had tried to prevent myself gazing upon him, but it had proved impossible.

His presence demanded attention, like some terrible accident to which people are drawn by appalled wonder rather than any genuine sense of empathy. In his hands he held Flagelleta, recently stripped of her little dress. The denuded minikin had been subjected to some kind of surgery. One arm was missing. The other limbs curiously transposed. And a vent had been cut in her abdomen. About her neck, tied to a piece of thread, was the corpse of the cockroach that he had kept beside his bed in a jar. 'She loved the games men played with death, where death must win . . .' cooed the boy, toying with the doll's moulting hair.

'I often think of your sister, you know,' I said. 'Now *Jane* was a good girl.'

'Jane's dead,' he answered, perfunctorily. Both my granddaughter and her nurse had perished in a boating accident. Little Ritchie had been the only survivor. My son's heart had been torn in twain. Remembering his tears, I could not help feel that he, and perhaps all of us, had been betrayed, then as now, by the callous detachment of his heir.

I found myself extemporizing an admonitory piece of doggerel.

> *'Gentle Jane was as good as gold,*
> *She always did as she was told;*
> *She never spoke when her mouth was full,*
> *Or caught bluebottles their legs to pull,*
> *Or spilt plum jam on her nice new frock,*
> *Or put white mice in the eight-day clock,*
> *Or fostered a passion for alcohol,*
> Or vivisected her last new doll.'

The boy's caresses of the porcelain amputee continued unabated. As did his slavering. But a tendency to essay an analysis of his paraphilia – and, I suppose, the more general disaffection revealed by his lamentable manners – was overtaken by the arrival on the green of a stout woman who seemed on terms of more than passing acquaintance with the sickening school of maidenly infatuation that had, by now, lapped the pond, and was again heading my way.

'Fools!' she exclaimed. The company started and then turned to her.

'I beg your pardon?' said one of the bolder girls.

'Fools and blind! The man loves – wildly loves!'

'Reginald? But whom? None of us!'

'No, none of us. His weird fancy has lighted, for the nonce, on the White Lady, Patience!'

'The White Lady? Oh, it cannot be!' they thrilled, in a chorale whose euphony was – due to my own sudden, intense, almost lyrical state of perturbation – lost to me, despite a certain taste I had for young women given to the shameless, stratospheric flights of the coloratura.

I got to my feet.

'Madam,' I said, engaging the stout one's attention. 'May I speak with you?' The woman looked at me a little sharply and then, with that resolve typical of the matronly kind, marched to where I stood. There, with feet planted wide and arms folded across her capacious breasts, she silently dared me to further utterance. 'Patience – you have seen her?' I enquired, nervously.

'You are new here, sir?'

'In a manner of speaking. But this White Lady you speak of – how is it that a wraith may enter into association with a human, such as this Reginald Pike?'

She shrugged. 'I am not sure. We have all had sightings of Patience, of course. The dead milkmaid is something of a legend. But I affirm that I have seen her and Mr Pike together. Sometimes I use the stables at Castle Thorn to go riding. It agrees with my health. And on more than a few afternoons, after I have returned from a hearty canter, I have seen strange goings on. Bah! Only yesterday I caught them in the dairy. He was eating fresh butter with a tablespoon. And today they say he is not well!'

'Only yesterday?' Only yesterday, I thought, she had as good as declared my brother her enemy. Why then should she choose to be so intimate? 'That's impossible,' I concluded. The woman was envious, deluded, perhaps a little mad.

'You are frank, sir. Overly frank, perhaps. After all, we have not yet been introduced!'

'Madam, I fear I am to be for ever denied that boon.' I turned my back on the garrulous hag and, taking the boy by the arm, began to traverse the green in the direction of the public house.

'It's but a fleeting fancy of his,' she called after me. 'It will quickly wear away. And then –' and her voice fell to a mellow, if penetrating, whisper '– oh, Reginald, if you but knew what a wealth of golden love is waiting for you, stored up in this rugged old bosom of mine, the milkmaid's triumph would be short!'

But her lovelorn ramblings had not the power to distract. The church clock had struck the hour. It was opening time.

*

The Order of the Black Knights was some five centuries old. It had been established in pre-Christian times at the height of the wars with the Netherworld. After the orcs had been driven permanently into their subterranean lairs, and soon after the first missionaries had arrived from the East, those knights whose device had formerly been the Null, the Zero and the Void took vows of poverty and chastity and became the mailed fist of the church militant. They dedicated themselves to securing the king's highways and subduing the marauding bands who wandered the wastes. At last, their military and financial power grew so enormous that they were seen to threaten England's autocracy. Persecution followed. They were accused of blasphemies. Crimes of the spirit and irregularities of the flesh. Many were arrested. Some were hanged. The others, stripped of their status, retreated into the Darkling Isle's wilder counties to offer their services as gentlemen of fortune.

One of their more notorious members had been Richard Pike the First, swordsman par excellence, orc-slayer of renown and my great-great-great-great-great-grandfather. The fact that I was something of an honorary member of the Order – if by the most distant of familial ties – and, perhaps more importantly, because I was the elder sibling of this particular detachment's paymaster, put the captain and I on easy terms. Not that he entertained warm feelings towards Reginald. On the contrary, I discovered that he and his men greatly resented the manner in which the old satyr had the local women at his beck and call. Some of his knights had taken to trumpeting 'that Utilitarian nonsense' as he put it, in a vain attempt to regain the ladies' favours. And the gruffness with which he expressed his disdain of stooping to such a course himself came perilously near to a mutinous reproof of his temporal master. I allowed myself a cautious, inward smile. The captain, far from being my brother's uncritical henchman, was, perhaps, an unlooked-for ally.

The strong ale did much to contribute to our ever-increasing bonhomie and, to this effect, I bought round after round, eager to foster, on his part, at least, manifold indiscretions. But try as I might, I could learn little about my brother and the tendencies he had lately revealed towards politico-military adventurism. The captain's attention was all upon the boy.

'Yes indeed,' he said, in reply to one of my grandson's queries, 'our mission is as it has always been: to extirpate the perverse, and so cleanse the planet. New manifestations, such as the Nephilim, have, of late, been our particular focus. But we also actively seek out human recidivists who cling to perverse creeds: those slaves in Mercia and Northumberland, for instance, who refuse to be emancipated, despite the efforts of so many brave men.' I put a hand to my mouth, in imitation of one inspired to meditate upon such a fine encapsulation of high moral purpose. In reality, I strove to hide a smile. The knights would often reveal themselves to be as much mirror images of the vices they deplored as the general public in one of its ridiculous, but, it seemed to me, increasingly rabid, fits of censure. Righteous hatred allowed an indulgence in fantasies and conduct that men like the captain normally would not admit to countenancing. It was a classic case of pointing the finger in order to divert suspicion. 'Let those slaves fall to the sword if they cannot walk true,' he continued. 'Let them go to the grave along with their pox-ridden masters. And let the lime and the worms take all their feeble-minded talk of love, death and transcendence!'

The boy stared past the captain at one of the buxom young serving-maids who carried tankards of foaming ale across the room. Then he sipped at his *cassis à l'eau* and shifted on the rough wooden bench. The hand that he kept upon his lap tightened about the doll. His knuckles whitened.

'The perverse is amongst us,' said my grandson. 'I see it. I see it everyday. We humans must hunt it down. Hunt it down without mercy!'

The captain beamed with avuncular pride.

'I have heard you have done a pretty thorough job about these parts already,' I said, addressing the black knight, but keeping a wary eye on the flushed, over-excited child. 'My brother speaks warmly of the way you and your men have sanitized his woods.'

'Ah, but it will not be enough.' He sighed, the light of zealotry kindling his eyes. 'I fear no amount of killing will be enough. Have you read your Bible of late?'

'Not for some time, I fear,' I said, apprehensive of the conversation's somewhat austere change of tack.

'I would refer you to Genesis, chapter six, verses one through four: "And it came to pass, when men began to multiply on the face of the Earth, and daughters were born unto them, that the sons of God saw the daughters of men that they were fair; and they took them wives of all which they chose . . . There were giants on the Earth

224

in those days; and also after that, when the sons of God came in unto the daughters of men, and they bare children to them, the same became mighty men which were of old, men of renown."'

Pushing aside his tankard, he leaned across the table, tapping the side of his nose with his middle finger. 'The passage is, of course, a prophecy concerning the last days. That is, those in which we live. The word that is translated "giant" is, in Hebrew, "Nephilim", which means, "those who fell, or the fallen ones". These Nephilim: they are fallen angels, the same rebel ben Elohim whose self-imploded universe – parallel, but quite alien to our own – infected Earth with the soul-particles to which we may trace the original contamination of the human race some four and a half thousand years ago. These creatures that haunt our reborn forests, whether physical or immaterial, represent a final attempt by evil spirits from beyond the confines of our own space and time to colonize us!'

I found myself studying the broken network of capillaries that lined the captain's cheeks, their disconnectedness symbolic, somehow, of my own fragmented understanding of the past. And not merely of the collective past, but the personal, too. Ever since Patience had died, a discord as profound as that of the Dark Ages had divided me from myself. And it often seemed that only the faint echo of ancient song kept me sane. But my aestheticism had failed me. Like other men, I had become unreal; unreal without being fictive. And in despair I sometimes felt that my jangling, off-key life would be resolved only if I acknowledged defeat and followed mankind into the blessed anonymity of history's aether.

I looked down into my tankard and forced myself to reply, knowing that if I did not re-engage with the world, then I might simply fade away. 'I always thought,' I said, 'that the tribes of the perverse had died out; become extinct, as eventually do all forms of life. Only the orcs are still with us, they say. But buried underground, in their Netherworld haunts, there to languish until the end. The Nephilim seem to represent something else entirely. Something new.'

'You are wrong! The perverse lives!' he replied quickly. 'It is manifest! It is everywhere! It seeks to merge with and corrupt the bloodline of Adam! Because of God's promise to send a redeemer through the first man's kin! By such corruption, it seeks to prevent the Second Coming of Our Lord, Jesus Christ!' He slapped the table top with the flat of his hand. His eyes shone not only with zeal, but with the mad, libidinous fire of the tribes, orcs, half-men and slaves who had roamed the Earth during the Dark Ages. For mankind was all that was left of the perverse. That we too would soon pass from the world was, I knew, a blessing. 'The boy is indeed right,' the captain continued. 'The perverse is amongst us. But Christ is coming, mark my words. And he will come with a sword. Let there be on that day an end to all flesh and a resurrection of the spirit of Man! "And God saw that the wickedness of man was great in the Earth, and that every imagination of the thoughts of his heart was only evil continually. And it repented the LORD that he had made man on the Earth, and it grieved him at his heart. And the LORD said, I will destroy man whom I have created from the face of the Earth . . ."'

'Yes!' piped the boy, his eyes grown large. 'It must all

end in the great death! The great consummation! The marriage of above and below!' The captain grinned and tousled the boy's hair.

'I like this one, indeed I do. Would you like to be a black knight, young Richard? Would you care to dedicate yourself to the extermination of the Nephilim? If so, be warned. We have only seen their shadow. There will be ones to come greater than any man can comprehend. Angel-demons, terrible and beautiful. But we will fight them unto the very last, will we not boy? We will not submit!' And he gave the boy's hair such a roisterous tug that I thought he would part scalp him. 'God damn, but he's a pleasant rascal!'

My suspicions of the captain vanished as of that moment. This black knight did not seem capable of much duplicity; his fanaticism would not have allowed it. Reginald, I decided, was acting alone. Or at least, without benefit of counsel. But why, I wondered, had he suggested this meeting? Perhaps simply to get the boy and I out of the castle grounds so that he might conduct certain business in private.

An assignation with Patience, perhaps . . .

If I were to test the supposition I knew I would have to disencumber myself of the boy's company.

'Would you show him round your garrison, captain? I'm sure Richard would be most interested to hear you recount more of your life and work.'

Though I believed the captain to harbour no ill-intentions towards the boy the stratagem, of course, was still rash. But the sudden urgency I felt to return to Castle Thorn and have it out with my brother overrode all sense of prudence. The boy's fidgeting grew colossal.

227

He pulled at the doll's hair and twisted its violated limbs. And then a sound, which was almost like a dog's whimpering, emerged from behind his thin, blood-drained lips.

'Really, Grandfather? May I?'

It was the only time, in our short re-acquaintance, that his moody truculence had given way to a rudimentary state of courtesy.

'I'd be very happy to show him all there is!' interjected the captain. 'Most happy!'

And so I left them, the captain quaffing his ale, the boy playing with his *cassis*, each finding in the other's company a measure of familial contentment greater than any I or my brother, or perhaps any other human, could provide.

Reginald called the trees that formed the avenue leading to Castle Thorn's front door cherry trees, but their resemblance to the few examples of that genus that had survived the mutative incursions of the Netherworld was cursory. Carmine of bole, bough and berry – a garishness that brought to mind a kind of vegetable maquillage – and festooned with lanterns, these fantastically clipped whores of the new parturition cast their toparian shadows before my feet, as if soliciting me to enter their embrace. Oblivious to their painted charms, I stepped over the outlines of heraldic beasts and the chimeric shapes of some of the more familiar Nephilim, and proceeded towards the castle.

The evening was close. The castle's grey coping seemed to deliquesce into the ashy light. But though indistinct, the windows of the dining room had been clearly flung wide open, the air so still that I could hear cutlery being set upon the table preparatory to my return. As I approached I heard another sound, less distinct, but so insistent that I came to a stop and strained to identify its nature and the direction from which it came.

The sound was like that of a steam, or perhaps even petrol, engine – a low, deep-throated rumble – and it seemed to owe its origin to the dairy. Immediately I recalled the details of what the village matron had said regarding the supposed tryst between my brother and Patience – 'Only yesterday I caught them in the dairy' – a tryst that put an ambiguous gloss on the evil events of the small hours. Was the ghost I had encountered in the forest truly the shade of my long-dead love, or some piece of diabolic stage machinery, trumped up by God knows whom? I determined to investigate, a sliver of jealous rage such as I had not felt for over fifty years – its ridiculous inappropriateness unable to dull its force – pricking at my heart, as if it would turn it to an ulcer.

I left the path and moved across the lawn as silently as I was able, trusting to the deeper shadows that lay hereabouts to conceal my progress.

The dairy was a comparatively small building, no more than a commodious shed, really, that my brother had had erected in order to conduct his experiments in automated farming. But it was, I knew, equipped with the latest electrical lights. Therefore I was surprised – the surprise swiftly translating itself into foreboding – to discover that the only illumination it boasted at present was the flickering that one associates with a taper.

Something clandestine was afoot.

I drew up to the door. It was ajar, a crack of feeble light allowing me to squint inside. And though the interior of the dairy was correspondingly dim, the sight that I was met with was infused with such a blaze of depravity that I involuntarily held up a hand to shield my eyes, blinded in equal measures by disgust, horror and recognition.

Half woman, half animal, the sphinx lay on an oriental mat, its chin upon the ground, its hindquarters raised into the air. My brother coupled with it, one hand sunk deep into the fur of the lustrous flanks, the other stroking the throat, then moving down the lynx-spotted body. Both man and chimera glistened, as if with the dew of night and death. And as my brother undulated his hips in sensual communion his leman purred, filling the air with that rasping sound that I had confused with some mechanical device. Tail coiled about human thigh. Then ears flicked, as if at a passing insect.

The sphinx turned its head towards the door.

Black satin eyes fell upon me. The eyes hardened, leered, became like polished jet. Then burst into flames.

I prepared to flee. But as I went to step backwards something emerged from the shadows that held me to the spot. Near where sphinx and human enjoyed unnatural congress was a woman. And yet not a woman, for she was, I knew, as unnatural, in her own way, as the therianthropic monstrosity on the mat; as unnatural as my brother.

Patience.

All eyes were upon me now. The hot eyes of the

sphinx, heavy with a surfeit of pleasure, those of
Patience – like fantastic moons shivering in some stagnant lake – and my brother's own, clouded, mad. The
old rakehell spasmed, cried out, his hands tearing at
flesh and fur; the sphinx emitted a shriek. And then
man and beast fell apart, and the sweat-slicked body of
Reginald Pike lay supine upon the mat, his ribcage
shaking with convulsive laughter.

The sphinx fawned at his feet then came to rest with
its head upon his knee, stretched laterally to the pale
exclamation mark of his head and torso. It extended its
tongue and ran it lazily about its lips. And all the while,
its eyes never left me.

With a small creak, befitting a modestly haunted
house, the door opened, exposing me to full view.
Patience stood on the threshold.

'Come in, Ritchie,' she said, her voice soft and sad.
'Come in, and let us resolve matters once and for all. I
have an itch to return to eternity.'

I entered. If it had not been for the two Nephilim in
whose presence I stood, one, if not consciously malign
then possessed, I would have supposed, of an
appropriately savage animality, the other, my own
Patience, translated by all that had transpired into an
unknown, equally alien, and perhaps far more
dangerous quantity, then I would have walked up to
Reginald, slapped his face, and demanded an
explanation for all that had passed since I had arrived
at Castle Thorn little more than twenty-four hours ago.
As it was, what with the sphinx greeting my approach
with an ominous growl, and the gossamer-like, if
strangely corporeal sensation of Patience's hand upon

my forearm, I restrained myself, bit my tongue and swallowed the strong, nay, almost poetic language of reproach that had risen into my mouth like a haemorrhaging of my very genius. It little mattered. I believe my thunderous visage said it all.

'I really hadn't expected such a display of mulish distemper from *you*, Ritchie,' my brother said.

'I want to know everything,' I replied, as dispassionately as I could, 'about your intentions regarding the title. And your homicidal intentions towards the boy. And, and . . .' I desisted before the apoplexy I heard knocking on the door of my skull made good its threat to make my acquaintance.

'And why I have a yen to copulate with the beasts of the field?' My brother smiled, playfully tugging at the sphinx's amber hackles. 'Pleasure is all, Ritchie. Pleasure is all.'

'The black knights,' said Patience, 'could not kill *all* the chimeras that live in these parts. And so it is that over the last few months I have been able to present your brother with certain gifts in lieu of myself. But that is all over. Tonight I am promised to him. I must, it seems, become his final, most absolute pleasure. The one he says will blot out what has until now been an immitigable pain.'

'Promised? But what you said yesterday, in the forest—'

I turned my back on her. And not only because of the heartbreak that she had once again occasioned, this time from the other side of the grave, but because I felt I simply could not risk taking my gaze off the sphinx.

'Ah yes,' she said, 'of all my gifts, it is the sphinx that

he loves the most. A sphinx couchant is, after all, part of your coat of arms, is it not? I think it satisfies his vanity, for he really does mean to become Lord Soho.'

'She gave it to me when news arrived of your son's death,' said my brother, slurring a little, as if with the intoxication of victory. 'She made me swear not to hurt the boy!' He again fell to emitting wild peals of laughter.

'But he wanted more,' said Patience. 'He always wants more. And tonight I have promised the last thing I have to give. Love must be unselfish, must it not? Please, try to understand. What I do I do for little Ritchie.'

'Because *I* have failed,' I said, miserably. 'Because I will always fail.'

'Because you are Ideal, Ritchie,' she said. 'It was wrong of me to ask for your help. You are not meant for this world.' Her voice grew strained, brittle. 'It does not matter. Reggie has agreed to let your grandson live.'

I ground my teeth so hard that the cattle stirred in their pens and began a sullen lowing.

'I can't allow myself to hope that he may be otherwise appeased,' Patience continued. 'Not after last night. Not after I discovered that I had inadvertently provided him with the very means to *destroy* the child.'

I shook my head furiously. 'Don't do it. He's not a man of his word. You must see that, for God's sake.' I held my arms at my sides, my big, stooped form bloated with such despair that it seemed to me that I filled half the dairy. Then, as my despair increased and my bulk seemed to expand the more, with several buttons of my waistcoat set to pop, I felt the void surrender to my mass. Despair was all. And yet it was at that very moment of utter hopelessness that I found the strength to fight back.

I concentrated upon Reginald. 'Modern thought is distinguished from ancient by its cultivation of the relative spirit in place of the absolute. But I am not a modern. I am a man, as you have so rightly intuited, who owes his allegiance to the past. I do not believe, as you do, brother, that good may result from mere expedience. No. Your philosophy is a mask under which hides the face of a jackal.' I swung about. My dead sweetheart looked upon me wonderingly. 'I believe in absolutes, Patience. In absolute values. Give the boy into my charge. Trust me. I *will* protect him with my life. I swear it.'

I am not sure what had prompted me to make such a declaration towards a child that, until then, I had longed to be rid of. Perhaps it was the thought of losing Patience again, if not to the grave, then to another, infinitely more sinister death. The death that was modernity, the shoddy, mean-spiritedness of an age I had spent my life trying to escape from.

But escape was no longer an option.

My brother grinned, mockingly. 'Ah,' he gasped, 'you and your absolutes, Ritchie.' He rolled on to his side, and, propping up his head with a hand, gazed up at Patience. 'Listen: rights, human or otherwise, are the result of law; from real law come real rights; but from imaginary laws, such as he – damned unacknowledged legislator that he is – from law of imagination come imaginary rights! He cannot protect you, my dear. Only I can.'

'Am I to be your pet then, Reggie?' she said. 'The last

survivor of the Nephilim, protected by Reginald Pike's *laws*? You tried to kill me—'

'Yes, because I loved you!'

'Ha!' I exploded. 'Love?'

'She was always a danger,' he said, as he disentangled himself from the sphinx and hauled himself languidly into a sitting position. He stared at me from behind a hank of disordered hair. 'A danger to me. And to you, Ritchie. She was always the one who would destroy us. Look what she did to us when she was merely human! And now her power is such that to love her is to risk losing the world.'

'It was always so,' I said.

'And we have always been her slaves. Slaves to the past! But if I cannot kill her, then I will make her *my* slave.' He looked Patience keenly in the eye. 'If you become my bride, I shall ensure that the Nephilim are granted the right to exist.'

I too turned to address Patience. 'Right to exist? He'll enslave you all. And the ones that offer resistance will be hunted down by his black knights.' I swung about. 'Isn't that so, Reggie?'

'Oh, why don't you leave well alone. You are committed to your aestheticism, are you not? Go back to your cloisters and books.'

'My aestheticism? I'll renounce it. Become an ordinary man. Ordinary enough, at least, to acquit myself of the responsibilities of a guardian to my grandson.'

He broke into such a fit of cachinnation as put his post-coital laughter to shame.

'Anything to best me, eh, Ritchie. You're as much a sham as I am.'

Patience darted to my side. 'If you are sincere, Ritchie,' she said. 'If you are *truly* sincere, then . . .'

My brother's laughter subsided. His brow corrugated with calculation, but also, I was pleased to note, a little fear.

'I hope you are not going back on your bargain, my precious. Your powers are confined to the forest. You cannot resort to bedevilment here. But my lovely pet Mitsou' – the sphinx put its head in his lap and rolled its head appreciatively – 'could, contrariwise, tear you limb from limb. That is, if you persist in assuming that pretty, fleshly shape.'

She put herself between me and my brother. Glancing over her shoulder she met my eyes. 'Ritchie?'

'I mean it, Patience. I will do as you bid. I will be the servant of the Nephilim. I swear it!'

'Ha!' cried my brother. 'Do you think the two of you can play such games with impunity!'

'Ritchie, listen,' said Patience. 'The Pikes are a line of great swordsmen, are they not?'

'That was a long time ago,' I said. 'All that is lost, along with our sword, *Espiritu Santo*.'

'But the sword lives. Inside you. I can sense it, Ritchie. I have few powers when I am away from the woodlands. But I know I have the power to look into your heart and awaken your spirit!'

She placed her hand on my chest. Its warmth transfused itself through the linen shirt and found its way deep, deep, into my essence. 'You have no blade within reach, Ritchie. Nor would you know how to use one. Your sword has always been language. Words. Cutting words—'

'Words,' my brother muttered, getting to his feet, 'words, words, words, words, words. Bah! Kill him, Mitsou.'

Unhurriedly, the sphinx rose, extended its forepaws, stretched – the lordotic arch of its back, perhaps, a gesture of submission towards its master as much as a self-pleasuring indulgence in feline calisthenics – and then, with an easy cruelty of gait, padded towards me, its black eyes brimful with malevolence.

Unbidden, the words came:

> *'Come forth my lovely seneschal,*
> *So somnolent, so statuesque,*
> *Come forth you exquisite grotesque,*
> *Half woman and half animal,*
>
> *Come forth my lovely languorous Sphinx,*
> *And put your head upon my knee*
> *And let me stroke your throat and see*
> *Your body spotted like the Lynx,*
>
> *And let me touch those curving claws*
> *Of yellow ivory, and grasp*
> *The tail that like a monstrous Asp*
> *Coils round your heavy velvet paws.'*

The chimera nudged its cheek against my thigh, looked up and uttered a deep-throated rumble of meekness and tractability.

'You've, you've—' My brother stamped his foot upon the ground. 'Oh, you've turned my lovely Mitsou into a contemptible little *kitten*!' And then he shook his fist, first at me, then at his wayward betrothed. 'It seems you do have a spell or two up your sleeve, my dear,' he added, testily. His frown compressed the more, the corrugations indicative of maturing violence. 'Ritchie has been one of those poets who affect a morbid deviation from the healthy forms of life. His work has been characterized by a weary, wasting sensuality; nothing virile, nothing tender, nothing completely sane; a superfluity of extreme sensibility. With your assistance, he might be able to charm a chimera, but I assure you his paltry effusions will have no effect on *me*.'

'Oh really, Reggie —' and I threw back my head '— I cannot be moved by such cheap hack sentiments. Except, of course, if it be to scorn.'

'Focus,' said Patience, close to my ear. 'Hone your words. Make every utterance razor-sharp. Make your words *cut*.'

'There's nothing *you* can teach me, Ritchie,' said my brother. It seemed his arrogance was such that he disdained to further defend himself.

'Literature can teach you, Reggie. Teach you a damn good lesson. Not by explicit preachment, not by express intent — as you would have it in your vulgar new world — but by *being*.'

My brother let out a sharp cry and put his hand to his cheek. When he took it away, a long, thin gash was revealed, as if from a riding crop. He looked down at his bloodstained hand, his eyes wide with astonishment.

'Patience,' he said, fighting for his breath, 'stop this — stop this this *instant*!'

I knew I had to press home the advantage. 'The poet

is a god-like creator of new orders of being,' I ventured. 'He is the proclaimer of new values, of new kinds of humanity.'

'No!' my brother screamed. He flinched, then doubled over, another wound manifesting itself across the opposite cheek.

'Morality is nothing without imagination, Reggie.'

My brother straightened himself and attempted to parry. 'Imagination without morality is a riderless carriage, out of control!'

'Control, ah yes . . .'

'Art,' he said, stuttering in his haste to summon up the requisite verbal fizz, 'art must be the handmaiden of morality!'

'And whose morality might that be, Reggie? Yours? "The greatest happiness of the greatest number"? I despise your good. I despise your happiness. Your high moral purpose is the same as that of the black knights: a feint, a veneer, a convenient piece of tokenism to convince the world that you are not perverse.' I glanced at the sphinx. It crouched at my feet, its eyes balefully fixed upon my brother. I went down on one knee and tickled it behind its ear. 'But we are all perverse, Reggie. Humanity carries the taint of the Dark Ages in its collective veins. How could it be otherwise after so many millennia of miscegenation? If the Darkling Isle ever comes to accept your philosophy, it will only be to mask its vices, as you mask your own. Humanity is corrupt. Doomed. The mirror image of a diseased past. And that corruption will out, despite our lip service to freedom and egalitarianism. All shall be revealed for what it is, Reggie, just as tonight you have been revealed. And then humanity – dissolute, murderous, depraved humanity – shall pass away and be replaced by its successors.' The sphinx emitted a low growl and pawed at the floorboards. 'Morality, Reggie? Your morality is that of the most desperate of hypocrites.'

My brother had wrapped his arms about his chest. He writhed on the spot in agony. 'And your precious imagination: is it not as desperate as me? Does not your goblin blood cry out for fulfilment? Are you not a hypocrite too?'

'Imagination? The extra-textual world will soon vanish. As unreal as the human race. For the Nephilim are coming, and mankind has had its day. If I am desperate, I am desperate to leave this world, Reggie, not to hang on to it, like you. Attune yourself. Listen to the song that will soon be all we have left of ourselves. Become one with it and work out your deliverance. For the grand opera is soon to reach its finale. And the only thing left of us will be our fictiveness. Yes, our *imagination*.'

He chewed at his lower lip. Blood dribbled from his nose and ears. And then his red, hangdog eyes became those of a cornered animal. 'Take care!' he fairly barked. 'When I am thwarted I am very terrible!'

'Of course you are, Reggie,' I said, ignoring him and turning to look up at Patience. 'But I say again: I am prepared to renounce my aesthetic quest. For your sake, I am prepared to enter the world.' My dead love knelt down by my side.

'You really will become commonplace, Ritchie?'

'I'll acquit myself of my responsibilities towards the boy, yes,' I said.

Her hand dipped into the chimera's fur and closed over my own. 'I love you, Ritchie. But then I have always loved you. What you do, this sacrifice of yours – ah, it is something the Nephilim will never forget.'

'I don't think,' my brother said, somewhat more quietly now, 'that you quite appreciate the consequences of thwarting me.'

I studied my brother's bleeding face, reluctant to press home. For, with Patience's declaration of love, it seemed that our duel – which we had been fighting, in one way or another, ever since we had been boys – was effectively at an end. Suddenly, his eyes became hooded, almost rapt, so that he seemed one of Christendom's less celebrated martyrs, Reginald, patron saint of cunning, perhaps. His throat contracted in a dry swallow. He moistened his lips. And I knew at once that our logomachy was about to become a death struggle.

'Suppose,' he said, 'suppose – I won't go so far as to say that I will do it – but suppose for one moment I were to *curse* you? It would be an extreme measure, no doubt. Still—'

'Don't do it, Reggie,' said Patience.

'I can be as cutting as my elder brother, my dear, believe me. No one has ever accused Reginald Pike of being at a loss for a few sharp words!'

'No, Reggie,' she said, 'it's over – you don't understand!'

'Listen to her, Reggie. The poetry of the *fleshly* belongs to the Nephilim, like the rest of the material world. Don't overreach yourself.'

But he was unwilling to heed us. 'I curse you,

Ritchie,' he began, 'I curse you in the name of the very goblinry we both carry in our veins. May you always be sequestered amongst your books, alone, without affection, devoid of the small comforts of the vernacular world. May you never know connection with another human soul. May you never know the peace you yearn for. May you die alone, without hope, and may the damnable Ideal that you say will provide refuge for your soul disclose itself to be metaphysical gibberish. May you and Patience dwell for ever apart. May that horrible grandson of yours torment you even upon your deathbed. May the curse of the Pikes take the little rotter to exile and perdition as it did the first of our line. And may you both . . .'

By now, my brother bled from so many self-inflicted wounds that he was too weak to continue. He took a few uncertain steps forward and then dropped to his knees.

And sensing its opportunity, the sphinx leaped from my grasp. Falling upon its erstwhile master, it knocked him backwards, its lips immediately seizing his own in a greedy, sucking kiss, its claws tearing at chest, ribs, hips and thighs so frenziedly that, within the interval it took for me to bound across the dairy and bring the impetuous creature to heel, my brother was no more than blood and bone.

I shook hands with the captain and then, less enthusiastically, with my grandson.

'You shall go to school, here, then, with the Order,' I reiterated, to make sure that he understood the nature of our contract, and that I would not have him turning up at my rooms in Magdalen until the Christmas holidays, 'and I will pay your board and keep until such time as you decide upon a career.'

'I *have* decided,' said the boy, calmly. His uniform – leather hose and doublet adorned with various fetishistic regalia and surmounted by a very conspicuous codpiece – was a miniature version of the captain's. It was also an unacknowledged homage to the psychic lumber all of us – but he, of course, more than most – carried about as a reminder of our schismatic racial past. But if my grandson did not, or could not, own to his own perversity, then he was at least amongst others of his kind. The Order, despite all that I might offer, or do, would constitute the child's only real home. 'I want to be like the captain,' he explained, 'and I want to travel to the East, to redeem our lineage from the mire. I want to regain the family title, if not for myself, then for my descendants!'

Responsibility? Someone once said it is better to be irresponsible and right than to be responsible and wrong.

I awarded them each a curt nod and then left.

The glade was as I had seen it before. Patience was waiting for me. Today, however, she was sans cow, as if that prop was supererogatory now that I had accepted her terms and surrendered, of my own free will, to the rough, bovine world.

I released the sphinx from its leash. It waited a moment, unsure of its freedom, and then gamboled across the glade to disappear amongst the encircling trees.

'You're wearing a tweed suit, Ritchie,' she said, her smile dimpling her plump left cheek.

'It is as I have promised,' I said. 'I am determined to become commonplace.'

'And the boy?'

I gazed round; pursed my lips. 'The boy? Oh, he's all right.'

'You *will* take care of him, Ritchie?'

'As much as I am able, Patience. I grow old. And the boy is . . . strange. No matter. My conversation, you may be assured, will henceforth be perfectly matter of fact. I will cut my hair, and have a back parting. I will be steady and stolid. And if there remains in me anything aesthetic, then it will be an aestheticism of the most pastoral kind.' I sighed, deeply, in a last concession to histrionics. 'Yes, I will indeed attempt to become the most *ordinary* of mortals.'

'Don't worry about being *too* commonplace,' she said. 'Be assured: the boy's fate will be *extra*ordinary.'

About me, the silence deepened.

'Is the world really to end?' I said.

'Your world, Ritchie. Aestheticism and morality are obsolete. Pleasure and pain – how could you and Reggie argue about such things? Little Ritchie knows better. Pleasure and pain, he says, are one. He will be the worst of your line, yet the one who will paradoxically revive it. And his son will sire the Nephilim's saviour.' She smiled. 'Something new is coming. Something transcendent.'

'Transcendent,' I said, softly. 'I am glad to hear it. I tire of history. Its repetitions. Its subverted song.'

She began to glow. At first, she seemed the girl I had known during my childhood and early youth, my madonna of the forest. I began to intone:

'A lily-girl, not made for this world's pain,
With brown, soft hair close braided by her ears,
And longing eyes half veiled by slumberous tears
Like bluest water seen through mists of rain:
Pale cheeks whereon no love hath seen its stain,
Red underlip drawn in for fear of love,
And white throat, whiter than the silvered dove,
Through whose wan marble creeps one purple vein . . .'

Then her aspect changed and she assumed the appearance of the girl she had been just before she had died, her face pale and covered in lesions. The fire of holy immanence burned away that pain. And finally, I saw her true self. An ultimate transfiguration that was both more terrible, and more wonderful than any vision I had ever been granted by poetry, music or art. For before me stood an angel-demon. Uncreated light. A hard, gem-like flame that pierced my soul with the same angelic spear that had wounded St Teresa. Consciousness without an object, or indeed, a subject. The bedrock of everything.

The veil was rent. Leaving this world, she dissolved into the Ideal.

I put my hand out, seeking to touch the still faint afterglow of her image. And in the soughing, fervent trees I heard the words, 'You cannot go where I go, Richard. No human can.' The contorted limbs of the new parturition fanned themselves and groped towards the sky. The evanescence receded. And the veil was again drawn over eternity and its vast, empty spaces of Love.

The days of normative existence were over. The

schismatic life forms of hell and heaven, of the Netherworld and Earth-Above, would herald a new Earth. A dream Earth, where intelligible structure would burn away its material bonds, to reveal a spiritual reality independent of this world.

I stood alone. Again, the forest had begun to make its sibilant call, urging me to depart and not to tarry. To re-enter all that was fallen and corrupt.

I was commonplace. I had always been commonplace. It was only the Nephilim who were extraordinary. Their destiny was unimaginable. I belonged to the past.

L'art pour l'art? I had always believed that art must lead *somewhere*. But now I knew it was a somewhere I was to be denied. Knew it as surely as I had known my brother's philosophy to be a political sop for the masses. An illusion, like happiness itself.

Roach Motel

I dismounted from the palanquin. The crowd had grown thick and my litter could make no further progress. I would have to go the rest of the way on foot. I paid my bearers, then, standing on tiptoe, scanned the square. A scaffold had been erected beneath the palace walls. Opposite the scaffold stood the obelisk, where I was to meet my contact. The granite column's obscene brass entablature reflected the light of the newly risen moon. Resignedly, I began to eel my way towards my objective.

I had never conceived that the Square of Heavenly Peace would be almost filled. Timur would have known, of course. Known, too, that the obelisk would prove the only marker amid this undifferentiated expanse of humanity. He had been our agent here for nearly ten years.

By the time I reached the obelisk, Pu-tin-pao, the imperial headsman, had mounted the scaffold. He wore a clean white apron over ceremonial robes. Ignoring the crowd, he began to sharpen the edge of his long, curved blade using a strop that hung from a bamboo stanchion.

'Good evening,' said Timur, looking down, his voice pitched an octave or two above the crowd's anticipatory drone. 'Come up. You will discover that we have an excellent view.' I ascended the half-dozen or so steps that led to the top of the plinth. As I drew level with him he turned away, disinclined, for the moment, to acknowledge me further. He stared towards the scaffold. In his bearing, he seemed as emotionally detached from the night's proceedings as the headsman. I rested an elbow on the iron handrail. A little way off, stalls had been set up. They sold fishballs, lanterns, firecrackers and rockets. Boys played with miniature wooden swords.

I wondered why we occupied such a favourable spot, isolated on a little stony eminence amid the surge and press of bodies. 'In my *other* capacity, I occupy a position at court,' he said, in answer to my unspoken question, but still not meeting my eyes. 'My face is known to this rabble. And it is a face that inspires fear. They will not disturb us.' His voice was lowered. Despite his bravado, I think he feared the 'rabble' as much as they feared him. The people of Cambulac would likely take as much pleasure in the death of traitors as they did in the death of impecunious young princes. 'A Persian has been the latest suitor to fail the test. He . . .' The voice had become little more than a whisper, his sentence trailing off into incomprehensibility. But implicit in its timbre was something I recognized: a hatred for his mistress as deep as love. Recognized, because, in a less literal, but more poetically apposite sense, Turandot was my mistress, too. I looked at him askance, studying his stony face, a face congested by long years of silent revolt. Hatred, yes, but no conscience, I decided. I was glad; I did not wish to place myself at the mercy of a man's conscience. I knew too well what undependable things they were.

I moved nearer so that I might hear him. 'Look, do you see?' he said, pointing upwards. 'The birds of carrion are circling overhead.' Several ladies-in-waiting had appeared on the battlements, vulturine in their black, diaphanous plumage and white, mousseline ruffs. Directly beneath them, the scaffold's backcloth parted to reveal a door set in the palace walls. A wave undulated through the crowd as imperial guards, priests, mandarins, dignitaries and courtesans all strove to get as near to the scaffold as they could.

The condemned man was being led on to the stage. He was young. Naked. And very beautiful.

'You know what you have to do?' said my contact.

'Of course.' I did not care for his clipped tone of voice, nor for the somewhat dismissive way in which he had received me. I was a Captain of the Order of Black Knights. He was a mere operative. The man should have been treating me with greater respect. 'Do you know who I am? Do you know of my patrimony? My lineage? My name?'

He turned and met my gaze. 'I do not wish to know,' he said, curtly, his face registering distaste and astonishment in equal degree. 'Who you are is of no consequence here. It is your assumed identity that is of importance. There is to be no mention of the past. No reference to blood, merit or social position except that which the Order has seen fit to bestow upon you for the purposes of this mission.' He resumed his former stance, abstracted, untouchable. 'I pray you are well briefed.'

'I pray you are too, sir,' I said. 'I know who *I* am. But do you know who *you* are?' I paused, breathing deeply.

At such times as I recalled my family's shame and dispossession, a certain bitterness would enter my voice. Since entering the Celestial City two days ago that bitterness had been compounded by a belated, if full, realization that the time of my passion was nigh, and that, soon, all would be over. 'You are a man,' I continued, 'who would, I believe, suffer a death more terrible than that which awaits this Persian should you fail in your duty and force the Order to expose you.' His cheek was afflicted with a barely detectable tic. 'And your duty,' I added, purging my voice of its acerbity, and allowing the rounded, fulsome notes of true, aristocratic disdain to ring through, 'is to get me an audience with the princess. Nothing more is required.' I sniffed at the incense-burdened air. 'Certainly nothing in the way of criticism or advice. I come from a *proud* line, one that is destined to be restored to all its former glory.' I allowed myself a fleeting, self-satisfied grin. My bitterness was, after all, misplaced; I had accepted all that had been done, and willingly, too.

'Nothing more is required. That's true. Nothing more.' If he was stung, he kept it well hid – tied up, perhaps, and locked away in the vault in which he had sequestered his passions. He gestured towards the gong that stood in the scaffold's roped-off enclosure. 'The first part's easy. The court officials will expect you to present your bona fides, of course. But the papers we have prepared for you are excellent. You have them?' I nodded. Timur's eyes narrowed as he focused on the doomed man. 'The second part is more difficult. But from what I hear, the Order has found, in you, someone with the requisite psychopathology.' His lip curled.

'The right motivation, as it were. Someone who can play this sick, sick princess at her own game.' He looked suddenly very tired. 'Let us hope that her bloody reign is at an end.'

The prince knelt. His flesh was bleached by moonlight. Each bead of sweat that trickled down his slim, powerful torso was like a droplet of mercury. He bowed his head, long, dark hair veiling his face and cascading down his smooth chest and abdomen. So refined was his deportment, so delicately sculpted his body, that, despite the well-defined musculature, he might have been mistaken for a young girl if his hair had not stopped short of the glistening apex of his thighs and the organ of generation the virgin princess had so cruelly disdained.

Timur gave a start, gasped, took a step backwards and once more pointed to the battlements. I looked up. The princess had appeared. The sight of her was, perhaps, the one thing that could provoke Timur to betray his feelings. I could understand why. Even at this distance, she was unmistakable. I had studied secretly taken photographs of her during the long hours of my briefing, but even without that advantage, I would still have known that it was she. She. The one whom I had dreamed of as a child. The one who had possessed me and made me mad, and demanded of me my career, my honour, even my family. The one I desired more than life. I had glimpsed her semblance before, in the faces and bodies of women I had sought out in uptown soirées and downtown brothels, but never with such absolute clarity. Those other women: they had been human approximations, evidence of the shadow that the lost gods of the perverse still sometimes cast upon this world. The young woman who ruled Cathay in all but name *was* the perverse. A goddess. The thing itself.

Turandot.

'You must prepare yourself,' said Timur, the stony face at last giving vent to the seismic activity of his inner life. I could not speak; I felt the ground shift beneath me as I contended with my own emotional temblor. I gripped the handrail. The crowd's roar was almost as loud as my heart's.

The time had come. To perform. To accept. To bring to conclusion.

To expiate.

My contact was speaking, it seemed, from the far side of the universe, his words filtering through dust clouds, vast regions where different laws applied. 'The gong. Set to. Go. Quick. Do not linger.'

The princess looked down upon the scaffold, raised her hand and then let it drop.

Pu-tin-pao swung his blade, effecting a swift, elegant separation of head and body. Out of the corner of my eye, I saw Timur's lips continue to move, but if his words had not been lost to the great swell of noise that greeted the decollation, they would have been obscured almost as effectively by the thud of blood rushing through my inner ear.

The princess and her ladies were slipping away into the shadows. For an instant, she turned and looked down upon her people. Her face was like the risen moon, a satellite that had swung through the Big Night of my soul for over seventy years, raw, incandescent, terrifyingly pure, governing the ebb and flow of my life.

I had had no more than a glimpse of her. A glimpse of black, corkscrew hair, of full, parted lips, the glint of jewels and the sheen of white vestal robes cut with crimson. But that glimpse had been enough to assure me that the die was cast, and that my blood, denied its birthright for eight generations, had come, if not yet into its human legacy, then into that other dark inheritance of my dreams.

I felt a hand upon my arm, urging me forward. The princess had disappeared. I turned; knew that my contact continued to speak only by the idle flapping of his lips; began to walk. My head was filled with such a commotion that I tottered. I was on the verge of insensibility and a convulsive riot of limbs. Timur's eyes grew wide with alarm.

I shouldered him aside. The next moment, I was stumbling down the steps, giddy with desire and trepidation. I remember little of what followed. I cried out. I cried, 'Turandot! Turandot!' of that I am sure. Sure too that the crowd, whose baffled cries soon gave way to mockery, parted at my approach. *'Another man fool enough to brave the princess's challenge,'* was the general tenor of the uproarious commentary. *'Let him pass. Let us be provided with further entertainment this beautiful night.'*

I staggered through the gauntlet, emerging unscathed. None had deigned to touch me. For a moment, I spun on my heels, confused. Lantern-cast shadows lay all about. Then I looked up. The scaffold loomed, its greatest shadows reserved for those who dared breach its perimeter. I ducked beneath the circumscribing ropes and ran on unhindered. At last, I stood before the lustrous metal disc that was set to announce my fate. Taking up the gong stick, I struck home, and heard a broad, mournful note resound throughout the square, informing Cambulac, imperial seat of Cathay, that I would submit to the Three Great Questions.

Who are we?

Where have we come from?

Where do we go?

The moon-flooded multitude had grown still. None spoke. The air was benumbed, infused with the opiate-like sonorousness of the gong. Its serial boom reverberated off the palace walls, and then, fading, became the ghost of a mantra chanted by those who had gone before. Those who had wagered all for the hand of Turandot.

'I had hardly taken you for a prince,' said the concierge, raising his eyebrows and inspecting my tattered robe. I had endured his derision since checking in some days ago and was by now inured to it. I was somewhat surprised however to discover that my newly revealed status had not gone *some* way to having him modify his opinion of me. I stared back. The eyebrows drooped; his expression became self-reflective. He pushed the key under the grille. 'I mean, this motel, it's—'

'It's seen better days?'

'I have heard the Darkling Isle has also seen better days,' he shot back, obviously nettled, even though he usually made no secret of his abhorrence for his place of work.

'Perhaps if this prince weren't so impoverished, he would not have to risk his life,' I said.

Somewhat mollified, the concierge nodded, in sage concession to plain speaking. 'If I were an aristocrat like you, sir, I might also risk the princess's challenge. She is rich. Beautiful. And now that her father is in his dotage, she practically rules all Cathay. Poverty is a great inducement to love and terror. For myself . . .' he paused, and his tired, suspicious eyes darted hither and thither, 'I think I would do anything, so long as I could put my present life behind me.'

The motel was located amongst the slums of the Outer City. On entering Cambulac, it had provided me with the anonymity I had required. Now that I had declared my suit and earned a somewhat unenviable renown, it consolidated my cover. Only a prince or lord of painfully reduced circumstance would choose to win the Princess Turandot for his bride.

'Yes, yes, if I were you, sir, I might truly be tempted to take part in the princess's bizarre, and, let it be said, altogether *wanton* challenge.' He whistled through his teeth. 'Fourteen men dead at her hand, though! That's enough to cool any man's ardour. Ah, the empire is not what it was. It is consumed by a lust for cruelty and death. Consumed by the old, unspeakable desires of those who lived here before us.' Again, he glanced to and fro, his rheumy eyes lighting up with apprehension. But the lobby remained deserted. 'I endanger myself by talking so freely. Yet what have I to lose? Even my daughter . . .' I turned my back on him and began to walk down the corridor. 'Have you seen her, sir?' he called after me. 'Milord? Your Highness?' he added, perhaps in the event that, should I answer Turandot successfully, I would either forget his treacherous remarks, or award him a sinecure. 'I hope the little chit doesn't bother you? You have only to say, sir. She's been a problem for us all.'

I continued on my way and was soon deep inside the motel's fusty warren.

I stopped opposite my door. Heard a susurration. Looked down. A cockroach emerged from the dirty plates stacked outside the adjoining room. I froze. The alluring bug tested the air with its feelers, then, after awarding me a look that seemed almost humanly cognizant of life's tawdriness, scuttled across the tiles. As it passed close, almost arrogantly close, I attempted to treat it to the heel of my shoe, but it escaped through a hole in the wainscot. The motel was, it seemed, beneath even this lowly creature's contempt.

If this were an omen, it was not one I cared to reflect upon. I could not bear to think that the princess might similarly escape me.

I turned the key in the lock and entered.

Looking about, I saw that my accommodation was as I had left it. I walked through the meagrely furnished dining area and into the bedroom. I opened the jalousie and filled my lungs with fresh air.

The bedroom gave on to a quadrangle. Carts, jalopies and a few rusty electric vans were parked haphazardly between trashcans and fire escapes. Balconies, each one enclosed in an iron cage, rose before and to either side, festooned with lines of grubby washing. At night, the noise of arguing couples, crying infants and, on one occasion, the report of a handgun being discharged, had often made sleep impossible. But this morning all was quiet, and now that I had surrendered to my destiny, and no longer fretted quite so much about my mission and what I had been sanctioned to perform, I felt that quietness extend to my spirit. Soon, I told myself, I would know peace and sleep for ever.

I turned. Slats of early morning light fell across the parquetry floor, extending to where my suitcase lay open, still, for the most part, unpacked. I crossed the room and stood before the wardrobe. I slid back its door. The sole confidence I placed in the motel's staff lay in their utter disregard for making up my room, indeed, for offering service of any kind, and not in any presumption of their honesty. But my uniform, I was relieved to discover, was undisturbed, as were my other valuables.

Slipping the indigenous robe off my shoulders, shuffling it to my ankles and then kicking the demeaning thing aside, I reached out and ran a finger down those emblems of my other self: the leather hose, doublet, riding boots, thick velvet cloak and cambric shirt that constituted the regimentals of a Captain of the Order of Black Knights. Then, taking them from their hangers, I laid them out on the unmade bed.

I proceeded to the shower. I wanted to look my best when I at last came face to face with Turandot. I lathered, washed, shaved, defecated and then some-what neurotically washed again. Immediately after towelling myself off, I walked back to the bed and strapped on the uniform. The cloak I secured to a hook behind the bedroom door, ready for when I should leave. The sky was clear, but it was nearing the end of autumn, and the air had, of late, begun to pink at my skin.

There was one thing I lacked. The family heirloom, *Espiritu Santo*. But that mystic blade had been lost for centuries. The only weapon I would be allowed to carry into the palace would be its *reductio ad absurdum*.

I stretched out on the bed. The night had been taken up with satisfying court protocol. At noon, soldiers would arrive to escort me to the princess. I had barely four hours to prepare.

I had not intended to sleep, but merely to rest and mentally rehearse my lecture. Sleep, however, had been too long denied me; it admitted no counterfeit; like an abused whore, who could no longer be bought off, it demanded recompense in kind. I seem to recall that, dipping beneath the surface of consciousness, I encountered Pu-tin-pao, in his little apron, sharpening his sword. The scene also featured my dead wife, estranged children and grandchildren. They entered stage left, knelt, then lowered their heads, napes exposed to the descending blade. The youngest – he who, if all went well, would become the next Lord Soho – peered up at me, and time came to a halt. Kicking, spluttering, gasping for air, I rose towards the light, and, opening my eyes, was confronted by the face of a girl peering round the connecting door.

'Oh, I'm sorry sir, I—'

With a convulsive jerk, I sat up. 'Who—'

'I was going to clean your room, sir, I . . .'

I swung my legs over the side of the bed and stood. The face before me: it was a mask, a hallucination, some kind of trick. It could not, I reasoned, be the face of the Princess Turandot. Yet it *was* her.

Did I still dream? I shook my head, clearing it of

muzziness. No, I did not dream. This was one of those 'across the room' moments such as I had experienced in the Darkling Isle, when, at a dinner party, I might find myself confronted by a beauty who seemed the realization of my visions. Disappointment, on such occasions, was inevitable. Blinking, I would discover, soon enough, that I gazed upon a woman who, if stamped with the goddess's imprimatur, was flawed by a debt to humanity.

This little beauty, this girl who, even half-obscured by the door, seemed as much an example of divine incarnation as the vicious young woman who ruled Cathay, was a qualitatively different kind of creature. I knew at once that, however much I might blink, I would never be disappointed, never discover that, on looking again, she was anything less than a distillation of my life's obsessions.

For, apart from the most obvious and cursory physical correlatives, there was really nothing human about her at all.

She came into the room. 'Extraordinary,' I murmured. It was not just her face, but her body, too, that approximated the princess's, though whereas Turandot had last night chosen to conceal herself in opalescent robes that seemed spun from moonbeams, her unacknowledged younger sister was turned out in the briefest and most shameless of rags. The penurious attire, along with the vulgarly applied make-up, suggested a sexual heat that had chosen to fan itself until it was on the brink of self-combustion. Had this chambermaid, I wondered, inadvertently afforded me a glimpse of the real Turandot? A Turandot who, perhaps, out of self-preservation, had attempted to conceal her own insatiability behind a glacial renown?

'I know,' she said, with a sly grin, and looking me straight in the eye. 'Everybody says it. I look like the princess.' If somewhat more gloriously common, I thought. Her face became serious. 'It's why I was expelled. Slave school's a real opportunity for girls like me. One day it's the slums, the next the palace. Dad was really angry I flunked. But when the headmistress noticed I looked so much like *royalty* there was really only one way things could end. Now I help Dad out around the motel.'

So this was the daughter of whom I had been warned.

'It's such a waste,' she said, 'because I know I'd have been a really good slave. I was born to it.'

Born to it? And how many others of her kind had recently been born to it? Born to inherit the Earth? According to the Order, the perverse, so long in abeyance, had, in one generation, begun to manifest itself in Cathay as at no other time during the last two thousand years.

Tentatively, with an exaggerated roll of her hips, she took a step forward. And then, lowering her gaze, so that she studied me through long, mascara-caked eyelashes, she took another step, the see-sawing pelvis achieving a degree of angular displacement that human flesh could hardly be expected to contain.

The sound of her: the *click* then *clack* of her high-heeled sandals as they made their lazy, percussive overture across the floor; the protestation of silk against skin as it strove to constrain her absurdly curvaceous body.

The smell of her: cheap scent applied with plebeian liberality, combined with perspiration and the heady aroma of dirty hair – all in all, the perfume of the gutter.

And oh, the *sight* of her. The sight of that scrap of clingy black chiffon. The single shoulder strap, so thin as to resemble an unwound thread. A neckline so low that, on the right side, where the strap's counterpart had snapped, fatigued, perhaps, after months of constraining the unconstrainable, the rouged areola of a breast all puppy-fat and buttermilk peeped insolently above the seam. The nipped waist gave way to runs, tears and ladders, where the tight, silken rag contended with the generous pelvic girdle, and then flared, in sublime ruination, over the gently rounded belly. Clearly visible through the distressed, ultra-fine denier, the umbilicus, decorated with a big, red slug of costume jewellery, glowed like a hot coal. The hemline was also torn, but artfully so. It formed a V, the frayed topmost edges revealing the sharp hipbones, the nethermost tatters barely covering the black, closely cropped fuzz of the pubic mound.

She stood before me, shifting her weight from one leg to the other, toying with the helical strands of her unkempt hair. In her neck, a pulsing, turquoise vein seemed to offer a correlative to the ever-quickening tempo of my own blood and its polluted heritage. Then, sweeping the disordered mass of locks over her shoulders, she continued her advance.

'Who are we?' I mumbled, unconsciously rehearsing the catechism I would soon have to answer in earnest.

'I'm Liù,' she said, pursing her plump, glossy lips. She might have been weaned on a diet of crushed strawberries whose dye had proved indelible. 'Who are *you*, stranger?'

'I'm not sure,' I murmured, a stab of fear in my bowels. 'At times like this, I'm not sure who or what any of us are.'

I was being a little disingenuous. If my own heritage was something of an enigma, even to me, then hers was clear. In the interregnum of irrationality that divided the Ancient and Modern, when mankind's perception of the world had become so skewed that it turned its back on its accumulated wisdom and embraced the dark joys of animality, various races of hybrids, known as the tribes of the perverse, had roamed the Earth.

'Sharkmen, bearmen, insectmen,' I numbly declaimed, more to myself than her, remembering all that the Order had taught me. 'And swangirls, fishgirls, sophisticated but down and dirty foxgirls, grisettes such as belonged to the Way of the Cat and Rat . . .'

Not that Liù belonged to any of those extinct genera.

No, Liù had roachgirl blood in her veins.

Her ancestors had been the lowest of the low, so aberrant that they had not been officially classified a 'tribe', even by their fellow outlaws. But for me the *roach* was the only genus – despite the undoubted attractions of those other pedigrees of girl – that had ever been worth studying.

'Oh, what are you, who are also my beloved Turandot,' I whispered, 'and what manner of creature am I?'

I was human. But the perverse, latent in me since birth, just as it was latent, these days, in all humanity, had become manifest and demanded my allegiance. I had surrendered to it. That was all I knew. I had no tribe. I had no extra-human identity. No reshaped forebears to call my own, except they be orc: those degenerate creatures living beneath the Earth's surface.

The chambermaid pressed herself against me, as if determined to heal the schism in my soul, that fundamental breach in my being. Then, raising herself on tiptoe, her arm snaked about my neck, and pulled my mouth down on to her own.

And finally, the taste of her, the feel of her, all five senses conspiring to undermine my humanity, to turn me back into that bestial man who would creep from his home and seek kisses, blood and female lamentation in the slums and ghettos of the Darkling Isle's wastes. That mouth: it was sweetened as if by an appalling diet of lollipops, sherbet, bubblegum and candyfloss. My tongue was some blind, famished beast that groped its way through a ransacked confectioners. Yet that candied succulence was underpinned by a base note of something darker, something bitter, something gross. The mouth closed, became a vacuum, my tongue sucked into its pink cavern so violently that I thought it might be torn from its ligaments. The sweetness was gone, and her taste had become unrelievedly pungent, the back of her throat like a sewer or drain slicked with her verminous essence. I bent over her a little more and placed a hand on her thigh, fingers closing upon the fringe of silk that played over the knobby articulation of her pelvis.

Her crimson fingernails dug into my leather hose. Then, ascending, they slipped beneath the doublet and shirt, scarifying my chest with slow, deliberate artistry.

And if I knew it was inevitable that the impression I had hoped to make at court would be compromised by bloody telltale signs of having recently consorted with the city's lowlife, then I did not, at that moment, care.

Suddenly, she drew back, our mouths disengaging with an audible implosion of air. Her face was flushed, twitchy, pettish, giving her the aspect of a child who had got up from her sick bed before she ought to, to wander about the house in a feverish daze. She placed her hand on my solar plexus and gave me a little push. So weakened was I from her embrace that I immediately sat down upon the bedside chair to my rear.

'You want a shine?'

'A shine?' I replied, somewhat perplexed.

She looked down through corkscrews of dishevelled hair, longingly. She was inspecting my boots. 'You've got a big day ahead of you. I can make your boots look really nice. It takes time, of course. Licking just gets the dirt off. It's necessary that I cover the leather with my vaginal secretions and then buff it with my *mons Veneris* to work up a shine of truly martinet gorgeousity. Is that okay?' Before I had chance to reply, she concluded, and somewhat peripherally, I would have thought: 'You're English, aren't you?'

I was a little taken aback. 'Yes,' I said. 'How—'

'Word gets round pretty quickly. But I sort of had you figured out long ago. Didn't have to hear it on the street. First time I saw that uniform in your wardrobe I just went crazy.' Room service had not, it seemed, been quite so unobtrusive as I had wished.

'You know this uniform?' I said, concerned. 'You know what it implies?' Centuries ago the Order had been persecuted, disbanded, and, to all purposes, forgotten. I had not thought it possible that, here, on the other side of the world, mere threads, buckles and a studded codpiece might provoke an ignorant slave girl to an intimation that I was more than I claimed to be, even if such girls *do* understand something about leather, its mystery and implications, that the average woman or man often fails to grasp. '*Do you know this uniform and what it means*,' I repeated, with emphasis, to the lust-deafened girl.

'It means you're like me,' she said. 'You have the dark fire in your veins. A girl can tell these things.' She really was too much to the point, as pert as she was perspicacious. I strove to calm myself. She knew nothing, doubtless, of the wider world, and, while speculation about my origins could hardly be avoided, I felt it unlikely she was capable, or even interested, in discovering the truth: that is, that I belonged to a secret society dedicated to upholding the ways of man in the face of the perverse.

I should have dismissed the girl. But if she was not part of the common order of things, then neither was I. They had looked for a sick, sick man to take on this mission, and – all credit to their thoroughness – had chosen me. I wondered whether they had known that the sickness, though it might spur me to do things others would baulk at, would also lay me open to dangers a more well-adjusted individual might have been able to resist.

'So much leather,' she giggled, looking me over from toe to crown, 'and so little time.' Again, she surveyed me, her gaze lingering, this time, over my crotch. 'Oh mercy me —' her giggles threatening to become uncontrollable '— how *codlicious*.'

I cast my gaze from the failed slave to the leather-shrouded object of her scrutiny. Sir John, my peccant ally, who was destined to be such a woe and wonder to the world. He was of late, alas, too often the object of ridicule. It was I alone who accorded him that 'Sir'; to the rest of the world, certainly to those women I had consorted with outside the purview of brothels, he had always been plain Mr Thomas.

I stood up, took a step forward, grabbed her by the hair and twisted a length of her greasy tresses about my fist. Her mouth opened wide, so wide, in fact, that I heard her jaw emit a subtle crack over her gasp of anticipation. She surely believed that I meant to force her down and take her with deliciously unnecessary brutality. Instead, I pushed her away, so that she stumbled backwards to come to rest half-leaning against the dresser, leaving, in my knotted hand, a few inky locks, and, in my knotted stomach, a pain that was unfamiliar: that of self-denial.

What a bore sex was. And when not a bore, what a horror.

I strove to ignore Sir John's barked imprecations and let him fret in his dark place of confinement, there to gnash his teeth and mourn that he no longer enjoyed the freedom that had been his in the Darkling Isle. My family had been promised much if I should fulfil my calling. Delicacy, professional delicacy, would, I decided, inform my actions till the end.

'You don't want to fuck me?' she said, neither incredulous, angry, nor bemused, her voice invested only with the sexual need that would long ago have burned away all other aspects of her personality.

'Do you know who I am, little girl?' I said, careless, then, of who I was or had been. Tired of life. This mission. Everything. 'My name is Richard Pike, tenth of that line. Lord Soho, if not for the machinations of my family's enemies.'

Her expression was as inane as porcelain. Not because she had withdrawn into herself – an interiority that consists merely of sexual appetite offers little sanctuary – but because, rejected, with her lust momentarily spiked, there was nothing left to animate her.

If she could not give me physical satisfaction, then she would, I decided, provide me with a sounding board for the relief of my overburdened soul. She was nothing. A shell. Of no import and of no consequence. How had it been possible that I had ever thought she might pose a threat?

'My erstwhile life was fake,' I said. 'As inauthentic as the role I have been forced to play, here, in Cambulac. It had to end.' I gazed into the fly-specked pier glass that stood opposite, to one side of the dresser. An unnaturally youthful eighty-year-old in black leather stared back, his grey face lined, pocked and brindled with the hereditary curse of the Pikes. I began to wonder where I had put my hypodermic. The drug that had shaved half a century off my appearance needed to be administered twice a day. That drug was killing me, of course, even as it lent me its vital lie. But that was of no consequence. I had time enough. Time enough to renounce the fraudulence of my life and embrace, once and for all, the only thing about me that had ever been real.

I extended a hand. The slave girl took a few steps forward, stopped, then lowered her head so that she might press her cheek against the metacarpus. Her skin, if no longer flushed by the urgency of desire, was almost equally hectic with rouge, but cool, strangely cool.

In me, the human is an unpredictable element. It rose, now, displacing the perverse. I heaved, a dry sob contorting my chest. But I was otherwise silent. And still.

I knew I could rely on Liù not to cry. And self-control had nothing to do with it. Just as girls such as her knew fear but not terror, obsession but not love, so too they knew self-pity but not the true sorrow that culminates in weeping. And I thought: How sad, to be so beyond tears, to be so beyond childhood, that its loss is impossible to recall. The coolness transfused itself through my hand. I thought of my own childhood in Epping and Oxford, the ridiculous dream I had had that I might myself become Lord Soho. A dream blighted by the creeping realization that I was damned. The coolness deepened. Her flesh was like ice. With the prospect of carnality gone, and therefore, the life gone too, Liù was a living corpse, her flesh as impersonal as chitin.

'Poor little cockroach,' I said.

'I know,' she said. 'I know what I am. They told me at school. I'm not Liù. Not really. I'm not even a slave. I'm something lower. A roachgirl.'

I sat down again and leaned back in the chair, relinquishing my role as comforter. 'Your ancestors,' I said, 'unlike other tribes, could not reproduce. Born

270

to humans, they were considered spontaneous mutations – of the perverse, but not belonging to it. A bastard
tribe, if you will. Midwives, faced with these abomi-
nations, would consign the newborn hybrids to the
sewers, and there, beneath the world's great cities, they
learned to survive. The other species of the perverse
always regarded them with contempt.'

'Don't you like cockroaches?'

'I do like them. More than you know. They've been
my reason for living. Roachgirls are so . . . so very
beautiful,' I said, not wanting to estrange her further by
explaining that just as some boys will take to natural
history and collect insects in specimen jars, then so too
will other boys delight in subjecting those same little
creatures to excruciations, plucking off their wings and
then their legs, one by one, before cremating them
beneath a magnifying glass. 'Very beautiful, indeed.
And even if the other female tribes were not extinct, I
would still dedicate myself to the most despised of their
number. For if roachgirls were never fully recognized as
a genus, *I* recognize you as such. You can keep your
catgirls, ratgirls, fishgirls and she-spiders. I sing the
order Blattaria! The *Blatella germanica*, the *Blatella
asahinai*, and, of course –' I leaned forward; she bent
down to meet me; I gave her nose a playful tweak '– the
Blatta orientalis!'

She pulled back her lips, exposed her teeth and
hissed with mock-insect pleasure.

'The princess is a cockroach too, isn't she?'

'Of course,' I said. 'Whether born in a palace or in the
gutter, perverse little girls like you are *always* roaches,
for these days the roachgirl is the sole form by which

the perverse can express itself. The other tribes are gone, like the dodo, the roc and the tyrannosaur. But the genotype of the roach has survived, living on within the physical and imaginative corpus of humanity and waiting only for some freak mutation of genes to herald its rebirth.'

'And the princess,' she said, kneeling between my outstretched feet and sitting back on her heels. 'She's *pure* cockroach?' A frown of dark suspicion creased her brow.

'A pure human–cockroach hybrid. Such as existed in the Dark Ages. A rare thing, these days. Perhaps a thing unmatched. The world must certainly hope so.'

'And that's why you prefer her to me? Because I'm more human than roach? Is that what you're saying?'

'Given the fact that you so resemble the princess, I think it likely you are far more roach than human. But you are not as those who lived in the Dark Ages. The perverse, in you, is distilled, but strong, nevertheless. Very strong. You are, in fact, the most desirable roach-girl I have ever encountered in the flesh.'

Her eyebrows – just visible beneath the curlicues of her bangs – became set in an attitude of child-like concentration. She pouted, and looked away, affectedly holding a hand before her face to study her manicure. 'Then why don't you *fuck* me?' she said, with a mortified huff.

I made a steeple of my hands and rested my chin on the apex of my well-chewed fingernails. 'I can't,' I said. 'I have to save myself for the one who is destined to be my bride.'

'I'm *desirable*, but not roachgirl enough for a man of

your discriminating tastes, is that it?' she said, with a most un-slave-like flash of anger. 'Not *pure* enough. Too human. Just a dumb chambermaid. Well, I hope your blue-blooded floozie gives you what you're looking for. I can't. It seems I don't have enough *insect* in me.' She met my eyes, hurt, yet defiant. 'I won't forget you,' she concluded. 'I won't.'

It was still early morning, but I decided it would be wise to make an exit. 'It's a matter of politics,' I said, getting up and taking out my pocket-watch as I stepped over her hunched, shivering body. She held her face in her hands, and contrary to my predictions, she did indeed seem to cry. 'We are pawns. Both of us. It is by sacrifice, and sacrifice alone, that we can hope to win. And now, my dear, if you will excuse me . . .'

If sex was a bore, a trial, a horror, then so too, it seemed, was conscience.

Behind me, some boys busied themselves putting my lectern in place. I coughed, to test the hall's acoustics. Finding them satisfactory, I rolled my notes into a scroll and held them behind my back. Then, raising my heels off the floor, I rocked to and fro and surveyed my surroundings.

Court officials swarmed across the concourse. They gathered about the imperial dais at the opposite end of the hall, their ranks swelling by the minute.

'It'll be either a funeral or a wedding, that's for sure,' said one mandarin to another as they proceeded towards the dais, oblivious of whether or not I overheard. 'But we must I suppose be thankful that in this life there are still *some* certainties.' There were, of course, some things I was certain of, too, though I could not bring myself to be thankful. The certainty, for instance, that I would not be going home, even if I should succeed in the trial. It didn't matter. Home was not to be found in this world. Or even in this universe.

More officials were entering the hall. Some cast me a quick, impatient glance, as if they had grown weary of supervising the princess's charades, and the men who, in volunteering themselves, perpetuated them. Others swapped infantile jokes about those who had lost their heads over the princess 'both figuratively and literally'. And a few of the older, braver men reminisced about the Middle Kingdom as it had been in the emperor's time, before its renascence of learning had, in this generation, been threatened by a second coming of the perverse. 'Perhaps it would be some kind of salvation,' said one such elder statesman, 'if the princess surrendered. After all, love may provide not merely personal deliverance, but prove conducive to the restitution of the commonweal. At least, it may prove so for those of us who still believe and place our hopes in the rediscovery of Man.'

Trumpets sounded. Men and women hurried to their stations. Conversation ceased. The hall was quiet, still and possessed of ominous lucidity.

The assembly bowed. Altoum, the emperor, had entered by a side door.

With the assistance of several bearers, the old man climbed to the top of the dais and assumed the throne. His only child followed, her retinue in close attendance. I had heard that the emperor, agonizing over his daughter's loyalty, sought comfort in the spies he had seconded to her entourage. Studying the ranks of her bodyguard, ladies-in-waiting and slaves, I could see that many were indeed human. Human and non-human alike, however, were left at the foot of the dais. Turandot ascended towards the emperor alone.

She seated herself upon the penultimate step. There was a hush. Then the thrice-made salutation of 'Ten Thousand Years!' filled the hall, the dying traces of that great cry ringing in my ears long after the court dignitaries had taken to their seats.

'Son of Heaven, I ask to prove myself,' I said. Despite the roachgirls who constituted the princess's harem of slaves – beautiful vermin all – I had eyes only for their exemplar, the princess herself, and was oblivious to Altoum until she chose to turn her head and look up at him. Wearily, he nodded, and, with a barely perceptible flick of his hand, signalled that the trial should begin.

The princess got to her feet and took a few steps down the dais. And then, for the first time, her gaze met my own.

'Two thousand years ago,' she said (and I realized, then, that she was the archetype of that slave *manqué*, Liù, not just in face and body, but in voice, too, if enjoying a greater degree of elocutionary refinement), 'when Cathay was still home to the tribes of the perverse, my ancestress, Lou-ou-ling, last empress of Albracca, was ravished by a conquering warlord of Atlantis, and died a horrible death. To her memory I have consecrated my maidenhead, that no human will think the New Cathay I intend to build may be so easily overcome. So it is I say that no man will ever possess me unless he correctly answers the Three Great Questions.

Think well before you make your attempt. The questions are three, but there is only one death.'

She was more beautiful than the visions I had had of her in sleep, or that sometimes swarmed about me in the treacherous shadowlands of daytime; more beautiful than when I had seen her picked out by moonlight on the palace battlements. My throat tightened. And my heart beat so fast that I grew giddy. Not even an intimate encounter with a body double, such as Liù, could assuage the shock of confronting her at such close quarters. I feared that I might be unable to continue.

Her headdress was like the translaterally arranged crest of a monstrous cockatoo, betokening her equally monstrous royalty. Her diaphanous shift resembled a shroud. It was similar to the garment Liù had worn, except it fell from neck to floor, and was as intact as her redoubtable hymen. Beneath: anklets, belly-chains and necklaces jingled faintly against what must have been perpetually quivering flesh. Jewels that coruscated like a new constellation fated to crowd the familiar, human lights from the sky. If Liù had been a glorification of the kind of seductiveness that wretches such as myself called 'cheap and nasty', then Turandot was its apotheosis. It was as if I viewed Liù through some magic lens that magnified 'the cheap' until it shone with numinous inner light.

'Who are we?' said the princess.

Then, after a short pause: 'Where have we come from?'

And finally, a malicious smile enlivening a face that was like that of a child who had larded herself with her big sister's make-up and was playing at being the Bad

Witch: 'Where do we go?'

I composed myself, stepped behind the lectern, took my pince-nez from a breast pocket, settled them upon the bridge of my nose, and spread out my notes.

I cleared my throat. '"Who are we?" you say.' I looked up, letting my gaze linger on the princess, and then let it roam freely among the assembled courtiers. 'Some would have it that we are not human, that we mimic humanity, but are dissociated from its template, that that template is lost, or even shattered, and that what is left is a mockery of its original. But since we have, these days, little notion of what that original was, except, sometimes, from the archaeological record, I will continue to use the word "human", at least, when referencing creatures such as myself, Calaf, Prince of the Darkling Isle, fifteenth in line to the throne of Her Majesty Queen Berenice the Second. When referencing *your* kind, however –' and I awarded the princess a cursory nod '– I must be more exact.' My arm sawed through the air. 'Look about this hall. Here we may find Europans, such as myself, and Atlanteans and Africans, too, as well as Cataians. Yet we are indistinguishable. For just as the Earth's once disparate languages have coalesced, so have those races of humanity that, in the Ancient world, were classified as Mongol, Caucasian, Atlantean, Ethiopian and Malay. There is, nevertheless, princess, a clear division between, say, a Cataian, such as yourself, and me. Why is this?'

The princess folded her arms. I readjusted my pince-nez and once more turned to my notes.

'The division I speak of is, of course, the one that cleaves sapient life into the camps of humanity and the perverse. In the dark days of the interregnum that division was profound. Some two and a half thousand years ago, as the Princess Turandot has reminded us, the perverse colonized Cathay; it was, for centuries, a stronghold of fox-people, cat-people, shark-people and all the rest of those hybrid fabrications that were the physical correlatives of alien desires. But after Cathay fell to human armies, a diaspora of the perverse spread out over the Earth's surface, eventually taking refuge underground.

'There, the tribes mutated, and became a single tribe, who, unseen for over a dozen generations, but still, it is to be believed, lurking hundreds of miles beneath our feet, have, for the most part, passed into legend. We call them goblins, orcs, and, today, the mention of them scares only our children and babes. We have, in effect, forgotten them. Their progeny, however, still walk amongst us: descendants of creatures born of couplings between humans and non-humans, men and women whose bloodline is polluted with traces of the perverse.'

Somewhat self-consciously, I once more raised my eyes. But my orc-heritage was as inscrutable, I deemed, as my identity as a black knight. For in me, the human and the orc met in a seamless celebration of the simply *ugly*. The princess remained impassive, seemingly unconcerned at what I had said. I had, after all, only reiterated what was general knowledge. My predecessors had had little trouble with this initial hurdle, and she doubtless considered my oration no cause for immediate alarm.

'"Who are we?" you say. You too, princess, are the result of a forgotten act of miscegenation, a coupling between the royal house of Albracca and a human. Over two-thousand years later, the pollution should have been so diluted as to be insignificant. That is, after all, the way it has been for much of humanity, most of whom would find it hard to gainsay the evidence that they carried the dregs of a sleeping perversity in their veins, but who nevertheless live fully human lives. In this generation, however, a curious teratogenesis has occurred throughout Cathay. A multitude of throwbacks have been born, humans who have reverted to the genotype of distant forebears. Most still have vestiges of humanity about them, but sometimes one is born for whom two thousand years of history might as well not have taken place, an individual in whom the fires of the perverse burn with a terrible purity. It has been the fate of Cathay that one such rare individual is the heir to the Celestial Throne. Today, a young woman who follows the Way of the Cockroach again rules a quarter of the world.'

Her hands came together in slow, derisive applause, her dismissive smile as cruel as formerly. No doubt she considered my answer too pat, too predictable, to give her reason to suppose I might succeed with her next question.

'Where have we come from?' she said.

I cleared my throat, the echo loud in the stilled, expectant air.

'Men of learning tell us that the Ancient world was infected with psychic particulates emanating from a parallel universe that had suffered cataclysm. These shards and fragments of alien perceptions and desires changed us, irrevocably. For such reason our descendants chose to remake themselves, so that their bodies conformed to the new sexual imperatives that had been instilled into their minds and souls. But what was that world, the universe that, in its destruction and collapse, adumbrated what we are today? Few are brave enough to guess. But those of us in whom the perverse burns bright have atavistic dreams. And visions. What is your earliest memory, princess?

> *Jack and Jill went up the hill*
> *To fetch a pail of water,*
> *Jack fell down and broke his crown*
> *And Jill came tumbling after.*

'At the age when you first heard that rhyme, you couldn't decide whether you were Jill or Jack, could you? You knew only that the essence of your universe was pain. And calamity.'

The princess had grown pale. She held a set of knuckles to her mouth, and bit at them with her small, bright teeth, lipstick traces lending the illusion that they had been worried to the bone. Some of the courtiers leaned forward in their seats, stirred from their torpor. I had begun to encroach upon dark, unknown territory. It was I who held the initiative now. I felt emboldened, determined to press on until I laid the secrets of this land called 'Turandot' bare.

'At about the age of five, a fissure opened up in the bedrock of your reality. And something erupted from your covert, subterranean self, to for ever after haunt you with hot, dark dreams. It whispered. It sang. It warned. It praised. You heard it in nursery rhymes and recognized its call in the illustrated books that your governess would read to you before you went to sleep. Since that age, you have lived in two worlds: this universe, where you find yourself exiled, and the universe to which your soul belongs, the dead universe that has appeared to you in dreams and longings.'

I gripped the lectern's sides. The wood creaked under the pressure. My cheeks had begun to burn.

'As you grew, so did those dreams intensify, and so did that other universe's imperatives wax irresistible.' I pushed my notes to one side. I had no need of such formalities now. I would improvise. For when I talked of Turandot, I talked of myself.

'Nursery rhymes and fairytales lost all traces of innocence. You turned to paintings, music, philosophy, the incunabula and similarly found these artefacts of the human genius to be limned with the dark, abiding beauty of your lost home. Nothing was untainted. Nothing was humanly pure. Wherever you turned, you saw, heard, thought and read of pain, disgrace and abjection, and knew these things to be signposts pointing the way back to the one place where you could realize yourself, but which was to be for ever denied you. Life has always had that bitter-sweet tang of knowing that you do not belong, has it not? That you owe your nature to a world that exists only in your imagination? As you grew, from child to querulous teenager, so did your plans. For to survive on this adopted world called Earth you knew it would be necessary to transform it. To colonize it, if you will, just as your ancestors did millennia ago: by using your authority to draw together other spontaneous mutations who shared your vision of imposing upon the world of their captivity the semblance of their dead, forgotten origins: a universe outside space and time which yet demanded rebirth. And it has been in this endeavour, princess, this dark but, if I may say, heroic endeavour, that we have learned not just who you are, but *where you have come from.*'

The princess turned to her father. 'He knows me,' she said, in an urgent whisper. 'Stop him. Stop him before it's too late!'

The emperor shook his head. 'No,' he said, with what almost seemed a grim smack of pleasure. 'I may not violate the sacred honour of the trial. He may proceed.'

Once more she folded her arms across her chest. Her brilliant eyes sought my own, as if she were contriving to blind me with some last, desperate flash of ocular haughtiness. But when she delivered her last challenge, the disdain she had meant to communicate was hopelessly undermined by the tremulousness of her voice.

'Where do we go?'

I attempted to rearrange my papers into some kind of order. But my hands shook with such violence that the task defeated me. My disquiet was a match for her own. Sweeping everything on to the floor I closed my eyes and relied on memory and instinct.

'Where? It follows, from my previous answer, that where you *hope* to go is where we, or rather some of us, have already been. The Earth has been colonized before, by the alien universe of which you, princess, are a scion. It achieved this by infecting the human world with visions and desires radically different from humanity's own, yet, at the same time, so abominably familiar that they found a ready place in the hearts and minds of something like a half of the Earth's population. The influence of the perverse waned, until the descendants of those reshaped humans we call "the tribes" became either extinct, or lost to the Netherworld beneath our feet. But the coming of a generation of genetic throwbacks, such as now infests Cathay, allows us to consider the almost unthinkable possibility of the Earth's *recolonization*.

'It is, of course, your most fervent hope, princess, that the children of the perverse – of which you are, if I may say, such a paragon – may again assume their rightful place on the surface of the Earth. A glory it will be for you if you are successful, if a tragedy for the human race. Humanity, after all, has recently begun to rediscover *its* true origins. During the high days of the perverse, objective knowledge was at a premium, and all science and technology was lost. For when your kind are in the world, mankind's perceptions become skewed. Humans cease to recognize the nature of their own universe, seeing it only through the dark veil that was cast over us when a transdimensional cataclysm brought the ancient world to an end under a rain of strange lusts and atrocity. My kind, that is, *man*kind, and your kind, princess, cannot, it seems, live together other than in a state where one party is either dominant or submissive.

'But I ask you: do you really want this victory? Have you ever *truly* wished to dominate the Earth? Have you not known, princess, from the earliest age, that the thing you desire above all else, is not triumph – no, no, not triumph at all – but annihilation? "Where do we go" you ask. There is no turning back the clock. Mankind goes on to rediscover itself, and you, princess, go to your doom. Such will it be for all your kind. And such is your kind's deepest, most secret wish. Death. The ecstasy of death. And a final, dreamless sleep.'

And such, I thought, is it for my kind too. No matter if the perverse, in my own veins, were so thinned by time that I qualified as human. I knew her, as she had said. And I knew, even before I stared down the length of the hall and saw her kneeling before her father, devastated, frightened, confused, that I had answered correctly and had won.

'Don't abandon me to him,' she said. 'Help me, Daddy! *Do* something.'

The emperor glanced down at the scribe who had hurried to the foot of the dais.

'Do the answers tally with the parchments?'

'They do,' said the scribe, his dolefulness as unconvincing as the emperor's chaste, disinterested concession to duty.

'Then the Princess Turandot must accept the prescribed edict: that she give herself to this man, Prince Calaf of the Darkling Isle.' The emperor seemed eminently pleased with the proceedings, and so did many of his courtiers. Marriage, they would have reasoned, would be sure to clip the princess's wings, the ambitious, overreaching beat of which had lately cast the shadow of madness across all Cathay.

I think she detected the suppressed laughter. Laughter that threatened to well up and resound throughout the hall. For when she got to her feet, her face betrayed the angry realization that she had been the agent of her own undoing. That, perhaps, she had always meant to be undone, but had never known it. Until now.

Fists clenched and held at her sides, her small body tense, she seemed determined that her reputation as an ice maiden should not be sullied by some inadvertent signal that she was prepared to yield. Her perversity, however, could not be so easily denied. It demanded its place in the scheme of things. She relaxed, her cold exterior melting before my eyes, her body, grown fluid and urgent of line and curve, a glaring advertisement to the measure of delight she took in her débâcle.

But she would not, I knew, yield without a fight.

'Would you, verbose dog that you are, take me in your arms by force?'

A dislocation occurred then, at a depth, that, if not unplumbed, had not been explored for years, a depth almost fathomless; and if the rupture had not enjoyed precedent – had I not only that morning experienced, with Liù, the unpredictable resurgence of my humanity? – it would either have so astonished me as to unseat my reason, or gone unapprehended. If, at an early age, a fissure had opened up in the Princess Turandot's sense of reality, and something alien had entered her, then I too had been similarly invaded, with the difference that my human self had never been entirely relinquished, nor had it chosen, of its own volition, to abandon me in disgust. Buried, it yet sometimes became so strong as to predominate, and I would undergo a shift of character so radical that it would be as if I had awoken from a dream, that other, cruel, perverted self unsubstantial, ludicrous even.

It awoke now. Unsure suddenly of exactly who I was, I felt unaccountably sorry for the young woman against whom I had prevailed, knowing, as I did, what was to be her fate when I indeed took her, by force or otherwise. My 'better self' was, perhaps, in the ascendant for no more than a handful of seconds; but it was enough to disrupt my sense of mission. The prospect that, earlier, would have sent ripples of thrilling anticipation through my body – the prospect of bedding Turandot – filled me instead with horror, as if I stood on a precipice, whereupon one wrong move would send me hurtling into a void, where I would know neither friendship, love nor any other human sympathy.

'No, exalted princess,' I said, drawing back from the imagined abyss, 'I want you burning with love. I will return to you this evening. If you can, by sunset, learn my name, my true name, I will relinquish my claim to you and accept death.'

With a sweep of my cloak I walked out of the hall, the confused squawks and hollers of the multitude of bureaucrats I had left behind rising in volume with each step I took.

It was not until I was in the street, with heralds already pronouncing Turandot's decree – that under pain of death, no one in Cambulac should rest until Prince Calaf's true name was discovered – that the balance between human and non-human levelled out in me and I came to a full understanding of my rashness. I remembered my encounter with Liù, and what I had told her. 'Do you know who I am, little girl?' I had said, betrayed as much by my human side as I had been in the Great

Hall of the People. 'My name is Richard Pike, tenth of that line.' I had bested the Princess Turandot only to throw the prospect of enjoying her to the winds.

Would Liù talk?

My experience of the Darkling Isle's own breed of slave girl is that, though rarely evil, they are often mischievous. Exhibitionists, as fundamentally infantile as they are animalistic, they desire constant attention. Being looked at, arousing concupiscence – the grand, universal itch – is, for them, as much a source of pleasure as the autoerotic routines of their wardrobe and toilette, or being commanded by, indulged and played with by their feared but adored masters. But when they are denied, when they feel a man's eyes stray, and their coquetry, as they perceive it, is defied and rejected in the manner in which I had rejected Liù's, then they will seek to reacquire attention by an act of disobedience or even treachery.

The passing automobiles filled the air with dust, obscuring the meaner forms of transport that an impecunious prince might be expected to employ. At last, I sighted and then waved down a palanquin. Scrambling inside, I curtly instructed my bearers to take me to the motel.

I was no longer on a level playing field. I no longer batted for the humans. My other self had come to the rescue. I knew, quite simply, that I would have to kill the little slave, before she volunteered my name, or before the princess's guards could interrogate her.

I stood outside my rooms. The door, I had discovered, was unlocked. I had told the concierge that I wished to speak with his daughter, and to bring her at once. Having recently heard of my success, and realizing that he spoke to a man who was about to become a power in the land, he had been eager, disgustingly eager, to comply. Surely, I thought, pushing the door open with the toe of my boot and stepping uneasily into the cloistered shadows, surely he hadn't been so expeditious as to send his daughter on ahead of me with the pass-key?

Evidently he had. The drapes shut out the day, and even though the late-afternoon sun could not be accused of untoward intrusiveness, I knew her immediately, even in the shadows. She lay on the bed, naked, her attitude somewhat curious, like that of a fairground contortionist, or a child felled by a pathological identification with a broken, favourite doll. I edged towards her, conscious that something was not right, but unable, for the moment, to make capital of my misgivings.

She was supine, calves tucked under her spread thighs, the high heels of her sandals furrowing the perfect hemispheres of her buttocks. The head rested on a pillow, her arms turned out in the fifth position of classical ballet, *en haut*, the fingers, with their long, red nails, tangled amid the halo of wild, corkscrew tresses. Her eyes were closed; a film of sweat glistened on her body. And when her chest heaved, and her breasts rose into the air, high, then higher on the swell of her ribcage – the deeply indented navel turned into a taut ellipsis by the unnaturalness of her repose – her habitual, scratchy breathing would transform itself into desperate gasps for air.

As I drew nearer I saw that she was not completely naked, but wore the elements of what might have been some kind of masquerade costume. Thin metal stalks protruded from her brow, fastened to a chamois headband. Secured to her back by means of a long, silver body-chain that snaked under her breasts, disappeared below, and then resurfaced over her hips to meet up at the fork of her crotch before again disappearing into the cleft of her buttocks, was an amberous, thickly padded cloak, the convex profile of which would have given me the impression that she sought to imitate an upturned turtle, if I had not already guessed the truth of the matter. The masquerade costume was a hastily assembled, home-made homage to her genus, and, in wearing it, Liù had attempted to assume the appearance, not of a turtle, but of a gigantic cockroach.

Then I saw the empty bottle by her side. The powder stains about her mouth.

I leaned over her. She opened her eyes. 'Is this how you like me?' she said. 'It's my own creation. A style I call *roach motel*.'

I glanced away, and, lifted somewhat out of time by my discovery, spent seconds, minutes, long minutes, perhaps, staring at the unstoppered bottle. Its label, surmounted by a skull and crossbones, read INSECTICIDE. After a while my attention shifted. On the edge of the counterpane was a sheet of paper. It lay next to the piece of cheap paste jewellery that had doubtless been precipitated from her navel by abdominal contractions that, initially at least, must have been extremely violent. I retrieved the fake gem, pocketed it, and

then reached out and grabbed the paper. Shaking it free
of its creases, and in so doing, peppering myself with
dots of bug powder, I saw at once that it was a suicide
note:

*I killed myself because I was expelled from school.
I would have made a good slave, too. I was born to
it. The prince isn't to blame. I just wanted him to
know the way I feel. The way I feel about all men in
uniform . . .*

Propped against the brass bedstead were a few fluffy
toys, a doll attired in the kind of black, chiffon rag she
had herself worn only that morning – it reminded me
somewhat of the doll I had had in childhood whom I
had named Flagelleta – and a few sacramentalized
objects taken from my own wardrobe, including my
spare codpiece and belt. They constituted the
impromptu altar she had sacrificed herself to.

'You're the Princess Turandot's now,' she mumbled.
'Soon, I'll lose you. I'll never see you again. Not that
you'll care. Me, I'm not even a slave. Not a real one at
least. I'm just a piece of trash, I know that, just a rotten
girl-cockroach. But even a failed slave can be a princess
for a day if she's willing to give her all. And you like
cockroaches, mmm? At least, I think you're the kind of
man who likes them when they've been condemned.
And this motel is condemned. Or should be. And all the
little roaches in it.'

It was all highly fortuitous, of course. A death, a
silence and a suicide note absolving me from all blame.
But she seemed to be taking a long time to go to slave

heaven. Time enough for the princess's guard to torture my name out of her.

Her eyes closed. She seemed to sink into a deep peace. I leaned forward and took two handfuls of lank, black hair, and was just about to twine them about her throat when the eyes snapped back open with such force that I dropped the improvised garrotte and took a step backwards. Those eyes: they were filled with such a muddle of love and desire, and presented such a sad corollary to my own miserable life, that even if the door had not at that moment been thrown open, I would not, I think, have been able to complete the deed.

I shot a glance over my shoulder, dismayed as much as any man, I suppose, who is surprised in his rooms, not only with a beautiful, naked, adolescent slave girl stretched out on his bed, but one whose unfortunate demise provided enough evidence to convict him, if not of murder – the note would absolve him of that – then of such questionable proclivities that years of blameless public life would be compromised for ever, and by nothing more than the expression on his face: a look that informed all that beheld it that he had been here before.

Liù was taken from the roach motel to its palatial counterpart on the other side of town. And there she was cruelly displayed in the Square of Heavenly Peace.

They suspended her from one of the bamboo stanchions of the scaffold, her wrists bound to the bracket that had formerly supported the executioner's strop. The ridiculous wire feelers still protruded from her forehead, like the sole remaining item of a party costume a sleepy child might cling to during a stormy night.

Soon, a crowd had begun to gather.

Turandot looked out over the square. The sun was low, its rays slanting across the rooftops. And still the slave had not responded to her questions. I stood nearby, the half-dead girl between us, Pu-tin-pao withdrawn to the far side of the platform, idly stroking the stock of his blood-slicked whip. The last thing she had said, an hour or so ago, was that her agony was a gift to me.

The sun disappeared. Night fell.

'You have won, Prince Calaf,' Turandot said. 'I should have known better than to attempt to wring a confession from one of my slaves. They practise a rather esoteric form of erotic yoga. They are made familiar with the discipline at school. A painful death, for them, is something of an apotheosis.' The princess turned to the dying girl and sighed. 'Ah, she looks so like me.' More so than ever, perhaps, now that Liù so luridly foreshadowed her own fate. And I fell to considering how intimate the princess herself was with 'erotic yoga', and whether her practice of it extended to making proxies of her slaves. 'What is it that makes you resist, child?' Her eyes narrowed, as if seeking something that she yet seemed fearful of discovering. 'Is it truly the yoga? Or is it—' The cruel lilt of her voice broke, so that she herself became as a child, lost, confused and filled with mysterious presentiment.

Liù raised her head a little. With glazed eyes she looked at me then smiled, saying softly, 'Princess – it is love.'

Turandot walked briskly forward, a hand raised as if to reward such impertinence with appropriate recompense. Suddenly, she came to a halt. The hand, and its long, red fingernails that had come within an inch of scarifying the ex-chambermaid's flesh, fell to her side. She averted her face and spun about, smoothing down the perpendicular folds of her gown, and then her thick, convoluted hair. 'Let her be suspended thus for an hour or so,' she said to the imperial headsman, 'that her writhings and moans may satisfy the prurient curiosity of the mob, and then have an armed guard encircle her, so that she may suffer undisturbed by any who, in a fit of misplaced compassion, might be so foolish as to attempt the *coup de grâce.*' She turned, and met my worshipping eyes with a long, hard stare. 'She would not, after all, appreciate it. Unless, perhaps, it were to be awarded by the dashing Prince Calaf?' I shrugged. 'But of course, for good or ill, you belong to me now. And I have a jealous disposition. Let her die, then, without benefit of a man's embrace.'

'Then you concede?'

'I intend to make a virtue of necessity, Prince Calaf. I belong to you. And you to me. These are the facts. We live with them. We move on.'

She offered me her arm. I took it. The executioner went before us and swept aside the curtain that screened the portal set in the palace wall.

'You answered my questions,' she said. 'How?'

'Because I am the same manner of creature as yourself.'

'You are perverse?'

'Not as you are,' I said. 'I'm human. Fully human. But it is strong in me.'

'Perhaps that is why I now concede to you. That, and the vision of this dying slave girl.' She looked over her shoulder and once more drank in the sight of tortured beauty. 'It is almost as if she *is* me. The me you talked about in the hall. The one who craves, not power, oh no, not power at all, but annihilation.'

I placed a hand over her own and urged her forward. 'It is time for us to go,' I said. She looked ahead, putting the sight, but surely not the memory, of the self-immolated slave behind her.

'Yes,' she said. 'It is time.'

As we walked through the portal I heard several voices in the rapidly swelling crowd begin to hum the first bars of a mournful yet somehow triumphant hymn.

We walked alone. The guards had instinctively understood, or else been previously briefed, that this was how matters were to proceed, come sundown and final defeat, and had left us to our own devices.

The palace's long, dark corridors echoed to the crisp tread of my boots, and the brittle, almost panicky report of stilettos. And if the non-human side of my nature was now, not so much in the ascendant, but on the threshold of establishing its sovereignty and banishing my human part to perpetual exile, then so was the princess's cold, insect-like exterior likewise being undermined by a soft, yielding inner life that longed to be extirpated.

'You seemed so cold. So distant,' I said, 'when I saw you on the palace battlements, and then again in the Great Hall.'

'I cannot surrender myself to myself,' she said. 'I have always known that. Not if I am to reconstruct the empire of the perverse. I cannot allow myself to be like that girl you call Liù. To lead my people into a new world, I must be cold. Distant. A virgin.'

'And what happens now that your deflowering is imminent?'

'I don't know,' she said. 'Perhaps it was all just a dream. A stupid dream. How could I ever be other than what I am? But then again, perhaps . . .' She brought me to a halt and then gazed up at me through thick, tacky eyelashes. She gazed in the same way as Liù had done when she had attempted to seduce me. 'No, I must be strong. What has happened has happened. I must live with it.'

'These are the facts,' I said.

'Yes. You understand me, Calaf. And as you acknowledge, you are like me.' Her voice betrayed desperation. 'The two of us could succeed in resurrecting the perverse where I alone have failed. You might be emperor, not merely of Cathay, but of the world.'

'Which reminds me,' I said. 'We are going to our nuptials apace. Is there to be no ceremony?'

'Tomorrow,' she said. 'And then your position as the most powerful man in Cathay will not be open to question. But have you won me for power alone, Calaf? Do you not want to enjoy me this evening?'

'I don't covet power. It is you I want. You I have always wanted.' I disengaged my arm from hers and touched her glossy, rubicund cheek. 'I have known you longer than you suppose, princess,' I added. 'Have known you ever since I was a young boy.'

She frowned, then tilted her head so that her vision was occluded by her bangs and their dusky volutes. 'I think I've known you perhaps an equally long time. When you spoke to me in the hall . . . yes, I remembered you from my childhood. Though you're the one I have tried to forget. The one I always knew would track me down. The one I always knew would love me.' She raised her head with such a start that her bangs flailed at her eyes, and she had to blink several times, and then brush away a few stray ringlets, before she could focus on me again. 'But I don't want to be tracked down,' she said. 'I want things to go on like before. I had such plans!'

I stroked her cheek, then eased my hand down to her shoulder, where it found the clasp that held the diaphanous shift in place. I unclipped it, and the length of fine, black silk fell to the floor in a soughing of pleats and folds. She stood naked, except for high, leather boots and the frigid adornment of her precious stones and metals. She moved towards me, ready to press her body against my own, though whether in true surrender or in the hope that she could win a reprieve such as the one I had granted her in the hall, I do not know. And not wanting to know until I came to the place where I might risk all, I drew back and, somewhat to her surprise and, I think, consternation, took her arm with cool formality, and led her on through the palace's corridors to our mutually binding fate.

We entered a low-ceilinged region, abandoned, perhaps, for centuries. Tussocks of grass erupted from between the cracks in the floor. Moss grew on the walls, and rich tapestries hung in tatters, victims of the murderous moth. There were few windows, but those we passed revealed that we still overlooked the square, if at an elevation that reduced the gathering crowd to insects.

There were other insects. I began to detect a rank smell. Cockroaches scuttled across the floor, dotted the walls, and, at our passing, would occasionally take to the air in hissing swarms. The constant susurration, the puddles that we occasionally splashed through and, above all, the overpowering malodorousness, suggested that we walked through a sewer. We pressed on, and – as if to bear my impressions out – the cockroach population thickened, and the walls bore evidence of faecal smears and daubs, a kind of cloacal graffiti.

'Unlike the other tribes, roachgirls could not reproduce,' I said. 'They were aberrations, mutants. Within this generation, you shall die out. What good will your *plans* be then?'

Taunting her, I had hoped she might put off the masquerade of realpolitik and become the creature she had been born to be. But I had merely pricked her into making one last stand, one final defiance.

'We shall die out. Certainly. But not before we have infiltrated the world's slave-caste system. That system will act as our underground network. The Darkling Isle is hardly unique in having had a population of submissives evolve beyond the walls of its cities. Humans who, over time, have become culturally and psychologically addicted to servitude. Such populations exist all over the world. I have trained my girls to insinuate themselves into those spineless, half-cretinized communities and indoctrinate them in the ways of the perverse. We shall reshape that raw, human material so that it reflects our own image, in the same manner our ancestors did with more worthy examples of flesh and bone.'

'Really, princess, you have *such* plans. Reshaping! This is ambitious! Particularly since the metamorphic arts of the Ancients are lost.'

'We shall not need ancient science. We shall have desire, Need. And it will be so strong that it will re-impose our desires upon others. The flesh will follow the mind. The reborn empire will be fashioned by imagination and will! *Those* are the engines of change, those the engines by which we will recast the body so that it be an expression of the perverse!'

'And this new world of yours?'

'This new world will be a slave world. The beauty and ethos of the slave will be so widely disseminated, and at the same time, so desired, that her kind will come to dominate the Earth, culturally, imaginatively and politically. Slavery will be at the heart of human concerns. As will abjection, the base, and all other stigmata of the Way of the Cockroach. In our pain and humiliation, in the filth and squalor of our low, abject lives, we will be the world's mistresses. Once again, mankind will have eyes for naught else but *perversity*.'

She seemed less eager to convince me than herself: that the slave she was becoming would prove triumphant, not in spite of personal defeat, but because of it.

I felt gooseflesh, and then a fibrillation of muscle as I held her arm tighter, determined, now we were together at last, that we should not be sundered, whether by act of man, god, or a reversion to our other, weaker selves.

At last, we came to her private chambers. It was no surprise, of course, to find them guarded. I was, however, surprised to see Timur. But any twinge of recognition that might have animated my face would, I knew, be so camouflaged by my palpitant state of sexual excitement that I looked upon him freely, without fear of arousing the suspicion of his underlings.

'Your cloak, please, Prince Calaf,' he said in his familiar, inflectionless voice. I took it off and handed it to him. The guards began to pat me down. 'He can conceal nothing, I think, in that skin-tight attire of his,' Timur remarked, berating his men for their punctiliousness. Then he looked at me. And his eyes became like slits. He resented the fact, perhaps, that he was constrained to acknowledge my impending royal status. 'Forgive the impudence of these mere soldiers. But I hope you understand that no weapons can be allowed to enter the princess's bedchamber. Guards will be present outside the door at all times. We cannot take chances.'

'I understand,' I said. He had underlined what I already knew. In his high-handedness, he had come here to ensure that I did not forget the mission's parameters.

The princess and I passed into the rooms where we were to celebrate our dark rites. The doors closed, leaving Timur and his guards outside. I heard bolts fall into place. I knew, now, that there was to be only one exit. The sole exit which the rare conjunction of desire and my conscience permitted me.

I stood within a slattern's palace of mayhem and

grime. The bedchamber was as filthy as the corridors we had recently passed through. Its ornate décor, its moth-holed tapestries soiled with unspeakable leavings, its broken, useless chandelier and cobwebbed shadows, evoked a luxuriant rottenness, a celebration of aristocratic putrefaction and decay.

I turned from surveying the choice, circumambient squalor and confronted Turandot, allowing myself – now she was so near, so vulnerable to my caresses – a certain leisure in my appraisal of her. My loins sprung to life only when confronted by abject beauty, the loveliness of the low, the lissomness of the lost, a beauty so extreme it was quite, quite contemptible. I had sung of such creatures all my life and prayed for the coming of another Dark Age, a kind of second Carboniferous, when the roach, clad in lineaments of girlish turpitude, would repopulate the world. What man would not whose own abnormal desires had allocated him the role of exterminator?

Liù. Turandot. Turandot. Liù. Ice had melted, and the memory of a slave's fire had been replaced by a princess's newly awakened sensuality. The contraries of high and low, worth and trumpery, ceased to have any meaning. For the goddess whose presence blessed at the same time as it damned, all these things resolved into one. Just as she was abject, so was she a creature of noble blood; just as she was the perverse noumenon I had so longed for, so was she something more, something unheralded, a creature – the revelation so sudden it almost unmanned me – capable of bestowing an unhoped for grace.

She walked to the big, four-poster bed. Her pelvis

rolled in time with her short, measured stride, the perilous heels of her boots silent in the carpet's thick, matted pile. Her long, black mane swung lazily from hip to hip; her jewellery clinked, like a thousand champagne glasses lifted in a toast; and the small of her back dimpled. The boots shone in the pale lantern light. Black. Glacial. No longer imperious but, in emphasizing the helpless voluptuousness of her body, ironic, and purposefully so, as if she had adopted the paraphernalia of a dominatrix to cast the submissive imperatives of her rediscovered flesh into more cunning relief. She turned; faced me; swept her mane over her shoulders to reveal firm, fulsome breasts, their areolae so red they seemed diseased, like cankered florets. Then she sat down on the bed's edge and leaned backwards, her expression quizzical, as if, even then, she had detected that not all was as it seemed.

I came to her, tore aside some of the mosquito netting that hung in ruin from the bed's gilded canopy, and, grasping her by the shoulders, pushed her down into the soiled silks and brocade. She stared up at me, half on, half off the bed, her legs making no attempt to close upon and shield the exposed, pink cleft that wantonly yielded itself up to a reconnaissance. I unlaced my codpiece. And then I gazed down at myself, a captain inspecting an errant trooper. But no; he hadn't gone AWOL. There he was, as always. No Private Thomas, no, not tonight, but a Falstaff, a man who, if something of a wastrel, and, indeed, a rogue, was also a man who, in times of national crisis, could be counted on to prove himself an Englishman through and through.

'Well, aren't *you* a maiden's nightmare,' she said, like

the vulgar slave she had become. The transformation was complete.

I was, for the moment, forgotten; her gaze was concentrated on my cartilaginous sword, the basest substitute, the lowest, most common denominator, perhaps, there had ever been for my family's lost heirloom, *Espiritu Santo*.

I was filled with a need to confess.

'Do you still wish to know my true name?' I said. Unable to avert her gaze from the mesmeric scrutiny of my netherparts, she seemed as unequally unable to speak. 'My name is Richard Pike, tenth of that line,' I continued, staring down at the dumbstruck princess, determined to have my day in court even though the sentence I would pass, and that would be passed on me, was a foregone conclusion. 'I really am an English lord, if a dispossessed one. But no prince. A knight, if you will. A member of the Order of Black Knights.' Her frown grew more marked, then, as if she sought to dredge up the significance of what I had said from a long-buried school lesson. 'My ancestors were stripped of the family title because it was discovered that they had orc-blood in their veins.' I touched my face. The marks, that might, in another place and time, have been interpreted as scars left by acne or pox, had, in the Darkling Isle, signalled that I counted among my ancestors those last living relatives of the perverse, the goblins of the Netherworld. 'The Pikes were exiled, made to live outside London's walls. They lived so, generation after generation.'

She had forsaken the vision of my apocalyptic penis to gaze up into my eyes.

'A black knight,' she said, quietly.

'Say rather a man reviled. Someone the world could well do without. A man here to exculpate his sins.' I put a hand to her cheek. She flinched, then relaxed and turned her head. Screwing her eyes shut with ecstatic concentration, she proceeded to kiss my fingers, one by one. 'They used ancient skills on me, you see. Ancient science. It wasn't enough that they had found a man with the right kind of psychopathology. They used artefacts: engines with strange powers that effected a modification of my body.'

I bent over and slipped my fingers under her rump, just above where the boots terminated, a few inches from the apex of her thighs. With a violent jerk, I pulled her forward, over sheets so stained that we might have been contending on a discarded mattress in some fetid back alley, rather than the bedchamber of a princess. Then, lifting the lower part of her body into the air, I brought her towards her nemesis. She managed one glance, I think, at the remorseless organ and the trajectory of her own sex, and then flung back her head, and bifurcated her thighs the more. 'The Pikes have always had something of an extreme, fantastical and outlandish interest in female flesh.' I coughed, in a self-conscious gesture of modesty. 'But I fear I am without doubt the most degenerate of my line.'

Her scream, the Order had assured me, would be interpreted by the guards outside as a nuptial holler. 'I am perverse,' I said, through gritted teeth. 'Perverse, like you. And people like us no longer belong in this world. We must leave it, and make way for the new humans.' And as I fell into a rhythm, I knew that the human was finally gone from me for good, and that, being damned for all time, I was finally free, too.

I stepped backwards. She flopped off the bed, her torso arching away from me, our contact now purely genitalic. Both she and I were aristocrats, but I had always known I would have her as if she were a commoner, exercising my lordly prerogative of 'minimalist contact'.

I let my eyes feast on the retroflexion of her torso, the sucked-in belly, the ribcage that strained at the taught, shivery flesh. Her thigh boots rubbed against the top of my leather hose setting up a squeak that lent the illusion that the bedchamber had been overrun by phantom rats. She shook her head, hair sweeping across the carpet and its accumulated filth.

'I'm the exterminator, and you're the roach. The Queen Roach. You are the ice which sets afire, which frees even as it enslaves. You are Turandot! It is my expiation, princess. They promised me that on completion of this mission, my forfeited lands will be restored and revert to my family. My son will regain the title. The Pikes will again walk with their heads held high. And they can do it. The Order is powerful! My family's shame and dispossession shall be at an end.'

I walked her towards the balcony, the princess like a barrow that had lost its front wheel. Her hands were on her breasts, caressing herself as I moved her over the littered ground, her hair trailing through lipsticks, palettes of rouge and mascara, decayed or calcified nuggets of food, chocolate boxes – their contents trodden into the general muck – and the excreta of house lizards, birds and stray humans.

On the balcony, I looked out over the square. A crowd now filled it as on the night of the Prince of Persia's decollation.

'And what is this mission?' I said. 'Nothing less than to assassinate the Princess Turandot, and so prevent Reason and Science from being once more suffocated by the influence of the perverse.'

I felt the princess twist in my grip. She tensed, tried to sit up, failed, and then threw herself backwards. The abandon she had so long denied herself enveloped her, like a deliciously toxic gas, and she succumbed.

'Guards,' she said, weakly, in a pro-forma nod to self-preservation.

'They hear only the cries of passion, the screams of a young woman on heat,' I said. 'I am here to kill you, Turandot. Do you wish it to be otherwise?'

She wriggled and squirmed, though whether in some last, half-hearted effort to free herself or in a frank attempt to take her pleasure of me while she could, it was impossible to establish. 'But your Order of Black Knights has had its day,' she gasped. 'Oh, don't you know it? You die, too, just like we creatures of the perverse. At last, I see the truth! Both perverse and human must give way to a new order of being. Creatures born of evil and light! It is right that I pass away. I know that now and rejoice! It is right that we both leave this Earth!' And then there was a catch in her voice that betrayed that ambition, mortality, retribution, had been forgotten, and all that was left was the desire to be lost. 'Oh, my love,' she said, 'oh my beautiful love! Take me. I am ready to be judged!'

The moon was high in the sky. I focused upon it as I

had the big overhead lamp in the operating theatre before I had gone under the anaesthetic.

The time had come. I let orgasm approach and then overwhelm me. The moon seemed to bleed, as if signalling the end of time. And in the nimbus of its glow, or perhaps, only in the iridescence of my own tear-sodden eyelashes, I saw those creatures that the princess had spoken of. The ones who, in England, we called the Nephilim. The Order averred that it had wiped them from the face of the Earth. But perhaps it was mistaken, or could not bear to admit the truth, even to itself. Ah, I thought, is this then all for nought; is my house to be reborn only to be destroyed by the angel-demons who it is said will displace us? With a spasm, a contraction, and a yell that split open the night as if it were a membrane and I the ravisher of universal darkness itself, my scrotum gave a small leap of delight – delight that was yet tinctured with an infinite despair – and the modified seminal plasma, which it was my prerogative to infuse, pulsed up from the little poison sacs that had been inserted in my epididymous, through my urethra and into the daughter of heaven and hell. My goddess, Turandot.

And there, as it made its way through the lesions thoughtfully provided for it in advance, it attained her bloodstream, and set out upon its task of stilling her heart.

Our screams of agony and fulfilment echoed about the great square and directed the gaze of the assembled multitude to the eminence upon which we stood. And in the interlude between our screams, when we would both gasp for life, I thought I could differentiate words amongst the crowd's growing rumble; and I thought that the men, women and children of Cambulac were saying: 'The princess declares that she knows the stranger's name – it is Love!'

And I realized then that I did love her, had always loved her, and that she had always loved me.

Her body began to convulse and twitch. The great mane of corkscrew hair whipped across the balcony's tessellated floor. *'I see it,'* she gasped. *'It's there. Waiting. Look! So beautiful. So fabulous. Our home . . .'* Long, self-scarifying fingernails raked at her belly, her breasts, fluttered, one last time, about the root of the invasive length of muscle that transfixed her, and then at last found a home in her locks, which she tore at, frenziedly, until, with one final, massive buck of her hips and a high scream of perfect purity, her limbs relaxed, and I felt the life depart.

The moon's rays were cool upon my sweat-slicked skin. A breeze ruffled my shirt and found its way into the interstices of my uniform. I looked over the square and then down at my beloved.

The princess had become still. Quite still. Her wet skin shone like wax. Oozingly, she slipped from my grip, a molten, precious statue recommitted to a forge, melted, and then poured on to the floor in an ecstasy of waste.

It was over. My wife and children: let them live, let them triumph, let honour be restored, but not to me. For this is all there is for you and me, princess. All that there can be. A moment of glory, and then shame and oblivion.

It was enough.

Like a man who has all his life been leashed to a mad, barking dog, I had finally loosed the knot, upped and ran.

The air was shrill with insect song. Beyond the balcony, in the middle firmament between the streets and the star-flecked sky, a myriad of cockroaches had taken wing, as if come to escort the soul of their departed queen to heaven.

I took the piece of cheap umbilical jewellery from my doublet pocket. I held it up so that its rubineous glass eclipsed the moon and turned it blood-red. I prayed that time would stop, that life might be for ever as it was in those too brief seconds when I had consummated my office, and given myself to the one I had followed, served, hated, loved and at last destroyed in the same way that she had given herself to me.

I stood, unmoving, receiving the adulation of my people, and waited for the dawn, or whenever else the guards might choose to check upon the princess's welfare. The Order – deaf to my entreaties for the provision of a double *Liebestod* – had, of course, immunized me, lest I die spilling my seed upon the ground. But there would be no escape. I had known that from the first. I had been snared by the world's great muddle of love and desire while still a child. But if I had lived the life of a cheat, rogue and savage, then I would die like an aristocrat. The peace within me was like a celestial hymn. I stood, chin tilted slightly towards the sky, and watched the moon rise higher, higher into the consummate dark.

Like the princess, I was going home.

Espiritu Santo

'*Roo-too-to-rooey!*'

I stood flush against the battlements. It was a little past midnight. And ever since my half-hunter had chimed the hour I had been baying incessantly at the moon. My hollers and shrieks had set up a sympathetic chorus amongst feral creatures, both animal and human, that prowled about the foot of my ancestral manor, had awoken my neighbours to angry remonstrance, and might well have turned the wits of the moon itself, if I had not been sure that, like the rest of creation, it was already quite, quite mad.

I had been meditating upon whether or not to consign my baby son, and then myself, to the pavings three hundred feet below. As on so many other nights during my two weeks of leave, I had, after much staring into the shadows that swirled meaninglessly about my bed, at last got up – abandoning my wife to her callous repose – and made my way to the top of the bell tower. Only on this, my last night before returning to the front, I had made an inspired detour to the nursery and taken my son from his crib before proceeding up the long, winding stairs. Procrastination had so often got the better of me that I had determined that one thing alone would take me to the point of no return and thus expedite my release: infanticide.

I swayed back and forth on my heels, my son held tightly in my arms. Pulling back the blanket I bestowed a last kiss upon his pale, almost limpid, brow. How beautiful he was. Richard Pike the Thirteenth, my first-born, destined to be the fifth Lord Soho, if not for the despair of his master and the cruelty of his dame. How unaccountably beautiful! His angelic features without trace of the contamination that flowed through my own veins. A contamination that had been with my family ever since the first Richard Pike had got an orc woman with child and acknowledged that child as his own. Bitterly, I recalled the old snatch that my father had sung in happier days.

'Oh slumber, my darling, thy sire is a knight,
Thy mother's a lady so lovely and bright;
The hills and the dales, and the tow'rs which you
  see,
They all shall belong, my dear creature, to thee.'

But the world had been taken from us. The orcs had returned in greater numbers, and with a pitilessness of will not seen since they chose to cloister themselves in their subterranean haunts some half a millennium ago. Humankind had retreated into its walled cities, and hill and dale, or rather, the monstrous explosions of putrid vegetation that they had become, belonged to the enemy. 'Richard Pike the Thirteenth,' I said, in a hot, tremulous whisper. 'Unlucky for some.' He began to cry. I extended my arms, holding him over the void. And then I rocked him.

Lord Soho

'Hush-a-bye, baby, upon the tree top,
When the wind blows the cradle will rock,
When the bough breaks the cradle will fall,
Down comes the baby and cradle and all.'

For me, the world was without prospect of joy. The war was to blame, of course. The endless carnage. The random slaughter. But a share of blame, and perhaps the greater share, could be as easily apportioned to my wife. It would be only a matter of time before my precious boy, grown to manhood in a world of perpetual bloodshed and maternal deceit, came to appreciate my sense of futility and desperation. Better this rough exeunt, then. There was, I knew, no other escape. Certain people, they say, carry something in their hereditary make-up that gives them a susceptibility to addiction. For some this means alcohol, drugs, food or sex. And for others, I suppose, a stupendous combination of all these things, and more. Intimacy was my addiction. A certain kind of corrosive intimacy. I had long promised myself I would leave Joan and never return. But I always returned, telling myself that next time, it would be different; that I had nowhere else to go; that this was all I was good for; that the cultivation of our unequal relationship, in which I played the long-suffering father and she, the spoilt, if beloved, brat, was indeed to be the purpose of my life, if its burden, also. For what else might a man like me – one of Nature's little mistakes – truly expect? Certainly not the rapport one expects to find in more symmetrical unions. Certainly not the emotional and intellectual reciprocity of kindred hearts and minds. No. I was trapped. And during the nights that I had stood crowing my agony to the stars I had come to the conclusion that the only freedom I would enjoy would be the freedom of the grave.

The baby grew heavy. His bawling, upturned face screwed itself into an inarticulate criticism of my motives, suggesting, perhaps – sweet, foolish boy that he was – that I might not have his best interests at heart. I averted my gaze. Readied myself to follow him on what would soon be his downward trajectory into blessed nothingness. Across town, beyond London's walls, was the red glow of encampments and trenches. Searchlights panned the skies, and, occasionally, a flare would illuminate the enemy positions. Sometimes, even the hell-mouth itself. And farther away, shrouded by the night, yet haunting me with such persistence that they might well have been visible, were the colossal forms that ringed London's hills, glowing in the depths of my mind like gold at the bottom of a dark yet translucent lake. Forms that watched over the tribulations of humankind with the cool detachment of the gods that some thought them to be.

The nothingness beckoned. And the knowledge that a failure of nerve would mean returning to a nothingness more bleak, more terrible, than anything death might offer, emboldened me. I prepared to commit my son to the void. And thereby irrevocably commit myself.

'Nooooo – not the baby!'

I swung about so swiftly that he was almost precipitated into the void by mischance rather than design. Stock-still, I hugged the child to my breast, the small of my back against a parapet, staring into my wife's tearful eyes.

'Please, Ritchie, not this way! Not the baby!'

'This way? No. It's always *your* way, isn't it?' I said, with the profound calmness of a man who has passed his mental limits, and is about to disappear into the black, dimensionless vanishing point of sanity. 'It's always what *Joanie* wants.' It had been a spring-autumn wedding. Or spring-winter, perhaps. She had been sixteen. I had been ninety-two. One of the Darkling Isle's few nonagenarians able to afford the pharmaceutical regimen that conferred rejuvenescence. No fool like an old fool, especially one relieved of the physical burden of the years, but not their superannuated hopes. 'If I had ever had a word of genuine kindness from you it might have been different,' I continued. 'But such kindness as I have had has been meted out by an arch manipulator. Admit it, you married me for my money. The chance to be Lady Soho. You've never loved me. Never.' The tears flowed down her plump, girlish cheeks. She shook her head and moaned.

'It's not true. I *do* love you.' But I was as inured to her cant as to her histrionics. And sensing my resolve, her aspect darkened, her white, faultless complexion suddenly an adult version of my son's, prune-like with mute reproach. My wife's method of control did not rely upon shrewishness alone. No. Her moments of surrender, her woman's tears, were as much responsible for the outlandish conditions of peace I would concede to as her tireless campaigns of verbal, and sometimes physical, violence. The tears gushed the more. And I must admit I felt my old, misogynistic heart weaken. But what tenderness I might have claimed if I had seized the moment and submitted to her puerile will was rapidly disappearing. Within moments, her more familiar plate-smashing, table-turning, oath-screaming fury would be to the fore. 'Give me the baby this second, Ritchie, or I swear, and on the good book, too, that I'll bloody well swing for you!' Her teeth were clenched, the steel coil that ran through the silly little street Arab I had married tautening in preparation for the offensive. Fists raised, she essayed a step towards me. 'Perhaps I do only care about your money. Why else should I have wasted my time on such a little toad of a man? Those horrible drugs you take might lend you the appearance of a twenty-one-year-old, but they can't straighten out your bones or rearrange your phiz. You're an ugly rotter, Ritchie. Always have been, always will be. But then, of course –' she held a hand before her own inestimably beautiful face, fanned her fingers and studied her exquisitely polished nails '– you're a Pike.' She looked me in the eye. 'Dear, dear –' she had begun to put on the 'posh' accent that always made such a travesty of her demotic vowels '– the things a girl must do if she is to stand a chance of rising out of Soho's gutters.'

I hissed. Ran my tongue over rows of sharp little teeth. Looked to the ground, where the moon cast my dromedary shadow across the flagstones. I rocked the baby more vigorously. His crying had intensified. 'What a cross child!' I said, giggling with self-conscious nastiness, content, for the while, to up the ante of my wife's melodramatic rant. 'I can't bear cross children.' Joan took another step towards me. 'Not too near,' I said. 'No, not too near, my sweet, or you shall never see little Richard again.'

The muscles in her face strained to contrive a smile. 'Times are hard,' she said, her voice calculatedly subdued, the pendulum of her temper once more swinging towards compliance and reconciliation. 'And you've been under a lot of pressure. But think. You don't have to go back to the front. You can hide. Here. Deep beneath the house. In the old dungeons. The crypts and cellars of Castle Soho.'

'And what of honour?'

'And when have you ever cared for honour, husband?'

'More times than you may care to know. I do not, I am afraid, possess your glib powers of mendacity. But what could I expect a little fool like you to know of *honour*.' She stepped closer. With one hand, I reached out for my crutch. I could spy no candlestick, paperweight or household article of more blatant lethality concealed about her person, but if she were determined upon some bloody recourse, then I would treat her in kind.

'Perhaps,' she said, her elocutionary pretensions attaining the level of the cosmically pathetic, 'perhaps, malformed gudgeon that you are, I have been more dishonourable than you suppose.' Her voice had become so low that I was forced to cock my head, the better to hear her over the lamentations of the creatures of the streets. I knew from experience that when she exhibited calmness such as this it always presaged a storm. Shrinking into myself, and preparing for the worst, I took hold of the crutch, put the crosspiece under my right armpit and made ready to raise the staff and ward her off with its long, pointed ferrule. 'Do you really think such a beautiful child could have sprung from the loins of a wretched beak-nosed hunchback like yourself?'

I looked down at my son, back into the eyes of my erstwhile child-bride, then finally at the flagstones, where the dwarfish, crookbacked shadow, with its skinny little legs and grotesque pot-bellied profile made all the more notable by a great, hooked nose that my wife had euphemistically called a 'beak', testified to the force of her argument.

'We Pikes have not all been hideous,' I ventured. 'It was inevitable that, with the dilution of the family curse, an heir would be born in whom there would be no trace of orc, or indeed any other element of perversity.' She continued on her stalker's progress, each footfall lithe as a cat's and suggestive of a vast, amoral grace. With one hand, I crushed the child against the broad, ermine-trimmed lapel of my dressing gown, the welling of love in my bosom translating itself into a covetousness of all that was still innocent in this world. 'He is mine. Every accursed corpuscle of my inheritance says so. He is the salve of my broken, twisted form. He is the Soho, the new Lord Soho, who will wash away the sins of his clan and inherit a new Earth!'

She stood a few feet from me, an eyebrow lifted in ironic disdain. There had been no median in this marriage. I had either to spoil her, cajole her, tickle her, tell her I would never leave her, or retreat before the barrage of her fishwoman's ire. But if her character knew only two extremes – that of a whining, though sometimes affecting, child, and that of a shrill, cheap-mouthed harridan – then tonight she had reconciled her opposites. And the cool measure of her regard chilled my bones.

'You were made a cuckold some time ago,' she said with an intrepidity that suddenly made me aware of what should have been the less than incredible truth. 'Now give me the baby. You cannot love him. At least, not enough to destroy him, surely? And you may be certain he will never love you.' She crossed her arms over a perilously low-cut neckline whose twinned improprieties of opulent flesh I had always found magnificently vulgar. 'Nobody can.'

'But you said . . .' You said you *did* love me, I thought. Said, on so many occasions, that you would always love me. Love me until the end of time. Though I had long known her assertions of devotion to be shallow, and almost invariably followed by pleas for hard cash, and though she had always revealed herself, in her little, everyday acts of dishonesty, to be an unprincipled liar, confirmation was still painful. Perhaps all the more painful in that I had long felt the abyss of betrayal opening up but had refused to believe, until this night, that it could devour me. 'You said . . .' I found that I had insufficient sobriety of mind to complete the sentence. Her bald confession – with its fleshing out of the phantoms that had haunted me for over eleven years – threatened to induce in me a fit of riotous crying analogous to that of my son's. My throat tightened. Became dry. As dry as the invisible threads that bound the universe together. That, like my mind, seemed about to snap, setting stars and planets free from their orbits and spinning into the black hole that was existence's icy heart.

But I did not cry. In place of tears, a cold anger swept through my body. I shivered. I ground my teeth together. I glowered. And then anger became disgust.

'You odious little whore,' I said. 'I've done everything for you. Bought you out of the brothel. Paid off your pimp. Given you a home, food, clothes, jewellery, French perfume and toys. Given you, for God's sake, a name, a *title*. All I've ever asked for in return is a little affection. Not much. Just a little. But how do you repay me? With lies, thieving and unfaithfulness.' I stamped a slippered foot upon the cold stones, the harsh noise eliciting a doomy if barely perceptible knell from the tower's disused bell. 'The gutter, it seems, is all you're good for!'

'Hand over the baby,' she said, lips trembling and cheeks crimson with alarm. 'Or I'll call the police and have you locked up!'

She came on. Joan was a small woman, but like almost all her sex, a good head and shoulders taller than myself. And so it was that when, with a hoarse whoop, I swung my crutch from the ground in a great arc that put its steel ferrule on a course that seemed certain to inflict a corporeal wound across her cheek that would for ever remind her of the pain she had caused Richard Pike, fourth Lord Soho, I toppled backwards with the effort, and my arm – which, in exerting itself, had to cope with the gross counterweight of my hump – dropped. Fatally dropped. For the sweep of the vengeful staff decayed to the extent that the ferrule cut not across her cheek but her neck, compounding a punishment that I had meant to be severe, but not, in the end, so mortal.

'Joan?' But I was already tipping over the parapet, the unnatural centre of gravity of a four-feet, ten-inch man with wasted legs but broad, powerful shoulders surmounted by a huge, protuberant mass of flesh and bone, carrying me backwards, now, relentlessly. The crutch pointed to the stars, and then, as I sought to regain balance, clicked and scratched against the stone coping, its noise, combined with the wheezing of my lungs, reminiscent of a giant bug attempting to skitter up an enamel wall. As sky and earth changed places I was granted a last glimpse of the rooftop: a ghastly tableau featuring a young woman in her nightshirt, one hand to her throat, a bib of blood forming over her breasts, her eyes opened shockingly wide, upturned and as white as if they had been bleached with carbolic.

My last conscious deed, before my powers of deliberation were lost to a great bowel-wrenching rush of fear, was to try to tuck the baby into an embrasure; but my legs were over my head before I was given the opportunity, and the next second I was tumbling through space, knowing only that, in deciding, after all, that my son should live, indeed, that we both should live, and that the horror of life was nothing compared to the dread vacuum of hope that would soon envelop me, I had let him slip from my grasp. Procrastination had lost out to mischance, and thought and action were, at last, unhappily consolidated.

The fall was long. Long enough to fill me with barren wonder. Not so much at all that I was bidding goodbye – for that, I decided, amounted to little – but at the dross which would follow me into the perpetual realms of death, the effluvia of crime, shame and infinite despair. My dressing gown flapped about my arms like the patagium of one of the enemy. Tumbling, cursing, wincing, defecating – the long façade of the bell tower receding with dizzy haste to have all done – I plunged to the level of the square's humbler abodes, their rooftops passing over my head as the parabola of my descent delivered me to the darkness immediately above the fenced-in square. I began to spin, a horizon of grey walls pirouetting in sympathy, a mad carnival of faces, glib with a horror that only I, that night, could claim expert knowledge of, silhouetted against spectral casements, dormers and oriels. Faces that, for all I knew, revealed a satisfaction at having the promise of sleep returned. Time distended. For a moment I had seemed to hover, and I pedalled furiously at the air, subscribing to the desperate illusion that I might re-ascend to the point from which I had taken infelicitous wing. But the universe could hardly be expected to neglect the foreclosure necessary to my doubly damnable state for long. The illusion evaporated; again, I plummeted earthwards. Below, dogs, cats, tramps, waifs and nameless discrepancies of what passed these days for 'human' looked up to identify the nature of the screaming form that they may well have momentarily thought to be an incoming shell, and then scattered, to leave only street lamps, a fouled pavement and a brutal *cheval-de-frise* of railings to greet me. I closed my eyes.

'*Roo-too-to-rooey*!'

But the ground, though it tore upwards with deadly conviction, hesitated to introduce itself. And then seemed to comprehensively snub me. I fell straight through cobblestones, basements, foundations and the full strata of the hypostatic aeons, as if they had not been there. Fell, until I came to a place of darkness and dreams, deep, deep at the centre of myself.

Dazed, I wandered beneath Castle Soho, padding through its vast network of passageways and vaults, alert only to the drip-drip of water, the scuttling of rats, and my own shadow going before me, unaware, for the greater part, of what had happened, or even who I was. My flesh was numb – so numb that I was convinced that it had been discarded, my nerve endings those of a spirit, perhaps, striving incompetently to apprehend the particulars of a yet unassimilated order, an ethereality of the damned. Sometimes, a voice would drift down through the beamed ceiling. 'Poor man! How pale he looks! I'll feel his pulse. One, two, fourteen, nine, eleven. Hi! Are you dead? Are you dead? Are you dead?' I walked on. The air was damp. I pulled up my ermine lapels, my head contracting into the dark recess between my unevenly distributed shoulders.

Despite the knowledge that I walked below my own house and the disjointed remarks that percolated through the stone, I might as well have been floating in some black waste of the senses, dead in spirit as much as body. Yet I felt an unaccountable calmness. 'He's killed his wife and bibby,' a second voice exclaimed. 'Would you Adam and Eve it. He's done them in proper. And him a lord of the realm, too.' Calmness left me. Not because the comment had been unjustified, but because I had detected a plebeian inflection to the speaker's voice, and because I knew I could be judged only by my fellow peers. Stung by the impertinence, I decided to respond. To defend the indefensible. But the words I heard coming out of my mouth seemed to belong to another, as if, in dying, my behaviour had acquired a coarseness appropriate to my new station amongst the lowest of the low: 'I have had a misfortune; the child was so terrible cross, I throwed it out the winder!'

I continued on my progress. In the past, when I had had more leisure, I had explored these subterranean regions. And, I had thought, explored them thoroughly. But I had entered upon a quarter where everything was unfamiliar, a multi-chambered enclave that seemed to pre-date the house above.

The mazy thoroughfares were lit; somebody had been expecting me. I passed under arches, some crumbling, others evincing more radical depredations, and then descended, by way of various stairways, ever deeper into the Earth. I came upon wine cellars, storerooms and armouries. Little remained to indicate their original function: a slew of cobwebbed, but empty, wine racks, a pile of moth-eaten books, a collection of antique musketry and swords. And from time to time I would come upon a human skeleton, confirming the rumours that those of my family whose humanitarian sentiments were, I like to think, less developed than my own, had employed these dark, dank underground chambers as places of confinement for those whose personal slights they had seen fit not to endure.

As I passed under an arch somewhat more imposing than those that had gone before I came to a halt, and not merely because the chamber in front of me represented a dead end, with no passageway or stair communicating with a connecting room or deeper level, but because of what punctuated that terminus's derelict shell. A sword that, in many ways, was like those that littered the forgotten armouries I had only recently left behind. And yet as different as telephony, radio, petrochemicals and plastics were to the age of swords that that solitary, glittering blade so potently evoked.

Turning on its axis, it hung in midair, a *perpetuum mobile* that might, I apprehended with the certainty that one only has in dreams, have performed its slow gyrations for centuries. It was a Toledo blade. A rapier. And its blue-veined steel reflected the candlelight that here subsituted for the prevailing electricity. The coruscation sent a kaleidoscopic array of circles, rect- angles, parallelograms and lozenges dancing across the walls. And by virtue of their variegated light I descried hieroglyphs and graffiti scored into the sweating, mould- encrusted plaster: signs and icons that my own experience of warfare had taught me were not the work of men, ancient or modern, but the fell work of goblins. I felt the hairs rise on the back of my neck. For it seemed I had penetrated the outskirts of the Netherworld.

'You have fallen here?' said a voice I immediately knew to belong to the sword, even though it emanated from within my own skull.

'I've been falling all my life.'

'Ah, like all your family.'

'I have no family. Not any more. I killed them.'

'I mean to say, this fall of yours: it has been going on for generations. You are merely the Pike who has hit rock bottom, yes?'

'I suppose so. We Pikes are accursed. And none so much as me, it seems. Born ugly, I was fated to do uglier things. It is as well I no longer walk the face of the Earth. But it is not so well I am still here in spirit. I wish to be gone. Comprehensively *gone*. To a place where there is no more pain.' Like attendant spirits, mocking my failure to achieve nullity, the colourful, geometric shapes continued to dance about the chamber in time to the sword's languorous carousel.

'I am not your judge, Richard. Neither am I some kind of preternatural anaesthetist. But I *am* here to offer you the possibility of atonement. Do you not know what, or who, I am?'

'My father talked of a sword—'

'Then he would have talked of *Espiritu Santo*.'

Abruptly, the sword stopped rotating. The chamber had been silent, without echo or other acknowledgement that our words disturbed the air and not just my mind. But now another, more palpable stillness had descended, one that had suddenly announced itself by way of a sort of inverted thunderclap whose reverberations left me isolated in a perfect and terrible limbo. A place outside time, but infinitely distant from eternity.

'The sword that was lost,' I murmured. 'The old family heirloom. The sword that, according to legend, represents the holy spirit of another universe.' I stepped forward. 'How is it I have found you?'

'Come nearer, Richard Pike.'

I walked towards the centre of the chamber. When I came within a few feet of the flashing sword, I halted, gazing into the hypnotic, highly polished flat of its blade. My reflection stared back, as if from a thin, elegant, funhouse mirror, face distorted by its cambered surface and made ridiculously beautiful. I laughed.

'Do you know who I am now, Richard?'

'You're me,' I said. 'You've always been me.'

'I have always been *with* you, that is true. I came into your family's possession many centuries ago, when the lost tribes of the perverse sought sanctuary beneath the Earth's surface. I was perverse too, of course. But not like the tribespeople. The cataclysm that destroyed the world of my birth – a parallel world that showered your own world with the fragmented consciousnesses of its inhabitants – left my spirit intact. And just as I had chosen this sword as a sanctum, and not a human mind, the better that I should retain my integrity, so it was that I chose to stay on the surface of the planet that the perverse was destined to one day rule. I slept. Slept through the countless wars between the Netherworld and Earth-Above. Slept in despair at the degeneracy of my people. In despair that they would never be reborn. It was the notorious orc-slayer, Richard Pike, who, of course, at last disturbed my slumbers. And I flew from the confines of this steel to find a home in his warrior's soul. For though I once disdained to deliquesce into so base a vehicle as the *human*, I had myself become as lost as my people, a diaspora of one, you might say, an exile desperate for the life that you so profligately enjoy in Time. So it is that, though few of your line have known it, sword and swordsman have since been one. You, Richard Pike, twelfth of that name, are the still living spirit of an otherwise dead universe. You are *Espiritu Santo*.'

'Yes,' I murmured, feeling the power stir within me.

'An angel. A guardian angel. An angel that will blow the trump announcing the last day. I have the perverse in my veins. I have always known that. The first Richard Pike got an orc woman with child, and—'

'It is not your orc blood that speaks, Richard. It is that holy spirit of place that antedates the Dark Ages, a spirit that existed before my universe died into your own, and which exists still, in the creature that is you and me. For twelve generations of Pikes I have been growing. Gestating in the womb that is your family's ancestral soul. And now I am ready to be born in flesh. To herald the end of this world, and the coming of the next. The world in which my people *will* be reborn. For humanity has run its course, and the dark, violent beauty of a cosmos that you cannot begin to understand will at last be resurrected, here, amongst those whose minds and bodies we first parasitized, but will now ultimately usurp, the Earth at last transfigured into the likeness of my home – a kingdom that passed away in cataclysm, but which will soon be restored in all its power and glory!'

The silence roared, urging me to fill it, if not with such rhetorical fervour.

'You speak of an end to time,' I said. 'But will there then at last be an end to me?'

'Is that all you wish for, Richard Pike? To leave this world?'

'I wish for an end – yes, for myself. For others, I wish that time should not so much end as be undone.'

'You wish to see your wife and child? You place your hope' – a note of querulous disbelief had entered the voice – 'not in the rebirth of my species but in the resurrection of your own dead?'

328

'Will you grant me that?'

'You will serve me. You have no other choice. We are one. It must be so. But yes, if it be your pleasure, I will allow your wife and son to tarry here on Earth. But not you, Richard. You must depart. You must go to where I presently dwell, as must all humanity that has not been granted our boon: the half-world that my kind have inhabited since we were expelled from our place of origin. The song that has been humankind must end. Only then may the great forms that haunt the forests of your Darkling Isle be released from the confines of eternity. Only then may they enjoy the Time that they have hungered for during the mournful days of their exclusion, the broken, fragmented days when they had hardly dared believe that they would ever again be whole.'

'My wife and child returned to life? You swear that it will be so?'

'Reach out, Richard. Touch me. Weigh *Espiritu Santo* in your hand. And *know* that it will be so.'

Tentatively, I reached out and threaded my fingers through the sword's filigree guard and then closed them over the ebony hilt. Immediately, I felt an intimacy that I knew was the counterpart of that which I had both desired and been addicted to all my life, but which I had hitherto never suspected to exist except as one of the comforts of illusion. This, I told myself, with a measure of wonder and bitterness, was the only intimacy I would henceforth have reason to exalt in, complain of and return to. And the only one I would need.

I made to lift the sword above my head. It fairly

jumped into the air, as if impatient to satisfy me, the blade light as gossamer and informed with an intelligence that, I knew, would be the commander of my arm and the caretaker of my spirit until the end, whether it be of myself or the world.

With the sword held high, and the candlelight playing off its blade so that the steel seemed like a tongue of argent flame, I filled the empty vaults with the battle cry of my forebears: '*Espiritu Santo!*'

And then, darkness. A breeze had gusted from nowhere and the candles had been uniformly snuffed out. Panicking, I floundered through a pitchy absence of form that might have represented the deep before God had created the heavens, earth and Richard Pike. As my cry reverberated through the labyrinthine depths its numerous echoes transformed themselves into voices. A multitude of voices, none of them my own.

'I never heard a dead man speak before, constable.'

'Brandy and water, somebody!'

'It's a miracle. He should have broken every bone in his body.'

'He might have wished he had. I'm not so sure I should be wasting my time on someone who's destined for the gallows.'

And then the darkness spread from my optic nerve and insinuated itself into the deepest environs of my brain, the small flicker that was my consciousness snuffed out as effectively as the candles.

I swooned, surrendering to the cool, velvet night. Again, voices. Manifold voices, and many other things, too, denotative of morbid curiosity having got the better of a population whose more respectable representatives should have been observing curfew. I heard the sound of sirens. And then there was nothing. Nothing save the knowledge – conferred in the brief intervals when a scrap of sentience would return – that I had been lifted off the pavement, put in a car and was being driven through the unquiet streets.

But it was enough to inform me that the promises of the sword called *Espiritu Santo* were as insubstantial as all else that had been conjured up by my dream-laden concussion.

The benches were full. Some lords and ladies stood in the aisles. Even the queen was in attendance, the gossip at court doubtless hinting that the day's business promised to be amusing, and that an hour or two spent in the ancient halls of Westminster might alleviate the tedium of a winter's day.

I was secured to an iron chair, my wrists and ankles shackled to its rests and supports, my feet dangling above the chamber's plush red carpet. The two men who had carried me in and set me down in front of the woolsack drew away, and the Lord Chancellor, looking up from a sheaf of well-thumbed notes, regarded me with rheumy-eyed circumspection. 'I always feared it might come to this, young Soho. I always told your father you'd come to no good.' The central heating was turned, it seemed, to maximum, and in my ermine robes and coronet I sweated like a pig, though not one, I hoped, that this gathering of cantankerous Methuselahs were going to make squeal, no matter how viciously they might stick me. 'I won't waste the house's time by expounding upon the events of the last forty-eight hours. Suffice to say that you, Richard Pike, fourth Lord Soho, have been summoned here as a self-confessed wife-killer, and, what is more, the murderer of your child and heir. A formal plea of guilty would be much appreciated. It will not have escaped your notice that this realm is at war. And your peers have more pressing matters to discuss.'

'Guilty it is,' I said. 'And do not lecture me about the urgency of a war that I have spent so much time, labour and blood in trying to end. This house, after all, has become known for its cowardly evasions, its inability to embrace the only solution left to us, fearful, as it is, that the radical technologies I have championed may destroy, not only the enemy, but its privileges.' I turned my head left, then right, treating my audience to the full repertoire of a music-hall villain's scowls, ogles, leers and dirty looks. Several women looked away, one – an old dame with the virginal, strawberries and cream complexion of someone a tenth of her age – taking out a lace handkerchief and pressing it to her mouth before giving a little cough of revulsion. 'Guilty,' I reiterated. 'Now let us have done with this.'

'But before,' said another voice, 'we have done with *him*, I beg leave to put a few questions to the prisoner, so that the house may be clarified upon a number of points.' I sought to identify the speaker from the anonymous morass of ermine. I succeeded only when he stood to take the floor. It was Lord Bayswater. A man whose descendants had been numbered amongst my family's bitterest enemies.

'Ah, Bayswater,' said the Lord Chancellor, somewhat put out of countenance. 'Really, is this—'

'There is precedent, my lord.'

'Yes, yes, there is precedent. Very well.' The Lord Chancellor sighed. 'But be concise, please. We have a busy day ahead of us.'

Bayswater swept back his robes, stood akimbo and gazed down from his vantage point, fixing me with his iron-grey stare. 'This assertion of yours that we hear about: that your wife declared, before you so barbarically slew her, that the child was not your own: was it this, Lord Soho, that put you over the edge, so to speak, if you will, hem, forgive my choice of phrase?' There was a swell of laughter amongst the assembly that died almost as soon as it had breached my ears. Not content to have me consigned to the lime, Bayswater meant to humiliate me, it seemed, to make my great name a thing of mockery. I did not wonder at it. He had always been jealous of my war record. Of the esteem with which I had been regarded at the front, and the influence I had wielded over the high command that had been out of all proportion to my humble commission. His purpose, now, was to undermine whatever influence I still had upon the house. And he would do so by having my fellow peers forget their horror of my crimes in their eagerness to utterly despise me. For whereas each lord and lady present – wretched, depraved creatures that they were – might imagine, or indeed contrive, a death for their burdensome spouse or offspring similar to that which I had perpetrated upon my own, they would not have dared permit themselves to have sympathy for one who had allowed himself to be so easily betrayed. A cuckold, in English high society, was beneath contempt.

'Hang me and have done with it,' I said, for what I hoped would be the final time.

'So you have said, so you have said,' replied Bayswater, airily. 'But we cannot simply stretch a man's neck, and especially not a fellow peer's, without trying to understand his motives. Or do you, Lord Soho, have such disdain for due process of law?'

'Law? You know as well as I do that the law of this country is arbitrary. Or if you do not know, then perhaps' – and I lifted my gaze to stare at the crone who, for the last twenty-odd years, had lived inside the body of a thirteen-year-old girl – '*you* do, madam.'

'I know that *you*, Lord Soho,' returned the monstrous anomaly that was my queen, with that engineered lisp of hers that so appealed to her present favourite, the sweet-toothed octogenarian, Lord Kilburn. 'I know that you, uxoricide and infanticide that you have so predictably revealed yourself to be, have always been one to give us *problems*.' Kilburn belonged to Bayswater's claque, and had, of late, filled the queen's ears with poisonous rumours as to my loyalty, compounding the prejudices she had long held towards any whose physical beauty was less than immaculate.

'Yes!' broke in Lord Bayswater. 'The tactics, and, indeed, overall strategy, that he has often recommended have been nothing short of suicidal! And these latest plans, this big push qualified by ancient diablerie – it is, of course, madness. Pure madness!' Like me, he was a centurion, but one who had been returned to a state of youth in which chiselled good looks had only been accentuated by the steely, not to say – for such were the tastes of the queen – brutal characteristics of his extreme age. 'It often seems that the man means to kill us all!' he added. I tried to remember when that leonine mane had been as grey as his eyes. When his skin had hung in great folds from his skeletal face. It was impossible. But if death was a dream to those whose coffers bought them a new, eternal youth, it was a dream that I would soon wake from. And then, perhaps, disencumbered of flesh and all its attendant illusions, my ghost would see things as they were: that England, behind its façade of zest and vigour, was a wasted, lifeless fraud whose gaudy renascence had been unable to relieve the logjam of the war. Only the most daring and extreme measures, I had decided, could offer a true hope for a cessation of hostilities. 'Let Her Highness remember,' my old adversary concluded, 'that Soho is one of those erstwhile mercenaries, a *black knight*, and that his allegiances have always been in question. Good God, it is a well enough known fact that the man has the blood of our enemy running in his very veins!'

'Same old song, Bayswater?' I said, tiredly. 'You were instrumental in having my family banished to the wastes. It took us centuries to reclaim our title. And now, not content that my line has been ground into the dust, you wish to take away my reputation, too.'

'We are not concerned about the prisoner's military career,' said the Lord Chancellor, taking out his watch and shaking his head, 'nor are we overly concerned about his genetic inheritance.'

'However much he may be ugly!' interpolated the queen, breaking into one of her girlish fits of giggles that were the delight of her admirers and the terror of her foes. The two exotic rarities – more pets, really, than guards – who stood to either side of her throne remained stony-faced, providing the only exception to what quickly became a sycophantic chorus of general merriment. They were pinheads. Specially bred, eight-feet tall, microcephalic, killing machines, the body-guards of choice for those traditionalists amongst the Darkling Isle's autocracy who found the modern fighting man, with his pretensions to worth and freedom, vulgar beyond compare. 'Ugly, ugly, ugly!' shrilled the queen, between bursts of uncontrollable laughter.

'That is so, Your Majesty,' said the Lord Chancellor. 'But if I may recall us all to the matter at hand: since the prisoner has pleaded guilty, we may, with Your Majesty's permission, dispense, I feel, with the need for a vote, and proceed directly to sentencing, and thus, as I have previously submitted, expedite the day's other business.'

'Then you admit it, Lord Soho. You cut your lovely wife's throat and dashed your little baby's brains out on the pavement!' vociferated the queen, giggling all the louder, like a child who cannot quite believe that it has dared to be so forward.

'He has indeed admitted it, Your Majesty,' said the Lord Chancellor, with barely concealed disaffection. 'And now Your Majesty, the question of—'

'Yes, yes, yes. I know. I *know*. But before I put a noose about his neck,' said the queen, 'let *me* put a few questions to him.' Bayswater bowed his head and sat down. The Lord Chancellor frowned, nodded, and buried his head in the voluminous papers that he still held in his hand, his shoulders quaking in what may have been the prelude to a sob of frustration. 'Now, Soho, let me ask you: did you love your wife?'

'Yes,' I said. Then smiled, sadly. For I don't think that I had known, until that moment, just how much I had loved her. 'She was a child. But not like you, madam. She was—'

The queen's eyes ignited. She banged a fist upon the armrest of her throne, leaned forward, and then almost as swiftly relaxed. 'In my curiosity to hear you finish, I suppose I must overlook your impertinence. Continue, Lord Soho.'

'I only meant that she had never been old, madam. And never, I think, could have become old, even if she had lived as long as us. She was an innocent. A true innocent. And if I sometimes thought her a shrew, it was only because every day I wronged her. She wanted to laugh. To play. To have fun. To be with her friends. She was the rose, the happy, lovely rose of all our dreams. But I locked her up in my big, cold house and expected her to be happy. Happy with toys and the company of an old fool! My flower began to wither . . .' Yes, she had been a child. My child. A child who could never be returned to me. The promise of that dream, when I had fallen through the Earth, was false, as counterfeit as the land that England had become. 'She *was* England,' I said. 'The last of England. I will never see her like again.'

'Do you regret what you have done?' the queen said. Her voice was purged of laughter. And though she almost whispered, her words, brooking no competition – a hush had fallen upon the chamber – were clear as a child's for whom the world held its breath.

'I can conceive of doing no greater evil.' I studied the saturnine faces of my fellow peers. One after another, they stared back, a carrion appetite lighting up their eyes, as they readied to scavenge for the last scrap of pain and humiliation that the disgraced Lord Soho might provide them. 'When we were first married, I would take her to the top of the bell tower and she would ask me strange questions, such as whether there were animals on the moon and whether Jesus and the Virgin Mary were man and wife. She would talk of her past, of a time when, sick and near death, she had gone to heaven and had never wished to return, for the angels, she said, were all children, like her, and sang to her with voices so beautiful that she had cried when her fever had at last broken. And I think, perhaps, in those rare moments, she did truly love me. But that was before I tried to make a lady out of her.'

'And she turned to others for more human solace. So sad, Lord Soho,' said the queen. 'I'm almost sorry I laughed at you.'

'Fear not, Your Majesty,' said Bayswater, standing up once again. 'This is one the *world* will come to laugh at. And surely for all time! But when we have finished with laughter, we must consider that this man has merely revealed his colours by murdering Lady Soho and his –' and the filthy old man with the appearance of a teenage boy could not resist availing himself of a derisive laugh '– or perhaps, let us say, *her* child.'

The silence that had permeated the chamber evaporated. And Bayswater's guffaws were echoed by the house, a drone of scabrous pleasure that grew in volume and became a discordant hymn signalling that

England's aristocracy was impatient to see the lord who had wed a street-girl brought to account, not for his crimes, and certainly not for his orc-blood – which, if truth were known, more than a few of my peers shared – but for being a gull, a fool, a dupe of the worst type, a creature they considered deserving of no compassion: a man so promiscuous of his better nature as to *trust*.

'Oh, fiddlesticks,' said the queen. 'I say we settle matters now. For all his fine words, the man's a toad. A slug. A cockroach. Seeing him at court has made me feel absolutely *sick*.' She picked the sceptre from off her lap and levelled it so that its obsidian orb pointed at my chest. 'It's death, Lord Soho. Death by hanging. And I don't care how much you regret doing your poor family in. But there is one thing you must answer me before I have them take you away. How on earth did you survive a fall of some three hundred feet without so much as a broken pinky?'

'I don't know, madam.' I said. 'I don't know.'

In concession to my exalted station, and the importance the Darkling Isle's autocracy placed on ceremonies of power and death, I was driven to Tyburn in a black, open-topped Vipera, the big limousine's running boards burdened with armed policemen to allay any thought the crowd might have of exacting a more summary justice, or – unlikely as it doubtless seemed to any but the most paranoid members of officialdom – to dissuade those misguided enough to attempt rescue.

I was allowed, or I should rather say, required to wear my robes and coronet. For the sake of greater ceremonial form. And to demonstrate, I think, to

London's starved, discontented multitude, that if a queen and her lords would brook no dissent from on high, they would certainly have no compunction in crushing those so low as to be normally beneath their notice. But if I was a lord of the realm, and one happy to display the accoutrements of a proud if disturbed lineage, then I was also a black knight, and prouder, perhaps, of the renown the Order had won in the war, than of the deeds, manifold but sometimes dubious in the extreme, of the Lords Soho who had preceded me. And so under my robes I had put on my knightly uniform. One that identified me as a captain of the ancient and élite unit it had been my special pleasure to command.

As we wound through Holborn and into Oxford Street, several Soho denizens – some of whom I thought I recognized – forced themselves to the front of those that crowded the way and saluted me with a choice selection of obscenities. I put an index finger to my lordly little crown and tipped my head in their direction, conveying a wish that their own journeys to hell might be as speedy as my own. I was rewarded with a bombardment of tin cans, stones and faeces – the traditional rotten fruit reserved, these days, for the cooking pot, so effectively had the orcs tightened their siege. Something ricocheted off my coronet, setting it at a jaunty angle, which, turning to inspect myself in a wing mirror, I found agreed with my mood so much that I let it stay that way. The crowd, oblivious to the shouts of the policemen to either side of me that the hunchback was to die, not by stoning, but by hanging, and woe to anyone who thought otherwise, continued pelting me with muck. I lay back in the soft, black leather upholstery and stared up at the rooftops, picking ordure from my soiled, white furs.

The city, I reflected, had changed much since I was a boy. Its elegant, spiralling buildings worked from the forests of living stone that the orcs had left behind more than five hundred years ago remained, recalling the days when the Darkling Isle had thought that those stones would be the enemy's sole legacy. But the old skyline had been scarred, and not just by the regular cannonades that reminded us that the orcs had returned and meant to stay, but by novel contraptions such as elevators, skywalks, blimps and aerials – symbols of modernity that proclaimed London's days of glory to be over, its renascence of learning buried in the shallowness and terror of the new.

I leaned over the side of the car. 'Fools!' I cried to the mob. 'My father liberated you! He pushed through the legislation that outlawed thraldom! But you are still slaves, slaves to the cheap, unfeeling modern world, slaves who know it not!' My father had only achieved what my family had immemorially fought for, of course, because England's autocracy had known that platitudes, nationalism and an insatiable craving for material goods were a more successful yoke than the old system of freeman and thrall had ever been, if only because the chains that bound slave to master had become invisible. In this modern world of ours, we had all become slaves, herded to slaughter by the crass forces of history.

We reached Tyburn. I was allowed to exit the car without the indignity of being frogmarched, or even having someone so much as put an authoritative hand on my arm. And with similar decorum, the constabulary who ringed the gallows parted to allow me to ascend to the place of reckoning alone. Putting my foot upon the first step, I cast a withering look over my shoulder, at pains to master myself by assuming the manner of a man who scorns the mean consolations of existence. Not a role so difficult for Richard Pike the Twelfth to assume, who had spent his life as an object of contempt, and had rounded it off by destroying the only creatures he loved, but a role, nevertheless, that recent events had proved was easier in theory than when one is actually called upon to tread the boards. I moved slowly upwards, one hand upon my jauntily aligned crown, the other sweeping the hem of my robes away from my feet, lest I break my neck prematurely.

I emerged on to the platform to be greeted by howls, catcalls, whistles, shrieks and a general cachinnation. I glanced at the hangman and the priest. Like those who had conveyed me here, they chose to keep their distance, the presence of one of the Darkling Isle's notoriously cruel aristocrats enough, it seemed, even in these revisionary times, to evoke a sense of the fearful social chasm that existed between us. I mustered my courage. Walked forward. And, with a somewhat ostentatious show of distaste, came to a halt standing upon the trap. No mischance would initiate the fall I must now suffer, I told myself. No freak accident would dictate the terms by which I would today face death. I smiled. It was a little, private smile of relief. And then, drawing my face into a look of vast condescension – the final luxury a condemned lord may, perhaps, offer himself – I turned towards the hangman and nodded. Obligingly, he stepped forward, slipped the noose about my neck and proceeded to tighten its knot under my ear.

Curtly, I refused the hood. 'I may speak a few last words, surely,' I said. Visibly embarrassed, the hangman bowed and retreated to the scaffold's rail. Since my hands were still free, I lifted them in an expansive rhetorical gesture that took in all of Tyburn, London, England, indeed the world, my body as unconsciously eager, perhaps, of exercising its vitality, as my mind was to expend its last energies in damning the mob.

'I say you are slaves still,' I cried. The crowd ceased its clamour, and, except for isolated hissing, hung upon my words like an astonished circus audience that watches a bizarrely apparelled little clown walk to the centre of the ring only to expostulate boldly upon the rest of humanity's inadequacies. 'For thousands of years your descendants lived outside London's walls. We called you the idiot people, fit only to wash our clothes, serve our meals and enliven our beds. And you loved us. Loved us almost as much as you loved your own slavery. So much had brainwashing – both ideological and chemical – effected a change in what was once called "human nature". But my ancestors redeemed you. Under their leadership, you renounced your servile ways, and took arms against the autocracy. At last, by the grace of my father, universal manumission was granted, in return for peace and the reabsorption of the rebel counties into London's fold. But what have you gained? Are you really so different from those cur-like men and women who were so eager to prove themselves chattels? You believe yourselves free; even boast about it. But you have merely exchanged one bondage for another: a subtle, clandestine slavery that is the curse of our modern world and which has made slaves of us *all*.' I paused to take breath. 'It is our slavery to the past that I talk of. The endless recycling of the past. To exhausted, reiterated, subverted human history. And to think we once dreamed that we might rebuild our world in the semblance of the Ancients! Impossible! For we are without a compass. Unable to determine past from present, present from future. That has been the price of our machine age. If you are no longer an idiot people, then I say you are a machine people. Slaves of a world without a centre, a world that will soon disintegrate under the force of its own contradictions. And slaves that you are, you find the truth inadmissible: that you, like the world you inhabit, are without souls, without substance. That you are still here, in time, means simply that the struggle between an illusory vitality and the fact that you are foredoomed has not yet resolved itself.'

Throughout my rant the mob remained quiescent. But as soon as I had let my arms fall to my sides and sealed my lips – for I had determined not to waste further breath upon this contemptible world – they stirred, pricked to fury. Their former boos, hisses and lonely shouts of guttural invective gave way to a huge roar of outrage and protest. And if the hangman had, until then, shown diffidence towards me, it was nothing compared to the nervousness that the mob now inspired. Forgetting rank and station in his hurry to do the general will, he fairly skipped over to the lever that would open the trap and prepared to satisfy those whose full-throated, if inarticulate, critique of my little speech indicated that a riot was in the offing.

Hurriedly, the priest read from his bible. Those of the crowd nearest to me redoubled their cries, desperate, it seemed, that I should learn their vile opinions concerning my less than Adonis-like demeanour before my ears were stopped up by death. I gazed down at them and bared my teeth. And as they gasped at this brazen display of the Pike family curse, I reflected upon that other emblem of perversity, the sword of my ancestors that I had dreamed of and which, at this moment of truth, seemed to stir within me, like a memory made flesh.

The hangman grasped the fatal lever. I threw back my head and closed my eyes. '*Espiritu Santo*,' I muttered, and grinned, wondering, in the few seconds I had left of mortal existence, why I had ever had such a strange dream, and why, more to the point, it seemed fit to recur just as I was about to fall once again, this time into a more imperishable darkness. And then, as time seemed to slow, I repeated the sword's name, the words eliding into a lusty holler, '*Espiritu Santo!*' The crowd, but for isolated whispers, was once more stilled.

'*He calls upon the perverse!*'

'*Upon his gods!*'

'*Upon the people of the Dark Ages!*'

'*He calls upon the spirits of the dead!*'

I descried an argent splinter cross the back of my eyelid, thrown into relief against the membrane's blaze of luminous blood by virtue of its greater brilliance. I tilted my chin, opened my eyes and instantly screwed them into painful slits, positioning myself so that I might bring the invading object into focus. Wheeling out of the sun, like a fragment of eternity, a glittering abstraction that recalled divine messengers such as described by the prophets of the Old Testament, came a sword. Silent at first, but soon to make a cool, rhythmic susurration as it scythed through the air, nearer and nearer, the blade at last revealed itself, and in so doing, revealed my destiny.

The trap opened. I fell.

My robes billowed. Like a drowning man who cannot help but submit, I sucked in two lungfuls of fetid air, wholly expecting to be smothered in the universe's oceanic darkness. But my lungs were to empty themselves not in terror, but in exultation. When the ground had disappeared beneath me, I had been staring upwards, frozen in the act of observing the comet-like appearance of the sword. Falling through space, in what should have been the last moments of my life, I still stared upwards. Thus it was I saw *Espiritu Santo* cross the square of sky framed by the open trap and sever the hemp rope just before my plummeting body could draw it taught. And I fell, not into oblivion, but on to the cobbles.

The rope snaked itself across my spreadeagled body. There was a moment of acute inner chaos, shot through with the conviction that my neck was intact. I rolled over, tore at the noose, pulled it over my head and then discarded it. I shivered. Felt, and then checked, a sudden desire to gag. Instinctively, I held up an arm; opened a hand. There was a flash of steel, and my fingers curled about an ebony hilt, exploring its contours with the familiarity of an old lover. A weight, a fullness of being, transposed itself to my mid-section, and then into my soul. The displaced centre of gravity that had hounded me all my floundering, half-capsized life suddenly righted, like life itself. I stood, and my confusion went, finding a more suitable host in the awed constabulary that surrounded me.

I made a few sweeps and passes through the air. The sword, though eager, it seemed, to communicate to my depths that it was possessed of an otherworldly massiveness, was paradoxically light to the touch. I shook my head. Laughed. My mind was clearer than at any time I cared to remember. The knowledge that I lived and that the sword was no dream, neither now nor when my spirit had passed through the forgotten passageways beneath my house, was like a light – a light that burned away the shadows that had clouded my thoughts and affirmed, in the white heat of recognition, that *Espiritu Santo* and I truly were one, and that I could do anything, anything.

Goaded on by the hangman, whose upside-down face peered at me over the lip of the scaffold, the two men who had been assigned to pull on my swinging legs should the drop have proved ineffectual closed in. Their assault was less than enthusiastic, and I slew them both with three nonchalant swipes, my robes swirling as I pranced across the straw-covered ground like an imp on an invisible pogo stick. Across my first victim's torso I swiftly carved, this way, and then that, a saltire – the only armorial emblem that that wretched pleb would ever own – and despatched the second somewhat less quixotically with an upsweep that opened him up from groin to chops.

A vast power coursed down my right arm. And when the same power filled my legs, I felt impelled to do something more than hop about as if on a child's toy – something that it was useless to query, or even to resist, anointed, as I was, with such a surfeit of preternatural energy that, if it were not to find expression, would surely kill me.

I raised my head and stared up at the hangman. The next moment I was leaping six, eight, twelve feet into the air. The sword leaped too, almost leaving my hand in its feverish haste to score old Jack Ketch through his hooded eye. The deed done, I dropped towards the ground. The blade came away. The hangman's scandalized visage receded. And as it did, his hands twitched, groping at vacancy, one of them finally clasping the offended socket, blood and brain oozing through the gauntleted fingers as he tried to discover, perhaps, why the world had turned red. Then, rising up on to his knees, he fell forward into space, impacting a second after myself. I jumped up and stood over him.

'*Roo-too-to-rooey*!'

A spectator to my own actions, as pathologically removed from humanity's concerns as the angels above, I gave him a cursory kick in the head and heard myself cackle something about how his dismount needed more work.

'Shoot him!' yelled one of the special policemen who had forced his way through the scrum of more cautious officers who encircled the scaffold. 'The man's a cripple! A damn midget! Shoot him for the dog he is!'

Following his example, a handful of trenchcoated special police shouldered their way through the perimeter, stepped over the bodies of the executioner's hapless assistants, dipped their hands beneath their lapels and pulled out their revolvers, forming an inner circle about me that mirrored that of their more hesitant colleagues, but which would, I knew, prove inflexible to anything but the most fabulous displays of violence.

'A cripple?' I said. The eyeball that had decorated the tip of my blood-slicked rapier was sent flying through the air with a single flick of my wrist. 'Perhaps. But have you heard of the first Richard Pike, the noted orc-slayer, and my distant forebear?' They pursed their lips and looked at each other askance, these big, brave boys choosing to conceal their apprehension somewhat unsuccessfully. 'He was famous for his unparalleled cut and thrust, the elegance of his parry, the noble élan of his eviscerating slash, and, of course, not least, his contemptuous jab to the genitalia.' One of the officers gave a brief, expectorant laugh. 'His spirit is my spirit, his sword my sword!' And then I laughed too, and so much more unpleasantly that the circle of policemen collectively took a step backwards.

I went in low, my rolling gait no longer that of a hunchback, but of a man whose resemblance to one of the lesser but more verminous creatures of the field lent him an advantage over his regularly apportioned fellows – the ability to hop, leap, jink and scurry like a rat or toad. The laughter increased – the spectacle I presented was, I suppose, somewhat curious – then abruptly stopped as, swinging the sword downwards, I relieved the man nearest me, not merely of his revolver, but the hand that had gripped it, too, leaving him staring at a bloodied shirt cuff as if about to angrily reproach his truant limb. And as *Espiritu Santo* demanded more blood, I was as good as my boast, cutting, thrusting, swaggering, eviscerating, and treating the last man standing to an impromptu castration, before any of my assailants had the chance to discharge their weapons.

I strode out from beneath the shadow of the gallows and all fell back before me, the derisive hoots of the crowd now turned to spunkless, if prudent, applause. But I had no time to acknowledge the accolade – a customary one, I would guess, for any adventurer with the distinction of putting Jack Ketch beneath the ground along with a good selection of his cohorts; whatever magnitude of energy and skills I had been invested with, I knew I had to escape, or myself die.

The crowd parted. I spotted the Vipera. Growling, and showing off my rows of gleaming incisors, I ran towards the car, the sword held before me in warning. My gait displayed the loping characteristics that had made me a mockery to my fellow men, but which, informed by the sword's transformative power, had become a fighting style that, if I should exploit it to its full, I was sure could put, not only Jack Ketch, but the whole world in its grave. And sensing that power, all drew back, hands held before their faces with the dread that men usually feel when confronted by the most august of omens or miracles.

The passenger door was open. I threw myself across the leather seat. Shouted at the driver to get out, hitting him smartly across the thighs with the flat of the blade to speed him on his way. Quickly, I slammed the door behind me, switched on the ignition, put the big car into gear and stamped on the accelerator, the plebeian horde scattering across Tyburn as I thundered through their midst.

I drove through the ruins of Bethnal Green. Streets where malnutrition and constant bombardment had sown an apathy that, I knew, could only assist my escape. As I travelled further east, negotiating a maze of ruptured sewers, burned-out tenements and piles of rubble, the streets became deserted, and apathy, if still prevalent as a kind of intangible miasma, no longer wore a human face.

Here, in the outer reaches of the East End, a strange deracination had occurred. The newspapers had carried reports of a newly diagnosed form of fugue, where people living beneath the shadows of the city walls had not so much forgotten who they were as become convinced that they were ghosts. Wandering from home, sometimes far, far into the wastes, they headed for another, less substantial world. My own flight from reality took me deep into this spectral land. For though I reminded myself I was no ghost, I knew I might well become one if I did not flee London and get back to the lines post-haste.

When I reached Dagenham the vast perpendicular of the wall became clearly visible over the rows of exposed, blackened rafters that constituted the skyline. Many centuries ago the wall's stones had been supplemented with titanic blocks hewn from the forests that the Netherworld had sown on Earth-Above during its many raids and incursions. And that stone, alive in a manner incomprehensible even to modern-day science, had extended the wall to a height comparable to that of Castle Soho. The stone had died, like the forests themselves, but in death, instead of rejuvenating into something terrible and strange, like the meta-morphosed woodlands surrounding London, had been subsumed into the wall's original masonry, with only a corbel that had the aspect of a branch, or an embrasure that seemed, at first glance, a gigantic bole, to suggest the nature, the dark, unnatural nature, that predicated our defences.

I put my foot down, heading towards a section of the wall that I knew, from the inspection tours I had carried out prior to submitting my most recent recom-mendations to the high command, was guarded by my fellow black knights. Men who, seeing my uniform and rank, and remembering my previous visits, would be unlikely to quiz me on where I had come from or where I was going, but simply open the gates and allow me through.

And so it was. I screeched to a halt; looked up to the grilled window that overlooked the approach road and barked out an order. The guard looked down, awarding me a perfunctory salute. The big gates creaked open. I was waved on. The car nosed under the great arch, through a longish tunnel – I never failed to wonder at the percipience of those of our forebears who, ignorant of the power of artillery, had yet provided future genera-tions with such substantial fortifications – and then, emerging into the desolate countryside that lay beyond, accelerated away as I pushed the Vipera to its limits.

The plain was so flat that the wall remained visible in the rear-view mirror long after I had clocked up several miles: a strip of black anonymous stone demarcating the spires and finials that lay beyond its compass from the frozen mud that flashed by and extended as far as the eye could see.

I concentrated on the road ahead. Even though it was near midday, the horizon still possessed its idiosyncratic red glow, which, at night, filled the sky above the front line with what seemed luminous, blood-drenched thunderclouds. Like most soldiers, my men were superstitious, and the sight regularly exacerbated their unhealthy proclivities to believe that it was the spilling of their own blood that was being foretold. It did not seem to matter how much I might assure them that the aurora was man-made, the result of the military-industrial complex I had been instrumental in creating and which, far from prophesying doom, was a cause for hope, even celebration; did not matter how much I emphasized that it was only with the aid of vastly improved materiel that we could even begin to think about bringing the war to an unconditional end. They knew they were to die. And would not be convinced otherwise.

Ruins began to dot the plain, the remains of villages, manor houses and farms. Before long, I began to pass through the outskirts of military encampments. The noise of artillery had become insistent, rumbling like a distant electrical storm. I braked, forced to slow down by a column of troops. They hobbled along either side of the road, covered in filth and so dazed that any one of them might well have fallen under the Vipera's front wheels if I had not exercised due caution.

The column thickened to such an extent that it

became impassable without recourse to vehicular manslaughter. I steered the car to the side of the road and got out, sliding *Espiritu Santo* between my belt and hip and then covering it beneath the folds of my robes. I knew where I was. A little way off, the great chimneys and flues that rose from factories deep beneath the Earth – factories we had taken from the orcs after pushing back their initial advance a quarter of a century ago, and which were now dedicated to manufacturing the most terrible weapons the mind of man could devise – spewed out their characteristic emissions and tainted the sky.

Resignedly, I began to shuffle through the oncoming human traffic, each soldier I pushed aside impassive, uncomplaining, as if to be treated thus by a little bantam cock in masquerade costume was something so common as to pass notice.

But if these war-weary troops displayed the same apathy that I had encountered in London's East End, I would soon, and soon enough, come upon those in whom I might expect to provoke suspicion. The tale of my escape from the noose would spread. And none who had not recently had their senses derailed by any one of the numerous disasters of war could not fail to form a mental association between the diminutive man in ermine robes and coronet who passed through their midst and reports of the base deeds of Richard Pike, Lord Soho.

My only hope, I knew, was to find Melchezidek.

My batman entered the dugout. My robes had been laundered and my coronet polished to a tee. He carried them in his outstretched arms.

'Are you sure you wish to wear these garments, sir? I would hazard they are somewhat *cumbersome* for the battlefield.'

I looked up from the maps that I had spread out over the table. 'I'm sure they are.' I stood and turned to the pier glass. Like my ceremonial robes, the uniform I wore was scrupulously clean. The leather doublet had been buffed to a fine gloss, so too the leather hose, riding boots, thick studded belt and matching codpiece. A scabbard, of similarly refined pedigree, was buckled to my side, the hilt of *Espiritu Santo* protruding from its calfskin mouth. I held out my arms, indicating that I wished to be dressed. 'But cumbersome or not, they are what my family has coveted for many generations. I am determined to die a lord.'

'A somewhat morbid sentiment, is it not sir, if I may be so bold?'

'It would be pointless, I think, to deny that I have a morbid temperament. I am, after all, a Pike.'

'And your father would be proud of you, sir. Your grandfather, too.'

'My grandfather? A monumental pervert, I've heard. Died out East, they say. My father? Well, I hardly knew him. His life was spent consolidating the return of the family's property, title and power.'

'You'll recall that *I* knew your father, sir. And I can tell you: he was a Pike through and through.'

The ermine settled upon my shoulders. I drew the fur greedily about me. It was cold. A sleeting rain had, that morning, come in from the north. My batman stooped – there was a quite audible *crack* – and placed the coronet upon my head. The sound of his protesting bones reminded me of his great age. Like most of the population, he had never rejuvenated; yet, despite being an old friend of the family whom I had known for over one hundred years, I could not remember him ever having changed. Outwardly, he was lean as a pipe-cleaner and straight as a board, if as ugly, or perhaps even uglier, than his master.

'You have been with my family a long time, Melchezidek. I feel you have known us *all* through and through.'

Just as you have aided us, I might have added, in times of peril. When I had fled London some three weeks ago, it had been he who, hearing of my escape, and that a warrant had already been telegraphed down the lines for my re-arrest, had tracked me down and taken me into hiding. Then, surprising me as much by his brazenness as by hitherto concealed, if very real diplomatic skills, he had approached the high command and explained to them exactly why the demands of civil law would have to give way to the more practical considerations of the battlefield. 'It is not merely that Captain Pike wishes to die like a soldier,' he had said, 'but that he is one of the few officers familiar with the technical details of the projected big push. One of the few who has championed the principles of mechanized warfare, the budget for which, I need not remind you, he successfully pressed in parliament, confounding those obfuscating scoundrels who roundly condemned the army's desire to research weapons of mass destruction. General, you simply cannot *afford* to lose Captain Pike.'

Melchezidek's ploy had proved successful. Something I found all the more surprising given that my batman had more orc blood in him than I, and presented an aspect, grey, wrinkled and horny, that was unlikely to instil confidence in a less genetically compromised human soul.

I inspected myself in the mirror, striving to look past the hooked nose, pot-belly and crooked back that constituted my own share of repulsiveness, and see into the self that had been revealed to me when I had lain unconscious at the foot of my ancestral home. The part of me that was *Espiritu Santo*.

'But the question is, Melchezidek, how well do you know the sword?'

'I always knew it would return to your family's keeping, sir. Just as surely as I knew that you would return to the front.'

'And what I have told you of all that I experienced when I fell from the top of Castle Soho, and for some reason survived, only to dream that I walked beneath the Earth: do you know enough to explain *that*?'

He cleared his throat and turned away, his face towards the retaining wall. Taking a step forward, he ran his hands over some of the shelves I had had erected, like an over-conscientious butler testing for dust. I had gone to some pains to make sure the dugout contained a few paltry reminders of home: a broken porcelain doll; an old cut-throat razor with a mother-of-pearl handle lying against a basin; a swordstick; the cast of an elephantine penis; a book of verse. And in addition to these oddments were contemporary and more impersonal artefacts that, like those reminders of my family's strange past, were reinterpretations, or perversions, of history. Vinyl recordings of *Le Nozze di Figaro* and *Turandot*; a gilt-framed movie poster of the beautiful starlet, Veda Pierce, the spoilt brat par excellence; postcards of Boucher, Fragonard, Watteau, and the autobiography of Giovanni Jacopo Casanova de Seingalt and the diaries of the Goncourts. But of late these things, in their bitter-sweet summations of my former life, gave no comfort, but only emphasized the impossible distance I must travel if I were ever to see their like again.

'Might it be true?' I said, quietly, addressing the back of my batman's head. 'The promise the sword made: might it really be possible to undo my crimes and bring Joan and Richard back to life?'

Again, he cleared his throat. 'All I know, sir, is that I've been waiting. I do not quite know why. The waiting has been as mysterious as my natural longevity. Yes, all I know is that you are the last of your kind, the man who must bring his race's fabulous iterations to an end. The coda, if you will, of an age. But as for more than that . . . I am only a man, sir. Or rather a half-man. A witch. Not even a player, but someone who has spent most of his time in the wings. What more can I tell you?'

I hesitated. The cold seemed to have solidified the air, so that I felt like a fly trapped in a piece of refrigerated amber. In subjective terms, my life processes had slowed to such an extent that my thoughts – racing forward, as they were, to find some conclusion – belonged to a world where men were born, weaned, brought to boyhood, manhood and then the grave in a single day. This day. This day, I thought, that promised to settle all. 'Am I and the sword one?' Each word chipped at the frozen stillness like a verbal ice pick.

The stillness fractured. 'If I am a half-man, sir,' he replied, 'believe me when I say with all respect that you have never been a man at all. Not that there are true men any more. All of us are infected with the perversions of mind and body that have riddled the centuries. It is just that you, sir . . . you are not of this universe. When the first Richard Pike asked me, shortly before he died, to bring his only surviving child home to the Darkling Isle, he told me of something that had happened to him, deep, deep below the Earth's surface. And he begged me, sir, to ensure that a similar fate would not befall his boy. That is why, when the second Richard Pike acquired the Soho title, I buried the sword beneath his house, hoping that, in time, the curse would be lifted. That is, that the spirit which had invested the sword, and subsequently, its master's soul, would be exorcised, and preside only over the Earth's nether regions, where it belonged. But during the course of the centuries, my hopes have been dashed. And I have come to realize that the curse may be lifted only one way.'

'It's all as I've been told,' I said, feeling something that was composed of dread and hope in equal measure oscillate through me like a radio wave from the beyond. 'Say no more.'

I strode forward, pulled aside the canvas flap of the dugout and, leaving Melchezidek behind, stepped out to confront a clear blue sky. The sleet had gone, and though it was still bitterly cold, the wind had abated. I knew, then, that this day, so meteorologically bland, would, in some as yet indefinable way, indeed prove wondrous.

I traversed the duckboards in a westerly direction passing row upon row of whey-faced troops who had been called up from the rear. Rats and frogs scuttled before me. NCOs shouted, 'Stand-to, stand-to!' At last I came to where my company of hardened warriors hunkered, ready to go over the top. They were all black knights. It affected me more than I can tell to see their ready salutes and smiles. Within London's walls, I had always been despised; a fitting subject for children's taunts. But here, where life and death were so inter-changeable, to the extent that one did not know, sometimes, whether one was a living man or a ghost, I had won, through various exploits on the field, a certain respect, perhaps even a modicum of renown. It was right that I died here and not upon the gallows. It was the only honour I was liable to salvage from an otherwise dishonourable life.

I came to a halt; nodded to my sergeant. Down the line, men loaded their rifles, fixed bayonets and crossed themselves, waiting for the order.

I crawled up the entrenchment. My sergeant handed me a periscope. I propped it up on the leading edge of the corrugated steel that reinforced the earth and peered into the eyepiece.

Smoke billowed about the enemy positions then cleared a little, and I saw that their wire had been broken. Great craters pocked the steaming earth. I waited, scanning no-man's-land for signs of activity. I could see no movement. All was as still as the frozen air. No snipers. No scouts. Indeed, nothing to indicate that the orcs in the trenches that were the counterpart to our own were still alive.

They were, of course. Experience had proved that they always were, no matter how heavy a pounding they took. That is why, today, our basic strategy was to change. The weapon that I had London's scientists working on for the last six months was designed to break the stalemate once and for all. It was a weapon that my critics said had been adumbrated, not by theorems, formulae and hypotheses, but by the ancient world's fables, arguing that the resources I had had allocated to research and development represented a vast waste of money and time, and that moreover, thing of fable that it was, it would never work. My more thoughtful critics, amongst whom I numbered Lord Bayswater, had argued the contrary: that the weapon had real historical antecedents, and that my attempts to remake it from the mathematically dubious recipes of grimoires and incunabula, would end, not in red faces all round, but in catastrophe. I myself well understood the risk. But I had seen too many young men throw away their lives for a few feet of bloodstained mud. No catastrophe could ever compare to the one we presently suffered.

I waited for the sound of the aeroplane. And as I waited, anxious that some unforeseen contingency had prevented it from taking off, the winter sun rose sufficiently to reveal the outlying hills. I adjusted the periscope's magnification to take in the familiar yet always awe-inspiring spectacle of the Nephilim.

How beautiful they were, those sentinel-like beings who held us in a kind of second siege. No matter that, like my batman, they were committed to a waiting game, and surprised us only by their unwavering patience. I focused on the golden body of what could equally have been a man or a woman suspended in a gelatinous sac between two great trees, glistening in the rays of the pendent sun.

The tree line that had, centuries before, been composed of living stone, and then, dying into petrifaction, been reborn as a great forest of flesh, presented a frontier between heaven and earth, the angelic and the fallen. The golden beings strung along its length, some said, promised to reconcile high and low, good and evil, and, yes, perhaps even beauty and ugliness. They were angel-demons. And they waited for us to depart as much as for the hour of their own nativity. The bodies within the folds and twists of the pink corpus of leaf and bough – their flesh either merging with or standing out from the surrounding, fleshly vegetation – left no doubt that the forest served as a womb.

We had long known the forests were pregnant with strange, new life. A life that we all suspected presaged our own end. Known with such clairvoyance that many had tried, unsuccessfully, to extirpate the chimeras and other, more powerful, spontaneously generated creatures that incubated in England's hills and dales. The black knights themselves had been to the forefront of such exercises. But the forests were dangerous. The life that slept there would sometimes wake, to deadly effect. And as the forests had grown, eventually to cover all of England, human life – or rather, what remained of human life – had retreated to its last line of defence: London.

Were the Nephilim the reason that I did not feel more than a numb despair for the loss of my wife and child? Why I did not rage, or cry with unanswerable sorrow? Perhaps. For it was not only a family I had lost, but a world. Whatever might happen today, the Nephilim would be the long-term victors.

I set the periscope down. In the distance, I heard the drone of a biplane. My men gazed up at the sky, expectantly. I took the whistle from the chain about my neck and put it between my lips. And then I pulled out my half-hunter. As the minute hand touched the hour, it chimed, a gay, tinny sound so lacking in gravitas that I almost expected it to be followed by a second, more deathly, knell that would upbraid it for its frivolousness. And I could not help but think that, though this might be the hour of our deliverance, it might also herald a time when watches would have no purpose, a time when human time would come to an end.

With a great roar, whose approach had been partly disguised by the drone of the plane, the armoured transports that would precede our advance trundled over our trenches, their hulls, bristling with long, steel spikes, lending them the appearance of mechanical porcupines, or weird engines of excruciation that might have enjoyed currency in the Dark Ages.

I blew a long blast on the whistle.

Then, drawing my heavy service revolver, and struggling up the rough, wooden steps, I was over the top, gun cocked and pointed forwards, walking as steadily as I could, and making for the gap in our wire.

I passed through; glanced backwards. My company were at my heels, rifles at the ready, a line that would, I knew, if the bomb should prove a squid, soon have to cope with the Netherworld's machine guns, the doom of so many of London's young men. I called to them to adopt my own pace, and not allow themselves to be panicked by the silence and the memories of comrades who had gone before. But their attention was wholly upon the skies as the signature of the plane grew closer. In the end, unable to resist the temptation, I too wrested my gaze from the wire that, several hundred yards ahead, paralleled our own, and looked up to scan the faultlessly blue sky.

I spotted the plane at the same time as my men, and as they broke into a unified cheer, I fought to make myself heard, with cries of 'Steady' and 'Eyes on the job, lads' lost to the general hubbub of joy and apprehension.

The plane was soon directly over the enemy lines. Then, as it continued on its journey towards the hell-mouth that lay beyond, it began to climb in preparation for releasing its payload: the great, iron casket that, even at the extreme altitude the plane strove to attain, was clearly, and forebodingly, visible.

As the drone of the plane's engines disappeared into the azure silence, and the plane itself shrunk to little more than a dot, puffs of smoke could be descried below its silver fuselage, as the big batteries that ringed the hell-mouth opened up. And, as if eager to compensate for the impotence of the flak, and the silence that extended from sky to earth, the *pop-pop-pop* of machine guns immediately followed.

I shouted. Told my company to regroup behind one of the ironclads. Then I transferred my revolver to my left hand and used my right to draw *Espiritu Santo*. We had covered a considerable amount of ground. But things were going wrong. As they always did. The leisurely walk across no-man's-land promised by the high command had been annulled by the plane's late arrival. However near or distant the enemy trenches might prove, I knew that we could not wait for the bomb to drop, or rely on the doubtful inviolability of the sluggish transport; we must charge now, if any of us were to survive. Or survive long enough, at least, to die like soldiers, amid the screams and lamentations of the enemy. Momentum was all.

Breaking cover, I raised the sword above my head, increased my stride and then broke into a trot. And those about me still on their feet followed.

I took one last look over my shoulder. We had left the ironclads behind. The main body of infantry, an army of some fifty thousand men, were in our wake, braving the hail of bullets with grim, boyish obstinacy, unable to quite believe, perhaps, that the innumerable corpses that already strewed the battlefield foreshadowed their own almost certain demise. I dare say I in part shared their disbelief, for I could not otherwise have so blithely led the vanguard of black knights into the chattering guns. The man next to me spun about, his tin helmet sailing through the air, and then, falling to one side, disappeared into a shell crater. I whirled *Espiritu Santo* above my head and broke into a sprint, leaping into the air as each enemy bullet pinged off a boulder or thudded into the earth, my ermine trailing behind me, my coronet bouncing up and down, and my heart ready to burst.

Ahead, amidst the muzzle flash and smoke, I saw that I approached one of the spots I had earlier reconnoitred: a length of ground where the enemy's wire had been broken. If we could only remain alive long enough, I thought, with a keen and dreadful thrill, we stood a real chance of storming their positions.

Of those black knights who clove to my ankles, a cluster of mines despatched at least half a dozen. For a moment, I stopped, inspected the bloody remains that lay about me, then made a brief, wary survey of myself. To my astonishment, I had not even been scratched. Angry, with an anger that banished all fear, and deaf to everything but the ringing inside my head, I pressed home the attack, crying out to those of my comrades who still stumbled in my shadow to join me.

I could see the orcs clearly now, their hornèd visages poking above an entrenchment. '*Espiritu Santo!*' I yelled. Their red eyes opened wide, then wider, as they came to a full understanding of our resolve. Taking heart, I urged my men on towards the perimeter of the wire; snaked through its rent network of rusted barbs; and suddenly found myself at the enemy's threshold. If their fire had become uncoordinated, it would, I knew, prove accurate and deadly enough at close quarters. But recalling the importance of sustaining the assault's momentum, and knowing that my duty was to lead, I jumped into the trench regardless. And was instantly surrounded by creatures with scaly flesh, forked tails, bat-like wings and talons. Demons such as were any Christian man's nightmare. Devils eager to usher me into their hell.

I emptied my revolver, killing three. Then, feeling my

sword-arm come to life, I threw the sidearm disdainfully aside and brought *Espiritu Santo* down upon the crown of the Netherworld soldier unlucky enough to have been bringing up his comrades' rear. The blade cleft his skull, spattering his brains on to the duckboards. The dark energy that filled my every nerve, muscle and sinew was so inordinate that I needed recourse to an ear-splitting scream to allay the pressure that I felt building up within me.

I danced, pranced, hopped, skipped and somersaulted. And all the while I performed my manic routine I chopped and hewed at the enemy. Very soon, I had no one left to fight, and was forced to pursue the one terrified orc still on his feet along the length of the trench before at last despatching him with a carefully chosen sword stroke.

I was alone, bereft as much of friend as of foe. I had been so consumed with killing everything within reach that I had been unaware that the mass of infantry, including my own black knights, had already swept across the front line to advance into the hinterland.

The point at which I stood had at some time received a direct hit from a shell. With no steps to be had, and with the usual reinforcements blasted away, I was forced to slither up the side of the trench on my belly, friable earth coming away in hands that, until then, I had not noticed to be so drenched in blood. As my head emerged over the top, my gaze happened to fall upon a part of the sky punctuated by a glittering point of light. One that, as I watched, gave birth to a second light that fell away from it, and that I knew to be my very own *enfant terrible*.

'Goggles!' I cried. But the noise of battle would have drowned out the order even if my men had not been so far away. I groped under my robes and quickly strapped on the eyewear that had been issued by the research and development people. The field turned murky as the smoked lenses filtered out the light – light that, very soon, I knew, would be intensified a thousandfold.

I got to my feet. The bomb was still falling lazily towards the hell-mouth. Forgetting the slaughter that transpired some one hundred yards in front of me, I studied its progress, transfixed by its minute, eschatological perfection. Then, out of the corner of my eye, I spied an orc emerging from beneath a pile of bodies. Disorientated, he rose and looked blearily about, and then, at last noticing my presence, held up his hands and stumbled forward to offer his surrender. With one eye still on the falling star of ultimate destruction that had almost reached the ground, I made a half-hearted lunge, skewering the creature through his solar plexus. And in the time it took my lips to form the dismissive sneer preparatory to awarding the interloper a forceful and particularly imaginative curse for proving such an unnecessary distraction, all disappeared behind a sheet of indescribable brilliance. Like a curtain descending upon a mad, extemporary piece of modern theatre, it signalled that the initial act of our drama had drawn to a close, and that, after this blinding interval, a dénouement would follow that, for the first time in twenty-five years, might have us driving the enemy back into its subterranean lairs.

With a whoop of triumph, I threw myself on to my face, next to the orc who, it seemed, had expired without need of my sword's further attentions. The flash began to dissipate. Wraith-like forms – of my comrades, the wire and a few disabled ironclads – delineated themselves from out of the epidemic of bedazzlement. Then I descried the desolate skyline, what remained of the refulgence now sucked back to its place of origin, so that the great plume of black smoke that rose out of the hell-mouth and into the blue – a blue fused with purple, so that the entire sky appeared like a vast, sickly bruise – was like a great, pale lantern, the war-tossed plain's sole remaining source of light. Darkness covered all else, the noon-day battlefield eclipsed by a dense, louring cloud that soon stretched from one horizon to the other.

I tore off the goggles and managed to stand. Some way ahead of me the bulk of my men were clawing at their eyes and screaming. Those who – less consumed with the lust of battle – had had the forethought to don their protective glasses continued their advance, if somewhat unsteadily.

But then came the wind. The wind they had told us of, and, with the wind, the scorching heat. Briefed as to what I might expect, I still stared, uncomprehending, at the sight of men and orcs as they changed from solids to liquids to gases even as they re-engaged each other in combat; still thought that I might dream. But dreams, of late, had proved so conterminous with reality that I could not long doubt the evidence of my senses. I watched, knowing that this truly was the end, as skin and scale peeled away from man-bone and orc-bone, and then the bones themselves superheated, so that, for a few beats of my lurching heart, the battlefield seemed alive with dancing, luminous skeletons, before assuming the appearance of a vast charnel house recently fire-bombed by some cosmic vandal.

Looking down at myself I decided that I too was having a cosmically bad day. I was no more than a scarecrow, a twisted, crooked template of 'humanity' festooned with strips of steaming flesh, with only the ermine that still clung to my shoulders suggesting that this memento mori had ever been Richard Pike, the fourth Lord Soho.

Yet I lived; impossibly lived.

I stood; scanned the four corners of the blackened plain and its unvarying prospect of devastation. The bomb had performed, alas, beyond my expectations. I made a little mental bow to some of my more intelligent critics, then, for want of knowing what else to do, gazed at the ground. My flesh dripped like hot fat on to the hardened earth. Bones followed, forming a pile, so that they came to resemble the remains of a wrecked xylophone. And yet, I told myself, I lived. Stood. Thought. Felt.

I studied my left hand. As the last piece of burned, tattered skin fell away, and the underlying bones joined those already heaped in a funeral mound about my disintegrating feet, and as all, finally, evaporated and was cast to perdition by the vestiges of the atomic wind, I saw that I had acquired another hand. One bright. Perfect. Immutable.

I ran that hand over my naked torso, and then my face. And though I had no mirror in which to inspect myself, I could tell, by that cursory appraisal of my rebirth, that I enjoyed the proportions of a young god. A god whose images I had seen in museums. A god betokening ancient harmonies and eternal truths. But I could tell, too, that something about the symmetry of my form was alien, truly alien, and that the truths that it embodied, eternal as they were, were as much antithetical to the world of the ancients as they were to my own time.

'Time?' echoed a voice inside my skull. 'That is what we have come here to rectify.'

How foolish, it seemed now, to dwell upon the *raison d'être* of this war. Of the orcs. And that I had ever placed so much store in defeating them. For the first time, I knew who I was. Not a lord, not a Pike, not even a man who had the blood of the Netherworld in his veins, nor any of those false fellows prefigured by my ancestors.

I held the sword above my head so that its tip was pointed at the fractured skies. I cried out its name . . .

My name.

And then I segued, once and for all, into dreamtime. The sword hoisted me aloft. Higher, higher into the combusting atmosphere I went, the land below shrouded in the smoke that drifted from the hell-mouth. I flew towards the hills, *Espiritu Santo* cleaving the hot soup of burning oxygen to leave a flaming slipstream arcing from the wastes to the spawning ground of the Nephilim.

I landed at the edge of the vertiginously deep and, as some would have it, bottomless pit out of which the orcs had sprung to renew their struggle with human-kind. It was huge. Some one mile in diameter. And it led directly to Pandemonium, the capital city of the goblin race that lay at the centre of the Earth. The city I, Richard Pike, had utterly destroyed.

Before me a great sweep of upland rose from the plain, ridged with that comb of fleshly foliage that divided earth from heaven, this world from the next. The forest seemed to tremble. Smoke billowed about its roots and threaded the red and pink branches. It was on fire. Not in the manner of the hell-mouth and the plain; its fire was a holy fire, a fire that called to the inferno of my own soul. Great tongues of spiritual essence licked and played through the interstices of bough and branch, at last to encircle the golden forms that they embowered.

The sword was raised above my head, no longer a blade wrought by mortal hands, but a tongue of brilliant, alien flame. It spoke. And I cried out an antiphonal response, our two voices becoming as one.

'Now the dwelling of God is with men, and he will live with them. They will be his people, and God himself will be with them and be their God. He will wipe every tear from their eyes. There will be no more death or mourning or crying or pain, for the old order of things has passed away.'

The forest erupted into a great arbour of incandescence. And its cry joined with the cry of the Pikes, the cry of Espiritu Santo becoming a hymn, a chorale announcing humanity's dispossession.

Pods cracked; colossal bodies disentangled themselves of vegetation – trees, shrubs, flowers, fungus and lichen burning away, like a veil soaked in petroleum and put to the match, to reveal the living temple of the Nephilim, the Form that had yet been only fore-shadowed by the Flesh.

A race of giants – men and women golden of aspect and possessed of terrifying beauty; beings who were both good and evil and who reconciled the contra-dictions of humanity's chaotic past – stood naked and alone upon a ridge from which all trace of the nurturing forest had vanished. Slowly, they began to walk down the hillsides, towards the plain and the detritus that was all that was left of the human race. And with them they brought their fire – a fire very different from that which had destroyed my physical body. A fire with a calorific content not of this world. And growing more intense by the second, it began to eat into the too-briefly enjoyed symmetry of my perfected form . . .

I collapsed, rolling towards the hell-mouth's crumbling edge, to come to a halt pillowed by a hummock of volcanic earth, so that I gazed down into the emptiness of the monstrous fumarole. The absolute silence of its sloping, vitreous walls testified to the pur-gative efficaciousness of the bomb, the secret weapon that had both blessed and damned. And the darkness at its centre, rejoicing in that silence, seemed to rise, and, after mixing with the smoke that polluted the air and sky, enveloped me.

'But nothing can kill Richard Pike,' someone said. 'No, no, not old Dick Pike, the slayer of Satan himself. For he is the champion of the disinherited, the broken and the lost. He is the prince of exiles, the lord of defeats. And Satan has no power over one who, in defeat, is fated to sing the last song and have the last laugh. He will always be with us, even though his immortality constitute a rack of eternal pain.' And I seemed to hear another voice begin to sing the national anthem. 'God save the queen and all the royal family! God save England's ladies and lords!'

'Bravo! Hooray! Satan is dead,' another voice cried. (We must have a good conclusion, you see.) 'We can now all do as we like!' (And that's the moral.)

'Satan, yes,' I mumbled, 'He wanted to take old Dick Pike away, to goblin land, for all his past misdeeds and fun and frolic. Take him away to the bottomless pit!'

'Goodbye, ladies and gentlemen: this is the whole of the original performance of Dick Pike, his time opera. And I remain still your most obedient and most humble servant to command. Goodbye, goodbye, goodbye!'

'Goodbye,' I mumbled, 'good—' Melchezidek stood over me. Unlike the time when I had dreamed of walking beneath my own house, and had heard real voices invading the walls of my consciousness, these verbal fragments, it seemed, had emanated from phantoms. Ghosts whose company I would – given the ludicrously pulped state of my body – soon make a surer acquaintance with.

My erstwhile batman had an arm extended protectively about my wife; lying in the crook of his opposite arm was Richard, my son.

'You're alive,' I said, looking at them through tear-spangled lashes. 'You've come back to me.' Disengaging himself, Melchezidek delivered my son into his mother's safe keeping. 'Joan?' I continued. 'Is it really you?' I struggled and, with one great heave, managed to

lever myself into a sitting position. And though I was a
spirit no longer, but only my old, ugly self, a pleasant,
ethereal numbness pervaded my burned flesh and
smashed bones, the beauty that had been mine for so
few sweet minutes conferring upon me one last
souvenir. 'How is it? How is it that you are alive? That *I*
am alive?'

'There are none living but us,' said Melchezidek.
'You walked here all the way from the enemy lines. For
a man in your condition, an extraordinary feat.'

'I flew,' I said. '*Espiritu Santo* lifted me up into the
sky.' Again, I surveyed my broken body. No trace of
transcendence remained. 'But lately I've had difficulty
knowing whether I'm dreaming or awake. To the
degree, I think, that I no longer care.'

'It is no matter. You have brought about the end of
time,' said Melchezidek. 'For the human race. And for
yourself. And in so doing you have delivered the
Nephilim from eternity.' I looked out over the vast, flat
plain. It was covered in blood, ruin and night. London
was ablaze. But in the far distance, shivering in the
convective air that destabilized the horizon, were the
colossal forms that had put their vegetative womb
behind them and walked away from this scene of death
and entropy into a new, inconceivable life. 'Your opera,
the time opera of the Pikes, and that of mankind, is
finished. The bomb ignited the atmosphere, and even
now a vast fire-storm rages across the planet. In
destroying the ancient enemy, humanity has destroyed
itself. But it is right that things are so. The Nephilim are
grateful.' He gestured towards mother and child. 'You
may see how grateful.'

'I did love you, you know,' Joan said. 'You were kind to me. Kinder than anyone had ever been before. It was something I found hard to understand. It was something—' A sob contorted her chest and she bowed her head. She looked as when I had first met her, the latest fifteen-year-old recruit of Madame Lotte's brothel in Greek Street. Her blonde hair was piled high, a few ringlets escaping to snake down her neck. Her doll-like face was that of an ingénue, yet also evinced a potential for infinite corruptibility. But because I had at once recognized in her an innocence that outweighed her apprentice wiles, I had fallen in love. I would take care of her, I had decided. I would make sure that the child who wore the crimson dress and six-inch heels, and whose face was larded with make-up, did not die.

She stepped forward, went down on her knees and, pulling the baby's blanket away from his face, showed me my son. 'They say he is going to survive. That I will survive too. That though all humans are even now becoming as ghosts, or fictions, then this one song, this finale of the Pikes, will remain corporeal and be allowed to walk the planet with the new gods.'

'But oh, Joan, is that such a good thing? To be alone, so alone . . .' She held Richard to my face, allowing me to kiss him.

'He will be fully human, that boy,' said Melchezidek, in a bracing voice that seemed designed to encourage my hopes. 'Not human like those latter-day men who lie dead across this plain. He will grow up without taint of the perverse. He will be free.'

A pudgy, infant hand reached out and began to play with the chain and whistle looped about my neck.

Wincing with effort, I took it off and slipped it over my little boy's head, as if it were a rosary.

'God bless you,' I whispered. 'If, that is, He has not died too.'

'He really is your son, you know,' said Joan. 'All that I said, it was—'

'He takes after you, Joan. That's why he's so fair. Whatever has happened, it no longer matters. Not since this world came to an end and history was rewritten. The past is a *tabla rasa*, now, just like the future. Both have a potential equal only to our love.'

I smiled and looked into my son's eyes, as blue as the sky had been before humanity had so polluted it. 'Good luck, Richard. All this wretchedness that you see about you will depart, and you will have a new world to play in.' I kissed him again. 'But now I think I must leave you. Isn't that so, Melchezidek?'

'It is the covenant you made with the sword.' He took Joan by her arm, gently assisted her to her feet and, as she stepped back, stooped and gathered my scorched body into his arms and lifted me. 'Mankind changes places with the Nephilim, just as you must go into the shadows in order that Joan and Richard may stay here.' I turned to take a last look at my family.

'Forgive me, Joan,' I said. 'I was mad, you know.'

'I was not a good wife, Ritchie.'

'You were what you have always been: a sweet, sweet child. I should have treated you better. I should have . . . I should have *spoilt* you.'

'But you did. I was a brat. Forgive me, too, won't you?' I saw that she had picked *Espiritu Santo* up from where it lay upon the hard, blood-caked earth. 'Please?'

'I love you, Joan.'

Melchezidek began to carry me into the hell-mouth. And as feet, waist, shoulders and then, finally, the head of my wife disappeared, and as she raised Richard into the air so that the last sight I should have of Earth-Above would include him, I whispered, 'The sword. Am I still the sword, Melchezidek?'

'The spirit of the sword is gone from you. You are cleansed. *Espiritu Santo* is now only a length of Toledo steel. The being it once contained, and which subsequently found a home in your family line, is the spirit of the New Heaven and New Earth.'

'And hell, Melchezidek?'

'Do not fear. It cannot embrace Joan and Richard. Hell is passing away, soon to be gone for ever, like the orcs. It has room in it now only for us.'

And so we continued our descent, Melchezidek stumbling as his feet traversed the black, friable earth. Wisps of infernal smoke played about his ankles, the pit belching its radiation-thick stew into the atmosphere to travel about the world and make its contribution to the discordant bars of the last act of the human race. Smoke. Fire. The screams of the damned writhing in eternal torment. The smell of sulphur. Ghostly traces of blood and violence and desperate, striving love. Soon, soon, that would be all that there was left of a man, poet, soldier, lover, an artist of extremes, a lord and the myth of *Espiritu Santo*.